THE STORYTELLER

Alan Sillitoe was born in Nottingham in 1928. He left school
at the age of fourteen to work in the Raleigh Bicycle Factory,
subsequently living and working in many different places including Spain and France. He has been a full-time writer
since the publication of his first phenomenally successful
novel 'Saturday Night and Sunday Morning' over twenty
years ago. He has written two books of plays, a collection of
essays, a travel book and five volumes of poetry. This is his
sixteenth volume of fiction.

THE STORYTELLER

Alan Sillitoe

Star

A STAR BOOK

published by

the Paperback Division of

W. H. ALLEN & Co. Ltd

A Star Book
Published in 1980
by the Paperback Division of
W. H. Allen & Co. Ltd
A Howard and Wyndham Company
44 Hill Street, London W1X 8LB

First published in Great Britain by
W. H. Allen & Co. Ltd, 1979

Printed in Great Britain by
The Anchor Press Ltd
Tiptree, Essex

ISBN 0 352 30698 x

CONTENTS

Part One

I

"I'm gonna smash yer ter bits."

Tom Baker's eyes almost closed as he spoke, and Ernest Cotgrave, looking into the slits, didn't believe him any the less for that.

"Boot yer," Baker emphasised. "Kick yer in. Rip yer." He pushed Ernest against the playground wall, and held him in the prison of two outstretched arms, palms flattened against the bricks. "Pull yer eyes out one by one, and chuck 'em over the gate to the caretaker's cat. That moggie's a greedy bleeder, ain't it, lads?"

Two of his mates grinned, mercilessly silent.

"Wain't I?"

The end of the world was close. Ernest wasn't small, but came nowhere near as big as the bastard pinning him at the wall. It was useless looking for a teacher to rescue him. They were guzzling tea in the common room, while he was about to be massacred. He made a silent though desperate prayer for a downpour of rain so violent it would send them soaked and panic-stricken to the sheds, jovial when they got there because they would then unite in deriding the forces of nature instead of each other. He had a vision so real of huge plates of rain bursting on the asphalt that he thought he was going to faint from that instead of at the sight of Baker's poised fist.

"Shit scared, aren't yer?" said Tom Baker. "Look at him, lads! Old Gingernut! Fizzled out. Stuff 'im in a jampot and chuck 'im over a cliff, eh?"

Ernest thought that if somebody would do him a favour by pressing a button to start World War Three, he'd be able to hold

9

Baker off till the four-minute warning took effect and they were scorched up together. There was nothing he'd like more, and yet, failing such a holocaust, he couldn't just stand there.

"I'm gonna pull yer nose off, and tread on it."

Ordinary sense told him that Baker would do no such thing, and that before a dismembering commenced, help would arrive from a teacher, or a policeman, or people out of the street responding to his screams. A lower part of him knew, however, that if this primeval and bloody attack were made, no one would come to his assistance. The teacher would say that his fate served him right, or call out that the sooner he learned to defend himself the better. A policeman, stuffing the bits of him that remained into a sack, would carry him off to the copshop because he would have ripped Baker's jacket while fighting for his life. And a woman rushing in from the street would say he deserved all he got because he'd nicked four bob from his mother's purse last week.

"He's gone all white: Pasty guts! What yer got to say for yourself? Hey, lads, shall I mek 'im spit chalk?"

This quieter threat indicated that time was getting short. Since the sky was clear, and there'd been no sign of impending war on the news that morning, he had to stop talking to himself. There were still ten minutes before the teacher's whistle pierced the solid noise all around.

Tell me a story, to take my mind off it, said a voice deep down to another as yet mute factotum equally distant. Let's save his bacon, said one to the other. He heard them talking above Baker's hectoring, though knew that even fifty clocks would give the same time, and show six hundred seconds of promised assault and almost certain battery still to pass. If the whistle immediately went he could still get ding-banged into a pancake on his way home for dinner. Those fifty white-faced clocks couldn't save him should they blow up one by one at the end of a four-minute warning.

One of the deep-down voices shot words to his lips and forced him to speak: "I've got an uncle who lives in a room full of clocks."

Baker's fist jutted under his nose. "Er! What fucking clocks?"

The voice didn't disappoint him, perhaps being more threatened than Ernest was by Baker if it failed to make Ernest's lips move. He wasn't interested in what went on down there, but something seemed intent on saving him. "He's been collecting clocks ever since he was born. There's alarm clocks, grandfather clocks, water-clocks, spirit-clocks, wick-clocks, candle-clocks, cuckoo clocks, crossbow-clocks, dandelion clocks, a factory clocking-in clock, and even a sundial in the garden. There is, honest."

The first, in withdrawing, was a gondolier floating backwards along the Grand Canal. It was the best time of his life so far.

"And eggtimers," he added. "When you go into the room, the clocks are all ticking, and you think it's a thousand rats behind the skirting boards, till you see 'em on the walls. They don't strike every hour at the same time though, because if they did the house would fall down. And the house next door as well. Maybe the whole row, like dominoes. So they go off all over the place, like an orchestra. My uncle sometimes tape-records it, and next day adds another lot. He's got hours of these tapes on a bookshelf, and can play 'em all night if he can't sleep. He loves to listen to 'em. It's like music to him. He's six-foot-four tall, and has got a beard, and was in the Royal Navy eighteen years."

It wasn't a good idea to say too much about the physical abilities of his imaginary uncle, in case Baker supposed he might intend calling him in as an ally, and so finished Ernest off there and then for his presumption. He decided to add no more in that direction, for the moment. Baker pulled his arms away, and listened.

"He used to send clocks back from Africa and America when he was overseas, as well as from Singapore and Pompey. Mam would store them for him. When he got his discharge from the Royal Navy he hung 'em in the front room of his house at Hucknall. One day *his* uncle died and left him a grandfather clock. The family laughed, because it looked like a bit of old rubbish. They'd got valuable things out of the will, but when Uncle George lugged his clock home he noticed it didn't strike very well. The pendulum didn't go, so he opened it up to mend it. He found four thousand quid inside."

"Pissin' 'ell!" It was as if only the mention of money made Baker anywhere near human. "What did he do with it?"

"He bought a bigger house to store his clocks in."

Baker was restless. He pushed his left arm back to the wall, and let his right go loose. Opaque grey eyes, aligned with Ernest's throat, moved slightly.

"When he was asleep one night upstairs, he heard a noise, so sat up, got out of bed, and opened the door. Somebody was down in the parlour where he stored his clocks. He kept a revolver under his pillow, and a cosh in the wardrobe, so he went back and got 'em. He's a big man, but he can walk without making a sound, especially when he's got no shoes on. And he hadn't got any on now. So with the cosh in one hand and the gun in the other, he went to the top of the stairs."

Eight boys were listening, though they were careful not to get too close and touch Tom Baker.

"Somebody was definitely moving about. He thinks they're pulling the precious hair-loom clocks off his wall and stuffing them in sackbags, so he starts treading down the stairs one at a time. They creak a lot, but he chuckles because he knows his clocks won't let the burglars hear him coming. He gets to the bottom of the stairs, and listens again."

Tom Baker tried to break up the picture of interest he knew his features must give, but his eyes were as fixed as mother-of-pearl buttons, his hands folded together, and his mouth half-an-inch open. Ernest, who saw the teacher coming into the yard, noticed the faint rattle of Tom's breath during pauses of his life-saving story.

"He crept to the door, one step at a time, and when he was close enough, he yanked it open, and then. . . ."

The whistle-noise, cutting across the playground, stopped every spin and jump. The moan from Baker belonged to a five-year-old, and put an idea into Ernest before the voice deep inside him could give words to it. He smiled at being saved from further trouble, though Baker was still too close for him to feel easy. If he took a swing at his enemy it would be more savage than any Baker could give because it would be compounded of revenge and self-defence. Baker rolled his hand into a fist as

Ernest loosened his: "Tell it me later, see?"

They walked to the entrance like old friends. Baker ran from the column and through a cloakroom. A teacher called him back, and he shuffled up like a dog expecting to be booted into the ground. They thought none the less of him. He was still big, and a bully. Ernest didn't stay to see what happened. He could always tell a story about it, and whatever he made up was bound to be true. When he laughed in class at his escape from Baker's steam-engine fists, the teacher threatened to knock his head off if he didn't keep a straight face and get on with his work.

That night he vomited across the back doorstep. He'd been sick twice in his life already, and each time thought he was going to die. The earth came through the bottom of his feet and out via his mouth. He was unable to tell his mother what was the matter. She put a hand on his forehead, but it was neither warm nor cold. He went to bed without supper, and couldn't remember what he dreamed, though in the morning he ate all his breakfast.

The suspense of waiting for more of Ernest's story disturbed Tom Baker's sullen equilibrium so much that before dinner time of instalment one he got into a fight with his teacher and was sent home for three days. It rained the whole of his absence, sheets of slate-grey water pounding the tarmac, and descending roofs and walls as if in deliberate pursuit of Ernest alone. The rain had a dozen different smells, but all of them were cold.

Ernest loved the rain, as well as hated it, because it coincided with those days of Baker's banishment. Looking at the windows, rain came down as if someone had fixed a plastic bag over the school but was having trouble holding it in place because there was a bit of a gale on. On the second day he walked slowly to the bus stop, not caring if he got saturated. When enough drops formed on his lips to lick, they tasted better than the hot tea he tried to sip as his mother was pulling the jersey off him that had got soaked because he'd left his mac open.

When the sun shone, Baker came back with a black eye from his father for getting sent home by the teacher. As he walked through the gate a boy near the bike sheds called "Hey, look! Old Baker's had knuckle-pudding for breakfast!" It was as if what Baker couldn't see he didn't hear, though his faculties, even under inborn disadvantages, were often sharp enough to keep a respectful silence about him. Anyone who recklessly threw out a remark might feel the weight of his whole body hurled for vengeance when in no way expecting it.

The teacher, still chafed by a grudge, threw Baker into his seat as soon as he came into the room. Ernest knew that no one could win. You lived from day to day, and hoped that nothing either good or bad would happen. When the teachers left you alone to learn what you could, and no one bullied you, and you daydreamed the playtimes away; when you went home and had tea and washed, and your mother and father were too busy with each other to bother about you; and when between tea and bedtime you ran about the street with pals who didn't want to fight because they had the same feeling for school and parents that you had—then you could take the risk of trying to feel happy.

Baker raced over at playtime and pushed him against the wall, bringing up a fist and knocking his head at the bricks. "Story, see? Or I'll chew yer, and spit yer out like orange pips. I'll pull yer legs off and play rounders with 'em!"

It wasn't a big bang, but Ernest felt tears close. "If I get a headache I can't think proper. Then I wain't be able to tell the story."

Baker's black eye made him more menacing, though Ernest might have felt sorry for his vicious injury if he hadn't been such a bullying bastard, or if he'd been merely stupid.

"Look, shit-house, I don't want yer to *think*. I want yer to go on with that story, see? I want to know what '*appened*. And quick."

Baker twitched a knee, as if to ram him at some random spot. Ernest didn't care to give in too easily: "There's a lot better stories in books."

Baker considered this possibility, then said, "Fuck books! I want yer to *tell* me a story, or I'll mek a corkscrew out of yer, and use yer for pullin' up paving stones."

Ernest could divert Baker's wrath by continuing his tale, yet because he no longer felt a scarified melting at the spine, the story would not flow as readily as before. Staring at the cloudless sky, he shuffled his feet, and hopelessly clenched his fists.

14

Baker smelled of onions. "Ain't got all day, Gingernut."

"I forgot where I was."

Baker's good eye widened. He tried to spread the bad one but, being like a lizard's, it wouldn't move. He came as close to a smile as anybody had yet seen. "I ain't forgot." He put his fist under Ernest's nose. The fist also stank of onions. "That uncle o' yourn come downstairs with a gun and a cosh, because a burglar was rummaging among his clocks. Now, fuckin' come on, or I'll push me fist up yer nostrils and pull the shit out o' your brains."

Such threats would have been funnier if Baker hadn't stood so close. A quick look at his purple eye (not the first mark they'd seen on him) led Ernest to suppose that the blows which caused it had been preceded as well as accompanied by the sort of abuse Baker threw at whatever victims he in turn could nobble in the playground. A blow swung his shoulder: "Come on, spunk eyes!"

"He went down the stairs one at a time, with a gun in his hand that had got six bullets in it."

Baker tapped him, but with a ghastly smile. "Er, you've told me that bit already."

"I've got to get back into it again, ain't I?"

"Push on, then, stoat-face."

"When he opened the door there was a bloke as large as life, getting his clocks off the wall and stacking 'em on the table, while another chap was putting them in cardboard boxes. It was like packing hats in Griffin and Spaldings shop. But they got the shock of their lives seeing Uncle George, because Uncle George was six-foot-four in his thick navy socks, and had a beard, and was dressed in his pyjamas, and had a gun in one hand and a torch in the other."

Baker clacked his knee-cap, a definite signal to stop: "A cosh in the other, not a torch. You think I'm a fucking fool?"

"Oh yes, that's right. No, of course I don't. A cosh it was. So Uncle George said to 'em: 'Put yer claws up, then, matey, and you as well, sailor' — pointing to the other one. They both had caps and rain-macs on, and one said: 'Here's a nice fucking how-do-you-do. I thought you said he'd gone away on a British Legion beano for the weekend?' 'That's next month,' Uncle George said. 'Now, you can put my clocks back on the wall. Go on, one at a time, and don't drop any of 'em, because if you do I'll blow both your bloody lids off. My gun here can tell time, and if you don't get going, smartish, it'll strike one-two before you can turn round and fall on your knees in front o' me. I used to chuck the likes o' you into the drink. Fed you to the sharks when I was in the Indian Ocean. I'd listen to 'em screaming as they got ripped to bits.'"

Ernest didn't know why this cruel flourish insisted on adding itself to his imitation of Uncle George, for he'd had no intention of making him anything but merciful towards others. But like most embellishments throughout the tale, he didn't consider that he had much to say in the matter, especially when they came out of the mouth of a big bluff grown-up like Uncle George. But at this indication of his darker pleasantries he noticed a glint in Baker's eyes which he liked even less than his murderous threats.

"That was *good*," Baker slavered.

"They put his clocks back on the wall. 'Now what, Captain? You caught us fair and square, but that don't mean you're going to turn us in, does it? You didn't lose your clocks, did you?'"

'Uncle George threw 'em a pencil and some paper: 'Write your names and addresses. And no lies. I'll remember you till my dying day. A chief petty officer never forgets a face. If owt happens to my clocks again I'll come and shoot the pair of you clean through your coal-scuttles.'

"They did as they was told, and off they went. Everything looked neat. Uncle George thought it was time to go back to bed. He was a good-hearted bloke, but dead tough all the same, when he had to be. Back in his bedroom, he staggers against the wall, a hand on his heart. His face goes bright purple."

Baker trembled. "What was up?"

"He went pale, and thought he was going to spew. His foot ached where a piece of shrapnel had got it during the war. He clawed at the wallpaper."

Ernest would have gone on, but didn't want a double-barrelled fist in his phizog. "Under his bed he'd kept a little tin trunk of his savings, and now it was kicked in and empty in the middle of the floor. The window of the room where he hung his clocks had been at the back of the house, and his bedroom window let onto the front, so while he'd been downstairs catching the two burglars at their business, somebody had shinned the drainpipes at the front, opened the window, and rifled his cash-box."

"Fucking arse-holes!"

Ernest nodded. "That's the sort of place our district is. You've got to be everywhere at once, unless you want robbing blind."

"It bleeding is." Baker knew wisdom when he heard it. "And then?"

"Then what?"

"What the fucking-hell happened next, snot-chops?"

"Uncle George howls like a dog. He learned it when he was a sailor. All sailors can howl, especially when there's a forty-foot wave or two on the sea. Nobody can hear 'em. They just stand outside on deck and howl. It isn't because they're frightened. They do it to keep themselves company, and maybe to try and get the waves to calm down a bit. Uncle George told me he did it once when he saw an iceberg, and because he howled, it drifted by the ship instead of smashing down on deck. Being a good sailor, Uncle George always knew when to howl, and he howled now because, seeing as how he'd been robbed of all he'd got, there wasn't much else to do."

Baker closed-in once more. "You'll fucking 'owl, if you don't gerron with this story. I don't care whether Uncle George 'owled or not, I just want to know what *'appened*."

Ernest was flattered, for this — albeit natural — request proved that he was telling the story with some ability. Yet what was to come next in his narrative didn't show itself so easily. One minute no further details were there, and suddenly three or four possible ways of carrying on the tale crowded into his mind. Baker aked why he didn't continue? Did he want to die? Did he want to be carried home on a shutter? Did he want lamming under a double-decker bus when it was halfway down the big hill from Canning Circus and going too quick to stop, so that if he saw home again it would be from the misted-up inside of a plastic bag?

Ernest had to admit that he didn't. "His first thought was revenge."

17

Baker cheered. "Dead fucking right. You can't beat a nice bit o' revenge."

"Uncle George would chase 'em to the four corners of the world."

Baker responded by grabbing Ernest at the lapels. "Cunt! The earth's *round*. I'm not fucking ignorant. It's like a football!"

It was, Ernest had heard, an oblong spheroid. Being caught out on a fact by Baker was like coming bottom of the school in a test. He'd known the earth wasn't square, but Baker thought he hadn't, and Ernest couldn't let him get away with a thing like that.

Apart from demanding higher standards of accuracy, Baker also wanted speedier action, and Ernest hoped he could live up to the challenge until no more story was necessary. He could make the actual telling of it better, but the ever-present possibility of being smashed by Baker's squalid fists told him he had better concentrate on the actual narrative, and veer away from the temptation to embroider in matters of style.

"Uncle George began his revenge trip there and then. He didn't care about sleep. He put on his coat, took his gun, picked a carving knife up from the kitchen table, and set out in the middle of the night to roam the streets looking for the robbers. 'They aren't going to fleece an old salt like me and get away with it,' he said, chewing a stick of black baccer, slamming the door and then locking it behind him."

'It was only half an hour since the blokes had robbed him, so he thought they might be still roaming the streets looking for more swag before they knocked off for the night. Searching for a burglar in Nottingham's like looking for a pin in a pudding, though you never knew you luck. George had plim. . . .'

Baker jerked an arm towards Ernest's ribs, but didn't strike. "*Uncle* George."

"Well, *Uncle* George, then. He had plimsolls on, so's he could go like a cat. He wore a dark coat, as well, and this rig made him nearly invisible. He knew the alleys and twitchells like the back of his big maulers."

Membranes of impatience slid over Baker's staring eyes. "Mek . . . summat . . . 'appen."

Ernest hardened his fists. He couldn't spend the rest of his life telling stories as Baker's personal entertainer, but the hour of George's clock-orchestra hadn't yet decided to strike. "Crossing Denman Street, he saw two men coming out of a pawnshop doorway carrying suitcases. Uncle George lifted his gun as he went towards them."

The thin choke of the whistle signalled the end of his instalment. Baker's mental condition at being cut from the opium-dreampipe was painful to see, as if each episode was the only peace of his life. Yet Ernest relied on Baker's savage threats, just as he needed the hated school wall at his back. Together they generated sufficient fear to force out another round.

Uncle George shot the two burglars dead, then discovered they didn't have his money. He got onto a ship at Liverpool which took him to Borneo, where he deserted and became a trader who met with all sorts of fantastic adventures, as well as more ordinary encounters in the jungle against deadly snakes and fanatical headhunters. Having — through many episodes — made a fortune, he changed his name and came back to Nottingham.

Baker suggested that Ernest take him to visit Uncle George at his big house in Mapperley, as if not realising that Ernest had been guilty of telling a chain of lies simply in order to safeguard his life. Baker almost pleaded, as if to meet Uncle George might reorganise his suffering world into some kind of tranquillity. "I want to see his garden you told me about, and then the two big St Bernard dogs he's got. Maybe *he'll* tell us a few more of his adventures, and let us drink tea and eat cakes while he does it. We can look at his trophies, and try tekin' that 'alf-inch machine-gun to bits. What about it, eh?"

Ernest, though flattered that Baker remembered so much of his tale, was frightened. Previously he'd been merely scared, whereas now he might be blamed for having driven Baker off his head. "I'd take you to see Uncle George," he began.

"Good old Ernie!" Such affection was more alarming than any menacing phrase. "I knew you would. You're my pal."

"Only . . ."

"Only fucking what?" The weather of Baker's temperament must have been born in the High Andes, because it could change, violently, by the split-second.

"But . . ."

"What do you pissing-well mean, cunt-eyes?"

Ernest was reassured that Baker could easily slip back to his proper place in the world. All the same, he wondered how hard his own fists were, and what force would come when he slugged them at Baker's mug like loaded thunderbolts.

From the time of telling his first story, Ernest started to grow, so that in nine months he was taller. Under the spell of his stories, Baker hadn't realised what had happened. At fifteen, he was soon to leave school, and Ernest felt no danger at being caught up again in the matter of height and build. Even so, to take a smash at him would be going into the unknown, with the risk of having both legs pile-driven into the asphalt from a terrible retaliation.

"Uncle George had to go to Switzerland. It was very sudden."

"Where the fucking-hell's that?"

"Near Holland," he said, unwilling to educate him beyond range of his story. "The coppers found who he was, and he heard they was coming to arrest him, so he drove off in his Rolls Royce, with his dogs in the back. *And* his clogs – in the boot. He was a great clog-dancer in his spare time, Uncle George was. In the navy he did a clog dance on the bridge for the admiral, and the admiral liked it so much he had all the other officers up to watch him do it again, and then he gave him an extra noggin of rum for his trouble. Uncle George was also a good storyteller. He used to entertain his messmates, and they loved him for it. I don't know why he is such a good storyteller, but p'raps one of his great-grandads was Portuguese. Uncle George said they tell smashing stories in Roly-Poly square, because his ship went to Lisbon once."

Baker stamped his boot. "Bollocks, get on with *your* fucking story, or I'll kill yer stone-dead."

"Uncle George went to London. He knew people in high places there, who helped him to change his name again. It's easy in London, as long as you've got money, and Uncle George allus made sure to keep enough o' that stashed away, because he knew that as long as you had money he'd be OK. He was followed all

20

the time, and had to be careful, so the only thing was to get out of England, quick. They were after him, but because he'd been a sailor, and because he'd lived in the jungle, he knew a thing or two more than they did, and gave 'em the slip.''

Baker let out a feverish cheer. "Good old Uncle George!"

"Things didn't look so easy, though, when he was walking on the ship. He'd sold his car in London, and put his dogs in kennels with a pal.'' Ernest drew away from the wall as if to breathe properly, wanting space for his thoughts (and fists) to swing in.

"Two coppers followed him along the dock, and one shouted: 'Stop, sir!' Uncle George thought of running, but he wasn't that daft. There was coppers all over the place. So he turns round, thinking they've twigged him, even though he's grown a beard, dyed his hair ginger, wears high heels, and got glasses on. 'Excuse me, sir,' the copper says, 'will you come with me?' Uncle George follows him into an office, and thinks, 'This is it, they've got me. They'll punch me up and kick me in. And if they don't, I've still missed the blinding boat, and they'll get me before the next one sails.' The copper points to a table. 'Does that wallet belong to you, sir?' Uncle George sees that it does. 'You dropped it getting off the train, sir,' the copper said. They check the name inside, and then give it to him, and he thanks them very much, shakes hands all round, and gives them ten quid for a drink . . .''

"Bloody-hell!"

"He always *was* generous, but it was close, just the same. He gets on the ship sweating like a pig. When the boat's half way across to France though, a terrible thing happens – to silly old bleeding George.''

Baker had other worries than these disrespectful words. One was shock, another was pain, and a third was blood. His roar crossed the playground like an invisible train, and served (almost as much as the teacher's whistle) to stop all activity.

Ernest jumped clear, and Baker's come-back threadled bone against bone. His reverberating knuckles, prised out in another flash to Baker's face, washboarded along the same gristle of the injured nose. Breath choked in him as if a paperbag had burst in his stomach. He wanted to run, but there was a wall hemming him in, so he clapped Baker ferociously on the ear.

Baker was trying to kick both legs from under him. He wore boots, studded. He jabbed his solid puddings out, though few came back in Ernest's face. Some brushed by his jacket, and had no stuff in them. Baker was shielding himself and, because it hadn't been as difficult to fight free as he'd expected, Ernest gave him a few more savage hits. "I'm going to kick you in, pull your eyes out and chuck 'em over the wall to the caretaker's cat; snap yer nose off and tread on it, push me fist up yer nostrils and rake the shit out o' yer brains. Fuck-face, spunk chops, cunt-eyes."

A girl shouted, "Leave him alone, you rotten bully."

Baker fell under his blows, and Ernest dived to go on thumping. A stronger arm pulled him up so fast that he felt as light as a flower of the field. "If you put as much work into your essays as you did in your cursing I'd be very pleased!"

The English master had him against the wall, and a bang at the face made orange sparks snap their fingers in front of his eyes. "You're a dirty-minded bully, aren't you, Cotgrave?"

A voice shouted loudly from deep inside: "Bollocks!"

The teacher's fist felt as if it were made of stone when it collided with his ear. "Go on, sir, do him over," the girl called. "He's a pig, hitting somebody like that." She pushed to the front. "They were just talking, ever so quiet, and Ernie Cotgrave slammed into him. I don't know what for." She took out a handkerchief and mopped Baker's face, who wondered if it might not be his lucky day after all.

He nodded towards Ernest. "I'm going to kill him for that."

Ernest wanted to tell the real story, but it would take a whole day, and no one would believe him.

"You lousy bully," they cried, and he still looked to see who was meant. Baker had been so enthralled by Ernest's story in the last months that he hadn't pummelled anyone. They'd forgotten his one-time ferocity, only knowing that for no reason Ernest had viciously attacked the harmless person that Baker now seemed to be. Even when Baker had been on the loose he had never been so wild as to draw blood, but only elbowed and jabbed, leaving few signs.

"I'll play the bully-boy now, Cotgrave," the teacher spoke, "and see how you get on. Come to the gymnasium, and we'll find the boxing gloves."

Everyone cheered as he was pushed across the playground. They'd listened to his story, but were ready to mob him now. Nobody stood up for him, and didn't care if he got knocked in pieces. He was learning, but thought the price too high.

His nose bled before the sparring finished, though it stopped on the way home, which made him feel better. He decided to end his career of being a bully, short as it had been, and take up boxing in his last months at school. It would always be useful for self-defence. Nobody would bully him again.

He felt a tap at his shoulder and, on the alert, swung with fists in the air.

Baker held a packet of Woodbines. "Fag, Ernie?"

He put his hands in his pockets, then took them out again in case there was treachery. He learned as much from himself as from others. "Don't smoke."

"I do. Since I was nine."

They walked along the Boulevard. "I was gonna kill yer last week," Baker said. "But I changed my mind."

"Ta."

He scraped a match along the sole of his boot, but kept the cigarette low. "Dad smokes, so I knock off a few now and again."

"Don't he say owt?"

"Yeh. I'll kill 'im one o' these days, if he don't do *me* in first. He ain't my dad. Mam got married again. I'll get a job soon, and live on my own. Then he can call me all the names under the sun."

"What yer gonna work at?"

He held up his scarred hands. "Dig, carry, lift. Don't know."

"Me as well. Gerra job in a factory." Ernest told him about an ambition that came from his day dreams: "I'd like to work on a ship."

"Like Uncle George?"

"Go through the Mediterranean. See Italy, and Greece."

"Tell stories," Baker said. "That's what yo' ought to do."

"You can't tell stories on ships."

"Uncle George did."

"He was in the *Royal* Navy, though."

23

Baker flipped the half-smoked cigarette across the road. "All sailors like stories, don't they? People do, as well. I liked that one about Uncle George. It were a treat!"

"Did yer?"

"He'd be a good bloke to work for."

Ernest told him the truth. "I made it up."

"I know yer did, yer old cunt." He put an arm over his shoulder. "There must be blokes like him."

Ernest liked Baker for remembering his tale. "Got to find 'em, though. They don't grow on trees."

"I wonder what did happen to Uncle George?"

Ernest couldn't stop his voice. "Went back to Borneo."

"Did he?"

"Only for a while. He's in Australia now."

Baker spat. "Just my fucking luck."

"He's married, with three kids."

"Wish he was my dad."

"He isn't though."

"Does he treat 'em right?"

"He bought 'em a pet kangaroo. *And* he tells 'em stories. But he wain't come back to England. Hates this rat-hole, like poison."

"Don't bleeding blame him," Baker said.

Ernest needed to explain Uncle George's attitude towards his native country more fully. "He can't stand it here. Everybody's against him. Work you to death, and rob you blind. In Australia he's got his own sheep farm, and rides his horse all day. In this country he lost his clocks."

They walked in silence, till Baker said, as if near to crying. "I'll go to Australia."

"Will you?"

"Soon as I fucking can. No cowing good here. I'm going to learn all I can at school, and then get out."

It was true that in the last few months Baker had reached the top of his class, though it wasn't possible for him to enter a higher stream in the time that was left. "I've got a brother," he said, "called Bernard. He's eighteen, and he's left home already. Works down pit, a real collier. I used to nick fags off him when he

24

was at home, but he threatened to slit my throat with his Bowie knife." He seemed derelict at recalling the incident, as if he would like to shed tears but couldn't. "We was close, me and my brother. *I* still am, but I don't know about him. He collects knives and bayonets. He's got loads on 'em. He'll kill somebody one day, because he's allus getting into fights in pubs."

"When Uncle George was in Borneo," Ernest said, to break this bleak mood, "he met a man called Fred Jones. Now, *he* was a right bloke. I know about him, because what George didn't tell me, my old man did. Fred had his own little aeroplane, and used to fly from one place to another, with people and supplies. He'd land his plane where no other plane could go. It had floats on it, for rivers and lakes. He had lots of adventures, did old Fred Jones."

They stood by a lamp post outside a furniture shop. Baker's eyes glistened. He tried to smile, but nudged him painfully. "Bet you've got a good story there, then, Ernest?"

"I have, an' all. He once chased a pirate ship, and set all the prisoners free. See you in the playground tomorrer?"

"All right, mate." It was hard to get rid of him. Even when they both left school Ernest knew he hadn't seen the last of Baker. He wondered whether he would ever meet his brother Bernard, and thought that if he did he might tell him a thing or two, no matter how many knives and bayonets he had under his coat.

2

He could smell the rain and taste it, as if it had been cooked and got cold again. It shot drenchingly down without giving him a chance to enjoy it with a slow-burning fag in his mouth. He hated it.

Walking on two sponges, with mac collar pulled high, he craved an overdose of shandy to soothe his bitterness. An hour ago his girl-friend had scorned him almost to death when he started reading a poem about a bloke who choked on a forkful of sickening chicken and chundered up chutney at a chinwag in a Chesterfield ṭake-away. She thought he had gone mad, yet had only laughed in order to get over the shock of hearing him spout something that rhymed in such a way that he clearly thought she should be staggered by its perfection.

The exercise book full of quips and funny rhymes was splitting apart at the staples. There was a lion's fierce face on the front cover, and arithmetic tables and metric conversions on the back that so blended into the shiny wash of blood-crimson they could no longer be read.

It was always risky to get sentimental. You let people see how soft you were, how vulnerable to their rotten core. He jumped cat-like out of Marlene's house as if she'd offered him a basin of ash and water instead of a cup of tea with milk and sugar in it. He was even more ashamed of his panicky skedaddling than of having read his poetry. If life had been interesting so far it was only because he'd rarely done what was considered by everyone to be the right thing; and the only right thing to have done in the present case would have been to finish his reading and then fucked her silly, which was what she'd expected, and so she would never forgive him for running away as he'd done. But who wanted to carry on courting a girl who was as dense as a black pudding? Especially as she was also as jittery as a chitterling.

Raindrops on the ledge of his collar, and those clinging to the overhang of his ginger quiff, and the few gripping the escarpment of his forehead, and the one or two clutching the knoll of his undistinguished nose, now developed arms and legs, and no doubt wore Captain Webb bathing suits as they dived beautifully down the Park Drive of his warm neck; or slid onto his cheeks, or even found his whitened sepulchral knuckles as he laid one set on the bar in the hope of getting speedily served.

He dislodged more waterdrops by a shake of his head, and called for a pint of shandy.

"Tristram! " the woman behind the bar screamed, for no reason he could think of.

"A pint of shandy," he insisted, shaking his head again to stop the waterdrops tickling his nose.

Her steel-grey eyes were unblinking. "I'll get our *bloody* Tristram onto *you*."

"What for?" She made Tristram sound like the biggest gorilla in Western Europe. He hoped he wasn't mistaken in seeing that her gaze became a little less threatening.

"Do you want it, or don't you?" she asked.

"What do you mean? "

"You called for a shandy, and then yer shook yer head as if you *didn't* want it. Our Tristram allus settles them as try to be funny. He drags 'em outside, and *kills* 'em. Got fined the other week, but *he* don't care, not our Tristram he don't. When he gets his hands on 'em, he *grackles* 'em. Can't stop 'im. But he's got a good heart, he has."

Was she clever, vicious, or as thick as tripe sauce? He was too intrigued at what was the matter to shake more liquid lodgers off his nose. "I just want some shandy."

"Why didn't you say so, then?" Fortunately, Tristram was too busy struggling with a spiggot in the side bar to bother, and now that things were sorted out she spoke kindly, which he thought was rare for a thin young woman with a big bust and a double chin. He looked in such a way as to make her think he'd noticed something nice about her, so she put his shandy down with a crocodile-smile, took his money, forgot to give him the change, and went to another sector of the front, where he was gratified to hear she was even less friendly while dealing with someone else. He waited in vain for her shrill threat to turn Tristram loose. The suspense made him forget the vengeful flop of the outside wind, and the humiliating snub from the girl-friend he'd thought of as his possible wife for life, even though he was only eighteen and she not yet fifteen. He took the limp exercise book from his pocket, to check that his quips were still legible.

"Are yer going to give us a tune, then?" asked a man by his elbow. Bright yellow eyes ranged across Ernest's face, and the man pushed against him because another half-dozen people had edged in from the monsoon.

The sight of his poems in this hall of boozers made Ernest feel as proud as a pig with a new squeal. He saw himself in the mirror above the skirting-board of bottles and half-measures, a well-set youth with a ginger crop, and a look of amazement at having scribbled anything at all.

He opened his demon notebook that was so sodden he felt sorry for the staples, who were sure to die of an overdose of rust. Then he closed it, not wanting whatever was written down to be held as evidence against him. "I'll give you a tale," he said, his stomach telling him he'd be sick if he didn't start talking.

"Hey, Clarence," a man called out who was smoking a thin cigar, "this young bogger's going to give us a tune — or summat."

The recoil-laugh from Clarence goaded him, but showed only the cobwebbed bed-and-lumber room behind his eyes, as vivid as a dream, so real it jolted him to promise, "I'll tell you a story-and-a-half, if you aren't careful!"

"A cock-and-bull 'un?" a man asked, hopefully.

"I don't know about 'bull'," his young and toothy wife laughed. "'Cock' though for me, any day."

The husband was ready enough. "Come on, then!"

"Not from yo'," she scorned. "It's a pintle! You only do it once, and you flop back dead."

"I'll tell you a gory story, not a stale tale," Ernest said, louder, hoping a shindig wouldn't erupt between man and wife before

28

he could do so. He lay his mac across the bar, and in so doing sent the next man's whisky slopping along the wood. But no murmur came from him because he too was fixed by Ernest's outcoming words, thinking he was either a young maniac about to go into a fit, which would be a treat for jaded Saturday-night eyes to watch, or that he had some proper tale to tell, in which case they might do well to listen.

"Come closer, ladies and gentlemen, fair blue-eyed ladies with pink frocks on, and stocky swart-eyed gents in jackets and fancy trousers!"

This was nowhere near what he wanted to say, but a malicious voice maintained its uncalled for spouting from his guts, and wouldn't be fenced out of things. He had neither a gory tale nor a stale story, and didn't know where his next word was hiding, though as long as he felt he must keep on or die he trusted that some pat phrase would rescue him. They weren't aware of this, and he certainly wouldn't mention it, letting them imagine that every word had been carefully rehearsed in front of a mirror, and listened to half a dozen times on a tape-recorder. Yet if they suspected it hadn't been, they were even more wrong, because he'd often done a snap run-through while going downstairs on a bus and glimpsing himself in the mirror set in the bend, or while pausing at a shop window to straighten his tie. He sometimes got in a quick grimace, or said hello to himself, in the tall porcelain urinal at the local Classic Cinema, or while having a few words in that fertile darkness behind the eyes before sleep's anaesthetic took effect.

"It's good old boozer time, and we're safe from the cold wet streets, so roll up, roll up. . . ."

"I'm not a marble!" a man shouted, and though they laughed, he could tell they wanted him to go on. His eyes were pressed by a dwarf's gleeful thumbs from within, and it felt as if they'd burst and leave nothing but two ragged holes, like embrasures in a fort from which tattered powder-black banners fluttered.

As words began tumbling free, the pressure eased, till he no longer noticed the pain. When he became aware of himself, during interruptions, his knees were like helpless elbows, and he struggled to stay upright by leaning at the bar.

"Roll up, then, and listen while I tell you something that you'll like to hear, not a gory story or a stale tale, but whatever unholy words come from my lips to tempt you into staying where you are."

They were restless. They weren't having any. Why were they stricken by him at all? "Lads and lasses, a tragic thing happened the other day. Don't laugh. It was deplorable. An old lady of ninety-six, a pensioner and a widow, got off a bus at Newark to go and see her son who lives there. It was a sad move, because she left her little hold-all behind on the bus, and in it were her sandwiches, her carpet-slippers and nightgown, but also — you'll never guess — *her life savings* of several hundred pounds in fivers stashed in a handbag. She'd walked off and left everything. Would you believe it? She was forgetful, but who wouldn't be, at ninety-six?

"She was going to stay with her son and his family for a month, and normally kept her savings under a mattress at home in Nottingham, but she felt it was natural that while she was away she ought to take 'em with her in case somebody broke in and helped themselves. So wearing her shawl, and bits of feather-and-tat, she got off the bus to walk to her son's place, leaving the money in the bus."

He'd got 'em. He was laughing inside because he knew very well he'd nailed 'em. His heart was in stitches. Would it go on being easy? They were quiet. He didn't care. His aches and hurts were gone. He was King of the Trent and Prince of the Leen because they even pulled noiselessly at the pumps so as to listen to his tale. Maybe even Tristram was lurking down among the beer barrels sucking up the soapy slops.

He didn't know whether to end the tale by narrating how she never found her money and so died of a broken heart — which would make them depressed and therefore dangerous; or finish by saying that she went back and found that the money had been handed in at the bus station, which would make them happy at the thought of living among a nation of honest and upright people — which would be a downright lie. Either way the tale would end too soon, and then he'd have to think of another. He knew in the fatal silence, getting longer and longer, that it wasn't enough to have the beginning of a story. An ending was necessary, and you needed to have it before you began, what's more. He suddenly realised that any ending was better than no ending at all.

He stood in silence, cauterised, burned-out, a cabbage-head full of fool's worms. He didn't know what to do or say. A glass fell over, and a woman laughed at the noise. Its sound went far down into his stomach, and lay grinding there till it set him going again.

"She lost her life-savings. Every penny was gone, with her sandwiches and Hushpuppies. The inspector went from bus to bus. Drivers and conductors searched for that hold-all of the poor old lady's everything. Maybe they hoped to slip out a twist of fivers for themselves before anybody could see them. Some people are honest, others aren't. You never know." He looked at them accusingly. "Do you? You might think you know, but I'm not so sure from where I happen to be standing."

He felt some demon set to drive them to fury against himself. He crushed it. Hold back! He smiled again, sweating onion juice under his vest. If I do this often I'd better carry a knife to cut myself free. It was blowing a gale outside. You couldn't normally hear it with so much babble and belch, but it was a pin-dropping silence he'd brought about.

"They telephoned depots up to twenty miles away, asking the people to frisk whatever bus got in. She was so shocked – the old lady – that she didn't know which bus she'd taken, whether it had come through Southwell, with its lovely minster, or travelled via Saxondale, with its you-know-what, that loony me will end up in one day – if I'm not careful.

"Her son had been late meeting her, and felt none too well when he did, and heard the news. He was a man of seventy-six, because his mother had had him when she was nineteen. She was frail, but he was on two sticks and dribbling as well. Some of the conductors thought he was the husband, or a brother, because at their ages it was hard to tell.

"The manager sat 'em in the ticket office on a form, and a girl brought 'em a plastic beaker of tea, to try and get some sense out

31

of 'em. When the money didn't show up, nobody believed it had existed, not for a while, anyway, until mother and son began to cry over it — passing the single beaker of tea back and forth like Darby and Joan. But they still weren't sure. It seemed a funny business, these two old fogies holding hands and sobbing at what looked like the loss of four hundred odd quid."

The landlord and waiters were pulling up pints by the dozen and hoving them across the counter because the suspense made everyone thirsty. It only needed somebody to order a drink for others to pass their jars along. The bar men and women were also interested in the story, and Ernest kept a sharp edge to his voice so that all would hear.

The cut-chaff stink of sour beer, and the swirl of fagsmoke, almost gagged him. Glittering light made his eyes ache, but as long as he kept talking the discomfort was bearable. Inner torment had no meaning at such a time. Memories were pushed under the mire and drowned. It was no laughing matter, being driven to find words that might, at a pinch, cure all maladies, and even control other ills that hadn't yet appeared.

"Half an hour later they got the news to the old lady's grandson at the football ground, passing it in between two goals lost by the home side. You can imagine what sort of a paddy *that* put him in. He arrived all of a bluster at the bus station, and kicked the door of the hut in, shouting, 'Why aren't you all on the buses looking for it?' The inspector was shocked at how he spoke to his dad and grandma. His dad had married young, as well, though his mother was in the grave. He'd driven her mad, because all he'd thought about was money, and he'd been on the dole nine-tenths of his life. In fact the whole family thought about nothing else but cash. They drove the people at the National Assistance office mad. The dole office had watched them grow up and expand as a tribe. As a family they made social workers' mouths water. The social workers loved 'em. Without such families they'd be unemployed. Anyway, the old lady's grandson was a six-foot bloke of fifty-six: bald, pig-eyed, bone-idle, and in a blazing temper. You *all* know the sort I mean."

Someone by the door shuffled, and muttered a few threats, as if he indeed *was* the sort, and lively enough to know it, and didn't (what's more) relish such a fact being pointed out to others. Ernest sensed this, so couldn't resist goading him further. "You see, he was a bully. He even lit a fag and blew the smoke at his dad's eyes. It was an accident, though, because nobody's *all* that bad, are they? "

A woman's voice was loud and bitter, "*Aren't* they? Huh! "

There's a story for you. Must talk to her. But there was no time. In any case, he had known her sort from birth.

"Some are, I suppose." He gave her a whiff of encouragement. "But he wasn't as bad as his daughter, who now shoved her tuppence in, having had the news, that her great-grandmother had lost her life savings on a bus, flashed to her on the television screen to detect thieving in a dark corner of the supermarket. She was a thirty-six-year-old woman with a figure like a bag of Bestwood Ashless, who'd married an argumentative man called Alf Squabble. The only time Mr and Mrs Squabble didn't was when they was in bed, and even then you couldn't be sure. Her six kids were clinging around the grocery trolley. They called her Supermarket Sally in the street where she lived, because she'd once given birth to a lovely blue-eyed kid in that place, between Biscuits and Soap powders, and they accused her of shoplifting when she got to the checkpoint, till someone vouched for what had happened, and said they didn't sell babies there, anyway. The manager realised his mistake, and awarded her a tin of beans and a packet of sausages, to make up for his stupid blunder.

"Forgive that little digression. Suffice it to say that the disease of marrying young, and the gift of procreation, was rife in that family. After paying up, and sending the kids home with the regimental supplies, she hurried to the bus station, and found the three of them looking noughts-and-daggers at each other.

"First thing she does is shock everybody by smacking her father right across the face. It sent an echo twenty miles and back. It reverberated round the county. It hit Southwell minster, clipped Newstead Abbey, and bounced off Major Oak. He was a dirty old bleeder, was Major Oak. He was in the Sherwood Foresters, and lost a leg in the Great War, but that didn't stop him one night getting into . . ."

"Get on with it."

"Thank you. Sorry about that. But can you imagine? A great beefy bully like him, wilting under a loud biff in the suet-chops from his lardy daughter? For nothing at all, as far as anybody knew. He'd always been a bit of a dirty swine. I don't suppose we'll ever know the truth, though his secret passion for malt whisky didn't help."

He was going too far, should never have let his glib tongue flap. He was like a cork bouncing on a wave-top, enjoying itself at the free movement, yet not seeing those carborundum rocks close by, with saw-teeth and snaggle-jaws.

"It's bloody far-fetched," a man shouted, with some justice.

"Everything in life *is*," he reassured him. "But listen, let me tell you what was written up in the *North Nottinghamshire Advertiser*. I expect you've forgotten, and in any case my version is better. I'll describe the trial, and the inquests."

"What was it, then," Larry Logic called, "a trial – or a bleeding inquest? "

Two queries to answer. They bled, all right. The bus station was a battlefield. No, he'd better not say that. They were getting belligerent. He had to hold them back, but the fact that they didn't look pleasant led him to say:

"Both."

They shouted for a happy ending which, in the nature of all things not very bright and far from beautiful, wasn't possible. Who could start a story that might have a happy ending? Not him. Another wail suggested they might demand a sentimental conclusion so strongly that he'd have to relent. There was no denying a crowd. A crowd could have anything, given its mind-less nature, especially when facing someone as powerless as him-self. Things might be different against tanks and machine-guns, but even then you couldn't be sure, if the crowd was big enough, and clever enough, and dead-set enough. From now on, he hated crowds. *Très Bon:*

"The woman's father turned chalk-white with rage and shame when his daughter slapped him in public. She shouted that it was his fault her great-grandma had lost all her money – *lovely* spotless money, she actually called the filthy stuff – that by rights should have come to her, and her children. She ranted

34

as if he'd pulled bread from their mouths, and made the poor little sods cough up half-eaten fish-fingers and prefabricated chips. Did they have to go on drawing National Assistance for the rest of their lives? He'd never had any family feeling, she screamed, tears in her eyes, as if she was the one who had been slapped. If he had, she bawled, (had any family feeling, she meant) he would have gone to Nottingham and brought poor old Grannie back in comfort on the train, then she wouldn't have lost that precious packet of four hundred quid."

His audience was quiet. He swelled with sentimentality, which he thought was pride. They loved him. Not bad for a first time, he told himself. They waited silently for each phrase. They were respectful.

"The bus inspector asked them to discuss the matter reasonably. The money would soon be found, anyway. But what he was really thinking. . . ."

"How do you know what he was *thinking*?"

"Stop interrupting — or Tristram might get you."

"Fuck Tristram," a deeper voice called. "I'll put that milksop in 'ospital anyday."

"I know what was going through his mind because he told me later. I got the whole story. He was an uncle of mine."

"Stupid fucking big-'ead! Kill 'im!"

"The bus inspector was thinking that when it *was* found, ladies and *gentlemen*, he hoped to God they'd be out of his office, because in arguing who it belonged to they'd tear it, him, each other, and any sundry spectators within blood spitting distance, to shreds of flesh and blips of snot. The bus station, and half its vehicles would surely end as a smoking bomb-site, not to mention a fair slice of the historic town of Newark going down under the flames of their savage greed!"

"Shouldn't wonder," some simple soul threw in, with deep conviction.

This interjection, on the whole a favourable one, unfortunately jacked up his self-esteem, which was the sort of encouragement he least needed, for it led to a further embroidering.

"The inspector, an amicable chap not long out of the army,

35

was beginning to have some effect in calming them down, when there was a knock at the door. It was a timid knock, but don't be deceived by that. A girl of about sixteen came in. She had an enormous belly pushing out under her Oxfam skirt, as if she was going to give birth to twins in the next five minutes. She went up to her mother, and whispered something. The mother turned white at the gills and pushed her back, telling her, in her outspoken way, to mind her own business or she'd knife her. Before I inform you what the pregnant girl said, ladies and gentlemen, I want to bring to your attention the fact that in this little hut at the bus station there were no less than six generations of the same underprivileged family."

"Chuck yer fuckin' pint over 'im," shouted a long-haired youth wearing an ear-ring and a headscarf — the modern garb of the Nottingham Lambs. Ernest wasn't too worried. If the suggestion had been to *chuck* the pint *at* him, he would certainly have trembled, for then the attack — albeit unasked for — would not have been merely liquid, but might have involved him in the reception, at some part of his undefended face, of the hard bullet-like pint-glass jar itself.

"You can tell he's having us on," yelled the hooligan's mate, sounding like the limb-ripping Tristram himself.

"I'm not codding you," Ernest pleaded. "By no means. And to prove it I'm going to pass this *empty* pint jar around, and hope you'll all be generous enough to put in what little contribution you can spare, and when it comes back to me I'll tell you how the day finished up at that unlucky bus station. You'll be surprised at what happens. There's a totally unexpected ending."

"Turf the bleeder out."

"We come 'ere to get *drunk*, not put up with 'is rigmarole."

If these comments had originated from the same person he might have forced the tale back to his own telling, but curses spread like steel darts, and the pushing began.

"Didn't you like my story?"

They'd listened from other rooms, and everyone was laughing. The first fist ran at him. They thumped him on his way to the door. Feet tried to trip him. It wasn't the vicious sort of treatment one might expect, for he got through without much damage, except that a hand more spiteful than the rest — from man or woman, he couldn't tell, and in any case it didn't matter — gripped his hair which, being fairly short, gave slight purchase. Jostling to safety, he tried not to look at anyone's face, for to do so would, he knew, invite serious blows. Yet it was impossible not to, and the glares that bounced back were rabid.

"Don't hurt the lad," the landlord bellowed. "He's done no harm."

The rain had stopped, though the wind still roamed. He'd left his coat on the bar, and as he turned to go back, probably at the cost of his life, a woman pushed it into his arms. "Come back next week," she winked. "We loved it."

He didn't know what had got him into such daftness. Telling tales in pubs! And for money? Show your teeth when you laugh like that, you ginger-haired bastard. Donkey-head. He lived a mile away, so the story of his story might not reach home. In any case they would be so drunk at chucking out time that they wouldn't remember much of what happened by Sunday morning. You live in hope, but you die in squalor. Maybe he'd leave home, and do it in Leicester. Never cack on your own doorstep. Move South to Northampton and, after a week or two at the pubs there, go and cheer up the car workers of Luton, which would be good practice for when he finally chucked himself into London.

He planned his future while hoping no one would remember his first fiasco. He'd learn from the flop of it. There'd be plenty, but with every one he'd get better. The day wouldn't be far off when he'd see money after sending the hat among the pigeons. Pub landlords would invite him to do proper performances, as if he were a piano player jazzing around the keys. He might get famous, and be paid by cheque instead of begging like a jester.

Plans and expectations ferried him through the dark. He held the exercise book of poems on his head to stop getting wet when the rain began again, and crumpled it into his pocket on going into the chicken-and-chippery to buy some supper.

A man in the queue babbled about his father.

Whose father?

The young, thin, old man's face with grey hair and false teeth, and big black bakelite National Health specs, repeated the desperate news.

Ernest felt the poisonous grudge of every pub ill-wisher crammed into his voice as he told him to: "Piss off! "

The man spoke again, the dreadful truth enabling him to ignore Ernest's unfriendly request. Such malice — for it was no less in such weather — was understandable, even to be expected.

"Don't get like that, Ernie, duck. I used to look after you when you was a little lad, when your mam was badly. I carried you all over the place on my shoulders. You was only two or three, don't you remember? "

He did, and said so. "But what did you tell me just now about my father? "

"Yer feyther? "

"Yer said summat."

"I know I did, my owd duck. An accident it was. Out like a light. I didn't see it, but that's what I heard."

Ernest knew himself to be the victim of one of his own stories. Without waiting for chips, chops, chicken or chutney — or even a chinwag in Chesterfield — he ran home to see whether it was true. He was sure a terrible mistake had been made. Live in expectation, and perish in the dust.

The big wheels and mudguards of a bus breathed at his ankles. I'll never tell another story, he screeched, leaping onto safe pavement. If it's true, I'll keep my claptrap shut, shrivel my heart and stitch my gob for ever.

He blamed the pub story for everything. While in thrall to such cock-eyed narration his father had stood up from the fireside to switch on the television set six feet away, and subsided as if pole-axed by a mattock of Scotch mist. He hadn't even been to the pub that night, and was dead by the time his wife got back from the beer-off with a quart of ale for his supper.

Even that was a lie. Everything was falsehood, and he had to get out of such regions or die two score years before his proper call. You could only lie with impunity when you were young. Sooner or later the time came when you had to fight through a jungle and reach the truth.

His father hadn't died on his way to the telly. He'd concocted that yarn to save his mother's already mortared and pestled heart – and his own kicked-in soul. Terence Cotgrave, with the quiff and cravat, and eau de cologne and silver fag-case, hadn't been in the house that night at all. Where he had been nobody was sure, "Till that woman," he said in a later story, "whom neither I nor my mother had known, was spotted by my aunt Winnie putting more expensive flowers on his grave than we'd ever been able to buy. We didn't care how he'd met her, but he had numerous chances at that garage he'd worked at as an assistant mechanic. The depth of his incompetence at that place was known only to himself, though suspected by others, most of all by a few of the unlucky customers. Now and again the manager would give him a car to work on, usually a foreign model belonging to one of the better-off clients, who were less likely to complain, and who knew little enough about cars, anyway. Perhaps the woman he was coming home from seeing on the night he died was one of these. Life's full of assumptions."

He was killed in a smash on the wet and misty motorway. Ernest heard about it after his stint in the pub that first evening, so he had killed him just the same. He was left with a six-figure map reference to where the pile-up had taken place, that the police had given him. The suit and shirts didn't fit, and he wouldn't be seen dead wearing the cuff links with antique cars painted on them.

A slender footbridge went high over the motorway, steep steps leading out of a conifer wood between Beauvale and Misk Hill. From the top he could lean on the parapet and, with a pair of binoculars, as traffic below rushed north and south in sun or swirling mist, just see the spot where his father's car had ignited on that fateful storyteller's night. As on a battlefield still full of unexploded bombs, there was no safe way to get at it.

He mesmerised the tarmacadam. Nothing would save him, or anybody. If he presaged his own death with a story he hoped it would be an improvement on a pub yarn, and hoped also that it would take the whole of a long life to tell.

3

After cycling through a burst water-main on Bath Street his flannel trousers hung wet around his ankles. A glance back from Carlton Hill, through the sore throat of shops and houses, showed an agitated pond of drab streets ending at the Castle, and at the General Hospital whose central tower rose like a gasometer on the skyline. To get his breath, he leaned against his new Raleigh machine, then took off his clips so that his trousers would dry in the long freewheeling descent. At Netherfield Crossing he counted twenty-eight wagon-loads of Nottingham products trundling by.

When the four gates swung inwards he pedalled his way to the street of two-up and two-down houses, hoping his Aunt Winnie was back from chapel. Most of the family didn't like her. At his father's funeral she had been the only person, apart from himself and his mother, dressed in proper black.

"What does that old crow want?" said a cousin, who added that she'd been born with a carbolic tongue and a worse temper. Her hair would be as grey as slate, if she didn't dye it dark, he said, and Ernest knew that her eyes could be as blue as red if her occasional painkillers didn't work. Her condemnation of their feckless ways was considered to be nothing more than malice. What his cousin said she wouldn't give you didn't bear repeating in anybody's earshot. Ernest assumed that only his yen for storytelling had made him overhear such things, and remember them afterwards.

Winnie was a member of the local Co-op Committee, and worked for the Labour Party. The more energy she gave, the more she saw was needed. She always had an opinion about people, and would ask a dozen questions between somebody coming in the door, and her giving them a cup of tea, and a slice of home-made buttered bread as if it were a prize at the end of a relay race. Deep lines from the flanges of the nose almost connected to either side of her mouth, an architectural grimness belying her generous and exploring spirit. She sometimes went into hospital — hence the painkillers — because of her liver which, at three-score years was, she said, no fun, though God doubtless knew what he was doing. At least it was easier to get into a hospital now, unlike those days before the war.

"Tell me another," Ernest thought. "I'm fed up hearing about them bad old days." He wondered which war she meant, because eighty-year-old Percy had been in those dreadful never-to-be-forgotten trenches of the Great War that a lot of ancient fogies mumbled about. Percy's pale face looked as fragile as an eggshell which, should you tap it with a spoon, might crack and crumble in, and show whether there was white or yolk inside. Perhaps to prevent anyone being tempted to this experiment he always smoked his black twist by the fire, but also maybe because in that position the most noxious of his fumes were drawn up the chimney. He was a little, hunched-up man who never took off his cap till he went to bed, and who was as alive to everything as if he were still fourteen years of age.

Ernest noted the piano, and the lock-and-key Bible, with other books from the library on top. There was a plant in a copper pot, with big green arching leaves, which he'd heard called an aspidistra. In a cut-glass dish on a corner what-not was a collection of beach pebbles and shells that Winnie had brought back from holiday excursions, two or three from each place which, mixed as they were, allowed her to remember the various piers, parades and esplanades, and perhaps to recall a positive whiff of the sea.

On the sofa was a black baby, dressed in pink and blue, whose wide-open eyes tracked every move. When Ernest held a finger to her face, the warm hand closed around with such a grip that he felt the panic of never getting free. He'd have to go everywhere the baby went even if he didn't want to, though when she grew into a young woman he'd climb into bed with her, and only then would she let go of his finger, in order to grab a stiffer one.

"It's Laura, and she's a real angel, aren't you, my little duck?" Winnie squeezed Laura's cheek, and Ernest winced for her, but she released his finger to smile at his aunt. "Laura's one of the Lord's children, aren't you, my love?"

She gurgled, and tried to lift up, and Percy came over for a look. "She'll be a devil at the tuppenny hop when she's eighteen." He went back to his fireside grandad-seat, which had a plaid blanket over the back so that the wind wouldn't get through at his backbone and ribs.

"She belongs to Albert and Jenny, next door. Albert works for the gas. They came in last week and said would I look after her while they went to Leeds for a couple of hours to see Albert's brother who was getting married. I expect they'll be home in a day or two. They know she's all right with us. Don't they Percy?"

"You tell 'em, my bonny lass!"

"They took us to Bleasby in their car last month. Had a nice little drink by the Trent, then came back here for tea."

There were dark patches under her eyes, and she sat down to stir the teapot. She worked three days a week at a corner shop, selling tinned beans and ginger-pop and cut bread over the counter, so with Percy's old-age pension they had enough to live on, though there was no telly or hi-fi or fridge or any of the stuff there was in Ernest's house — except an old wireless on the sideboard. He handed Percy an ounce of twist: "I brought you this."

Percy held the yellow-orange box to the light. "Fancy a lad like you giving me things. What a jammy devil I am! It's my favourite smoke." Dottle hissed as he knocked his pipe against the fireplace. "I'll be sending Indian telegrams till midnight!"

"I don't like him to smoke more than half a dozen a day," Winnie said. "It's wicked stuff. Wicked price, as well. *And* it stinks the house up. He's allus shuffling across the yard to the lavatory when he smokes too much. Drink that tea, or it'll get cold."

It was scalding, though she had finished hers already. You could hear Percy making a fair go of his by the fire. Laura swung her head from the settee as if she could do with a guzzle as well. Maybe slooshing tea when it was too hot had turned Winnie so sallow and ruined her liver. She reached to the mantel-shelf for a bottle of rose-hip syrup, filled the large teat of a dummy, and plopped it into Laura's mouth.

"She gets the gripes. Don't you my love? Don't you, then, my little duck?" Laura's eyes closed in an enjoyment that no one over the age of three can know about, as the syrup went down like sand out of an eggtimer. "How's work?"

The buttered toast was halfway to his mouth. "Still making plywood. I had a raise last week."

"Serve the boggers right," Percy called out. "Never did pay enough. Sweated on the railway sixty years, I did, except for five in the army. I'll show you that dagger one day. Ain't looked at it since I put it in the cellar with the rest of my kit. Used to carry a bit o' sharpening stone in my haversack. Kept it like a razor. Jumped into the mud-'ole near Passchendaele, and it was either him or me. So I ran it up his gut before he could do me in."

He cackled as if ready again for the same bit of fun, and Ernest knew he wasn't lying. Winnie told him not to be such a filthy old beast, and covered her ears. Sometimes Percy would torment her by going over it again and again. Fifty years had gone by before he started telling the tale. Ernest wondered why he was doing so now, when he'd not long to go before dying himself. Even in those Great War days he couldn't have been much above five-feet, a little old bantam youngster trundling forward under his own weight in kit, holding the rifle-and-bayonet but slinging it down so as to take out that terrible knife, and gut the German as some of his own mates lying in the muddy trench had already been gutted.

Winnie turned. "You aren't thinking of changing your job, are you?"

Her brown eyes looked full at him, and at such a gaze he had to come straight out with what was on his mind. Maybe it was good to know at least one person you couldn't lie to.

"You don't go boozing, do you?"

"I have a shandy at the weekend."

"That's bad, at your age."

Laura's empty dummy fell onto the rug, and she screamed for it back. When Ernest put it into her mouth she screamed again

43

because it was empty. "I tell stories, for entertainment."

Winnie rocked her till the house was quiet and he wished it wasn't. "I've never heard of such a thing."

He tried to laugh. "I spin a few yarns, and they pass the hat around. Earns me a quid or two."

"That sounds like begging." She wasn't the sort to leave you alone if she thought something was bothering you. "You can't be hard up with a job like yours."

A vertically narrow picture on the wall by the stairfoot door, in a plain brown furniture frame, was of a lighthouse in a stormy sea. The scene was grey, and precise, and a beam shone sharply on boiling waves rising up as if to put out the light. And on a curling crest was a rowing boat, heading for a valley between the waves, a movement towards disaster that would soon cause it to smash against the base of the lighthouse itself. Ernest looked at it, as if to get guidance, but only found confusion. "It ain't begging. I work for my living in the factory all week, to get money I live on. It's like playing a piano, or a banjo."

"I daresay it is. What kind of stories?"

"Tales that just come into my head."

She folded her arms, and sighed. "Do people like 'em?"

"They clap when I've done, and want me to go on."

Last Saturday night, on passing the hat round, a jokey swine dropped some crisps in. Another bloke threw in an empty fag packet. But somebody else put in a fiver.

"Do you mean to say you stand there, telling lies?"

"They aren't lies."

"They're *tales*, though."

He had to justify himself. "Your Bible's full o' tales."

"Not the sort you tell. You don't take after me. Nor your dad, either. It's a good job poor Terence ain't alive to hear you."

He drank his tea. Thank God he wasn't. He'd be as jealous as hell if he was. He couldn't tell her that he'd started his storytelling on the evening of his father's car smash. "I just stand there, and start to talk."

"As long as you make people happy." Curiosity led her to repeat the question: "What sort of stories?"

"About things that happen, to people like us, mostly."

She laughed. "I'd like to hear you, only I don't go in pubs, as a rule. I never knew one of our lot would be able to tell stories and earn a few coppers. But I suppose there's a need of it. As it says in Job: 'the ear trieth words, as the mouth tasteth meat.' "

These few words shone through at him like the white glittering rays from the lighthouse in the picture of desolation. He was glad that he had come to see her: "I like that saying."

"Aye," she said solemnly, "I learned a bit by listening to the preacher, and reading the Book. Some of us are going to Matlock soon, to meet people from the other chapels. I like Matlock. It's lovely to go in a boat on the river, if it's a sunny day! I'm hoping Jenny'll be back next door by then, so's she can look after Percy. Not to mention our Laura." She tilted the teapot, but only got half a cup, as black as tar. "Shall you go on with telling stories?"

"It makes me feel good," he admitted. "And *I* don't do it, in any case. It's something inside me as does it."

She made more tea, a blacker pot than the first. He'd be weaving back and forth on the way home, for it looked twenty times more potent than a gallon of bitter. He thought it a good thing there was no breathalyser for this sort of tea.

"If you've got a gift," she said, "you've got a gift. Tell *good* stories, though. Lies will get you nowhere. If you tell lies, God will take your gift away. He destroyed whole cities because wicked people told lies."

He didn't like it when she talked as if she met God once a week and put him right on a few people she knew. "I'll just remember what it says in Job."

"Read the rest of it," she advised. "It's a lovely book, Job is. Awful!"

He swallowed the tea. "If Albert and Jenny ain't back home, I'll look after Percy when you're at Matlock. Laura, as well."

Percy came to life on hearing his name: "I'll smoke twist all day if you do. They'll think the chimbley's on fire! We'll rummage round the cellar and find that dagger. Look at it again. Good for my eyes. Hold it tight. Get some grip in me veins! Mek me think I'm back in the mud. King o' the Mud, I was. Over the squelchy bags at dawn. There was a song about that. Can't remember it, though."

45

The words put real pain on Winnie's face, and Ernest felt sorry for her, though he wanted to hear the tale nevertheless. She took her knitting from the sideboard. "He can never talk about it unless he swears. I'd better put Laura's bottle on."

Ernest thought it might be his only way of annoying her. It was hard to see why he wanted to, yet everyone had to get back at everyone else, or how could they otherwise bear the sight of each other? His own parents had made a good enough job of it, and that was more than a fact. Maybe he'd put that into somebody's story, as well.

"It beat me fair and bloody proper, it did" – though Percy grinned when he said it – "Pissing down with rain near Passchendaele. Up to my bum in mud, then as high as my chest. Shells plopped in. Chucked it in yer eyes. Needed a pudding-spoon to get it out. It was grey, but the rain was acid, and stung your face. Bullets zizzing, all over. More frightened o' falling. Didn't know what was under the mud. Terrified me, all that slime. Sergeant screamed and bullied us on, poor bloke. Gerry machine-guns must a been up on a bit o' dry land. Didn't think about it. We'd been shelled all night, and hadn't slept a wink. Couldn't even lift me gun to fire because I was too tired pushing through the slosh. There was sulphur in the sky. Some didn't try. Stood crying. I felt like it myself. But I went on. Up for Old Nottingham and Lovely Manchester, they said I shouted! I didn't know what I bawled out. I didn't think. You can't fight, and think as well. Got me rifle and started to shoot. I allus get strength from somewhere. Shot standing up. No firestep. Arms like logs o' wood. If I knelt down I'd be up to my armpits. If I laid down I'd be right under. A real bleddy tattar. Got forward, still on me feet. Then I was close enough to chuck a bomb. Face in the slush when it went off. I run in, and bayoneted one. Don't suppose he saw me. He was tireder than I was. I was only a titch. He must have looked level, and didn't see me because I was under his eyes. Pushed me bayonet right in, then twisted it and yanked it out. Then I got another with me knife. Up the crotch. Blood all over me. Still, we captured their mud-'ole. 'Think of it as the middle of Berlin,' our Colonel had said. No officers with us by this time. Only twenty out of a hundred and forty. Laughing

46

mad. Loonies, we was. We 'ad some good times! Stayed all day, but it was nearly as dark as night, scoffing Gerry grub and puffing his fat smokes. It was funny mud, because it smelled like tinned tomatoes. We couldn't get back to our own lot. Nobody could come to us. Get killed if they tried. Machine-guns swept us from every-bleddy-where. The Gerries came for their trench back, but we shot 'em like pigs. They shot us like rabbits in a burrow with the lid off. We pulled out at night, anyway, the six of us that was left. I've still got me knife. Never part with that cleaver! It come in useful for good old England, that knife did. I was blindoe-drunk when I got back. 'Good old bleddy England!' I was waving an empty bottle of Gerry brandy. I'll tek that knife wi' me to Hell in case there's trouble. Put it in my bury-box when I die, will you Winnie? If *you* don't, Ernie will, wain't yer, Ernie, my owd?"

"All right," Ernest promised.

Winnie looked up, glad that the yarn had spun itself out. "It's God you should pray to, not England. Them wicked war days is over." After a pause, she added, "At least, I hope so."

Ernest had known Percy since he was a kid, but it was the first time he'd heard the full yarn of his knife. He felt sorry he couldn't use it in a pub tale. If he tried, they'd trample him underfoot and throw the bits of him that remained out by the piss-house door.

Who else but a senile old chokka like Percy would want to remember a thing like that? Yet the tale worried Ernest. His dreams would recollect that grey sky raining mud and bullets and shell-splinters, and he'd wake up groaning with fear. His wife would nudge him with a sharp elbow. Sometimes he was in a trench whose walls dripped sludge, and suddenly a dwarf-German soldier gripping a razor-sharp knife came for him like the spark of a cobra's bite. He didn't relish what Percy had passed on to him, though he could just as easily have got it from a book, or from hearing a story on the radio.

Winnie helped Percy to bed. There were sighs from both at every step. Winnie's kind words at each meant a long pause, so that Percy could get breath. She'd never borne children, but Ernest had always looked on her as if she'd had at least half a dozen, and even if she had, Percy would still have been her favourite, King of the Old Mud Pies, and fit for any story Ernest might one day tell.

4

Every time he flung himself into his leather overcoat the weight nearly knocked him to the ground, as if a live thing with a long-standing grudge against him had latched onto his back. The coat weighed like chain-mail, and stank of polish. Without heavy and regular doses of polish its outer covering turned into blotting paper.

Though he sweated half to death, he told better stories when he performed in it. Wearing it made him look as if he were going to leave any moment, especially when standing with one foot forward, with two hands hovering to button and belt it up. They liked that, because it created uncertainty. The open coat made them listen, whether or not the story had a mediocre beginning.

"Ladies and gentlemen, this garb on my back – well, I'm going to tell you how I got it, and what it means to me." They thought his story was both homely and vivid, a moment of living truth when he wore the actual garment. He learned slowly, and hardly at all. Any success was due to inspiration, helped by various improvisations. His wit despised the sweat of learning. He preferred going head-first into a story, and hoped that the heart would follow. There was danger in methodical self-instruction, because what you took in could easily pack up and unlearn itself from your brain. Ambition told him to rely on inspiration, and put himself at the mercy of his own spirit. It worked, at a price. He never knew when a pack of his own invented characters wouldn't suddenly become so real that they'd surround and then rend him ear from arse. He laughed at such a daft idea, which was no sort of story at all. Most of the time, he felt that he performed in a television screen, and that everyone in the pub had

49

their eyes fixed on him. He was real, and in colour, and talked, and they hadn't bought a licence to switch him on. All they had to do was drink, and listen.

He first saw the leather overcoat on a tatter's perambulator one weekday summer evening, under a bit of old mangle, an electric-light bracket, and a plastic bucket with a hole in the bottom. The coat – he told them – trailed assertively over the handle. The belt-buckle tapped at the kerb as the tatter pushed his elegant though battered pram up the street. Ernest was tired after eight hours in the plywood factory. "Where did you pick that up, mate?"

The tatter sensed a deal. He stopped his pram by bending down and turning a brake handle to the left, "It's none o' your fucking business, *mate*."

Ernest didn't know whether to smash him in both eyes, or laugh. He eschewed the former course, because the tatter was ruggedly built under his buttonless sports jacket, which showed an impeccable gentleman's waistcoat between flesh and vest. He might turn out to be one of those educated failures who had taken to the streets for a bit of real life. They were often vicious, and would stand no nonsense, being firm believers in Drop-out Liberation. A couple of Nottingham Lambs set on such a bloke in Slab Square the other week, hoping for a bit of kickabout fun, but two minutes later they were bleeding like stuck pigs, and shouting for the police to pull him off.

Ernest grinned. "I'll try it on, if you like."

"How much will yer give me for it?"

"It'll smother me."

"Not in winter, it wain't. It'll *mother* you then!"

Ernest touched it.

"If you want to make it look smart you rub polish in, and when you put it on in a storm the rain'll run off and over your wellingtons. A good hat, and you're wetproof," the tatter lectured, in a suspiciously posh accent all of a sudden.

"I'll try it."

The man scratched his beard, picked something from the middle of the bush, threw it onto the pavement, and stamped on it. Ernest swore he heard a muffled scream. The tatter then pushed the mangle-rollers aside, and held the coat for Ernest to slip his arms into as if they were in the best of men's outfitters. A button was missing, and a tiny hole in one arm near the shoulder suggested that a jealous husband had aimed a poignard — or knitting needle — at the retreating wearer. It would be impossible to run far, but it looked a treat for wrapping up in so that nobody would be able to kick you to death. It was an effort to lift his arms after being at work all day, yet such a heavy coat made him feel a different man.

"How much?" — knowing that the rogue had picked it up for five bob.

"Ten quid."

"I'll give you one."

"Ten."

"I'm a working man, not a millionaire."

The tatter squinted. His left eye was bloodshot. "I've got to live, as well."

"You will, at that price."

He whined, and started to cry. He enjoyed being treated as a human being, and was determined to get the most out of it — while it lasted. "I gave *nine* for it."

"Nine what?"

He put it back in his pram. "Not bloody marbles."

Ernest offered two pounds.

He snarled, "Piss off" — and pushed his vehicle away.

"Three."

He turned, and glared at Ernest as if he didn't like people with freckles and ginger hair — though he wouldn't say anything about that for the moment. "I wasn't born yesterday, you schizoid bourgeois ponce!"

Ernest knew he'd been right to suspect his origins. "Neither was I."

"You must have been." He went down the street, whistling one of the Brandenburg Concertos, but when he reached the corner shop Ernest ran after him. "How much do you want?"

The tatter looked wise, and spoke gently: "It's worth all of fifty, son."

"Not to me," Ernest said glumly, wondering whether the man

51

weren't an out-of-work actor, or an ex-newsreader.

"I've never seen such a coat."

"I'll give you four." It couldn't have come from a dustbin in this district. He'd probably been calling for old rags at the big houses in Mapperley, going from one to another and ripping a bit off each privet hedge in rancour whenever nobody answered his knock. He tried the handle of one such door, found it unlocked, went into the hall, saw the coat with his beady eyes, and came out with it. Ernest knew his tricks all right.

"I've got my rent to pay," the tatter said, now with an American accent. "I don't live under Brooklyn Bridge."

"I'll be squatting under Trent Bridge, though, if I give you more than five. I'm late for my tea."

"Ten." He was as stubborn as Gibraltar. As for the fact that Ernest's sumptuous tea might be getting chilled on the table, he wasn't moved. "I know what I paid for it, man."

If he stalked off in order to call his bluff he might never see the coat again, and the tatter would flog it on the next corner for his asking price. On the other hand if he did walk away maybe the man would grovel back up the street on his belly and say he could have it for five bob. But he was tired of the game. The bloke might go on for hours changing accent and character from one story to another. The longer it went on the healthier he looked. He thrived on it, and Ernest knew he couldn't win with this Jack-of-all-Personalities but Master of None. "I'll give you eight pounds for it."

The tatter became a sullen old tramp again. He hauled the coat up, threw it across Ernest's shoulders, took the money with what seemed like telescopic mandibles, counted it twice, and was around the next corner before a check could be made to see that the rest of the buttons were all there.

The reason that the marriage in my story tonight is different to everybody else's, he went on, edging into the mainstream of his evening's peroration, is because the woman in the case fell in love with the coat I'm wearing. That's why I don't unload it until – or unless – it's bedtime. I wear it everywhere, as if it's stuck to my shoulder blades. If she had fallen in love with what was in my breeches, as the old saying goes, we could have understood it, couldn't we? But she saw the glistening back of my brown leather coat (he turned around, to show them) which only an hour before had slurped up two tins of the best saddle polish. It was a greedy bleeder, though I was greedier in those young days. There was a hard frost that evening, and I was all wrapped up in it with nowhere to go, standing as warm as toast at that request bus stop waiting for the next to come along, while the town hall clock bonked six from Slab Square.

One of my favourite pastimes was to set out for nowhere in particular. It was the potent action of a negative mood that allowed me to drift aimlessly without touching any part of reality, but only so's there'd be a better chance of getting closer to it than if I charged head-on. The danger was that it might draw me through deceptive calms and into a fatal whirlpool that would suck me out of my carefree life completely.

When the queue moved, and we came to the step, I let her on first. I then followed her upstairs, and plonked myself across the gangway in case she thought I was trying to click, which I was, though without much caring whether I succeeded or not. There was always a better chance of getting what I wanted that way. I was also too proud to be suspected of trying, and wouldn't dream of pushing up on the same seat like a dirty old man. In any case, my coat took so much space that I needed a seat to myself.

The conductress came up.

"One to the Whirlpool, duck," I asked.

"Eh?"

I held out my money. "Whirlpool."

She didn't know whether to laugh, kick me in the shins, or stop the bus and wait for an inspector. "Where's that, then?"

It might be a slang name for a place she should have known about, but didn't because her mates had sent her to Coventry without her knowing it — for something she didn't know she'd done.

I gave in: "Terminus."

"Why didn't you say so in the first place? Whirlpool! It is, though, at times, a proper bleddy whirlpool at the depot!"

She turned to my future wife, who wanted a ticket to Colwick Bend, and got it with a smile. We were the only two on top.

53

"Where was that place you wanted a ticket to?" she asked me.

"I forget."

"No, you don't."

"The whirlpool."

"Why did you say that?"

"It just came into my head."

"Did it?"

She was older than me, so I didn't feel shy. "Life is a bit of a whirlpool, isn't it?"

She admitted that it might be.

"One minute it's calm, and the next you're getting sucked under."

"You don't *look* as if you've just had a nervous breakdown."

Even off duty I couldn't help entertaining people. "I haven't."

"That's good, then."

"I don't think I ever will, either."

She laughed, as if to say, "We'll see about that."

"You're having me on," she said aloud.

Only honesty will help win a woman like this, I decided. "The whole of my life's a nervous breakdown. I was born into one, and I'll die out of one. A nervous breakdown from beginning to end, but I carry it well, don't I? That's why I'll never have one of the sort you're hinting at."

Her light-green eyes were duller than they need be, and I could tell she felt better at hearing what to me was unimportant chat. It was right up her street. She also saw I was different, though different to what I didn't stop to wonder, which was a pity. I gathered later that she saw me as bright and vulnerable. My words were a bit of a challenge, and also a comfort to her. What a laugh! But I haven't come to that yet. She didn't know that I felt much the same about her, not from the way she spoke, because she hadn't said much, but from how she looked.

She was tall, almost stout, and nearly thirty years old, with short black hair, and an extremely pale face. She looked generous, and fundamentally distracted under the sheen of her all-knowingness. I soon found out (but you never discover anything till it's too late to do much about it, though too late for what, remains a mystery till it really is too late) that she always

54

knew exactly what she wanted, and usually got it, being far better at such half-buried zig-zags than I was, which meant that I couldn't blame her for what happened.

She was the manageress of the packing department at a hosiery firm up in the Lace Market, and her distracted expression – she told me, when I mentioned how attractive I found it – erased itself as soon as she walked onto the shop floor in her black patent-leather, medium-heeled shoes. The girls were afraid of her, even in these days.

She had a raffia shopping bag on her knee, and had come from visiting her mother in the General Hospital. "She fell down in the market and broke her leg. I reckon she's going a bit senile, though she's only seventy."

"I'm sorry." Her fingers were cold. She pressed my hand. I was a stranger, but a harmless one. "Just hold on lightly," I advised, "and they'll warm up quicker."

She pulled out a cigarette, so I fumbled for matches, but she flipped on a lighter without waiting. "I like your coat."

That's how it started. She admired my coat, ladies and gentlemen. Our relationship began as a casual affair, otherwise I would not have married her. I don't honestly believe she would have wedded me either, if she'd known. It didn't seem that we were courting, or even dabbling seriously on the sofa. (As you can imagine, however, we became veritable gluttons for hearthrug pie.) But if we had fallen heavily in love we'd have dropped harmlessly out of it long before getting married. We just didn't know how to drift apart.

In her decision to marry me, which she made to herself quite early on, Marion was naive, because she only detected the simpleton in me, and not the storyteller. When I made up my mind to marry her (all unbeknown to her) I was naive, because I saw only the woman in her, and not the mother who would one day wish I had never been born. When two people think they're onto a good thing with regard to each other, it's bound to be a disaster. The powder trail was long and loving, but it was also explosive, and in fact is still going on, sizzling in a slow-moving fuse through every acre of the jungle.

At the time of our first encounter I didn't have anything better

55

to do with my life except work, while Marion was at a stage where so many things were making her miserable that she didn't know what to do next. Out of despair she believed that whatever she did was bound to be better than what was. What could we do except get married? She took the pill, and wasn't even pregnant. She knew what she wanted, though, because what is despair except the purest sort of lust? And I knew what I wanted, for what is sloth except the deepest form of greed?

Such a story, warped by innaccuracy as it is bound to be when told out of my mouth, could not be related in a single session, nor even in the total blackness of the night that lasted from a leap year's end to the next. But he stripped his matrimonial saga clean in public, and enjoyed it. He took his time. He employed gobbets of his never-ending mal-liaison with Marion to pad out various tales. He was still married, and hadn't yet started to kick and thump against the tin walls of the family psycho-box with sufficient violence to make it drop to pieces, but took the story, before the evening was out, beyond the birth of their daughter. A son was expected at any moment, otherwise Marion might have been with him, having more or less subdued her embarrassment at seeing him standing on a platform at the end of a pub's best room reciting stories for their food and shelter.

She had not, however, heard him tell the tale of how they met, or describe their early married life, or relate how the ending of their union was going to come about. He decided to push the narrative as far as the divorce which hadn't yet been sprung on her. When life was dull or intolerable for a storyteller he could always shape his destiny by describing events which hadn't yet happened, but which the relating of might well bring about, though sometimes he lost all account of what he was saying, and told of occurrences which seemed so preposterous that it was out of the question for them ever to become reality and plague him in any way—or so he hoped.

While we were married — he was always able to choose a phrase that at least someone among his audience would remember—our children were in many ways like the poor bloody infantry: they spent most of their days waiting for something to happen, and the rest of the time going over the top. When they did, they saw mam and dad already there, throwing mud at each other by the ton.

After a few false starts and several near misses he called his story *The Loving Couple*. He didn't like titles, but skill increased, and therefore his status, and so landlords and club proprietors insisted on them, and he saw no reason to be ashamed of a poster which blazoned one in the pub window and on the door, together with his name, and even bigger words in day-glo green which said LIVE ENTERTAINMENT, as if the performer had recently graduated from the rigidity of the Waxworks' Museum to a growling stance behind bars at the zoo.

A few weeks after first meeting Marion – his story continued – I went home with her. She made it feel a great privilege, going into her house, though it wasn't much to look at. Nowadays it would be crumbling under the bulldozer, and she would be living in a high-rise hencoop in Radford. But she made me some bottled coffee, and put a plastic bag of teacakes on the table. "You've got a long way to walk back."

"I'll get a bus." I was as slow as flowing treacle when it came to the uptake.

"Could be too late for one."

Her mother had been sent back fit from the hospital, but was already in bed. Marion faced me across the formica-topped table that her mother had set for breakfast. She had, in her dotty way, laid the knives and forks opposite to where they should have been. Marion was rearranging them while she looked at me over the Siegfried Line of cornflakes, sauce bottles and sugar bowl.

It was the first time I'd seen her without her coat. She took my heavy covering, and held it in her arms as if I were still inside, then laid it across the sofa. So far, we'd only had a few kisses in the dark when saying good night, but I'd always hoped for something else.

Her dress was cut low in front, and her marvellous white breasts were quite large and slightly veined as she leaned towards me for my empty cup, which she took to the sink and washed, then put on the rack to dry.

A hooter sounded from Colwick junction, and I used it as a signal to stand up and put my arms around her. I could never act of my own free will since I bought that bloody coat. Even a train whistle had its uses. I squeezed her hand, but her pressure was firmer. "There's no hurry," she murmured, as if telling herself and not me. On our way from the bus stop a full moon had shone.

I kissed her forehead, ears, lips, and the top of her bosom. The walnut-cased clock on the shelf pinged midnight, signalling a brand-new day, in which only one event, it seemed, could take place. My fingers stroked the back of her neck. It was as if I'd drunk a molotov cocktail. I couldn't reconcile what was happening now with the way she'd tidied the table and washed the cups as soon as we'd eaten. Her hands were stroking my arse, and then she pushed me away to get at my front. All I wanted to do was get my tie off, and breathe. I felt her hump through the dress, and was wondering why I'd been so slow, though nothing mattered any more because here I was. She undid a couple of my shirt buttons. "Let's go upstairs. We shall have to be *very* quiet."

It was like trying to climb a tree with a thousand bells on it, because every tread let out a shot of noise. I debated whether I'd have time to take my shoes off when we got to the bed. You can laugh all you like, but for a moment it seemed a very important problem. I didn't want to get the sheets muddy, nor even the counterpane. I was fastidious in those days.

She went first up the wooden hill, and I followed her into a room. With the door behind us, she led me into pitch darkness. It was so black I thought maybe there's a bottomless pit at the next step waiting to swallow me up for ever. I'll go on dropping till my light's snuffed out, and that will be that.

There was a single-bed on the other side of the room. I'd undone my belt and zip on our way across, and fell onto her with my ramrod already out. She slipped her tights off, and I was into the slippery warmth, and she grabbed me firmly and swore a few times, so that I already felt her coming. Maybe she'd thought of it for a long time, just as I had. I'd been with a few girls, but this was something I wasn't used to. There was no time to take my shoes off — even if I wanted to anymore — nor my tie. She moaned and grunted and ground her cunt against me, and my hand under her arse was being hammered flat as she went up and down. I tried to hold off, but couldn't, and didn't care whether I

58

did or not because she was jolting all she could. Her cries got louder, and were joined by mine – of pleasure such as I'd never known, as if my backbone was pouring through my prick, and then I almost blacked out with rage that I'd shot so quickly when I'd wanted to make it last.

We were still in the throes of it when a sound started up from the other side of the room that hit me like a bucket of freezing water in a heat wave. She stopped as if pole-axed, though the tremors in her cunt continued, and I became a statue, as if I'd been put up in a city square and had to stay like that for ever whether the pigeons shat on me or not. My mutton-dagger had turned into a pintle, and flopped out of her marshmallow.

I hoped I was hearing things, that I'd only gone mad and was dreaming, that the diabolical baby would turn over and burrow its way back to sleep, but the cries got shriller, and full of panic, as if some foul demon were about to carry it back to the womb, and Marion pulled from under me and went across to the cot. I heaved my soaked pants and crumpled trousers up, assuming, quite reasonably, that our fun was finished for that night at least.

She switched on a night-light by the crib, then came back with a baby in her arms. "She's my sister's, and I'm looking after her for a while."

"Why didn't you tell me?"

"It's no bloody business of yours."

"You could have said something."

"I thought she wouldn't wake up."

The little bastard was put back to sleep, and we went down for more coffee. While Marion looked at me across the table, her dress still undone, tears were coming out of her eyes. "We'll never leave each other," I said. Later we went upstairs again, and slept together all night, and I remember it as the sweetest loving we ever did.

Her mother died a month later, of a massive cardiac arrest. After three months, Marion and I got married. I was twenty-one, and it wasn't till afterwards that she told me the baby girl was hers, so within a year I had two kids. I was so young that I wasn't able to worry about such things, which meant that Marion had no hard feelings against me.

The house was owned by her mother, and went to Marion, leaving only the rates to pay, which wasn't much on such a slum. Both having jobs, we were able to buy a car, and drove out to pubs at the weekend. Then she got pregnant again and had to give up her work. Don't think I'm racing ahead, and that I intend to fill in the juicy bits later. Oh no. There are more vital parts of the tale than that. It's sufficient to say, and to conclude on for the moment, that we were as happy as the day is long, though in the end it turned out to be almost as short as a winter's day in Finland.

We'll take a break now. I need a drink to slake my throat. I'll tell another part of my story later, because there's still a lot left. It's amazing what can happen when you buy a coat!

5

"Don't it ever 'appen," a woman asked, as a second neat vodka was sliding through his gullet, "that yer ain't got a story in yer?"

He hesitated. If Operation Barbarossa had started at the precise moment he would have choked. The vital cords of his throat might have caught fire. His stomach would have blitzed itself to a cinder. You never knew when anything began. All wars started before the first shots were fired, certainly before the field-commanders were born.

But when this young woman, smelling of gin, sweat and make-up, put a booted foot on the artery of his spirit, he could only wonder whether it was a gesture of love, or an act of war. He'd never know, but didn't want to let her go before trying to find out.

Not only those who were wise and well-bearded in the ways of the world, but even this dumpy woman with buck-teeth that were made for biting other nipples than her own, grey eyes for viewing all the scandalous permutations of an orgy while eating from a bag of chips, and long blonde hair that you must kiss your way up and down in order to get at her vital part, could step on man or woman's jugular without knowing she'd done so. Her mouth was small, and came out of full cheeks, but if she was ugly, she still looked a treat to go to bed with. Probably had a couple of kids already, and a husband at the back of the crowd. Her slightly plump Nottingham chin was tucked under, and made her look attractive, as well as sluttish and thirsting for a change at any cost, so that he wanted to get at her knickers, and grapple on the floor with her. He sensed that she wanted to do the same with him. If such a weighing up wasn't love at first sight he didn't know what was.

"I mean," she said, with a wonderful smile, "it would with me."

People often answered their questions for him, unable to wait, hating the silence they had provoked. Yet silence is wiser than speech, he thought, who spoke so much. It's also stronger north of the Trent, and they were ten miles that side of it right now. The further north, the thicker it gets, till total silence prevails and you can't find wisdom because the ice-age cometh and conquers all. But that was part of a story, no less, and he didn't need to pander to the south while in the north.

She didn't like silence, and he could love her for that alone. His vodka finished sliding in. "Not so far. Not with me."

"You tell 'em well." She blushed at complimenting a man, though happy to do so since few men did the same for her. Praising a man made her feel independent, which was necessary for a woman with a ring on her finger. "I don't know how you remember so many."

He looked for the furious visage of a husband about to raise a fist from the crowd. "Have a drink?"

A smile made her mouth pleasantly hungry. "Gin, then."

"What's your name?"

"Eileen."

"Stories" — which was the least he could tell her — "are ten a penny. Open any newspaper, and you find a dozen. I puke 'em by the score at breakfast time."

"I can see you do."

People who knew him for a storyteller assumed, before meeting him, that he was ten years older than he was. The advantage in knowing this was that it helped him to act a little wiser — at odd moments. "It's how you tell them that matters."

He hoped the barman wouldn't take his money for the drinks, but he did, though he refused to believe that everyone in the world was uncharitable. The man simply had a quota to fulfil. "Cheers!"

Eileen clinked her glass with his. "I'm surprised you don't get on the radio."

"One day, I might."

"Or the telly."

"I don't know whether I want to."

Her mouth rested open, so that she could ignore such stupid modesty. His talent had holes in it. "There's stories, and *stories*," she said.

He laughed. "How do you make that out?"

"There's some stories that haven't been told yet."

A man had said the same to him only last week. "Like what, lovely Eileen?"

She touched the sleeve of his leather coat for luck. "I know a dirty old man called Len. He *is* dirty, proper dirty, because of all the shitty tricks he gets up to. He's got such stories as 'ud make your hair stand on end. But he's shitty, though, real shitty. And he's full of the most marvellous stories. I can't understand why he's so dirty-rotten, that's all. Goes together, I suppose. If you heard him, you'd know what I mean. Last week in his little Yorkshire cottage up on the moors, he told me and Bernard about a man who *was* a storyteller but ended up with his throat cut because he put everybody's lives into his stories. A man came out of one of his own stories and cut him to bits. He just sat there telling us. It went on for hours. Laugh? I'll say we bleddy-well did. It was all blood and shit though, in the end, that's the trouble. But he's a proper card. Sometimes he talks like us, and at other times he does it posh, like a BBC bloke on the wireless. We just call in for a lark to listen to him. He ain't allus there, because they say he lives a lot of the year in Nottingham, but now and again we take a chance on finding him at home."

A hand pulled at her. "Come bloody-on, then. Are you going to get me that pint, or aren't you?" The man glared at Ernest, daring him to start something. He was the same build, but a few years older, and paler, and with bluish marks on his cheek. Ernest had seen him a long time ago, but the situation was such that he couldn't take time off to wonder about it calmly and decide who he was.

The lurking ally might have been a workmate, from the way he stood. He had a ginger moustache, and his grey eyes were glazed as if he always had to end the fights that the man with the blue-marked cheeks got into, and had become punch drunk in consequence. There were blackheads on his lumpy nose, and he wore a sports jacket, collar and tie, and a cardigan.

"You effing ponce," Eileen's husband said to Ernest. "Leave my wife alone."

The man hesitated to strike, and commit himself to the mangrove swamp. Ernest absorbed one blow after another: that of meeting such a woman when both of them were married, and now the shock of hearing about this storyteller who had already woven him into his net like an expert poacher out in the blackest night with a cosh in one pocket and a search-lamp in the other.

"She may be a fucking whore," Bernard raved "but she's *my* fucking whore, see?"

Ernest disliked the rancour and bad breath of this ferocious husband whose tight heart was ready to burst because he thought Ernest was trying to grapple with his wife's breasts. Too late to do anything about it. The third blow was that he must ape his way back into a story, which seemed a negative prospect after that glitter in Eileen's eyes while she recalled the old man's ensnaring tales on the Yorkshire Moors. He remembered that his story had concerned the cycles of his own life, but something now told him, in a mixture of foul words and friendly advice, to use no more of it tonight, but to put it in cap and bells so that it seemed none of his concern.

He felt drunk, which was new to him, on a mere three vodkas. Maybe he'd tell about where he'd worked at fifteen, starting life like a fish whose mouth searched eternally for its own tail, and woe betide anything that got in the way. He was in a perpetual race with his ravening soul, which bullied a head-start because his tail had leapt out of the womb one second before his head. From then on he'd tried to catch it up, the Devil's own work, as flesh raced the spirit in a tribulation which would go on till that part of his life which insisted on proving him to be alive had flaked away.

When he addressed his audience with quips and tales, he felt the fluvial stream bed below, and saw shouldering torrents of water on which his solitary head bobbed around in the millrace, choking him before he could tell a story whose only purpose was to keep everyone, but himself most of all, under control, while he floated helplessly towards clapperboards and rapids.

Aware of his progress towards interior death, he was often afraid of going too fast in telling a story and inadvertently ommitting nuances out of nervousness, of avoiding explanatory depths due to embarrassment, and of leaping across parts which might not be understood. He was also fearful of giving his tale too slowly, of dragging the humour so that they failed to notice it, of becoming nasty and snarling when the joke appeared too crude even for them. He sweated with terror at putting in too many circumlocutionary lacunae, which, in the beer and smoke fumes, might send them to sleep. He had nightmares of side-stepping the main issue by describing in great detail the prior life of an insignificant person who had nothing to do with the plot. This would either send *him* to sleep or, even worse, cause him to lose track of the story and forget his main character in whose fate they by now took a profound and personal interest. If this happened he'd have to invent a new person, place or incident, and thus alter the whole tone of the story, thereby contributing to the ruination of its success for that night at least, and mixing the perceptions of the audience so brutally that they could do nothing except get up and kill him. Or he might ramble too slowly in his narrative by putting everything in he could think of. Not knowing what to leave out, or not caring whether he ommitted anything or not, might prick the audience to fury because he appeared to be deliberately and maliciously boring them, thereby showing his ultimate contempt. Threats of violence from all quarters might then bring him beneficially to his senses – or so he hoped.

"Make us laugh," someone shouted, goaded by silence.

"We want summat spicy."

"Ar! That's right. *Racy!* Sex, and a bit o' football. Tell us how the manager of Ossington United went on a package tour to Russia and got lost in a knocking-shop in Minsk!"

He never begrudged a bit of audience participation.

"That was in London – or was it Nottingham?"

"It wore Leicester," the same man shouted.

The fifty-year-olds wanted orgies and flagellation. The

twenty-year class craved straight stuff, as long as it was all clean and proper sex. The women hoped for a bit of porn as well. But he hadn't (so far) dished up that sort of fissionary material.

It was five years since he had turned his talent into a profession, and though he never ran short of stories, his narrative energy sometimes collapsed before he'd quite done with one. His spirit, which he thought ever-obliging, might pack in at a vital point due to an ungodly weariness that even the domineering will itself finally had no control over. The cogwheels seized up as if boiling sugar had been poured in the sump tank.

During a sentence which had them in thrall his mind could empty, his mouth stay agape, hands fall to his side, the left shoulder slope, and his right knee go forward. God help me, where was I?

To cure most cases of this flash eviction of the faculties, he smiled, straightened himself like an old-time soldier, winked like a fellow-thief selling you your own watch, wagged his finger like an incompetent parson, clenched his fist like a true-blue communist, and hit himself – quite hard – on the top of his melon-head, then spouted the first thing that came into what of his brain remained:

"He only *thought* he was getting off the train in London, accompanied by his girl-friend, did our unfortunate Joe. He put his foot towards the platform, fell six inches, and yanked his ankle in such an anti-clockwise direction that instead of going with Avril to the nice hotel he'd booked a suite in, he was taken away unconscious with pain on a Red Cross stretcher to get his sprain seen to."

He could afford to smile, having bayoneted his way into a story. "Avril was a tall young woman nearly thirty-five years of age, with short black hair and gorgeous busts. She had a pale face that looked a bit common by now, though not as common as all that, so don't get ideas. After her boy-friend Joe had fallen down and done his ankle in, the kindly Red Cross man looked through his wallet and found his home telephone number, then got in touch with his wife to say he'd had an accident. His wife was full of tears and panic when she heard this. Joe had lately become very distrustful, creating trouble whenever she wanted to go out alone, unless it was for shopping or to see his mother. This unwarranted jealousy led her to believe that *he* might be carrying on with another woman, and she made up her mind to catch him at it if she could, even if it meant following him to London. A sprained ankle was as good an excuse as any, for she assumed that the man on the phone had been one of Joe's pals posing as a Red Cross bearer. She had to admit that he'd sounded very convincing, but Joe had always been too careful for her comfort.

"Thinking to trap him this time, she asked her brother, with tears in her eyes but rage in her heart, to drive her straight down to London in his Hardback Ten Thousand motorcar. They'd reach Joe at the outpatients' department of the hospital in a couple of hours, and would then see whether his story was true or not. If it *was* true he might not have had his ankle seen to yet, which would save her and her brother the bother of pulling off the bandages to see whether any bruise or wound was hiding underneath.

"And Avril? Well, tall swan-like Avril with the black hair and pale green eyes and dignified half-concealed bosom that every man wanted to get his hands on, looked horrified and appalled at this sudden catastrophe to her dirty mid-week idyll. She stood aside as if she didn't know Joe, and ignored the double plea of his white and staring eyes as he was taken away by those lovely Red Cross chaps who do a marvellous service at London's railway termini. What else could she have done? If you want to know, she hopped it double smart to a pub across the road, and when she got there had a double gin, and wondered what the hell she was going to do now.

"It was a violent switch in her expectations. She had come to London for a sexy twenty-four hours away from her husband, and then Joe, the damned fool, stepped off the train and did his ankle in. He deserved to be left alone for doing a thing like that. It was almost as if he'd deliberately planned it because at the last moment he either felt afraid of her, or had lost his nerve about doing it on his wife.

"And if that wasn't the case, it served him right for letting her down by not taking care of himself. There couldn't be much love in him. Certainly no consideration. It was just like a man. In fact she was beginning to feel proper sorry for herself — not to say indignant — so had a cheese cob with her next drink, and wondered whether she shouldn't go back to the station and try to find out what had happened to Joe after all. If that was impossible she would take the next train back to Nottingham. She stamped her foot under the table. She was bloody cross."

Ernest was firmly in control, up on his platform. They were quiet. "She certainly didn't intend, ladies and gentlemen, to look the length and breadth of London for somebody who had broken his andle when she'd been just on the point (because that's how *she* saw it) of pulling him into bed and having a good time with him. But we must give her her due. She made an effort. She walked back across Euston Road. She climbed that flight of spew-stained steps strewn with beer-tins, from the pavement to St Pancras Station. We all know those steps, don't we? — those Odessa Steps that Notts Forest supporters often slip and break an arm on after surviving a riot in the stands, twenty pints of wicked London piss-beer, and a punch-up in Piccadilly Circus. They were the steps she went up, and who do you think she saw coming down? You'll never guess. That's what I'm here for. It's my profession. I'm a storyteller. If *I* can't tell you who it was, I don't know who can. All right, I'll get on with it. It was none other than Ted Bingham, one of the managers at the hosiery firm she worked at.

"Ted was a bit of a lad, who would strut through the packaging department of the factory so that he could look over any new girls who had been set-on in the last twenty-four hours. His hair was wavy-dark, and he wore a good suit and a flashy tie. Being thirty-nine, he looked twenty-nine. The only thing wrong was that he had a purple patch on the left side of his face which many people found impossible to look at."

There was a cry of anguish from the snuggery door, "It's just not damned-well *on*, mate. I don't believe he'd have a strawberry mark on his face, and still fancy himself the cock o' the walk."

Ernest gave himself up to the luxury of anger. "Who's telling this story? You, or me?"

"Well, he wouldn't, would he?"

68

"Come on, who?"

The interjectionist had ginger sideburns, and tears in his eyes. Maybe his wife was pregnant, and he had to be home in half an hour to look after their two kids, so that she could then take a turn for gin-and-lime at the pub.

"*You* are," he mumbled, "but, all the same. . . ."

"All the same bloody what?"

The man turned away, to reveal one whole cheek of dense purple. Ernest felt his own face losing blood, its palor emphasising even more the difference between them. He wanted the floorboards to split, and drop the man out of sight, to take the disfigured interfering bleeder off to oblivion where he belonged. He hated him, couldn't stand the sight of him, thought he shouldn't be allowed to go around with such an unsightly mug.

Then he regretted his barbarous reaction. He felt properly contrite. That purple patch was the mark of a priest, or at least the brand of a king who had come down in the world. It was wrong to pull its bearer through a gauntlet of scorn. Ernest felt he ought to put his arms around him, kiss him, draw him gently onto the stage, and publically promise to look after him for the rest of his life. He recognised a companion of the depths, a man blasted on the outside just as he – Cotgrave – was undoubtedly scarred within. They were two of a kind, and the man had been right to shout down the lock-stock-and-barrel of his story. He could coddle him, mother him, feed him the juiciest titbits out of the best *Good Food Guide* restaurants, make his bed, wipe his nose, buy him nicky hats and natty suits (and paper handkerchiefs) and comfort him in the ice-cold battering rain that would fall on them both when they sat abandoned in the middle of a wasteground around which traffic plied all day and night, lights glowing from great buildings that vibrated with the laughter of people who loved and gorged and guzzled and sang that rousing chorus whose last line went: "Fuck you, Jack, I'm all right forever."

"Shut up, then," Ernest snapped, unable to escape his true self. "Let me tell my story. You're spoiling everybody's fun. You're an eyesore. You make us feel ashamed of ourselves. Do you understand me, Scarface?"

"It ain't his fault," he was told. "Just get on with it." There were some good folk left in the world, he noted. Others spoke to the same effect, as he'd hoped they would. Their tone of reprimand was by no means threatening, as if they suspected that his taunts against Purple Chops weren't seriously meant, or as if the man had been set there especially to manifest himself at dull parts of the act. Maybe he was his brother, Charlie Cotgrave, who was on permanent social security because no one would employ him with such a face in case he depressed the other workers, and who was only too glad to make a quid or two. It was a hard way to earn it, somebody thought, way ahead of the rest, but on the wrong path nevertheless.

There was iron in Ernest's heart, though he tried to disown it. The best that could be said for him, which was very little, was that he wanted to melt with the warmth of pity. But his ranting would not be harnessed, and the spiteful voice inside, that made his tale true, dominated his better feelings so that they had no opportunity against it. He would barter mother, father, wife, children, friends and certainly countrymen for the mere telling of a tale whose happenings disappeared into uselessness as soon as they left his lips. Compassion was not for storytellers. They neither gave it, nor claimed it. But Ernest felt inner terror, knowing that before the end of *his* story, he would be made to atone for the sins of the rabid voice that spoke through him.

"Avril recognised Ted Bingham. It was impossible not to, given the nature of his affliction. He was handsome and personable. She wouldn't have mistaken him anywhere. A strawberry face doesn't mean you have to crawl around like a dog, as long as your spirit is big enough to keep the wound in an insignificant place. In short, it was impossible not to recognise that jaunty air of self-confidence, especially in London, and on the steps of St Pancras station. Ted Bingham looked, and walked, as if he ran the world. When he too spotted her, and said hello how are you, you would have thought they'd spent weeks making a well-laid plan to meet here and at this time. They went back to the pub for a drink, and she told him her adventures of the morning.

"It's impossible to say who got the dastardly notion first. It might well have been Ted because he remembered, walking

70

along the corridor on the way to the main office one day, over-hearing Joe remark to one of his fellow-travellers on Ted's straw-berry glob. Ted, good natured though he was, never forgot such a slur.

"The upshot was that he and Avril decided to go to the hotel at which Joe (now lying in a hospital and nursing his injured ankle) had booked the suite. Ted would claim to be Joe, would even limp if need be, and they would take the man-and-wife accommodation as if to Brighton born. Avril knew that Joe had booked the room under his own name of Brown, so when they got there as Mr and Mrs Brown, the desk clerk merely requested Ted to sign the register, and handed him the key to the door.

"It was a magnificent double room with bath, overlooking the park from the fourth floor, furnished in the pleasant style of the 1930s, with a little dash of mock Arabia Deserta to bring it up to press. They were too young to be nostalgic for the one, and too old to hanker for the other, but shall I tell you what went on in it? Do you want all details down to the slightest moan and groan? Shall I extol every item of their slap-and-tickle? Every inching of their huff and puff? Ted had a reputation, and Avril found that it wasn't misplaced. In other words, he was good at it. Blokes with strawberry marks often are. Some chaps are made impotent by the possession of such technicolour scars, but others, who make more than the best of a very bad job, are driven on by it. Like a combine harvester, they learn to do everything at once, which is usually what the ladies want. Avril certainly did. She'd had her eye on that scar for some time, and was more than ready for a lick or two. After the excitement of the morning the only way to get calm was to have something positively titillating. Ted Bingham had come to London to see his brother Harold, but he phoned to put his visit off till next day. Harold was pleased at this because he'd sensed for some time that Ted-the-Tomcat had an itch for his wife, and she a yen for him.

"Ted deftly hung the DO NOT DISTURB notice on the aluminium knob outside before closing the door. Then, they got stripped. I can't put it plainer than that, ladies and gents. All that lovely underwear meant for Joe came off, piece by piece, for Edward Bingham. The scarfaced bastard couldn't believe his luck. They leapt into each others' arms, and played roly-poly on the counterpane.

"I don't want the police to be rung for, or to be the cause of our fine landlord flushing, and putting on the towels to save us all from fits and fevers. . . ."

"Boo!" they called.

They whistled.

"Spoilsport! Kill 'im!"

He lifted his hand for silence.

They obeyed. I'm too young to die. He could be king of the dung heap anytime he liked. He smiled: "There's a twist to this story that none of you expect. I defy any to guess what fate has in store for our mad passionate lovers!"

"You don't know your bloody self."

He swung hard onto this one, knowing you couldn't have the subverting spirit of sanity rife in the place. He could turn the rest of them loose on this prime specimen of interruption, and get him ripped arm from leg — if he so wished. But his malice wouldn't deepen, though he could, out of spite, make him apologise, by threatening not to finish his story. No, he couldn't, because he would not get his fee if he walked out with all the trimmings left unsaid. Anyway, he felt no rage. If his intentions spun too readily into the realms of malevolence it was only his story that suggested the route, a narrative that would eventually suffer by it.

"Do *you* know?" The crowd would like him all the more for being magnanimous.

No response.

"I'll tell you. Our lovers spent six hours in their bliss, lost to everyone but themselves. This was unwise because, as we know, to be isolated from your fellow men cuts you off from what the rest of your fellow men are doing, in which case you can always bet that some fellow-man, or even fellow-woman, is shifting around in the outside world and getting ready to do you a mischief.

"While pumping the living daylights out of each other, during this seemingly perfect assignation (though there can no more be a perfect assignation than there can be a perfect murder), they didn't remember to wonder, as they should have done, what had happened to Joe. Are you following my gunpowder-train of thought? And what about Joe's wife? you may ask. Well, as already related, she had been in such a hurry to get to her poor maimed (yet possibly gallivanting) husband that she'd persuaded her brother to drive her to London in his Super Roadhog Mark One motorcar. The trouble is, cars are less perfect than trains. A train can be late, but sometimes a car doesn't get there at all. No matter how good a car it is, it can break down, and that was what Sid's car did on the motorway, something so seriously wrong that when it got to the garage the mechanic said it wouldn't see any road again for at least three days because it would take that long to get the spare part from the factory (which in this case happened to be just fifteen miles up the road) and fit it on. If it had been a little Japanese Cherry Bum car he could have got the part sent special delivery from Tokyo in thirty-six hours. So there was no hope of them reaching Joe at the hospital that day. Or there wouldn't have been if Joe's wife, Edna, by now mad with suspicion and jealousy, hadn't got a hire-car to bring her through the last lap to the Smoke.

"Joe hobbled out of the outpatients' bottleneck on crutches, and flagged a taxi to take him to the hotel where he had reserved a suite. At the counter they said there was none in the name he had given. He extracted his wallet to find out what his name was, and then to prove his identity. Bank cards and driving licences were spread all over the counter, when he suddenly remembered that he had booked his suite under the name of Brown, not Smith – as he'd first thought of doing. He pointed this out, saying that his secretary had made a mistake, but they told him that Mr and Mrs Brown were already in their room. Joe swore that Mr Brown couldn't be in it, because Mr Bloody Arnold Brown was standing here before them, wasn't he? He stamped his foot, which was very painful on a sprained ankle, and called them all the bladder-heads under the sun."

They were in such stitches of laughter at Joe's misfortunes that you'd think they'd all been run together with a sewing machine, he noted. "When Joe gets upset he falls into a broader sort of Nottingham speech than he'd normally like to be heard

73

talking. On this occasion, he shouted so loud and wide that he finally persuaded the stupified onlookers that somebody must be in his room under false pretences. When they burst in (the manager holding the DO NOT DISTURB notice in his hand) Ted Bingham – alias Old Strawberry Face, to Joe and his cronies at the factory – was about to clamber onto Avril again. Joe must have thought he'd get *some* benefit from his sprained ankle, for he began clouting them with a crutch as he hobbled around the room with the aid of the other. It seemed as if he'd unwittingly stumbled onto a new cure for sprained ankles, though for the National Health Service to set up such situations would be rather expensive both in monetary and emotional terms.

"The manager phoned the police, to stop this trio of foul-mouthed Nottingham trippers wrecking his forty-quid a night suite. At this point, Joe's wife Edna walked in, having traced them by a superb piece of detective work, and the rumpus really got going. She swore so foully, and with such passionate intensity, with tears nowhere to be seen, that Teddy Bingham immediately fell in love with her. What happened to those two is a story all its own."

"You're a bloody liar."

"He's sending me up the fucking wall," said one of the Nottingham Lambs, who seemed to follow him everywhere.

"I'll scrape him off the floor in a bit," said his mate. "He'll be a right fucking strawberry mark before I've done with him."

"Which brings me to another interval, ladies and gentlemen. I don't know whether *you* are dry at the throttle, but I'm parched." He wrestled out of his leather coat, as if to punch his anger away on that, though he was merely folding it, to set it on a chair behind.

6

"I don't believe a word of your rigmarole."

"Why not?"

"Ar, well, because I don't."

"Go on, tell me."

"I don't reckon a good Nottingham lass like Avril would be so rotten as to play that sort of trick on Joe. Nor would she do it on her own husband, come to that," a more reasonable member of the audience tried to assure him.

If it had been Strawberry-face he could have had a real go at him. But it wasn't. He had to be careful. "What I've told you is true, every lying word of it. She was rotten to the marrow."

They clapped. They laughed and whistled. A man with a growth on his nose came up with a pint for him. "That was a good story. Somebody was wanking off at the back, but I had tears in my eyes."

"I'll tell you why I know it was true," Ernest called, pressing a hand on the pain in his stomach, after the warm suds of beer had gone down.

There was silence while they waited. In one sentence he would bend his diversionary tale back onto the straight and narrative line, thus proving, to himself at least, that there was no substitute for inspiration.

His conviction was reinforced after a stint at a club some weeks ago. The audience at *that* place wouldn't listen. A couple of Nottingham Lambs screamed every time he got close to the microphone. His story was no worse than normal. In fact he'd thought about it all day, and pondered much on the main facts. He worked a few choice phrases into it. But they wouldn't have any. A few minutes got him into a story, but they stopped him dead. He saw the studded leather jackets glinting in a far corner of the club. When an elderly shunter told them to stop howling, and let everybody hear Ern Cotgrave's story, they pushed him against the doorpost and threatened to burn his pension book.

"The bus got into the village where his lady-love lived." They weren't the only ones. For more reasons than he could understand, it was a bad night. They hated him. They considered him a show-off. He stood up there, and thought himself better than they were. He was a queer, and one of them shouted as much: "Cum 'ere, you fookin' poof, an' fight like a man!"

If he stepped down, they'd kill him. The club manager stood at the back, white-faced from more than his ulcers, terrified of being seen to walk off and phone the police. Ernest was secure, as long as he stayed on board his ship of the stage. He liked the hollow sound below when he tapped his feet. It reassured him, but only just. A shandy-glass lifted above the heads and tables. It was shown, but wasn't thrown.

He pulled the mike out of its clip and brought it towards his mouth, but ordinary human civilised speech was impossible. He unclipped the black lollipop all the way down. Another wave of howling made him flinch as if a burning blanket had been thrown in his direction. They sensed he was about to try going on with his tale.

Because speech hadn't helped so far, he saw no reason to use it again. They laughed at their easy victory. It had been a mistake to try telling a tale before the pop group and striptease. He lifted his leg, the thigh horizontally out, and the calf vertically down. The tide had come in as far as it would go. They would drown him in screams again if he tried to speak, but the crack of their laughter diminished slightly as he stood on one leg for more seconds than any in the crowd would be able to match. They hated show-offs, but recognised physical endurance — or ingenuity — when they saw it.

The mike in his left hand was a fancy arrangement shaped like the head of a bull rush. It was on a long enough lead for him to pull it around, as he maintained his fixed position on one leg (he hadn't done physical exercises, and specialised in this very one

76

every morning for the last five years, for nothing) and sil-houetted himself as if intending to thrust this cock-shaped microphone where he might, he supposed, have shoved it if he had been what they had vociferously accused him of being a few moments ago.

The freeze was successful. The longer he endured, the more silent they became. He maintained the statue of obscenity so long that soon there was silence. When one Nottingham Lamb's nerve broke, and he shouted for Ernest to get on with it, the other Nottingham Lamb told him to shut up or he'd sink his boots into his cooking-apples.

They waited, but Ernest had no intention of doing the expected. He never had had. They wanted him to try again. In a silence such as that hall had rarely known, with the switched-on microphone close to his arse, he spoke into it, for their delectation, the longest and most splintering fart either he, they, or anybody else had ever been heir to. Suitably broken into various rhythms, cut into dots and dashes, the mike magnified loudly the sombre metre into rolling drumbeats to all corners of the hall. It went on like gale force nine, flattening and then burying the minor attempt they had earlier made against him.

When the last echoes ate each other somewhere behind the furthest coloured lightbulbs, Ernest placed his left foot back on the boards, slotted the microphone in its socket, and gave a bow to signify the end of his labours for that night. He made his exit to respectful clapping. Like all inspired actions, it had been carried through with so little thought that he'd hardly been aware of what he had been doing. The manager was pleased with such a sensational act, but Ernest pushed him aside, and never went back.

"I know the story to be true," he said in his present place, "because it was my wife it happened to. And her name was Marion, not Avril – that's all."

He stood with a leg forward and his chest out, and drank the whole of his pint while their applause pummelled the floor and ceiling.

"She told me a month ago, and didn't make me promise to keep it a secret, either. That's the sort of woman she is. In all fairness, she had just found out about something I'd done. She was a good sport, which is why I'm getting so that I can't stand the sight of her. She can't tolerate me, either. The moral gangrene we generate together is too much even for *us*! Why are people that way, when they could be so happy?"

"He'll cry in a bit," a bully-voice prophesied, and Ernest knew he couldn't insult the owner of that big drum-box like he'd taken down Purple-Cain a short time ago. It was a wild sort of trade. You could drop from being King of the Muckheap, to getting crushed underfoot in five seconds flat if you misunderstood the reality of a threat, or didn't react at the right time and with the proper tone to an unnecessary reproach. Dealing with the taunts of your audience was an extension of storytelling. The two were inseparable, though there were times when he wished they were not, and that he could be divided from his spectators by a canyon too wide to be crossed. Yet without the powerhouse and storage-silo of their lives he would be a mere pleasure-shell fattening on the earth, and no more a storyteller.

"It takes a *real man* to cry," he responded. "And who isn't one of those from time to time?"

"What about a *real woman*?" a real woman shouted.

Tears were coming up, but his heart refused to let them out. "Here's another true story, about one February day, when I was eleven, and went with my pals to Martins Pond."

"Used to go there messen as a lad," a friendly voice called. "Fishin', and swimmin'."

They liked it when he mentioned familiar places, which confirmed that he'd been born and brought up on home territory. He might not be very nice, but at least they'd consider him one of their own during a Mongolian invasion.

"We walked two miles along Wollaton Road. There was a freezing black frost, and the trees were bare, but we joshed along, running in circles now and again to keep warm. Buses created a draft that made us cold. We'd left our topcoats at home, but kids are ever feckless. We had scarves and mittens though, and my cheeks were hot, and my eyes felt bright at getting away from the house and heading for a place where we could do some sliding on ice. The sky was grey, but for all we knew or cared it could have been full of sunshine.

"As soon as we got through the broken hedge I was entranced by the shine of the ice. I'd expected it to be grey, like slate, but it was closer to black. The pond glistened, as big as a lake, and smelled like washing-up water, and cold gravel, and then it reminded me of bread being toasted, that my mother held on our long three-pronged plaited fork before the fire. There was also the pong of coal burning in the grate, and fresh tea being poured. It was strange to smell such things before you were going to die.

"It was marvellous to fall all over the place. We didn't think about the long walk back. We'd often brought newts frogspawn and tiddlers in jam-tins from the canal, though there'd be nothing like that today. We'd have walked twenty miles for this. The other side of the pond ended among bushes and a swampy zone. As we slid, it was hard to believe there was water underneath, and easy to imagine that the ice went right to the centre of the earth.

"The length of our slide was pushed far out, and clearly marked when we squinted back at the beginning of it. I heard traffic from Wollaton Road and the village, but all noise seemed to stop when we looked at each other and got breath together.

"I walked till I was on my own. I often wanted to be alone. I'd just drift away, and say nothing, and nobody minded. It was quiet. The others were a long way off. There were big round patches of white on my part of the pond, and as I stood between two of them I heard the sound of a dog yawning under my feet. The growl of tiredness made me laugh, so I stood still to hear it again. Even though I didn't move, I was no longer cold. There was a breeze on my face, but my cheeks were frozen so that the wind felt warm, as if there were different layers of temperature in the air.

"There was a colliery just over the canal, and I wondered if the miners far down weren't hacking away at coal under my part of the pond. The teacher once said they dug galleries in all directions once they got low enough. I was a bit frightened at the idea, so began walking towards my pals. They stood at the edge of the pond and waved at me to get off it. It's hard to run on ice. I'd slip like a dog with three legs, but I tried to walk quickly, all the same. I smelled toast again, taken off the fork and put on the table for butter to be spread.

"Then the dog barked louder than ever, and the sky moved. Something crackled around my ankles and cut them, and I fell through teeth. I remember waving, though not shouting. My head was in the dark, and I closed my eyes, thinking I'd go blind if my eyeballs got wet. I reached to switch a light on. I'd fallen into a room with no walls, though it had a lid to it, as I found on pushing my arms up to get out. My mouth was closed so tight I thought my teeth were breaking. I also knew that it would be better not to think, otherwise I wouldn't be able to breathe again.

"There could be no dark that was darker. The water was a locked box. It wasn't cold as long as I moved and let my hands roam at all angles looking for a lit tunnel by which to get back into that room where hot toast was being put on the table.

"The iron on my chest was so heavy I couldn't shout at its weight. Being so frightened lit a fire and sent a flame to my stomach. This darkest wet darkness, so far from the sky, was being dead, and in one way I liked it because I'd be able to tell people what it was like being dead when I saw them again. Water was all around, and weeds were wrapped over my head. If I sank to the bottom I'd walk among mountains. I wasn't thinking, so much as having lit-up pictures stab my eyelids.

"My clothes wrapped me, and I pushed hard against the slate-cold solid ceiling, but went down and down, like a tadpole mauled by a cat. I wanted to roll into the smallest fullstop of a dot that it was possible to get into, but water pushed knives up my nose, and my arms spun like a windmill because a tentacle-monster that had grabbed me by the ankles was starting to eat me. I was dead, but could still be gobbled in its red cave.

"The earth rolled, and pinned my arms, but they shot out again, one of them grabbed by the toothless mouth of the dragon. I tried to pull free. If I didn't succeed I'd be sucked into flames. I was dead already, and wanted to sink deeper into the blackness that was getting warmer. I wanted to be on my own for ever, so that I would never want to be alone again. But if I followed the

80

way my arm was being pulled I'd be thrown into the fire and be really dead.

"I saw myself twenty times my size, and watched the legs of me crumbling like bread. The bread floated in lumps and crumbs, and fishes snapped at it. Then the arms began falling into bits, and minnows swam out of lumps of bread as they broke open. Bread grits drifted in the water like dust.

"My other hand was caught. Two of them were trying to tear me in pieces. My head was in flames. There was no point in struggling. My legs were also held, as if four monsters were fighting for me. I was worried about where they'd throw my arms and legs when they began to come off, and whether it would be possible to find them again. The blackness I'd been hoping for since falling through the ice rushed into every part of my marrow."

A man standing near the bar gulped the remainder of his beer, then fell heavily to the floor, his pint jar clattering emptily as he went. He was the one who, earlier, had referred to his wife as a fucking whore, and to Ernest as an effing ponce, and who until a few moments ago had looked like the last person prone to fainting. But he had, and lay still, and a waiter passed a glass of water, hoping someone would feed it to him, which someone did. They were too fixed by Ernest's possibly tragic tale to give more first aid than that. The man shifted, and was pulled up so that he could hang on to the bar-rail. He was pale, but rugged and hard-faced, with blue marks from hewing coal down one of his cheeks. He looked as if he might go again at any moment. Had he been working at the coalface under the pond when I had fallen in? Ernest wondered. He was too young, but maybe his father or his brother had. Am I foretelling his own death? he wondered; and was that why he had fainted?

"They pulled me out of it, just as I was about to enter heaven and be the happiest person there. I didn't get back to life till I'd been three weeks in hospital. My mother told me that I had entertained the nurses and other children with incredible and colourful stories, though the tale of how I'd drowned was not one of them. Tonight is the first time I've told it."

He was lying. He'd spun it often to himself, though it had

found, like a patriotic march played by the BBC Block-and-Tackle Band, it would still be obvious that they'd been stated too often before. Thus it was that an aphorism born a cliché became a homily in the flash of an agonising twitch. In the meantime he had to manage with what bits of gristle were thrown out from his disintegrating marriage, because up to now he hadn't known how to make other things happen to enrich his life.

Marriage had everything. It had to have, at the moment, but those unique and intimate cat-and-mouse details, precious mementoes to every loving couple, were so few in scope that all marriages ran on identical fuel, and were ultimately exploded by matters more or less the same. No two unit-couples were alike, he was always careful to state, yet every pair who couldn't stand the sight and sound of each other finally parted for reasons that could be counted on a person's hand who had had the misfortune to be born with only two or three fingers.

The music he could play on that eternal theme was endless. Comfortable nudges of recognition livened the audience with appreciation. He told things as if they had happened to no one else in the world but him, recounted an experience with such soil and saltiness that when it did happen to the chosen few in the audience at some future date, as it was statistically bound to do (if it hadn't already done so) they would recognise part of themselves like old friends or distant relatives. He made up most of his stories. But occasionally he used himself directly in order to influence his life into changing for the better, or in the hope that would begin to make sense again.

"Eileen, where are yer?" Bernard wanted her back, with a his soul. He stood looking at the shadows where he knew h might find her, but not able to move and begin the search, in cas he should do so. Perhaps he was afraid of entangling himself in Ernest's nightmare. Ernest imagined the man's sensations o murderous spite mixed with cowardly indecision, but they wer drowned by Eileen's words as she trembled close: "Kill him fo me."

His hand was already under her skirt. "One day I will."

He knew her feelings even better than he knew her husband's at the moment, and so wouldn't let her go. He wanted to pull he knickers off, and suck her bushy little cunt till she came all over his face. Then he'd push into the swamp and bang both her and himself to death.

7

The old man stood by a line of palings in the Arboretum. "I recognise you," he said to Ernest.

"Do you?"

"I heard you telling stories upstairs in Yates's Wine Lodge three months'ago. You were interviewed on Radio Nottingham next morning. Am I right?"

"It's more than possible." Ernest spoke out of politeness. He wasn't interested. In fact he always wanted to disappear into the earth when a possible 'fan' accosted him. It often felt as if a clawed hand were trying to pull out his liver, and rub it in his face till he suffocated. He was also pleased, and wanted him (or her) to go on with their praise. In the present case the man hadn't yet admired him, but Ernest decided that if he did he would state that no credit was due for giving out such interesting stories, because in fact everything about their telling was so effortless. It wasn't work or turmoil or trouble in any way whatsoever, but as if someone or some*thing* – call it God, if you like – took him over and told the story *through* him, so that there was no need at all to praise him. Really, there was no need.

He divided the world into those who believed him when he said this, and those who didn't. Those who were convinced that story-telling was without effort were naive beyond all imagining. Those on the other hand who thought he was deliberately playing down that wear and tear of his heart which a life of such self-exposure and vampirism entailed, were evil nuisances because they would not let him get on with whatever halfway state was really the crux of the matter.

"You spun a fine yarn," the man said, after a while. "You do quite well at it, let me tell you."

"Nice of you to say so," Ernest responded ashily. He felt gloomy, and not at his ease. The noise of traffic beyond the park railings irritated him. The sky looked as if it were conspiring to do him in. It wasn't difficult to understand, after such a night of love with Eileen.

"It was the best story I'd heard for a long time," the old man told him. "Almost."

Ernest sometimes turned blind in face of unstinted admiration, unable to remember the features of those who had, genuinely or not, indulged him. Since the tone of the man's affirmation seemed to qualify his praise, he couldn't help but look more closely. He was about sixty, which of course would explain it. Most of his other admirers had been younger. The man was dressed in a grey tweed suit. He wore a tie, and a tie-pin with some kind of jewel. He had on a trilby hat and a gaberdine overcoat. There was an odour of expensive sandalwood after-shave. His shoes were highly polished, and he held a straightheaded walking stick. He was the sort of man who dressed in such a way that you couldn't tell whether he lived in the city or in the country, which made Ernest think he was single rather than married.

"I sat at the back of the room, and don't suppose you saw me."

"I don't see anyone," Ernest admitted. "If I thought there were people in front of me I'd freeze up."

"It reminded me of the old days." The man's grey eyes twinkled one moment, and were dead the next. His thin-lipped smile, however, never faltered. "You don't seem interested in my views."

He was turning out to be a bore. "What days were those?"

The man cleared his throat gently, as if it were a sinful noise he made, then tipped an empty Players' packet through the railings with the end of his stick. Ernest didn't like the way he took his time over it, though you couldn't expect much more from someone so well-dressed. He looked the kind of person who never made mistakes, and who couldn't therefore be very likable.

"I was a storyteller once, just like you," he said. "But not anymore. Old storytellers aren't much in demand, though that wasn't why I gave it up. Young ones like you have it easier these days, with lots of Live Entertainment going on in pubs. As long as you can keep thinking young, you can go on for ever. Or so I assume. But I had to stop, and there was a rather special reason for it."

Ernest found himself listening like any member of an audience, and it wasn't a pleasant experience. He wished the man would say whatever he had to say, then leave him be.

"I told my stories in prose, and some in verse." It was as if he'd read Ernest's thoughts, which was not impossible for a storyteller. "The verse went better, as far as I was concerned. At least it did in those days. I took a few turns in theatres, though I got more satisfaction when I worked in pubs."

He drew a neatly tied packet from his coat pocket. Ernest wondered whether he had misjudged him for style, and whether he wasn't now going to eat his midday sandwiches. But he unwrapped a loaf-end of stale bread which he broke up for a brace of gaudy mallard males swimming in his direction. When he opened his overcoat, as if his motions with the bread were a job of real work, Ernest noticed that he had an elaborate watch-and-chain arrangement across his waistcoat, with a golden Star of David attached. "I read a couple of weeks ago in the *Evening Post* that your mother had died. Sorry about that. I suppose you told a story about it before it happened?"

Ernest sweated. "It was somebody else's mother in my story."

"It always is. Don't be upset, though. Storytellers can't help that sort of thing. If people had any sense they'd keep clear of us – though it would be very hard for our parents to have done so, wouldn't it?" He pulled out a half-hunter and clicked it open. "Right to the minute. I've been coming at twelve o'clock for many years, and those ducks know exactly when to paddle around that headland. They must pass the knowledge on from one generation to the next."

"Ducks are intelligent," Ernest agreed, for want of anything to say.

"Mallards are. Buck mallards, all green and blue. I did a long stint at storytelling. Started in the nineteen-thirties. I dressed a bit different to what I do now." He chuckled at the memory. "Clogs and scarf, that's how I began. It wasn't a special rig-out.

88

It was all I had. I spent most of the day in the warm public library, where I could sit in peace. When I ran out of stories, I said to myself one day while reading a novel: 'Damn your eyes, plagiarise!' I was already doing it with humanity, just as story-tellers had always done. There was no turning back – there never is. I read the novels of Arnold Bennett, Wells, Alexandre Dumas, Bulwer Lytton, as well as some Hardy and a bit of Meredith. You name it, I read it. Only the good was good enough. You can't put second-best over on people in pubs. They'd sniff you out a mile away. They didn't want modern stuff, mind you, as good as some of it was. *A Passage to India* just didn't go down. Neither did *Point Counterpoint*. I thought they might like *Sons and Lovers*, but when I tried the first instalment they threatened to hang me with my own muffler and batter my brains out with my clogs. When I did a bit of *The Plumed Serpent* some damned bully chased me outside and broke my arm. Still, when I got out of hospital, I was able to recite the poems of Rupert Brooke, and I earned more money than I'd done for weeks. It's funny that they didn't like most of the modern stuff, now I look back on it. I don't suppose it'd be different today, either. But Robert Graves was all right. They lapped up those Roman yarns. I went for three months on 'em. Crying in their beer over Belisarius, they were. I didn't make much money, but enough to scrape by on. It eked out my Dole, though I had to be careful, because if one of those Means test chaps popped in for a pint and knew I was drawing the Dole when I passed the hat around, they'd have stopped it altogether. It was social buggery, in those days."

It was easy to see why he'd cracked as a storyteller. He rambled too much. The gobbling ducks made Ernest feel hungry. Yet the man had an easy-going aura about him, and Ernest wondered when the change had come from clogs to the finest hand-made boots. "Did you get taken up by the films?"

He balled the paper, and threw it to a wire litter bin ten yards away. His aim was accurate. "The war put paid to my story-telling."

"How?"

The man's eyes lost the twinkle they'd had while feeding the mallards. They hardened. "It's not easy, storytelling."

"I never said it was."

"You'd better not. It might seem so, at your age. But it gets harder."

"Thanks for nothing."

"'The Lord GOD hath given me the tongue of them that are taught, that I should know how to sustain with words him that is weary. . . .'"

Ernest shivered, though he wasn't cold. "The Bible?"

"Don't you know it?"

He caught the man's heartrending pity at his ignorance. Ernest saw no point in lying. "Not that bit."

The man didn't deign to pin down chapter-and-verse. He was snappish. "If you don't know the Bible, you don't know anything. There's a conspiracy to stop kids reading it today. It's the biggest crime since the war. They get telly and lollipops, but no Bible. How can a storyteller live in a society that's never read the Bible?"

Ernest was glad to change topics. "Is that why you gave it up?"

"Oh no," he smiled. "I went on a bit after the war started. There was more money about. I didn't want to get a job on munitions, though I did finally occupy myself with war-work, of a peculiar sort."

Ernest was beginning to admit that he had the style of someone who might indeed have once been a passable storyteller, but, because he hadn't heard of his prowess in the trade, he assumed it had come to nothing. On the other hand, people in pubs have notoriously fickle memories, where they exist at all, and the praises of the best storytellers have forever stayed unsung. He put up a hand to wipe away a tear, but his cheek was as dry as tinder.

"One night," the man related, "somebody in a pub heard me performing a story. It was a Thomas Hardy night. I was reeling off a couple of Wessex tales transferred, as best I could, to Nottinghamshire. But that wasn't the thing that impressed my eminent listener. I always ended my 'programme' with a piece in verse that ran for five minutes or so. They were in strict rhyme and metre. I'd studied prosody, and read all the poets, let me tell you.

You can't be a proper storyteller, and not be well-read."

Ernest had read since childhood, and was fed up with the man's patronising tone. "You don't need to tell me."

"These verse-tales, as a rounding-off feature, were always popular. On this particular evening my piece was about a rough Nottingham family who had been evacuated to a posh house in Oxfordshire. I forget where that idea came from. The kids got into all sorts of scrapes. You know the thing: terrorising the gentry. I did it in a kind of 'Eskimo Nell' ballad form and, if I do say so myself (and I do) it brought the house down.

"They wanted an encore, so I did a shorter piece about a family stricken by scabies in an Anderson air-raid shelter during an alert which turned out to be a false alarm. They liked that, as well."

The man walked away. He'd finished feeding the ducks. He knew his power, and wasn't surprised when Ernest caught up and fell into step. If there's one thing a storyteller likes more than telling stories, it's hearing them — though he'll never admit it.

"I was imbibing my second pint, and had just pocketed a quid from the landlord — a lot of money in those days — when somebody at my elbow said in a quiet and pleasant voice, 'I think we can do something for you.' He was about forty, fairly well-dressed, and obviously not a Sherwood Forester. 'My name's Greene,' he said, 'Graham Greene.'

"He was a sallow chap, a bit puffy, but it gave him an amiable expression, if you know what I mean. He had soft, kindly eyes, the sort that didn't deceive because you knew there was plenty of steel behind. 'I think we can put your talent to better use,' he informed me.

"I'd read a couple of his books, though I hadn't told them. I'd thought of it, but hoped to do so later in the war, as people grew more sophisticated.

"The upshot of meeting Mr Greene was that I got a job in London at the Ministry of Information. A secretary typed my funny poems, which were then cyclostyled by the tens of thousand and sent all over the country to help the war effort. They were sold in pubs for a penny each. They were also black-marketed, pirated and plagiarised. They turned up everywhere —

as they were meant to — from the United States of America to Deep Down Under."

At the park gate Ernest thought the man would walk out and into town, but he made a very precise semi-circle, and doubled back towards the duck lake. "I never could write 'em myself. Not properly, anyway. I had the grammar, of course, but not the patience. When I wanted to learn a long poem I merely jotted the rhymes in a penny notebook with arithmetic tables on the back. I didn't see 'em written properly till I got that little underground room and a secretary in Whitehall. I did scores of 'em as the war went on — about rationing and air-raids and the call-up, mostly. I put in all the grumbles and grouses people think of in wartime when things are short and life is dangerous. There weren't many grumbles I couldn't think of. I knew 'em all, and it was better, the government thought, to let them go out in pamphlet form like this, with hawkers touting them in pubs on a Saturday night, and knowing what complaints were in them, than have grumbles and rumours going around that they didn't know about and so couldn't scotch.

"I once did a piece about Churchill at a banquet, describing all the food he ate, and what cigars he smoked, and the brandy he put back by the pint; and there was a tetchy letter in *The Times* complaining that such seditious trash shouldn't be allowed to circulate on the streets during the Present Emergency etc, etc. But in fact the poem ended by saying how good Churchill was, and that we as a nation had 'to feed our good old Winnie, With the best grub from New Guinea' — otherwise he wouldn't be able to lead us to victory. The bloke who wrote to *The Times* wasn't to know that Churchill himself had seen it, and had a laugh over it. I've still got his fan letter. J.B. Priestley showed me some of my stuff printed in Russian, though the bloody Soviets never paid me a bean — for a whole book of them. Even the Germans printed a few that they had captured off our sailors and airmen, and turned the text round to suit their own crackbrained ideas. I met George Orwell once at the BBC, and he told me he loved 'em. Said he'd do an article about them, though he never did. Somebody tipped him the wink not to, because it was all very hush-hush.

"I even helped, in my modest way, to deceive the Germans in Operation Overlord – about what spot the Allies would land at in France in 1944. If you remember, we wanted the Germans to believe that our armies would go straight across the Channel and start the invasion near Calais or Boulogne, and not in Normandy, where we did in fact go. So one of my verse-epics had a couplet in it which went 'When we get across to Calais/We'll be dancing in the Palais,' and it was arranged that a copy should find its way into German hands, where it presumably did the trick. The ordinary British people trusted my pamphlets because they knew that one of their own sort had scribbled them down, got them typed and, as they thought, had them put out illegally from some local cellar. They bought 'em like hot cakes. Even a few ink smudges and spelling mistakes were left in, to make them seem genuine. I expect that at some future time people will collect them as examples of anonymous folk poetry. No doubt they'll say how war brings it out of people who, when they are pushed, can make up their own ballads. You know the sort of thing.

"Some of 'em were dirty stories, done mainly to amuse but also, and this was bloody ingenious (though it wasn't my ingenuity), to make them seem authentic. I didn't write those. They were done by some famous poet whose name, as far as you're concerned, Cotgrave, I've forgotten. But it was all in a good fight, which we won, thank God, otherwise people like you and me would have been done in.

"I was all right in London during the war, because I had a well-paid job as a temporary civil servant, plus so much on every thousand sheets sold, which left me comfortably off when I quit. I kept my job till after the war, because they needed me for as long as rationing lasted, though I must say I wasn't very busy. I bought my little house in Nottingham from the proceeds of my talent, if you'll forgive me for calling it that, as well as a cottage on the Yorkshire moors, but I won't tell you where that is, because I have enough people popping in, to listen to the odd story or two that I still can't stop myself telling. Every few years I treat myself to a Mediterranean cruise, which helps to keep me civilised. A storyteller certainly needs something like that now and again."

What an inflated bastard. Ernest flipped a cigarette-end into the water, and the mallards, though they still hoped, didn't come for that.

"I could say it was my lucky day when I met Graham Greene in the pub, yet from that moment my career as a storyteller was over. I never went back to it. Writing so much to order through the best years of my life had killed it stone-dead. If the war hadn't started, I wouldn't have prostituted myself in the way I did. But it was fate. No storyteller can get away from it, otherwise we wouldn't be storytellers. But the truth was that I was finished even before that meeting in the pub. I'll tell you why. In those days, around the beginning of the war, apart from the novels I plagiarised, I still had to tell the sort of stories which I got from ordinary people. But a time came, and it came sooner than I liked, when such tales were no longer so easy to come by. Those who knew me for a storyteller kept their traps shut when we met on the street, though they were often happy enough to see me. People are better liars than they think, when they imagine they're speaking the truth. They'd shake my hand as if they were proud of me, make a stale joke or two, smile and touch me for luck, but there was no longer the hugger-mugger anecdote, or any juicy elbow-gripping gossip, or the beery smell of tittle-tattle, or glassy-eyed revelations from the place they worked at. I thought this was because life had gone dull on them, but they were holding back for reasons best known to themselves. It made me feel alone, though not lonely. They were still friendly, but didn't confide. I was left out of things. Though they wouldn't provide me with tales, they still liked to hear them. Fortunately I'd heard so many in my life that my imagination could feed on the permutations for as long as I had enough energy.

"Though I might not need them, their stories helped me to tell the ones I did know with deeper feeling. I understood why people no longer told me their troubles, and it didn't make things easier, If they told them to me they thought they might hear them rehashed in a pub the following night, and their friends and family would see through the disguise in which they were too flimsily wrapped. They were right, of course. I couldn't hate

94

them for it. If you hate somebody you're even less likely to get a tale. They sensed – wrongly, in fact – that I disliked them for no longer confiding in me when we met on the street. They tried to hide their lack of trust, and we passed it off in meaningless handshakes. In spite of all that, I knew that, providing I performed my tales well, it wouldn't matter if I told the same ones twice. There aren't more than ten good plots in the world, anyway – or so I'd read.

"I thought of leaving the town I was brought up in, and going to other places to pursue my storytelling career, so that I wouldn't have to rely on people inspiring me with their threadbare yarns. But I was reluctant to do so because, in spite of a lack of stories, I could make use of my imagination for a while, and swivel the plots around so that each tale seemed like a new one.

"The tale was important, but the way I told it was more so. During the telling I was often in an unnecessary hurry, like a near-impotent man who comes too quickly. I had to decelerate, yet still keep peoples' interest by spinning along artfully, and making sure I didn't reach the punch-line too soon. (You tend to do that yourself, by the way, or so I noticed in the pub the other night.) I needed to settle them into a mood, wherein I could put over details that didn't seem as if they were going to become part of the story, and when it was obvious that they were, move from one half-concealed titbit to another, zig-zagging step by step to the summit, so that they were boggle-eyed with impatience. What they thought of as the high spot turned out otherwise when I finally hit the real climax.

"I had 'em rocking between the iron-legged tables, spellbound at the bar, tearful in the shadows of snuggery or gunroom, taking them through such an emotional experience that – hard luck to their mothers and wives – they'd be knocked out till the morning after. You have to court 'em, Cotgrave, not rape 'em, show respect for their human spirit.

"I also told stories in order to find out why I was alive. But when I found out why I was alive, would I be able to go on telling stories? You'll understand my dilemma one day. I was as far from people as the moon is from the earth, yet at least I discovered that they were worth all the love and respect I could dredge out of

95

myself. I'd pondered a lot in the insomniac shadows of full-moon nights. I made each story my obituary, shaped it into a statue of eggtimer sand. I had to query, in pain and weariness, why I was alive if I was not to kill myself one hot afternoon before a thunderstorm, or die one pint-of-bitter dusk without having much say in the matter.

"Faced with a sphinx-like audience, I also asked myself if *they* were alive, and whether they knew or cared, and if they did care whether they were only listening to me in the hope of finding out. There must be some connection between me and my audience below the simple level of storytelling, I thought, and it seemed up to me, rather than up to them, to find out what it was. And given the state of me and them, divided as we were like the Grand Canyon from Devil's Corkscrew to Bright Angel Creek, then what the hell was it? But the real question didn't come till later, by which time I hoped to have – but still haven't got – some kind of an answer, and bring forth the precious from the vile. Certainly, Graham Greene shelved quite a problem when he propositioned me in the pub that night. I jumped at his offer as a way out of my quandaries."

He stopped, from exhaustion. He looked older than sixty, tired and done-for, as if he should never have been a storyteller or as if, having become one, he should have died twenty years ago. Writing rubbish for Whitehall, even though it had been in an emergency, had shrivelled his heart like a Dyak's head, Ernest thought.

He leaned against the pond railings, and when Ernest asked if he was all right he snapped his hand away. Storytellers were like that. They'd ignore the warnings of their bodies till they dropped dead. Neither friends nor doctors nor wives could do anything for them. They thought God would look after them, which was, of course, the height of selfishness. They were often unconscious on the physical level. Ernest knew the feeling, though it was only real when he saw it in someone else.

"I'm all right," the old man retorted. "It's obvious to me, though, that *you're* not. I noticed it in the pub the other night. My opinion is that you could do with some advice."

"You think so?"

96

He smiled at having annoyed him so easily. "Don't be offended. Do you know what's the greatest book ever written?"

"*Moby Dick*?"

"Don't guess. The one I have in mind is a patchwork of stories within a story within a story, a compendium of spoken wisdom coupled with endless actions of insanity wherein both are only reconciled in death."

He wanted to tell him to bollocks, then thought of all the books recently praised in the Sunday papers and weekend reviews. The stranger's mind seemed to be wandering. Or perhaps he really had been a storyteller, judging by the ease with which he slid from one topic to another. If Ernest had a hat he would have taken it off to his snakiness.

"I know it's hard not to be offended if you're a storyteller. We're born offended at the air and light as we come out of the womb, and we die offended at the idea of the air turning itself off like a tap at the end. And everything in between offends us whether it's offensive or not. But don't let's be offended with each other, there's a good chap. We've got to feel easy now and again, and it's rare enough for one storyteller to meet another. Sound advice offered from the goodness of the heart should never be refused, however."

The man made him feel like a juvenile delinquent: he wanted to knock him down and run away. "What bloody advice are you trying to give me?"

"It's fine that you have a healthy reaction to criticism. But the fact is that you go at your work too hard. You'll kill yourself before you get anywhere. I can see from your eyes that you'll be dead or finished in a year if you don't use less breath. You'll get bronchitis. It's the smoke and fumes. Flattens a lot of us, sooner rather than later. You're self-taught, aren't you?"

"Yes."

"Good storytellers usually are. It's about the only trade in life you can teach yourself and make a success of. Well, another thing is that you stand up too long. But all *that's* physical, and finally not much to worry at. It's the words that come out of your mouth that matter. I used to think every story came out of your soul, whether it was good or bad, sharp or sallow. The soul is an eternal pool-spring of water, so that what you take out automatically goes in again, from underneath. It never runs dry. The more you take out, the more goes in to fill it up. That's what I used to believe. You don't have to believe anything. The better you tell your stories, though, the closer you are to your soul, and when you're close to your soul you don't have to believe in anything like soul, heart, spirit, or politics or philosophy. Just keep telling your stories. That's where *you* are now. I remember as if it were yesterday. But be careful. Treat it well. Don't let anybody advise you to talk unnecessarily on this or that."

"You can rely on me," Ernest said.

There was silence, and then the old man laughed. "The greatest book in the world, and you couldn't tell me what it is!"

The air around them wasn't quite without hope. "*Wuthering Heights*?"

His sneer suggested a really vicious nature, but he clearly controlled the worst of it. "Oh my God, no! You can stuff that Yorkshire rubbish. That's for Americans and Londoners. It's comic-book nonsense. 'Wuthering-bloody-Heights' — that's all I hear. I'm tired ot it. I'm damned-well bloody sick and tired of it!"

"What is it, then?" Ernest shouted so loud that a policeman looked in their direction.

"You won't thank me."

He gave in. "I might."

The old man smiled evilly: "*Don Quixote*."

"Shit!"

"It's not by any means."

"I read it when I was seventeen," Ernest said.

The old man resumed his bland expression. Ducks still scooted, in case more bread was forthcoming. "Funny, that you're the first real storyteller I've ever met. I'm happy to know the trade isn't finished. It's almost as if I can die now."

Ernest didn't like hearing his profession referred to as a trade. Pickled-cabbage veins mapped the veteran's cheek. He felt almost kindly now that he'd mentioned death. "A storyteller never thinks about dying, does he?"

"Don't worry, I shan't jump over the railings. I can swim. It's just that for a moment I thought I was getting into another story, and that always makes me feel as if the end is near."

Ernest hated him so much that he wished a fork of lightning would obliterate him from the face of the earth. "You're having me on."

He came to life again. "Am I?"

"You old bore. Life's too short to bother with people like you."

"I don't think I'm joshing. One storyteller can't lie to another. Mutual honour is the only kind of solidarity we've got. It wouldn't do for us to compete. There can never be enough story-tellers in the world."

Perhaps there was something to learn from him, and that this *was* the way storytellers talked when they met. They must treat each other gently, with commiseration, as if they were a dying species, and as if only they, its members, were interested in preventing its final disappearance.

Yet Ernest was too mystified by this old storyteller to be convinced that he had ever been one. The man's laugh had energy and imagination, which only emphasised the impossibility of them being used in storytelling. On his own admission he was not a storyteller anymore, though there seemed no apparent reason why he shouldn't be, judging by the story he had told, which Ernest had not believed a word of. The old man obviously wasn't so spent that he had lost all desire to spin out a good yarn, and if it did come from a geriatric it need be no less enjoyable for that. He should be at the height of his powers, not wallowing in an ash-heap of self-pity at the rainbow's end.

Ernest's ninth sense told him that the man had suffered an appalling psychic disaster that had had nothing to do with his wartime experiences. It was as if his brain had been scooped out and put back the wrong way round. Ernest wanted to know what had happened, in order to prevent a similar doom overtaking himself. But he knew that if he asked, the answer would not make him any saner. Solidarity did not extend that far. He had the feeling that he was looking at himself in twenty years' time, so whatever information he received would make no difference, even if it *were* the truth which, under the circumstances, it could hardly be.

A silvery glitter of rain pattered on the lake. The old man

adjusted his coat collar. "I've always got some tune or other playing in my mind, a forceful nonentity-jingle which insults the intelligence yet insists on being heard. It's been happening for as long as I can remember. The only time I'm not aware of it is when I'm telling stories, or talking to you. It makes my life hell. Even in my sleep I know it keeps on, because I wake up tired."

Ernest wanted to escape the beam of his baleful talk. Also, he'd never been able to tolerate rain, and being under two calamities at the same time was more than he could bear. "I'll leave you to sort out your own problems. I've got a performance tomorrow at a university, and I must think about what I'm going to tell."

This made the old man smile, so that he looked younger than at any other time during the whole encounter. "That'll be exciting, taking such a risk."

"Risk?"

"They stand no nonsense."

He was beginning to dislike him again, never having met anyone who sent him from hot to cold so quickly. "I'm not going to feed 'em trash."

He grinned, a wise old shaman of the tribe. Then he farted, perhaps as a last despairing attempt to prove that he really was a storyteller, a noise so long loud and various that it sounded like an old wooden battleship-of-the-line breaking up. "The first place I got thrown out of was a students' hall. But that was before the war. I expect they're more enlightened, these days."

Ernest laughed at his malice. "It's no use trying to frighten me."

"I'm not. But there are dangers. A storyteller survives, if at all, by '*Der Durst nach Wahrheit und die Lust am Trug*' – in our language: 'The thirst for truth and the delight in deceit.' Not that such a playful conceit fools anybody. All the same, storytelling has responsibilities." The old man's mind seemed to be wandering.

"I know."

"Do you? Have you ever performed before coalminers? If so, don't do it again. They're all right as a bunch. I've nothing against colliers. In fact some were to be counted among my best friends in the old days. But I'm talking about one in particular, who has got it in for you. He was in the audience at the pub last time, and I saw him looking at you with a knife in his hand. The knife glinted, but his eyes didn't."

As far as age was concerned, Ernest felt they had changed places. He leaned against the railings. The gaudy mallards drifted away. By dislodging a stone into the pool of his fear the old man was trying to make a story out of him. He would not allow it. If anyone was going to knock a story together about Ernest Cotgrave he would do it himself. In fact he was already well into the middle of one.

Ernest tried to look less pale than he felt: "It can't be that bad."

"Don't bank on it – or tilt at windmills." He held out a hand for Ernest to shake. It was extraordinarily warm, but his face looked pinched in the raw air. "Good luck. I have to get back for my dinner. But don't forget: being a storyteller always changes you sooner or later into someone else. It did me, though don't – for God's sake – ask what or who it changed me into. Never smile. It's the smile that starts the transformation. That's where it begins. Leonard Orgill's my name, alias George Psalmanazar. I'll pray for you from now on, and try to forever hold my peace. I'll visit you once more, though."

Ernest, as if all the world's aliases were eating him away, walked out of the Arboretum gate onto Waverley Street and down Shakespeare Street to Milton Street.

8

"What shall I tell you?"

Left-wing students gave him the feeling that he was going up in the world. He had made contact with the middle classes, (by and large), so it was important not to start with a bad impression.

He was known, and he was not known. On the circuits they had heard of him, and he was called on sufficiently often to earn enough money for his keep. He saw himself as a gentleman of leisure, a jester, an itinerant patterer (and one-time preacher) for whom the word "work" no longer had meaning. He spouted, and the cash came in. If he pouted, it didn't.

He sometimes felt as false and fraudulent as George Psalmanzar, that historic personage (in spite of Leonard Orgill claiming the honour) who was an imposter of grand, and occasionally tragic, proportions as he lied his way through one saga after another and palmed it off as the gospel truth. Where Psalmanazar came from nobody knew. Some said it was France, others guessed Russia, while not a few remarked that Switzerland seemed more the place. He told his friends that it was Formosa, that beautiful island off the China coast. He said he was born under a bush in 1679 from an Amazon mother-queen of the most powerful tribe of that place. His mother had been loved by a kindly Portuguese Galiot captain, and when she died in matricidal battle he took young George to Europe. So George said. His lies were frightful, his imposturings fruitful, for when he grew up he composed a fake dictionary and grammar of the Formosan tongue into which he translated huge parts of the

Bible. In military service with the Duke of Mecklenburg he met a rascally and equally lying get called William Innes, chaplain of a Scottish regiment, who fell with satanic relish into assisting George Psalmanazar's literary and biographical forgeries. Innes was something of a topographer, and together they produced maps and monographs of fictitious countries, islands of fabulous riches for which gullible marineros set sail, and from which adventures many never came back. Psalmanazar and his crony of the cloth also invented *people*, fictitious (and charitable) magnates towards whom the indigent and hopeful, the quacks and sharpers and would-be shapers of the world made tracks. Grand houses with grounds like minor kingdoms sprang up in far off provinces and counties, which the travel-book hacks in Grub Street soon fabricated into their inaccurate tomes.

Innes, scenting the bad wind brewing up, high-tailed it to Portugal, though not before being appointed chaplain to the Forces there. Psalmanazar's productions thereon lost their refinement and subtlety. His inexactitudes were finally rumbled, and the powers of vengeance closed in — at which, near fifty years of age, he went down with a serious illness. It was, he remained conscious enough to utter, a dose of the Great Formosan Doxy-pox which would strike anyone who came near him with a swift and terrible fatality. From being the great liar of that or any other age, he recovered, and took up mere hackery, and among other things wrote a life story which gave an account of his impostures, half of which was also lies, though most people believed in his redemption and took it as the truth. He died at over eighty years of age, lying to the end, crying out that he was going back to the lost paradise in the middle of the mountains of felicitous Formosa, a place he had never known, though who could say with certainty that he would not see it at last?

That's enough, he said, of George Psalmanazar. Shall I tell you a tale of Jean-Jacques Trousseau the Secret Transvestite? He kept falling in love in order to stop himself turning normal. When he could fall in love no longer (the human spirit can take only so much punishment) he raped an ape and got shot for paederasty by his fellow animals. That was a very short story. But I can tell you another, though it's not my wish to get you so incensed that you burn down this fine university, where you smudge the walls with nursery drawings, and aerosol dirty words on gates and doors. I don't think you're out to *destroy* the place, however. You only want to take it over so that you won't have to learn anything anymore. You want to do highly enjoyable things like sitting on the grass all day (when it isn't raining – and who can blame you?) – or lounging in the halls drinking tea and talking about socialism, while being careful never to bring real socialism about by accident in case it sends you out to work more effectively than the tolerant (or non-caring) capitalism that lets you have such a good time. It's one of life's little ironies, except that it could be quite a big one: the hope that what you want doesn't happen because if it does it may not be quite what you thought it would be when you so ardently desired it from the warm bosom of your never-never-wind-in-the-willows land. I love you for it, and long may your good fortune last.

Some were amused, which proved them to be fair-minded and easy-going, and indicated, perhaps, that the first part of their education had taken hold. "I could tell you," he said, "never to fall in love, seeing that if you love someone you can't like them. I could tell you never to like anyone, because if you like them you can never fall in love with them. Either way, you're safe. But it's stories you want, so listen to this: 'The Lord GOD hath given me the tongue of them that are taught, that I should know how to sustain with words him that is weary.'"

"What the hell is that *crap*?" someone called.

"Book of Isaiah, chapter fifty, verse four, which is too good for the likes of you, though if you want to prove me wrong, get more of the Bible into your heart. I wish you would, because I wish you well. In the meantime, I'll return to the safer ground of stories. We all want them, even me, so that I can tell them to you. There's the rattling good yarn about the man who suddenly had enough money to send his three children to boarding school. His wife then went into the looney-bin because she was so lonely. He felt free for the first time in his life. But that's a bourgeois story, and I assume that you socialists want to hear a proletarian tale. Who can blame you? You're here to have tea with a chimpanzee. Does anyone know my definition of a paranoiac?"

"You," someone shouted.

He couldn't think of a narrative that would hook them, and so make his two hours an easy time. Whenever a story eluded him, one was on its way. He always began his sessions not knowing what the hell to tell. A paranoiac is someone who is under the delusion that somewhere in the world there is a person he can trust. Therefore he distrusts everybody until he has found him, which he never can. There's no such person, and no such system which can produce that person.

"I once knew a man" – he said – "who hated his wife for twenty years – for some unimportant thing or other. Suddenly he hadn't the energy to carry this hatred on any longer. Or maybe it was his better nature breaking through. Anyway, having lost the will to hate, he had nothing left to live for, so died of cancer. She was only forty, and got married again. Where there's a will there's a way. Or so my wife told me."

"Cut the shit," said a heavily bearded face.

Ernest took off his leather coat.

"Give the fellow a chance," someone advised in a highborn accent which, under the circumstances, Ernest was glad to hear.

"I'll tell a story in silence, if you like. Have you ever felt that slightly ridiculous silence of the man who has nothing to say? I have. Have you ever felt the silence, which is even more ridiculous, of the person who has so much to say that he ends up saying nothing? Life's full of the silence of continual and meaningless noise. The world would be intolerable if everyone managed to speak. Blokes like me wouldn't get a word in sideways. In print it's called Grub Street and Hack Lane. These days its been turned into a Motorway. But I'll get back to 'The Notebooks of Batty Jack' and tell you about my days in the factory, and how I nearly got the push. It's a tale to warm the cinders of your socialist realist hearts."

"Why don't you get that chip off your shoulder?"

"I do – often. But when I get it off one shoulder, it jumps onto the other. Besides, I feel a story coming on. It must be a story, because I want to piss."

"Jesus!" somebody moaned, in what Ernest hoped was only mock-despair.

"He had a big chip on *his* shoulder," Ernest called.

"I'm going to scream," a girl said.

"Don't do that, duck. Let me go on till I've earned my forty quid."

"Thirty" – from the man who had organised his performance.

"Thirty-five."

"You agreed to thirty, in writing."

If only I could faint, he thought, from a weak heart, a minor stroke, a peptic ulcer, a split spleen or a bout of the Baltic flu, and wake up in hospital so's I wouldn't have these hammers hammering at every bone. A private room in a clinic with colour telly, a phone, and three meals a day, with no real aches and pains, but buxom nurses to hold my hand as I sign my autograph on their starched caps. From my window I'd see a half-built building with men swarming all over it for their daily bread, a sight which would make me feel so faint I'd just have the strength to hobble back to bed and pull the clothes over my head for an afternoon nap before the tea-trolley was wheeled in.

When I was fifteen, he began, I stood outside a plywood factory where I'd been told there might be a vacancy for such as me. I listened to whining saws and planers roaring like aeroplane engines, and watched a van loaded with bundles of wastewood trundle down the street and turn the corner by a newspaper shop. The factory was a high old-fashioned building, dull-bricked from age. Windows let in the winter sun. Bandsaw and plane noise died down, and from a department upstairs came the sweet noise of girls singing, helped by music from a radio. I enjoyed trying to imagine what they looked like. It sounded a happy place to work in, but I should have known better. They were singing to stop themselves going off their heads. I threw down my fag-end and went up the office steps.

A woman opened a pigeon-hole and asked what I wanted, as if I'd just climbed out of a barrel of boot polish. When I told her, she banged down the wood and opened the door. "I'll inform Mr Thursdon."

The small room had a couple of chairs and a map of the world for company. I realise now that the map was on Mercator's projection, and was out of date because most of it was coloured red to mark off the British Empire. There were little diagrammatic clocks all along the top and bottom lines of longitude to say what time it was anywhere in the world, and I'd just altered the times of a few of them with a bit of pencil, and drawn moustaches on some, when I heard the door click, and Thursdon the manager came in.

He had short grey hair, thin lips, and a pain in his eyes that he obviously liked because it meant that he was still living. "You want a job, do you?"

I stood up. "That's right."

"Didn't they teach you at school to call people 'sir'?"

I was a quick learner. "No, sir."

"We'll give you a chance, then. If you work hard, and trust in God to help you, I see no reason why you shouldn't stay a long time. It could be a permanency for the right person."

So this was what it was like, I thought, being in the big world of work, not like it spouted from the cosy pop-land of radio and telly. It wasn't God I believed in, but the end of mankind, because I'd be sweating my nuts off for nine quid a week. My mother thought it good enough news when I got home, and dragged everything out of drawers and cupboards to look for a pair of old trousers but, not finding any, sent me up the street to buy some overalls.

The air in the bottom two floors of the factory was thick with sawdust rising in clouds from sanders and saw-teeth like the bad breath of a wooden dragon. After a few days, my spit turned orange as if, Ralph Brittain on the tablesaw said, I'd caught a stiff dose of good old-fashioned consumption.

Yet it was my first job, and gave me a fine feeling to clock-in like any workman at two minutes to eight every morning. It was near Christmas, and I turned off the street to sniff a mixture of warm glue and yesterday's wood-dust, a pleasant smell which was the only homely thing about the place. I held my card steady in the clock-slot, and smiled at the snappy ding that followed, then put it in the rack on the other side so that Thursdon could tell at a beady glance who was in, and who wasn't.

A lorry backed against a raised platform on which were stacked faggots of waste plywood that another lad and myself had brought up from the Cellar Department where all boards were finished off. Part of my work was to load the lorry, which only took a few minutes. Then I had to carry hot ragged-edged boards from the first floor press-room down into the cellar for trimming and finishing. I was a halfway boy, a catch for odd jobs when my own went slack.

Tom Baker, an old school pal, had also started work there. In his blue overalls he fancied himself as a boxer. He was a bit meatier than I was, though not so tall. His close eyes gave his face a look of frank, honest, take-it-or-leave-it anger. A smile was rare, and only appeared through a snap exposure of his teeth, which movement didn't in the least affect his eyes or the permanent crease on his forehead. His angry face came from continually trying to smile, even when there was nothing funny within living distance. I think his only ambition in life – at that time – was to smile, though even later he never quite achieved it in the way most people do. The skin of his face refused to let him into the world of smilers, and he wasn't too insensible to know that he'd suffer for it all his life. But everyone, including the foreman, treated him carefully because of his angry face.

With strong arms and big hands he toted finished plyboards from tablesaw to fillers, from sanding machine to inspection tables. Teased by the women scrapers, he rarely answered, though he'd sometimes lay his angry face against the back of a warm neck, then draw away with an attempted smile while the woman stood too amazed to crack him one. Or, free from binding up wood-waste, he'd approach the row of girls who damped and scraped the strips of gummed brown paper from over plywood cracks, take one in a Valentino embrace, gaze at her with his look of anger (that he tried changing to one of passionate concern but in which he only half succeeded) then pretend to drop her – though not before trying for a quick kiss on the throat – sometimes just as old Thursdon walked into the room.

A woman called Audrey Bergin loathed his antics and he resented this, though he didn't deprive her of a Zulu silhouette whenever he passed behind, arms and legs going with a sufficiently frog-like speed for her to know from the rims of her eyes what he was up to. She threatened to scoop *his* eyes out with a pair of scissors if he didn't stop his gallop. Not that he was outright crackers. He just liked a bit of fun in the humdrum day among the dust and noise of that large underground bunker.

Audrey was a straight-backed blonde whose thin face was set off by blue unsettled eyes that could become piercing if they deigned to fix you. She was on hot bricks for her divorce and, thinking herself a notch above the rest of us in the Cellar (which nobody could blame her for), began an affair with Radcliffe the foreman. He made her the supervisor of the testing tables, at which she could reject or pass all finished boards with the judgement of her micrometer eyes.

Me and Tom sprawled on the high stack of boards for tea-break or dinner-hour, chewing bread and cheese, and sipping tea from our flasks. We chinned about what was going on in the factory. Tom ripped strips of veneer from the top board and sent them like javelins over the edge. "Radcliffe ain't a bad foreman. Whenever he wants you to do owt he never *tells* you to do it. He *asks* you."

I soon put him straight on that one. "Maybe, but you still get your cards if you say no."

He thought about this, for what seemed like ten minutes, then: "It's better to be asked, than ordered to do summat."

"I'd rather be told, then it's all right saying no. If you say no when he *asks* you, it makes you feel a bit of a bastard."

Tom's latest javelin-skim fell out of the air like a German Starfighter, and his grin became angry. "I didn't think of it like that. They just don't know how to treat people."

He was upset. I shouldn't have pointed it out. You had to be careful with a lad like Tom, but I was too young to bother with such niceties – shall I call 'em?

I slid off the boards to go back upstairs, the fading note of the tea-break buzzer like a dying bluebottle stuck in my ear. When I'd stacked enough boards to keep the cellar going for half an hour, and after I'd been for a piss and a smoke, I went through the canteen whose mixed smell of coffee and cheese-rolls always set my mouth watering whether I'd just eaten or not.

I climbed the steps to the top floor where the thin layers of veneer were hoisted up from the street, twenty fragile flopping long sheets in each pack handled as carefully as silver foil. The women I'd heard singing, before deciding to come in and ask for a job, would search along the grain of each outsized wafer, and cover any splits with strips of gummed paper.

The veneers were then put into cold presses, on the floor below, to flatten the wrinkles. Another stage down, and the large sheets of wafer-wood were glued and crossgrained into a board and fed into hot presses to cement them together. An hour later they came out scorching, but stiff enough to be stacked by the wall, till yours truly carried them five at a time to the Cellar for Ralph Brittain to trim the ragged edges on his saw. After being scraped, puttied and sanded of their final blemish they were taken up to the loading bay facing the street – by me and Tom.

I cottoned on to the process inside a week because, apart from being interested, I was often sent on errands around the factory. The various crossgrained layers of a finished board, heated together and cemented, relied on each other for strength. Without one of the veneers, or with inferior glue, or a lack of weight in the presses, the durability might weaken and fall apart. Any blemishes or cracks were filled, glossed and polished by a bit of old factory know-how, and unless you took a sledgehammer to it, a sheet of plywood was strong enough to last till replaced by another new lot. You could bend it, which is the secret of a good finish, and I knew that a person could be just as flexible, and hard at the same time.

On Friday afternoon, when the floors had been swept and rubbish bundled away, I was still too unsure of my inner self to mention such thoughts to Tom. Yet they occupied me so that I was no longer myself. I stood there with an idle and will-less stare which made Thursdon say that nobody worked anymore when he came around with the wage-box and caught me at it – though there was little he could complain of so near to clocking out time. How could he or anybody know what was packed inside that vacant gaze? I wasn't going to spend my whole life there like some of the men, sensing as I did that fate had other plans in store. But Ralph Brittain said, after observing Thursdon flood me with the old-fashioned look, "If you get the sack, you'll have nobody to blame but yourself."

Tom Baker came to work with the *Daily Mirror* under his arm. He'd scan the headlines at tea-break, but go back and read every word during dinner-hour, when he sat on the warm boards with his back against the wall. He'd fill in any forms he could find, and at three in the afternoon, when I glanced through his discarded newspaper, even the tiniest form, whether indicated by a scissor-sign or not, connected with some advertised tent or bicycle or piano-accordian or book-club or holiday at Benidorm, was neatly pencilled-in with his name and address, and a tick marking the kind of article or explanatory pamphlet he wanted. I once saw him snatch a leaflet, half-hanging from the letter box of a house, advertising televisions, and that same afternoon in a corner of the Cellar I came across his block-capitalled name and address put neatly on the dotted lines for a demonstration of the marvellous sets pictured all over the paper. He never sent the forms in, except football pools, but he liked seeing his name written where it might have some influence if he took the trouble to put on a stamp and trot to the pillar box.

It was easy to catch forty-year-old Radcliffe's bachelor-button eyes love-sicking Audrey Bergin from above his production ledgers in the corner office. In place of the ring she'd taken off not long after starting work there, she now had Clarence to curl around her little finger. He was a short, slim, pink-faced chap with a little quiff, who smoked continually and coughed in your face when he spoke to you, as if the germs were a gift from God that he wanted to share with everybody. He and Audrey walked down the street with arms latched every night, Radcliffe risking his reputation by being seen with a woman who hadn't yet got her leave-ticket. You could tell by one of his eyes that he felt embarrrassed, and by the other that he enjoyed what he was doing. In spite of the scruples, which you saw he must have when he lowered both eyes together, and after seeing everyone else's on him, he revelled in his blonde angular piece of smouldering love. They came to work on the same bus every morning, so he helped her off with her coat. He'd have tied her apron in a bow at the back if she'd given him half a go-ahead.

The trouble began when Tom Baker thought he'd score off Audrey for the times she had ridiculed his mimicking games.

That morning I'd brought in a hi-fi magazine which had half a dozen forms on every page. Far from thanking me, and going to the toilets for an hour to get stuck into filling them up, Tom became moody at seeing so many, and stowed the magazine behind some boards. I didn't realise I was spoiling his fun, and that he only liked filling in whatever he came across by chance.

At dinner-hour when the Cellar was empty, he went up to the stack of boards which were all but finished except for inspection, took a dozen off as though handling a pack of sharper's cards, and leaned them against another stack. I'd come back from buying a packet of fags, and he didn't see me watching from behind a pillar. He chalked something on a board in big red letters, then replaced those he had slid from the top. He looked around, but was too embarrasssed to notice anything.

When he'd gone I slipped across and saw that he had written: AUDREY IS A TARTAR. I had to stop myself laughing in case someone heard me, but stood awhile at the the idea of Tom carrying out such a daft bit of annoyance on a person who, being in very tight with Radcliffe, might make his life in the Cellar hard if she guessed who'd done it.

Wanting to save Tom from the worst of himself, I began to rub out his message. Maybe she *was* a bit of a tartar, but it wouldn't help in the cause of peace to let her know it like this. Working from right to left in my leisurely way I just had time to make a good clean job of the last two letters when I heard someone coming down the steps.

The only other exit was through a wooden door and into darkened corridors of storage shelves leading to the boiler room, so I threw the boards back and got away, before whoever it was could blame *me* for what now remained on the piece of plywood.

When I offered Tom a cigarette later he acted as if nothing had happened. The second part of the day was always his best. In the morning he could be as thick as creosote, and impossibly slow on the uptake. Yet after midday his brain was often so nimble you wondered whether he was the same person. I assumed it was this bright side that led him to fill in forms, and also to chalk his little anonymous message to Audrey on the board, which I hadn't made any better by trying to rub out.

I went home with him that night to look at his new bike. It was a racer he'd seen in a shop-window and, having paid on the spot, carried it home through the rain, on his shoulder, because he couldn't bear to get the thin tyres muddy. It hung from a hook specially screwed into his bedroom ceiling. We sat on a wooden chest, gazing upwards, smoking a Gold Flake between us, admiring the polished frame.

What attracted me even more, as soon as I went into the room, was the style of his pin-ups. They weren't the usual stark-naked, big-titted, legs-spread-out-and-showing-the-universe stuff, but rows of plain (though sometimes smiling) females in jerseys and blouses clipped from knitting patterns and sweater designs and jumper advertisements and women's magazines of the sort that was old fashioned, but that sold by the million. The furthest he went was to have the odd cut-out of a pin-up in shimmy and bloomer underwear from a mail-order catalogue.

"Bleddy good, ain't they?"

I complimented him. What else could I do? He was living proof, if anybody needs it, that you never stop discovering things about a person, no matter how simple you might think they are. The sudden remembrance of how he had referred to Audrey as a Tartar on the plyboard came back to me, and I saw that the use of such a word fitted in well with his modest class of pin-ups. This was even more strange when I recalled that at school he'd had the foulest mouth imaginable.

Next morning I was bringing a list of sizes from the main office for Radcliffe when, passing Audrey's table, I saw her turn a certain board over for inspection. Though it was upside down, my reading was quicker than hers. She was curious at such big writing, and swivelled the piece to see what it said.

The words made purple spots in her cheeks, and her long fingers backtracked as if they had been sprayed with a thin coating of acid when she read: AUDREY IS A TART. She picked up a rag to wipe the insult clean, but it hovered over the first letter of her name, then was thrust into her overall pocket.

"Mr Radcliffe, will you come here a moment, please?"

He walked briskly, as if expecting a touch-up, but when I knelt to tie my shoe lace by the tablesaw he looked like somebody in a circus who'd got a beetroot on his shoulders instead of an ear-nose-and-throat-bonce. He moved the plywood sheet around as if it were a chess board and he was set to play Bobby Fischer after he'd already been beaten fifty times by a kid of ten. I felt sorry for them both, and wished Tom hadn't been so stupid, because whether or not Audrey was a member of the oldest profession (and she wasn't) was her own business, and nobody else's.

Tom was bundling wood-waste by the doorway. Anger and pleasure began a war of attrition among his underfeatures, but pleasure suddenly assumed an hegemonous position at seeing his message take more effect on Audrey than any previous shadow-jumping behind her left eye, though he was surprised that she should shout for Radcliffe to come and have a look.

Waiting for boards to come off the presses, I'd jot ideas for stories in a penny red-covered exercise book that I kept in my over-all pocket. Thursdon once saw me, through his wire-framed spectacles, stuffing pencil and book away, so I made as if to adjust the strap of my overall. He carried a sheaf of papers under his arm, and stood with legs slightly apart. Half of him was in shadow by a heap of untrimmed boards, but the part I saw showed a lapel with three tiny medal-ribbons from the war like a side view of liquorice allsorts. Once a month they looked spark-lingly new, as if just back from the cleaners.

My activities put a twinge of suspicion across his sanctimon-ious mug. Maybe he thought I was writing a betting slip, which he'd have liked still less because he once caught a couple of the Cellar lads playing cards for pennies: "If ever I see you gambling again, I'll dismiss you on the spot!" I heard his tread scraping up the steps as he went away.

I draped my lunch-bulging jacket on the pegs. Even before the work buzzer stopped I'd turned into the pressroom, lifted three boards that had gone cold from the night before, and taken them for walkies down to the Cellar. The bandsaws were already screaming.

Though I hated work I liked the weight pulling outwards from my left hand, and pressing heavily on the other, both maulers padded to stop the splintered edges slicing my flesh as I bent side-ways and lifted a double and often triple pack of boards, and felt the cannon-ball tension in my legs when I toted them down the stone steps, slowly because such a half-hundredweight made me top heavy, and prone to crash my nut against cold granite should one foot be misplaced by an inch.

My mind was gripped by the morning's radio news, that the Americans and Russians were threatening to blow each other up if either made a move in the wrong direction. I wondered what I'd do if the Bomb whistled down, regretting that while you could buy tellies on tick you couldn't hire-purchase a quick-firing rifle with ammo to match. It'd probably cost less, and a rifle would be worth more after the Bomb had dropped and everybody was going mad for food and Burnol. With a rifle I'd pick off any Reds or Deads who wanted me to fight for them.

In the Cellar everybody was working sluggishly, as if they'd also heard the news. The heavy suspicion puzzled me. Audrey was bent by her neon-lit table twiddling a micrometer, her face redder than usual. The lines on Radcliffe's mug stood out more as he supervised a change of width in the sanding machine. Tom Baker's hump was almost as big as the sack of shavings he was tying up beside the planer.

Ralph Brittain whistled no usual tune as he jerked his table towards the circular saw. He was a hefty chokka of sixty, with a head like a battered apple, topped by a foliage of grizzled grey hair that looked as if it would defend his bald spot to the death. He lived in the next street to where I was brought up, and I recognised him the first day I stepped into the Cellar. He spent every day trimming plyboards, fixing one after another against the set-squared lines of the jig, clamping it down, and trundling the table forward on its roller-skate runners into the saw. He seemed slow, but he never let up, demolishing the heaps of plywood I carried down from the presses.

I dumped my boards. "What's up? Have we got our notices?"

He undid the top button of his boiler suit, giving me a look as if it would tell all I wanted to know. "Radcliffe thinks you had summat to do with that writing about Audrey."

I felt the tingle of a minor rabbit-chop. "He ain't sure?"

"Says Audrey's upset about being called a whore."

My toe-caps cleared a lane through the sawdust.

"A tart," I corrected him.

"A tart, then. Any woman would be."

"He's crackers to think I did it." I shoved my hands in my pockets. "Not that I'll bother telling him I didn't. Do him good to think what he likes."

Ralph aligned another board. "It worries him that he can't openly accuse anybody."

I slung a few sticks on the horse for bundling. "You know who it was, don't you?"

He nodded. "I wain't say owt."

I was sure they'd never be able to blame it on me, whereas I wasn't so certain they couldn't do it to Tom. After a couple of questions he'd boil up like a pot of beetroots and bawl out it was him, sack or no sack.

Halfway through the morning Radcliffe stopped me by the steps, where nobody else could see us. "You heard what someone put on a board about Audrey, didn't you?"

I stood my plysheets against the wall. "I have."

"I'm trying to find out who it was."

Hesitation would have meant guilt, so I banged it out straightaway. "I can't think *who* did it."

He was embarrassed by his own glare, his eyes not quite hard enough to see through it, which was something to be said for him. "Thought you would, like."

He expected me to confess.

"I'll not rest till I get who did this. If there's any behaviour I don't like, it's using filthy language – nor writing it, either. In front of a woman, it's worse." His face whitened at this long speech, as if wanting to make me pay for it by catching me a swipe with his knuckly fist.

A smile was close, yet a blinding rage made me want to crash my load down and take to the streets for another job. But I had to pay my board on Friday, and take a girl out on Saturday. The laws of life clung to my back. I wasn't a lone wolf who could live on his wits, or by telling stories. In all jobs you had to put up with people who set you leaping around like a nit on a lousy ape. Too much temper robbed you of the ace of guile, that valuable king-card of patience.

Radcliffe then wagged a finger at Tom's crimson chops. Tom denied everything. He didn't, as I had thought he might, come alight as if he'd been struck along the rough edge of a box of matches, but went, flushed and humiliated, back to his work, while Radcliffe returned to his production lists, having told Tom that both of us were marked as having our heads too often together.

Radcliffe's suspicion broke the rhythm of Tom's working movements. It cut down his speed, which drove him to brood even more. He was the sort whose sensitivity lacked intelligence, and therefore the humour that would have allowed him to step aside from his trouble and see that it wasn't so important. Maybe in the long run he was better off that way, because it prevented him from harrassing people beyond the limits of what they could stand.

His simplicity made him the barometer of the Cellar department because he was always first to be affected by its mood, often sensing a change before anyone else, which set up in him a boisterousness that helped to hurry it on. He imagined that if he worked too hard he got pains in various places which might lead to cancer, rheumatic fever or a rupture. If people got ill it was only because they foolishly ignored, or were too daft to notice, the ample warning of minor aches that was always given.

He was morose the rest of the day, and I should have been as well, for both of us were under the smoke of suspicion. The only time he was free of gloom was at dinner-time while laboriously filling in a form on the back of his newspaper for details of a compact, easy-to-build, bargain-of-the-year gardening shed.

When Thursdon handed us our wages at the end of the week, he said we needn't come in anymore. My narrow pride wouldn't let me complain, and in any case I didn't have the energy after such all-day work. I slipped the pay-packet in my overall pocket, and turned aside to finish sweeping sawdust into a corner.

The two screams seemed to shoot from different directions, and from various people. The first was deep, as if a man had been hit unjustly (and unexpectedly) in the guts, and it came from Tom who hadn't been hit at all. The second scream came from Thursdon a few seconds later, who had been hit, and hit by Tom

— as he was halfway up the stairs. Thursdon's scream was high-pitched. Tom's was full of rabid indignation. Thursdon's was the outraged scream of a man who had never been hit in his life, at least not since that piece of shrapnel struck his left shoulder in Libya. When Tom lashed out again, the third scream from Thursdon was in a much lower tone, as if a world of experience had already passed between that and the first blow.

Tom got in three good thumps before Ralph Brittain and Radcliffe pulled him off. The guilty ones do most damage when they're rightfully accused, and it's often the innocent who fold up quietly when they're pulled in for nothing, quick to concoct reasons why they ought to feel guilty, since they're already paying for it. If they didn't do this, they'd go off their heads. To strike out like Tom Baker might make it look as if they deserved what was happening to them. In any case they'd feel too un-civilised to lash out, and to stay civilised is a luxury they cling to till the end, like those millions in Russia who got put down for nothing. If Russia had been a nation of Tom Bakers it might have been different.

Be that as it may, (and who knows how it may have been?) I didn't join in dragging Tom off Thursdon's back, though I would have if he'd started to half-kill him. My heart wouldn't have been in it, however.

After Tom had been thrown onto the street, Thursdon (having spruced himself up), came down from the office and told me that I hadn't got my notice after all. Speaking on his *own* behalf, he'd be happy if I stayed, because he didn't like injustice, and wouldn't want to think that he had sacked a man who hadn't anything to do with calling Mrs Bergin an unmentionable name.

Getting another job would have meant finding myself in a strange place again. An inability to adapt quickly had had me in its grip since birth. My idea of hell was having to make an alter-ation of any kind, especially in my place of work, which had become almost as important as ordinary life outside. Nowadays it's the other way. I get panicky if I'm not for ever vulnerable, and in a strange place that's more of a threat than a promise.

So I stayed. Thursdon wasn't a bad bloke, after all. He had tried to make amends, and that was good. Every year or two he took off alone on his favourite kind of holiday, a shipboard cruise around the Greek and Roman sites of the Mediterranean. His favourite ship – whose postcard-picture I'd seen propped on his office shelf when I went up with a message – was the *Psalmanazar*. Unless he booked nearly two years in advance, he didn't get a cabin. Last summer he'd travelled on it, which explained his amicability in the first months of my employment at Trowell and Moors, Plywoodmakers Limited.

I didn't find out what happened to Tom for a few years, until I read about it in every newspaper, even the London ones.

9

He asked for a hemlock-and-soda, as if no other drink would bring him back to life.

"There's only coffee," said a girl in dufflecoat and jeans.

The second part of the session would be spent mainly on questions, and any discussion that came therefrom, though he hadn't yet ended Baker's tale. "That's all right."

She had dark ringlets over her collar, a flattish nose and a roundish face, and gave him a plastic cup with steam on top: "I liked your story."

His lips scorched. "Thank you."

"It was *real*."

Which was more than he could say for his *English* coffee – the usual boiling water which had had, at the most, an acorn dipped in it. "Real?"

A student, peeping from ripples of ginger hair and beard, knocked his shoulder, fraternally. "Straight from *the people*, man!"

"I made up every word of it."

"Tough industrial situation. Why don't you tell how they went on *strike*?"

His hand burned, so he changed his cup to the other: "And set fire to the place?"

"Out of sight!"

"Wouldn't be any use. There were sprinkler valves all over the place, as I remember. When the factory goes up like a paper elephant, an ocean comes down from the ceiling. The usual fire-and-water touch. In any case, what if the good honest sons of toil marched out of the factory, and burned the university down?"

The man's eyes narrowed at Ernest's vicious and outlandish supposition. Others hissed with him. "You being fucking funny?" said the man who was like Jesus in anything but spirit.

When he stood on the platform again the same girl spoke up. "How did you start telling stories?"

"To answer that question would need a whole evening, which would cost a few bob more than tonight."

"You're a mercenary sod."

Because he had worked in a factory, they'd expected a stocky squint-eyed bloke with neanderthal arms who wore a cardigan splashed with beer and food. Or they'd hoped for a thin-faced shop-steward who'd smoke his fags to the core, and flash sharp eyes as he told them what was what on the industrial front, while acknowledging that students knew more about the workers' problems than he did.

Ernest was glad he had never been a student, for if he had it might have cost him his objectivity on this sort of occasion. He was too much an amalgam of ignorance, opinion, and individual spirit not to realise it. This admission, which he made, that such an ordinary experience might have robbed him of clear judgement or the possibility of just comment, was itself an objective statement of sorts – which they might have respected him for. After all, no one was perfect – certainly not a storyteller. In any case, he hadn't been brought up to expect a stint at some university.

This statement mollified them, and set their anger towards those nebulous others who had prevented him taking his rightful place in an orchard of academe. I might have been a thorn in your sides. They laughed. "We have quite a few people like you, and they're no trouble at all. They like it even more than those who were born to it!"

A group near the door was talking together. Either they were university versions of the Nottingham Lambs, or anti-Zionist Brownshirts of the sociology department whose fathers were in the Foreign Office.

He had to be careful, or they'd rip the zips out of his boots and hang him upside down with his own Italian tie. No rough stuff, but maybe he should be taught a lesson, because such working-class fellows often pretend to be as worldly and well-educated as you – he saw one of them thinking – and wouldn't admit that students had the superior political know-how of mentors and leaders.

They explained all this, but he considered them to be somewhat confused. He was the storyteller, or speaker (as they had referred to him in their letter) so they must not expect him to question *them* in the hope of learning anything.

"You may know the facts of life, man, because you worked in a factory" (they were reluctant to take that from him) "but you can't see the wider view. What could you see from a workshop Cellar?"

Safety lay in telling more of his story about Thomas Baker. Curiosity was not dead. The hissing stopped. Give him a chance. A one-time worker deserved that, at least. I'll reveal everything, in good time. He'd be silent till doomsday if they didn't come up with a query. In pub or club they clapped a bit, then turned back to their pints. Here, there had to be *questions*. Information was the last thing these Utopian jelly-babies ought to want.

"Didn't you belong to a trades' union?"

He felt as if needles swirled around the spin-drier of his guts. "Both Tom and I were members. I didn't see any sense in it, because what was the use of striking, if you lost your job? Or if you stayed out so long that the factory went bust?"

"No business ever collapsed for that reason, man."

The rest cheered.

A hand went high.

"Yes?"

"Didn't Tom complain about unfair dismissal?"

"You mean after he tried to thump the living daylights out of the general manager? I don't think he had much of a case. The thing about Tom was that somewhere among the rubble of his violent landscape were a few seeds of reason and justice, which he was quite capable of extending to the feelings of others."

No one wanted to know about that. "Wouldn't the rest of the factory have gone on strike with him? Where was working-class solidarity?"

"For Tom? For batty old, form-filling Thomas Baker? Excuse

me while I giggle! Come out on strike for Ned Ludd himself, that insane, snot-dribbling, hump-backed, frame-breaker from Nottingham? You mean to say we should have downed tools (or sweeping brushes in our case) and swarmed into the streets and stormed the Council House in Slab Square for *Tom Baker*? Not on your red belly-button. Tom was glad to get catapulted into daylight on that memorable day instead of being frog-marched to a cop-shop. A better fate was in store for him than for those who stayed behind. He had the obsessional drive of a real work-man, and didn't go on the street to make *revolution*, either. Nobody ever made revolution, anyway. Revolution made *them*. Everybody wants to get on, and those who can't make it inside the system, try the short cut of revolution. If they fail they can always go back into Big Daddy's office or factory (they've got to eat, after all) and do quite well in it. Revolution is the middle-class football pools. Sometimes, somewhere in the world, it's bound to pay off. But Tom wouldn't qualify for an entry form. He never came across one in all those newspapers and magazines he looked through. He just went home on that fateful day with a lump on his shoulder as big as the world, and filled in what other forms and football coupons he could get his hands on, till he'd calmed down enough to go out and look for another job."

"We know what to do with traitors like you!" one of the anti-Zionist Brownshirts called from the door.

A self-indulgent demon drove him on. "Listen, local bigwig though you may be in the Left-handed Wankers Party, I'm a traitor to nobody, except maybe to myself, (and I won't be that for ever), though I'd need to have you for three weeks on a cruise-liner to explain that fact properly, and such a trip would cost us both a bit more than we could afford."

A voice, more knifely for its sharpened reasonableness, said, "Mr Cotgrave, it seems to me, and possibly to the rest of us, that you in fact are something of a Luddite yourself, albeit merely vocal at this stage, and that in a spirit not entirely unlinked with malice you egged on Tom to attack his employer. Would you care to explain why? You deliberately failed to complete your erasing of his relatively harmless message on the plywood board."

You couldn't win, but by knowing you couldn't from the very

beginning you knew that you couldn't entirely lose, either. "It was an accident," he told her, "a factory lark. Maybe I did it so that ten years later I'd have a story to tell."

An American stood up, and he was comforted by her calm tone. "Seriously, Mr Cotgrave, don't you think you're betraying the workers with such tales? I mean, would they approve of you examining their underprivileged existences in this biassed way? Would *you* consent to someone doing it about your life? Your whole performance really is a betrayal of the working class."

He sweated. Everyone was on her side. Even he would be, if he wasn't on his own because no one else was on it. He'd never felt such intense collective antipathy beamed on him. There seemed little to do except bend his head and admit she could be right. They thought that working people hated him for not being one of them, and so *they* felt free to hate *him* for betraying the working class. He stood condemned for having followed a private and obsessional drive to tell stories which, after all, was a prolonged attempt to break through a ceiling of ice that had always held down his spirit.

He couldn't answer. They clawed him back to the earth and the streets, by telling him he had ceased to belong to the group from which he had cut himself off, but to which he had never really belonged. They told him nothing. He had no wish to belong to *them*, though they were puzzled that he did not want to.

Yet he didn't. He might be humiliated, but he was alone, and that was a prize no one could touch. Beset from all sides, your only strength was, he knew, the solitude of knowing that there was no one else between you and God, and that was something which could not be taken away.

"Do you hear? No one can rob me of it. Not Jesus, King, Pope, Queen, Trotsky or Mao Tse Tung. Neither priest, nun, don, guru nor telly. If I talk to God (and I sometimes do, because a storyteller often has no one else) then I speak from my own heart. You can laugh if you like. Not that I think God is made in the image of man and so is an equal of man. If I thought that, how could I or anyone look up to Him? When in doubt, ask Job. I speak direct and without fear to that brain or beneficence or

124

machine-like malignity that made the universe and therefore us."

They weren't interested, and asked no questions on that matter. They were puzzled. He had mystified them, so he was safe. But he had disappointed them, and they were also sullen. To know that there were some questions one could not answer was the first step towards enlightenment, but such a state also threatened him with despair, resignation, and that besetting sin of all storytellers — idleness. Avoid questions, he told himself, especially if you know the answers.

The fact that he had survived so far gave such openness to his smile that they also became silent, and general silence was a state in which he always felt at an advantage, because it was up to him to break it, and he was never afraid of that.

I owe it to you, he resumed, to tell you what happened to our hero, Tom Baker. Knowing him has taught me that less self-knowledge comes out of those blessed from birth by sensibility than from those who are not born with it but spend their lives trying to attain it. By making a pretty pattern with noughts and crosses on every football coupon, Tom one day got the news that he'd won £295,000 pounds, which proved to whoever's capable of listening that if you stick at something long enough, let it eat you to the marrow both waking and sleeping, you're bound to get what you want in the end. His success scored a place in every newspaper, because when asked, on being handed the cheque, how he'd spend so much money, he answered: "Fill in forms!"

He didn't go to work any more, because it had been his ambition, ever since he started, to pack it in as soon as possible, as it is of every free-born Englishman who has passed more than one day in a factory. I suppose you think that's a shame, and that if socialism ruled they'd love every minute of it? That must be why you're so hot on socialism, to keep the workers where you've decided they belong on the supposition that it's better that they should sweat in a factory than that you should. It's quite justifiable, believe me, but at least you ought to admit it. If you did, the workers would understand you more. If they came out on strike you'd shoot them like dogs. They would in Russia. All right, don't get hot under your sweaters. Tom bought a bungalow and sat filling in forms to his heart's content. He sent a lot of them off, and soon had elaborate hi-fi systems, remote-controlled colour television sets, a chronometer-watch on each wrist, as well as fully programmable pocket calculators on every occasional table and what-not.

In no time at all his garden was full of rejects and throw-outs, things that had gone wrong but were cheaper to buy again than get repaired. Such forms that Tom filled in, and all the gaudy advertising matter that so dazzled him, had been devised, drawn, written and got together by ex-students, some of whom started off as Maoists but then found, after getting their degrees, that they couldn't keep a family on a constant perusal of the *Little Red Book*.

Tom was a born gambler who, suddenly rich, wanted only to conform, and I suppose I should go on to say that he lived happily ever afterwards. But he married a girl who read about his hobby in the newspaper, and scribbled on the back of her photograph that she also liked filling in forms. They met, married, and soon had three kids who, after starting school, learned to read and write so that they too could fill in forms on the backs of comics. They were a very industrious family as they sat at the table of an evening laboriously but pleasurably writing on their dotted lines. Tom vetted each form in the morning to decide which would be sent off with a cheque.

Muriel, his wife, could hardly pull herself away from the table to fix scampi and fritters in the micro-oven kitchen, though she soon learned to press the right buttons for an electronically-operated dumb-waiter goods-train to come smoothly into the TV theatre-room station with a four-course dinner steaming on its flat-cars, so that she missed little of what was happening on the three television sets. There was never a happier *working-class* father than Tom who, with his family, could whizz through his fortune without going to a shop or department store and face the embarrassment of buying goods over the counter, which explained why he no longer had that angry look stamped on his face, though he still hadn't learned to smile. Even the sight of post office vans loaded with parcels couldn't draw the correct shape of one to his lips. In the beginning he tried, but the failure each time left him so unhappy and confused that he preferred silent dignity to achieving what was, at the time, his ultimate aim in life.

One young postman said to his face that he didn't need a guard dog with a smile like that, and Tom was about to rush along the crazy-paving path and knock him about a bit, when he remembered that he was rich now, and so wasn't expected — especially by the neighbours, but also by his wife — to get into brawls any more.

Muriel walked into the bathroom one morning, and saw him trying to force his lips into that shape and line of carefree gaiety which he thought should have been his by birth. He was so enthralled, especially when one attempt so nearly succeeded, that he reddened at the neck. He stepped back at the shock, and almost trod on her feet.

"It's no good, love," she told him tearfully, "there's only one way to do it."

She'd been aware of his inability to smile ever since they met, but had thought that her love, together with his getting accustomed to all the things that riches could buy, would eventually dissolve the muscles of his face enough to allow him to smile like most other people. But it hadn't.

They went by train to London, a tense and anxious couple of hours. The surgeon at the Harley Street clinic, a specialist in matters of the face, saw immediately that Tom did indeed need to be operated on if he was ever to smile properly.

Tom wasn't alone in the clinic. Two other men and a woman had come in for the same thing, so it was obvious that the surgeon knew his work. At sixty pounds a day the accommodation was, even at that time, expensive, but Muriel reminded him that he deserved only the best.

The transformation succeeded — to a certain degree. He was able to smile, and it didn't look too artificial to those who met him for the first time. Others thought it a little stiff, but didn't say so. The children shrieked when he came home, and for a while refused to look at him. Marion wept, because it was just successful enough as an operation to enable her to see what a real smile on his honest face would be like. All in all, Tom was rather pleased, and for weeks spent more time at the bathroom mirror than he should have done. If he was disappointed at all, (though he never said this) it was that he hadn't been able to acquire his smile simply by filling up a form or two.

For a few years they were happy – completely so. They could get all they wanted by sitting snugly in front of their individual tellies, in their own warm bungalow, (which they loved very much) and filling in forms. I said Tom *was* happy because, as we know, nothing stays the same. In less than ten years he was bankrupt, and had to go back to work. Muriel abandoned him because the fun had gone out of their lives. Everything they'd bought by form-filling either fell to pieces or lay in the back garden under rain and sunshine. The best stuff was carted off by Muriel, including the children, and the contemporary-style, wall-to-wall Persian carpets.

"You want to hear my last word on Tom? I don't blame you. He wouldn't let me get away with less. I never did scorn his passion for form-filling. It kept him happy, and did no one any harm. In some countries they might fill them in for him, and only expect him to put his signature at the bottom. Tom would be among the shock-troops of the freedom-loving form-fillers if that came about."

"Bullshit!"

"I didn't ask you what you had for breakfast. In any case, I can only hope your grant allows you something slightly more palatable, though perhaps *you* wouldn't notice. When a simple soul has freedom of choice the possible complications know no bounds. Be that as it may, and it certainly was in this instance, because one result of Tom's rocket-like upshot and downfall was that when he lived alone again he was too stricken to fill in forms anymore. What did he do? He went to night school, and improved his education."

"Capitalist lackey!"

"Every trade's useful. I knew someone who was a gentleman's gentleman, and now he owns a chain of hardware shops. There's no one more content. But Tom educated himself, and became a humble but satisfied teacher. I once called at his place of work, and saw that the kids loved him. He was stern, and able to keep them quiet because his angry expression had come back just enough for self-preservation. Tom, always fascinated by the sort of general knowledge that children loved, gleaned a lot of it from books and comics and newspapers (and, I admit, from some of the forms he had filled in) and though it wasn't of much value in itself, he used it to stimulate the kids and ruffle their curiosity. He taught them how to ask the sort of questions whose answers widened the limits of their minds. Those with the luck to be in his class were the envy of the school. The year below could hardly wait to take their place in it, and the year above, having already benefited, never forgot the times with Tom. He had the knack of teaching them as if he were showing himself things for the first time. The happiness I saw brought tears to my eyes. Tom had found something useful to do at last."

"You sentimental *bastard*!"

"Sentimentality is a safety net that stops us falling into a profundity of feeling that can't be understood. Right?" Ernest called.

"Right!" some of them agreed.

"Right. You accuse me of betraying Tom, and also the working class, but I never heard *him* mention the phrase 'working class'. That would have been sentimental in the extreme. If I had used it he would have laughed. Yet perhaps I did betray the 'working class', and if I were a student I'd do the same — except that, being a storyteller, I can't think like that."

"Bollocks!" a girl called in a posh voice.

He wiped his sweat.

"You socialists are put out at the idea of me 'betraying the working class'. How nicely you fart-boxes put it. If it existed I'd betray it, because let me assure you that no one among those you lump together as a 'class' would blame me one little bit. They'd do the same if they could, and jump for joy about it, and bash in anybody's smug mug who tried to push them back where they were supposed to have come from. If I've learned nothing else, I've picked up that much. The reason it bothers you is because in your class-raddled hearts you realise that I no longer know my place. Whatever you are, and wherever you are, society rides you like a bag of coal on a starving pig. I don't think in terms of 'working class' and 'middle class'. I can't mull on revolution. If a revolutionary situation came about you'd use all those whom you call working class to do the fighting, because in a revolution (and the civil war that's part of it) at least eighty per cent of the dead are of that class that you are supposed to love. You'd end up killing far more than you'd save. And when the revolution was over you'd make sure those who were left called themselves working class for the rest of their lives and kept their places so that they'd know exactly where they belonged. Your politics is the art of keeping the working class eternally oppressed, in which you drive people into what you want them to be for your own benefit.

"Those who rebel, against both Marxist and pop-capitalist culture, only escape by becoming something other than what they would normally have been if they had been left alone. What you think they are then is only a facade, and the real character (which isn't really them, but they're hiding inside it till the danger seems to be over – though it never is in their lifetime) is one which in reality has taken them over from their imagination. It is more disfiguring to them than dangerous to their oppressors, but they are left with no alternative but to escape into that refuge-world of their own imagination. Such people, who can't accept what the world bombards them with, are prepared to lose whatever they have in order to evade those social theories which they distrust and don't want to be part of. But by losing in this way they do so with more dignity than if they accepted the world on its own terms. Apart from those people there are enough others left who – call them the good old working class if you like, but in truth they come from any class – with all their inborn sense, want no truck with any revolutionary-isms. At least they haven't so far, though I suppose enough mismanagement might bring them to it. They're wary about voting for worse chains than they've got at the moment. Better the chains you know, than the chains you don't. There are some people, though, who want to make chains for the workers better than daddy ever did, and make 'em pay for them, what's more, out of their wages!"

A girl screamed, which forced a stop-light into his brain.

"Kill him." The 'H' had been used: whoever had shouted

didn't care to be taken for working class any more. The situation was fluid.

"All power to the *real* workers" — a call which rendered him helpless. "Power comes out of the barrel of a gun!"

He sprang — verbally — into action: "In my day it came out of a barrel of beer — and it tasted better."

"Fascist bastard." That long 'A' frightened him, for a moment.

"What about the Third World?"

He dredged up what he could. "When God made the world he didn't use fractions. Neither will he think of first-second-or-third when He destroys it. In the meantime, it's every man for himself — and every woman."

A groan of disgust rolled between them. Someone clapped: "Hoo-ray!"

I'll need him before the night's out. Why can't I keep quiet? Progress had slid out of his grasp. Once let loose, that ranting demon must have its say. He'd used it; it would use him. Every sin must be atoned for. Thought leapt into speech. He told them. He could never remember the point at which the change came: "Nothing's free, not even socialism. Ask anybody in a Russian prison camp. Ask any bloke or woman if anything comes free in this Land of Threadbare Hope and Clapped-out Glory. Free medicine? Free schools? The people pay for it. Why shouldn't they? Somebody's got to pay for it. But it's not *free*. They pay for their own dole or national assistance when they're laid off. If socialism reigned, they'd pay for it just the same. There'd be no one on the dole under socialism, you say? There'd be full employment? Excuse me while I cut my throat! I'm unemployable. I'm even prouder of the fact that I don't need to be employed. If socialist or capitalist offered me a well-paid job I'd tell them where to stuff their deadly offer. I earn enough money by story-telling; I don't need to work for a living. I haven't worked since leaving the factory when I was twenty — and that's almost as many years ago — but in those early glad-to-be-forgotten days I was only waiting to knock-off work for ever. Everyone wants to come in out of the rain, and they want me to get in from it, too. But Cotgrave doesn't want to. Cotgrave doesn't care. Cotgrave doesn't compete in the labour market and do some poor be-nighted sod out of a job. Strikes don't frighten him, either, so he's not interested in bringing in socialism to stop 'em for ever, and to get full employment. Strikes? They're not the way. It's all a fraud. You people think that the place must get smashed to pieces before you or anyone learns anything. Maybe. I hope not. The workers want a rest. They're not bone-idle. They're soul-weary. They want a full life – like me, like you. Their resources have been, and are being more than ever, squandered by the better-off. The workers have had enough of everybody, except each other. They've been kept in their place too long, and now the lid's off. And they've been kept in their place by you as much as by others, because you can only offer an authoritarian system which will keep them in their place just as firmly. Everything has to be much more easy and fluid than that – yet more serious, also. People want dignity, responsibility and moral example, and no socialism that I've ever heard about gives even one of these. Who cares? As long as *they* don't. It's when they begin to care that I'll worry. When they care in the way that the better-off want them to care they might knuckle under to some Big Daddy or other, and the likes of me (and at least some of you) will be the first to get it."

"You're not working-class," some shouted, a tone of great injury in his voice.

"I never said I was. I'm not one of the gaberdine swine, either."

They laughed. They thought he was mad. He was shouting above their protests.

"You haven't told us about the Third World yet." They'd ride him to the end; but he'd ride them, as well.

"All right. You want to help the Third World (and who doesn't?) but where do you think the money's going to come from? Where will we get the food? Who'll eat one meal a day from now on?"

One or two hands were uncertain and half-hearted. A few of the audience still rocked with deadly laughter. The Brownshirts looked grim.

"All the grub and stuff for the Third World can only come

from that mob you call 'the working class'. What are you groaning for? You'll have to make *them* give up food and clothes and pop records, and motor cars and Majorcan holidays, because if you loot only the rich everybody in Africa will get a bristle of a toothbrush, a splinter of a transistor, a crumb of slimming bread and half a kidney bean. In no time at all the rich will be dead and the Third World still groping for enough to eat. Abolish the rich if you like (and perhaps at your peril) but will you do away with yourselves as well? Not on your life. If you had your way you'd drive around in Landrovers with machine-guns and loud-speakers on top, wearing long beards and berets, and with cigars in your gobs, calling in your posh voices: 'Work! Work!' – between excerpts from the Collected verbal pigswill of Lenin, Stalin and Chairman Mao: 'Work is noble. Work for the State! All that you produce will be shared for the good of everyone else. Produce more, work more, come on – work, you bastards, because we need production, we've got to have more tanks, planes, and rocket-artillery to defend your freedom to keep you working-class piggoes where you can't threaten us anymore – er, sorry, we need more weapons to defend all us working-class chaps (sorry: blokes) against the wicked, vicious, imperialist, money-grubbing, mother-selling capitalist hyenas and their lick-spittle, running-dog guardians of feudal, robber-baron landlordism who want to rob us of our marvellous paradise that you all love so well, don't you? Don't you, then, eh?' If you *think* the truth you'll begin to see that there is no truth, though I suppose that if ever you get to that exalted state you might not be able to speak at all. You wouldn't be able to talk about what the working class would do, should do and, by God, ought to be made to do – if only they listened to you. When socialism has abolished death I'll vote for it. Let's get back to Tom Baker and his life."

"You've killed him, you fascist!"

"I haven't. I saw him the other day. He was very much alive. He reads the Bible – what you might call the Old Testament if you'd ever heard of it – to his school kids for fifteen minutes every morning. He makes it live for them. He doesn't tell them to actually believe in it. He doesn't need to. He wants them to believe in themselves first. Yet he does advise them to listen and take in what it says, to love the beautiful language it's written in, language that you can't normally hear anymore, nor read anywhere, either. If you nice people invite me to come here again (though not on a Friday night) I'll explain why, after all I've said, (and I hope there's no hard feelings, though I can see that there might be) why I'm still an idealist who believes in the innate goodness of man, and of his triumphing in some small way over the inborn evil of man, and the possibility of everybody helping each other, and working hard, and getting together to make a better world even for storytellers. I'll tell you why I think it possible for earth to be more of a heaven than it is. But the cobwebs of all vile and masochistic concepts have to be blown away. The twentieth century must first resolve itself, and I hope you'll forgive me for having tried to give my views this evening. . . ."

10

Because someone was following him, he presumed that wherever he was going he would get there in the end. There was even a moon for company, so he couldn't get lost. He was simply unable to find his car, which was as much a home as he was liable to have between here and the house which Marion had finally raged him out of.

He and Marion, too long in wedlock, had only separated when they had become sufficiently like each other to see that a fair division of their composite personality was the only way back to the noble self. Whenever he thought about it, he made up the story. It was endlessly repeated. It ran through his mind whether he wanted to reacquaint himself with it or not. When it ended, it began again. By now he was word-perfect. Like everything else, he had little control over the matter.

The story to himself started when he speculated that he had tried everything to make his marriage with Marion bearable, which was not to say that she had ever backslid in that respect, either. The honour he felt at giving her her due was cheap at the price.

He'd made up tales of his affairs with other women to amuse her, and there was, he decided, no greater love than that. It was impossible to say why she had been bored, living with someone like him. He considered it her most effective ploy, to appear so consistently and oppressively fed-up with him and with her own life, though mostly with him. He regretted that he had not thought of using such a tactic first. People who lived together defeat boredom by hatred, he thought, so to help cure her boredom (and maybe get his own back) he made up tales of his (not

135

entirely fictitious) philandering.

She did not realise that his confessions were as fake as he was himself. The quarrels were vitriolic and searing and went on for days. He couldn't wait to get home after a performance, so as to carry on where they had left off.

After a while she forgave him. They were happy again. But she followed him everywhere. His story went on train lines. He wondered whether hers did. She looked through his clothes and searched his papers for letters and addresses. She was up early every morning to be first at the mail. On finding nothing she felt guilty at not having trusted him, and took his breakfast up on a tray so as to feel better, a measure which set off more fights because he let the tea and food get cold, which she swore he had done out of malice, whereas he'd only been rendered helpless by her tenderness and concern.

In a few months the tension passed. No human soul could maintain such laser-rays of love and hate. He was shorn to a skeleton. He was afraid to stand on the bathroom scales and witness another lost pound. He would get cancer or TB. He was being eaten by something worse, and as yet unknown. The mutual indifference was killing him. So he became bored. Out of shame, and then sheer terror at such a fate (which was worse than death for a storyteller), he made another confession of treachery to Marion which — so the story continued — was brewed from the endless spring of his undying love. For how could a storyteller bear to see his wife bored? It was a negation of all he believed in. Being bored, she was incapable of giving him that undivided attention which he thought he deserved.

She looked forward to each over-elaborate account of his misdemeanours but, suspecting that they were not true, did not create the same dynamic encounters as before. She stayed quiet, and shrugged his yarns away. When this Part Two of his tale got almost no attention, he thought it was because *she* was having an affair (again), and *he* then looked among her coats and dresses hoping for clues as to who the villain was. He got up early to meet any mail shooting through the wooden slit. On witnessing this, she assumed that *he* really *was* having an affair and that he only got up first to hide any letters from his girl-friend. As far as she was concerned, his 'second series' of confessions were, again, only a cover for his actual carryings-on. She set the alarm even earlier, (but he heard it too), in order to reach the front door before he did, which meant that, fragmented by lack of sleep and the sharp pains of profound distrust, they collided on the mat over circulars, income tax demands and other bills, and started the day with deep yet intimate ill will towards one another. The children saw them scrabbling on the coconut matting, tearing at bits of paper.

One night he came back from a gig and found 'Now it's my turn' written in lipstick on the bedroom mirror. Underneath, in barely visible letters, as if she'd tried hurriedly to erase it, was added 'Smash passion'. He'd had his turn many times already, and it was obvious that she suspected as much from his various hints.

She came back after a few weeks. In his vast misery he wanted no more to do with her. There was nothing he could say. He was silent, which made her fall so passionately in love with him that she was unable to resist the temptation of informing him that it was the first time she had done so. Their marriage survived that statement. The perigean tide receded. They trusted each other, and the children were happy again.

His story swung along until, one evening, she heard him telling the tale of their marriage and of his fake confessions in a pub, describing all vicissitudes, right up to when she could stand it no longer and went away. It was Part Three, and she listened while he created a narrative of her departure with one of his friends to London, and from there of her journey to Majorca, which she did not see how he could have known about, but which even in its details was true. It was as if he'd paid someone to follow them. He also narrated the circumstances of her coming back to him. The intimate facts of the affair, and of the reunion, were boiled up and poured in. There were tears of laughter in everyone's eyes. They screeched. They howled. They nudged each other and lasciviously winked. She had never known that he was so popular. He was a comedian. They were entertained with far more skill and panache than when he had told similar stories to her. That, too, was something she wanted to kill him for. Near the end of the tale she could listen no longer and, in her loathing, added a conclusion of her own.

He could never have foreseen such a fracas, although, as he told her later in order to save face (when they were in bed, and she had to change the blood-soaked bandages where the stitches in his flesh had come loose after so much pounding around in their love-making), he had enjoyed every moment.

In the pub, she picked up a weighty pint jar (empty) and threw it with such force that it ripped his forehead. Whether she regretted it before or after the jar had powdered itself, and splintered itself, and made a rainbow of great beauty before his eyes, she neither knew nor cared. For his part, from within the protection – as he thought – of his much appreciated story, he was in no condition to worry about anything except, it seemed at that moment, his life. He ended his performance in a welter of blood, such a flood that, after the icy contact and the flash of glass, made him wonder whether he weren't at the point of death.

The glass hit him like the blast of some primitive firearm. He could have sworn she had shot him. The next sound, confirming, anyway, that he was still alive, (though he didn't yet know in what condition), was of the audience applauding so loudly that passers-by outside looked in at every door.

Such violence, under the cutting lights of a public house, gave him a notion of what real life could be like, showing that it was, after all, possible to be the chief character of an actual story instead of making up events from which everyone but him took some advantage.

The landlord wanted them to do the same act the following week. There had never been such Live Entertainment. Ernest agreed, except that it had nearly killed him. The landlord tended them like two Hollywood stars who had stumbled into his Nottingham pub and put their life's experience into an unforgettable show. Should they agree to do a whole season, his establishment would be crowded every night. Drink would flow like money, but Ernest didn't fancy having his forehead pounded to a bloody mush week after week. Neither, as he said to Marion, did he think much of the pub's arrangements for its walking wounded. They'll have to alter that for a start, was how he ended Part

Three.

Not even that kind of love could last. He wondered indeed what sort would have endured. Only that which was no love at all might have stood a chance, and neither of them could tolerate that shallow existence. The conclusion was that they were never intended for each other, and would have been better off if they hadn't met. He could spend whole chapters on such speculations.

Though their latest uplift into violence was promising, it was still not the sort of love that could last very long. The torment boiled again, and continued for two more years. It went on just too long for them to relish staying together. During this time they didn't even have to taunt each other. They lived in silence. He said something, which was aimed at her, to himself. He imagined her response to it as if he had said it aloud. And then he followed her supposed response by formulating a shattering reply to it and, taking the generated pain and statements of great spite and gravity into account, he released, still in silence, the impacted venom of the brooding days and nights, which broke over him, all by his own fault, its devastation as when a newly constructed dam in a previously notorious famine region of China bursts at some full moon or other to lay the lush and smiling countryside waste for ever. Thus it was the same in both of them. Their arguments went on in utter silence. They stared at each other night after night across the table or from chair to settee, too blocked by intense and inner conversations to say a word. He was a storyteller, and it shrivelled his heart. She was a woman, and died under his wrecker's beam. The fear that his ability to tell stories would vanish became primeval. Marion felt dead already, and knew there was nothing left except to come back to life. He remembered one of their last talks, when she told him: "A woman isn't complete until she's married, and then she's finished. It's all right for a man, but a woman is condemned to death as soon as she's born, and there's no reprieve for anybody who marries your sort. I've had enough. I want to know what it's like to live."

There was no more to say. It was the silence — and that alone — that parted them.

Only when he felt himself hanging onto the world with his

139

fingertips did he notice that there was black under the nails. They also needed filing. He wondered what Marion would say if she knew he was so close to oblivion. Couldn't he live alone, and yet keep himself decent? But she wouldn't care anymore. He was dead to Marion. May she live long, whoever she was with, even if she lived on her own. Even if she'd shacked up with old no-nose, strawberry-face Bingham.

He ground his stomach into powder in order to wish her well, and wondered if she were doing the same for him. The stress on his intestines was more intense when he thought about her in a mood of charity and toleration than when he stood up before a stormy audience to quieten them with one of his stories. This pointed to the fact that instead of her wishing him well in his solitary life she was probably hoping he'd fall into hell as quickly as possible and never crawl out again. And if that were so he knew he couldn't blame her at all. And if he could, it wouldn't make him feel better.

Whatever she thought, and however it was, she would never die out of his heart. It was as if love were a wound that never healed. But at least it left you with a wound to live with, proving how generous an affliction it finally was to the human spirit.

She'd got her job back at the factory, and in every possible way he was, as she had often put it, 'superfluous to requirements'. They were too different as people, and she had hated his storytelling because he had mangled her up in it. They were separated by every psychic galaxy he could put a name to, had bent themselves double in order to get away from each other, and had then got so far away that it was inevitable they should meet again. But even that was not possible anymore. They had gone through their separate black holes, to find something at last which resembled ordinary human daylight. But it was dull. It was empty. It was peace for her (maybe) but blight for him.

Being a storyteller, he would never let her know that he was hanging onto the world with his fingertips, unless he wanted to make her suffer and cling to the world in a similar manner. He didn't care to, because he had learned long ago that if there was anything worse than one person being miserable, it was two people hooked the same way who were close to one another, especially if one of them was you, and the other your wife. Mutual misery made both feel twice as bad, instead of half as bad. The idea that trouble shared meant trouble halved was an abomination. Or had been between him and Marion. If he was depressed and she wasn't (and it worked in reverse, as well), her sympathy made him feel that she was eating him up. If Marion was in anguish, and he wasn't, he felt that she was only using it as a method of getting at him, because it put him in such despair that she was soon cured of her unhappiness. The human condition that they had inherited pointed to the conclusion that there was no end to it.

In short, it seemed none of anybody's business to share your fits and miseries, certainly not to *want* to, in spite of a possible social worker pleading with you not to relax your fingertips and slip into oblivion, in case you set a bad example to those who, applauding from below, might be persuaded into the same flying stunt after your sackbag body had burst spectacularly at their feet. And he or she, thinking to share your dead-end, ashtip feeling, might also be hanging with their fingertips but, glancing side-on, would talk you into keeping your grip till men in white overalls hauled you to safety, then pumped you full of toleran and equanim and stabilim and conformerim and fuck-you-jack-I'm-all-righterim, and sent you reeling and dead-headed back into the world of bottled sunshine and tinned orgasms.

Where were the upright, God-fearing, hardworking, other-directed versatile inventors of yesteryear who thought of no such matters? What had happened to the idiosyncratic self-opinionated captains of former times? He knew that even to ask such a question meant that he was not one of them, but he tried hard all the same and felt that there were too many people between man and God, too many laws, too many questions, too many social demands called love – but no real love at all. His life was a failure, so there was nothing for it but to go on, and maybe create a failure so monstrous that it would be the one success of his life.

No one had come from the students' hall to see him safely back to his car. Like a man in the desert he walked rightwards to counter the pull of the heart and stop himself going in circles.

The rowdy ending to his performance had made him lose his memory. They hadn't tried to get him drunk, for which he thanked them. If he'd been as full of beer as he was of bile he'd have zig-zagged for ever. Groups of people strolled between the blocks; he was content to skirt the buildings whose zone he had penetrated but whose inner *festung* was out of bounds to him. As soon as he thought of the car as home, a built-in compass turned him towards it. A fine drizzle curtained the moonlight. Looking at the battered but lovingly cared-for Humber Hawke Estate of ten years ago, his affection was tempered at the possibility of the battery being flat, and of him being stranded for the night on this unholy island of higher learning.

He was exhausted in all his flesh and senses, but the car had its comforts. He sat in the familiar fag-smoke and rexine smell, and hooked a basket from the back seat kitchen, and took out a flask of coffee. Steam coated the windows of the dining room. Everything blinded him, but he didn't mind because it also cut him off. The electric side-light was so dim he fixed a lit candle above the dashboard in a pan of its congealing wax. The lozenge of flame was a comfort to his soul, and he thought of buying a brass antique holder for both safety and ceremony.

A tap sounded at his window, and he thought that emissaries had been sent with orders not to let him off the campus with two legs on his body. The face was smiling, a finger indicating that he let her in. At least, turn down the window and talk, her eyes said. She had given him coffee halfway through the evening. Maybe they would try to damage him in more subtle ways, by getting a tele-photo shot of him rolling her tights off, then send the negative back to his wife. They were not to know it was too late.

"Go away."

The doughnuts were stale, but fatty and sweet. He wondered where he would sleep tonight. It seemed like three in the morning, instead of ten o'clock. It wouldn't be the first time he'd kipped in a lay-by but, still mentally raddled from the session, he fancied something more opulent, such as a good snore and a few farts in a snug four-poster. The idea made him even more tired, so he moved sufficiently to reach the imitation rosewood glovebox above the fireplace for his hip-flask and a Simon Bolivar cigar in a tube.

It was a car equipped for all emergencies. In the forecourt of every gig-place such as pub, palace or campus he turned the car round on arrival for a quick getaway. You never knew. He'd needed it more than once. He also made sure the fuel tank was sufficiently full to get him to Cornwall or London at one go if he were pursued; or, if the mood overwhelmed him, he'd get almost to Edinburgh should he choose to go north. It was hard to say how far or in which direction he would aim, in his present state of split infinity. Certainly his car was self-contained. Besides a wooden box of eat-and-drink he had a first aid kit, an entrenching tool, a set of maps, two extra bulbs of gas for a quick brew-up in lay-by or field, a down sleeping bag, binoculars (Japanese), a prismatic compass, a Bible, a story-pad, a pocket calculator, a rubber-coated, drop-proof flashlight, a wooden box of Monte Cristo cigars given by a well-wisher, half a dozen bottles of good claret from Ehrmann's wine emporium, a pair of black and white track shoes in case the car packed in and he had to run across moorland, as well as a length of tow-rope with which to hang himself if the spiritual fibre went totally and all of a sudden to ash. He hoped he was prepared for everything, yet never felt sure of it.

The brandy burned, and the cigar tasted like privy-matter from King Cob the First. He wanted to be alone, to blab no more my lady, nor walk in the ways of the righteous till he had got himself into one body and brain again. She banged on the window:

"I want to *talk*."

He felt like bawling dirty stuff, yet it was bad to be foul-mouthed with a candle burning so close. The wax dripped his soul away. Hot globs fell on the patched upholstery. In brilliant electric light he could swear with the fulness of a steely heart, but not by the civilised shadow of candlelight.

Cigar smoke bounced from her face. Through the window she saw him in a mist, illuminated by an assegai-point of flame. He took another gulp, then screwed on the stopper and returned it to the unrefrigerated glove-box. The candle was too dim, but it was impossible to fit a chandelier with seven branches from the ceiling so that it flooded the space with irrepressible dazzle as he lounged in a lay-by with Radio Zombie wanging away.

Her lips said 'Open up'. He liked her teeth, and the back of her throat, and wondered whether she was a fish in the zodiac trying to get in and gobble him. He opened the door to the rear seats. "Welcome aboard! Don't step on the washing-up."

She crunched plastic cups and paper plates underfoot. "Phew, it's warm in here."

"The decks haven't been swabbed for a fortnight. The crew walked out on me — the bone-idle bunch of cut-throats. Something about not getting their pay." He smiled at her in the mirror. "Coffee?"

"No thanks." She undid her dufflecoat. "I'm awash with it already."

He liked her flat nose and round face, and the frame of dark ringlets. "I hope you approve of my mock Elizabethan, postwar, pebble-dash, galleon-style, lethal landship of the late sixties?"

She settled in. "Bit small."

"Why did you follow me?"

The smile filled his mirror, then moved slightly leftwards. "Wanted to talk, I suppose."

He turned his face close. "That'll be a real holiday, after my stint."

"I thought you liked telling stories?"

"I do. Keeps me saturated with the past. I only read histories and memoirs, though. I'd dry up in a fortnight if I read novels and stories. They eat the same carcase I feed off, and that's no good, because maggots would meet their cousins and fight to the death over the inheritance. I've got to have my own special corpse, but not a dead one."

"You're a vampire," she decided. "How boring! I'll put a beefsteak through your heart."

He nodded. "I thought I was going to need one on both eyes after getting away from that lot. Do they always turn into a lynch-mob so easily? Where have all the peaceful intellectuals gone?"

144

"There are some things you don't know. Every university has a Heavy Brigade, trained to smash the National Front."

"They don't need to practise on me."

"You goaded them."

"It's just that before I start I have to give myself a punch in the midriff to stir the demon. I come on breathless, pale and in pain, so that hell can let itself loose."

"Do you ever tell stories to individuals?" she asked. "I mean, if I had enough money could I hire you all on my own?"

He opened the flask and passed a cup of scalding — but real — coffee. "Search the map pocket in the back left door, and you'll find a packet of sugar. It's between the galley and the chart-room."

"I don't take it."

"Could you afford to hire me? Or would you have to live on chip-butties for a month? I don't think you'd get a grant from the Arts Council. You're not rich, are you?"

"No. I have my own flat, though."

He shook his head. "It would have to be in a proper hall, with rows of chairs, even if you were the only person there. I have to lose myself in space, otherwise I'd crumble in the middle of a peroration, like a newspaper on fire when you can't see the flame till the print turns black. But I've told tales for charity, so I can do it for love. I put on a show once at my Aunt Winnie's Co-op Club. She and Uncle Percy loved it. But I couldn't tell stories across the cornflakes on a kitchen table, or relax in a deep-angled, leather-bound settee with a whisky and soda staining the Scandinavian what-not. I've tried it at parties, and it didn't work. Such domesticity is an insidious serpent-spirit crushing all invective, intuition and inspiration — as we say in the trade. What's your name?"

"Valerie."

"Gold, or Silver?"

She didn't know whether to smile. "How did you know?"

"I'm asking, that's all."

"Gold. But how could you tell?"

"I couldn't. Call it inspiration, the aching retina of the all-knowing. 'The silver is mine, and the gold is mine, saith the Lord of hosts' — according to Haggai. Israel is my everlasting love, but don't let's talk about it. Those bastards back there would cut me off without a pen, pick, or a shovel if they knew."

She nodded.

"You and I understand each other," he said.

Or did they? The question went through them both. He wondered how many more times he was destined to fall in love. It didn't matter. When it stopped happening he'd be dead. It was an occupational hazard of storytellers. It drew people to him, and pulled him towards them. His cold hand reached for her warm hand. Both had enough strength to squeeze, as if trying to get at the blood inside.

"What do you mean by 'understand'?"

"Don't spoil it," he said. "I love you."

"Why?"

"Because you love me."

She smiled in her spiritual pain. "How did you know?"

"Because I'm not afraid to give words to things. What have we got to lose? Even if innacurate, inappropriate or inept (I'm having a good innings tonight) they help to define more exactly what we are. One word leads to another, and suggests meanings that you either suck in or blow back. As long as you aren't afraid to rummage in your toolbox of words, and pull them out so that emotions fly onto them and stick."

She thought it pleasant that they could talk of love so easily in this foul-smelling, smoky motorcar with a stub of candle dangerously burning, sipping coffee (that got rapidly cold), feeling the squeeze of his rather big hand, and looking into his worn freckled face that didn't know whether to weep or grin. His features were indeterminate, clownish one moment, stern and normal the next. He was indeed a funny bloke, but she didn't dare mention it. She had once said such a thing to a boy-friend, and he'd hit her, an experience even more frightening now that she thought about it.

"It must be love," he said.

She felt for the latch. "I just came to tell you how much I enjoyed your story."

"Stay with me, and I'll tell you another. I need you. I'm afraid

146

to get out of the car. The ship will sink. The captain always goes down with his ship. I'll stand on the bridge drinking brandy, my cap at a slanty angle, a shine in my eye as the water creeps up my trouser legs. I'll never be seen again. I'll be a handful of dust heading for the stars. I'm scared to drive. The speeding car will hit a ghost coming across the marshes. I'll disintegrate in a puff of dust, or fly off a cliff and hit the peppermint briny. I'll strike a coaster amidships and sink it. I can't think straight. I've given my backbone away, scraped my insides dry. I'm not asking you to stay, because who can say whether it would do any good? A crisis is coming, but was I ever the worse for that? It's a lock-gate lifting me to a higher level of perception. But I might get drowned in the changing level of water, or crushed by a sudden conglomeration of barges set on the same collision-attempt at elevation. That's neither here nor there in the universal scheme of darkness. We all go together when we go – if not before, as the old song has it. When looked back on from a certain point in time and distance the whole ten thousand years of civilisation will appear as a flicker on the universal horizon. So let the crisis come. I'll steer my frail little motor-coracle like Jim Hawkins and see whether I can safely reach the treasure island of sanity and philosophical calm. Now you're crying. I'm sorry, love. It can't be that sad for you, can it?"

"Yes," she said. "You know what you're doing, don't you?"

"No."

"How did you get that scar in the middle of your fore-head?"

"The valley of death? My wife tried to kill me in a pub."

"You lead a violent life."

"Do you know what I thought when the tankard flew at me? I thought: I'm making a story, instead of telling one. I was drunk on that treat for days. Something had happened to *me*, and when I told a story about it in a pub the following week, pointing to my bandage, they loved it."

"Do you always destroy everyone you meet?"

"I suppose so. One day I'll find somebody who can destroy me."

He passed the flask, and she took a bigger drink than he would

147

have thought good for her. "Don't rely on *me* to do it."

"Sometimes, after a gig, I talk all night, and get no sleep. Every performance takes three days out of my life."

"Is that all?" She wiped her eyes on a Kleenex. It was impossible not to laugh. They looked at each other and laughed again. Self-control, except during storytelling, was a luxury his temperament did not allow. If it did, no one would tell *him* stories. Endless talking stopped him being the silent man that everyone would have respected. You babbled on in Babylon, and they thought you were nothing but a loose-lip. They had to talk, in order to stop him talking.

"If I slipped into oblivion there'd be no one happier," he said. "If my eyes closed and I never woke up, my troubles would be over!"

She was alert, and curious. "Would they? I don't believe it."

He didn't care whether she was in love with him or not. The moment had passed. She was like the sister he'd never had. "I mean," she went on, "if to close your eyes meant you'd die instantly, would you do it?"

She was trying to trap him. Why had he let her into his private land-boat for a spiritual basket case? Everything that happened was his own fault. It was proved time and again.

"If you just rest your eyelids together, you'll die!"

He blinked. There was a carving knife under the seat. The time had come to cease telling stories and make one, to stop living through others and take a crocodile snap out of his own spine for the first and last time. He made as if to scratch his ankle, but couldn't find the knife. Maybe it was under the other seat. Should he drive to a lonely spot in the marshes and commit hara-kiri? Or race up to Sherwood Forest and suspend himself from a lower branch of Major Oak, his last sight the mistletoe (and ice-cream-eating tourists) before eagles put out his eyes and beagles chewed off his feet? Telling stories for so long had eaten into him like a disease. Except for storytelling his spirit was dispersed. His body was dismembered. How could anyone who was rotten with indecision decide whether or not he wanted to die? Those who couldn't make up their minds must surely belong to God, for who else would own them? And why did a person unused to action believe that to commit a crime was the only way to live? To kill from a position of inactivity would be a third-rate jump to an extreme. Raskolnikov, who murdered to prove his freedom, was a self-indulgent villain, using an intellectual argument to wake himself up.

"You can't even decide whether or not to close your eyes and die!" she taunted. She put a hand on his shoulder. "Let's go to my place, and I'll make you something to eat. Then you can drive home to your wife."

As soon as she said it, he knew he wanted nothing better than to sit under an electric light and eat a plate of scrambled eggs. He recognised disinterested human kindness when he heard it. Perhaps in a few days he'd drive up to see Marion, and find out whether it would be possible for them to live together again.

He turned on the ignition, surprised that the engine choked into life. Such a ready response worried him, though when the car was moving, and Valerie had left her back seat to join him on the bridge, he felt the black weight of the evening lift sufficiently for him to feel human again. "Can we sleep together when we get back to your flat?"

She said nothing for a while, so he knew there would be a negative response. "I suppose you try to go to bed with a girl after every performance?"

He laughed that she wanted to argue. "Forget I spoke. That sort of thing only happened once, for me. She was a collier's wife, and her husband is still out to kill me because of it. He collects bayonets and knives, and is determined to get me. I split with her after a week. Or she left me, rather."

"I'm sorry," Valerie said. "Were you in love with her?"

"I was, but don't be sorry for me."

"It's her I'm sorry for."

"I'm in an easygoing frame of mind," he said, though he didn't sound like it. "That's why I asked you to sleep with me. But I'll settle for some supper and a mug of tea."

"I'm afraid you'll have to," she told him.

At the first red traffic light, he found the razor-sharp bayonet under his own front seat, and wanted to throw it out of the window, beyond temptation. He didn't. You wouldn't discard your friends so easily, would you? he asked himself.

II

When he woke up in the morning he thought he was dying. He fumbled a way out of bed, put on his dressing gown, and went to the bathroom wondering whether he would manage the few steps necessary to get there.

He did, and stood at the mirror assuming that if he could lift his right arm there was hope. If he could raise his left, he was still alive. There were more certain grounds for optimism when he faced his reflection in the glass, though his wavy ginger hair, light brown eyes, the few freckles on his left cheek, and well-shaped lips, told him that what he saw was the greatest barrier to his understanding. He hadn't fought through to it so far, and wondered if he ever would.

The fact that things could not go on as they were gave him hope. As a child he used to ask himself why he was alive, and now that he was middle-aged he asked himself why he was dead. Wondering what had happened between then and now meant that he might have stumbled on a way of coming back to life. Every morning he went down to the mailbox, bare feet on gritty carpets, to see if there was a letter saying he'd got his three-week job on the Mediterranean cruise liner *Psalmanazar*. As an evening entertainer he'd be an antidote to the daily doses of antiquity handed out to the passengers. He looked on it as a joke. You reach reality through jokes. Did he want the post? If he didn't care enough, perhaps he'd get it. No joke was too abominable, or funny. And they never denied reality.

It took half an hour for his features to shake into place after washing and rubbing them dry. He thought that if anyone else could have looked at him out of the mirror, then that person, blessed or cursed with such a unique experience, would have sacrificed his sense of vision in vain. To get into such a spiritually difficult position merely to see something which had no importance would have had a humiliating and final effect. Only if the mirror shattered would he cease to be as dead as he felt.

Traffic rolling along the street consoled him. If the piss hadn't turned to blood while coming out of his bladder he felt justified in entering the kitchen to see what he could find for breakfast. If he was hungry when he got there his chances of surviving the day were fair to middling. Optimism was a fool's mushroom, however. It was envenomed to the core.

Life hung on a floating thread of cotton. Knowing he might die at any moment (though there was no reason why he should) kept a sense of reality in his heart. It made the world more interesting, and so was cheap at the price. Whenever he slept more than seven hours he felt that his kidneys were disintegrating. That extra hour in bed had given the piss more time to boil around his innards and poison them.

Peace at last. His story remembered how his mother shook that nipple back into her blouse: "No more, you greedy bleeder!" – from which point he began to leave the home he was born in, especially when his father added: (may he rot in peace) "He'd suck you dry, if you let him." At eighteen months the sky was blue. Their words were unintelligible. Their firm tone might have told him that it was his last bout at the nipple, as he tried for the umpteenth time to pull himself upright by the table leg after his mother had put him decisively down. It's not how you're brought up, so much as what you become that matters. If he'd been weaned at twenty-one the shock would have been as great. It was an effort to stop telling stories to himself.

Meaning to steer free of them all, he had shut the door of his two-roomed flat on Clarundel Road. London was the place to hide. It was bolted from the blue and barred against the black night because they were after him, and that was a fact. They'd never find him in London. But they would not leave him alone, either, and who could blame them after all he had done? Four horizons of blazing fire had been set on him by way of vengeance. He had offended in every possible way, and there was no escape.

Almost every day a madman on the telephone said he had a jungle knife and would chop him in pieces. And he wasn't the only one. Marion had put detectives onto him because she wanted a divorce and he couldn't be bothered to say yes, or sign any papers. Next week he would go up and talk to her. An insane cousin just out of the looney-bin was demanding money — with menaces. Some Maoist students were hounding him, and fascist scumboys last week shied a brick at his window but missed.

They were mere skin-chafes. Eileen's husband was after him in a more determined way. He was a collector of knives and bayonets, she'd told him, and had sworn on a Bible to get Ernest even if he had to pursue him to the ends of the earth. In so many words he had said it and, remembering what Bernard looked like, Ernest had no reason to disbelieve her, nor to hope that anyone with such a pallid face, and with blue streaks of ingrained coaldust down one of his cheeks, meant other than what he said. In order to tolerate the threat of this single fanatical would-be butcher on his trail, and to keep his mind equable, Ernest invented a story whereby another mob was continually on the loose for him.

Yet even though they *were* after him, he was determined that nothing would explode his peace of mind — as he put three beef sausages under the grill, and stabbed them with a fork to let the venomous fat run out. They wouldn't find him. Let anyone knock at his door and he'd smile till they went away. Let the telephone ring and he would stand on one leg till the distant rattle stopped. Let a voice scream for help from the street outside and he would watch television till he could no longer hear it. He certainly wouldn't run down to help and get caught in an ambush. Forty was a good age at which to change into second gear, from which to enter a higher form of life and not fall for such elementary ruses.

Let them talk earnestly of pestilence, famine, earthquake and ecological doom on radio or television — or the fact that God was dead (though they never mentioned that) or that ELIJAH RULES, which he had seen painted in pale blue on a half demolished row of W11 houses, with not even an "OK?" after it, so sure were they of themselves that one day Elijah really would rule – and he'd go and get sloshed in a pub, providing it was dark outside, while they discussed the ills and tribulations of the world in his absence. Let all voices endlessly expatiate, let a dozen fists clatter on his door, let every voice roar for his attention, and by cutting them dead he could live in the peace that came from having the strength not to respond. Let a war commence and his tranquillity would be absolute. If the Day of Doom dawned he would go out with eyes closed and meet Elijah anyway. When the engines of war warmed up he would throw off his boots and die in bare feet.

Last week his doorbell had rung one afternoon and, on opening it (but standing well to the side in case a fatal dose of double-barrelled buckshot should attempt to precede his visitor), he saw Leonard Orgill standing there.

"What do you want?"

Orgill gave his usual faint smile. "I'm in town for the day, and thought I'd call to see how you were."

The afternoon sleep still dampened Ernest's brain. "I'm all right."

"Aren't you going to ask me in? I'm bloody snatched, standing here."

Any visitor from north of Potters Bar reminded him too achingly of Marion for him not to respond hospitably, though he was suspicious in case Orgill was scouting for those who had made it their life's mission either to kill or maim him. "Sorry. Come in, and sit down a minute."

Leonard took off his leather gloves, loosened his overcoat, unwrapped his scarf, leaned his stick against the dresser, and took the chair closest to the gas fire. "I've just had lunch with the girl – woman now – who used to type my ballads during the War. Miss Smythe's her name. She's still single, but has a nice house in Ealing. She offered me her big front room there, but I don't think I'll take it, though I may stay there tonight. I can still get it up, now and again."

"Is that all you came to tell me?" – you dirty old bugger, he added to himself. 'Shitty' was the word Eileen had used, and he never stopped wondering why.

"Of course not. I wouldn't say no to a cup of tea and a buttered scone. The only thing Smythe can't make is tea. Nobody can in London, not proper tea that we're used to! She can make cocoa, but not tea. It's sodding cold outside."

When Ernest came in from the kitchen, Orgill nipped away from looking through his books, and helped him to steady the tray to the floor: "I've been making investigations about you."

"Milk or lemon?"

"Those buns smell good. Lemon."

"Look, mate," Ernest said, "I can't have you here long. I've got a performance this evening at a library in Hammersmith. I'm busier since coming to live in London. I do schools now, as well."

Putting two buns on his plate, Orgill exclaimed, "Good for you! I shan't stay, don't worry. My time's just as valuable as yours. But I did think we had some friendship between us, and this is only a friendly visit, after all."

Ernest wasn't hungry. "I'm glad to hear it."

"You see" – Orgill, though greedy, ate very neatly for a story-teller – "my investigations have led me to the conclusion that you're not Ernest Cotgrave at all."

"No?"

"You're somebody else. And that someone else in another person still."

Ernest laughed. "But isn't that other person posing as another bloke called Ernest Cotgrave? We all come full circle, in the end."

"Well, that 'other person' ain't Leonard Orgill, and that's a bloody fact," Leonard Orgill said.

Ernest was happy that he'd annoyed him. "We'd better talk about the weather." He fetched a packet of cigarettes from the mantelpiece, and offered one.

"I haven't finished my tea yet. Then I'll smoke a cigar."

It was, as Orgill had promised, a friendly call, though it took an hour to get rid of him. Ernest didn't like casual visitors. Saying goodbye, he remarked: "And you're not Leonard Orgill, either, are you?"

Whoever he was, Leonard Orgill fastened his overcoat, took

up his hat, scarf, glove and stick. "Now you're waking up. I wondered when you were going to say that. This visit won't quite make a chapter of my come-back story, but I suppose it'll fit in somewhere, if I can catch it when I chase it through the maze!"

Woodworm, rising damp and deathwatch beetle worked in silence, and so didn't interfere with him, proving for the time being that the world was held at bay. The only sound was that of sausage skins bursting under the grill. Let them turn off the electricity, and he'd burn a chair in the fireplace. He wouldn't notice if they stopped his newspapers, because with so much loss who would need news? Let them cut off the sky, and he would bury his head in the sand.

He was safe and at peace, even from Leonard Orgill, for the moment – as long as he told the story before *he* sorted it out. If they did anything it would be when he didn't have a roof over his head (and Orgill knew it), or a penny to his name, or a pair of clean pants to his arse, or a new place to run to. Any fool knew that. They would chase him to some desolate moor and set on him with flails and shot guns, coming out of fresh wind and sunshine towards him on whom the cold rain beat down. His only hope was to land that three-week gig with the shipping line, but because it was his safety net there was no surety that he would get it. The plot-lines of a storyteller's life often did fall neatly into place, however, so maybe he would. Once on the ship he'd be secure. It was a close secret, and he was certain no one would follow him up the gangplank. And if they did, he could always jump ship at Naples or Smyrna.

He was fatigued, after getting back late from a performance last night. Waking up had always been his bane. He hated going to bed and loathed vacating it in the morning, but it was essential to do both for some twenty-five thousand times during his life – or would be, if he was lucky. The ideal existence would be where it stayed between nine in the evening and two after midnight, a perfect time for the sort of spirit he'd been born with as if (and he had never asked his mother while she was alive whether it was true or not) he had actually been pushed into the world in those bland hours.

Be that as all of it might well have been, a storyteller could not be expected to wake up easily, otherwise he might discover, when he reached his shaving mirror, that his nose had altered shape, or that his eyes had changed colour, or that a sudden smile showed a gap between his teeth that had not been there before; or that there was no penny-space where one had previously stared. On the other hand he might see that his hair had switched its tint to an even more than flaming ginger (a perfect candidate for the wicker-basket, but then, weren't all storytellers, according to the Druids, whether they had red hair or not?), or that it had turned Exodus purple, or Job black, or Isaiah green, or Benjamin blue or Ishmael red. Or that a third eye had broken through in the middle of his forehead, formed itself complete during his night's baleful dreams, taken on colour and eyelashes when he had woken without effort. Or he'd look at himself in that stained, cracked mirror and find he had no ears. A revelation of such inadequacy would make his heart almost stop, till on looking close he noticed that at least he had *one* ear, and so was better off than he'd supposed, at which his heart would pick up speed because he could not afford to be optimistic in even that small aspect.

A poignant sensation would arise, because such facile transformations would signify a fundamental change to anyone looking at him who had said goodbye only the day before. To alter the colour of the hair would make the skin different, diffuse the pinpoint eyes, give more importance to his chin, flatten his nose, narrow his forehead, and make him feel even more unnecessary to the world. If there was one thing he couldn't thank his parents for it was that neither of them had had ginger hair. It was passed on by his grandmother, and the fact that he had never been able to show gratitude to her (because she had died before his birth) had always been a matter of regret.

What faced him in the mirror was not his real self. There was much room for improvement. He saw his image the wrong way round. To see himself as others saw him he would have to cease being himself. It's no use saying it's impossible, he thought. The first step is to try and find someone from whose viewpoint to look at me. But before this can happen I have to get myself into a prison or a zoo (or on a ship, maybe), so that I can be sufficiently framed and immovable to be observed for that amount of time to make the mutual examination useful.

Above all, he was terrified (though trying not to feel so as he cut into his sausages) that he'd wake up one day without this terror of death, bereft of this squeamishness at daylight, chagrined at his vanished dreams, and in awe at mulled memories that plagued him till he'd shaved and eaten. Such a state might signify that he would never again tell another story, that at his next gig he would stand up in Miners' Welfare, works' canteen, university hall, bingo club, small-town theatre, wedding celebration or funeral wake, or by the war memorial plinth outside a railway station (or having embarked on a suicidal ad-libbing session in an attempt to pacify the lads coming back on a Football Special when their home team had lost, and luggage racks and lavatory bowls – and each other – were already going out of the windows as the train went through Constable countryside), and his mouth wouldn't move, his epiglottis would go in a flash from flesh to plywood, his jinxed recollections twist themselves into gibberish. He'd nod and mime and tilt his head into a soundless laugh as, from the darkness, the mob hurled pint-glasses, then came for him wielding the handles of one-armed bandits with the intention of breaking him so completely limb from limb that he might as well have been carried off at an early age in that wicker basket and burned with the rest of the unfortunate redheads by the Druids.

Between mouthfuls of bread-and-butter and sausage, he smiled because the morning had begun with his grudging acceptance of the day. There'd never been any alternative, though occasionally he was stricken by an undercurrent which suggested that maybe it would be an improvement if he one time woke up with his mind blank and tranquil; (it couldn't be tranquil unless it were blank, or blank unless it were tranquil, worse luck for him); or that on some stage he became so frozen in his storyteller's act that he wouldn't recover from it, his limbs sprung together after ritual dismemberment, whereby he'd stop telling his shallow stories (always in great demand) and instead spin out God's own narrative from his innermost tripes; expound a story that would not only hold them spellbound or shake them to pieces with laughter, but produce fundamental terror, causing blood to spurt from their noses and maggots to inch from under their feet; to make the walls and boards of the building swirl along the street as if a tornado had got it and it alone; a story that would originate from the pressurised fire of the earth's centre shooting up and into him through his heels, and coming down through the clouds of the cold blue sky and in by the top of his bovine head. The two would meet and give power to a tale, as if the world had never heard of Job or Genesis, Ezekiel or the Psalms, and solo he'd thunder chapter and verse for the first time on earth during one of his performances. He'd feel the proof of God's existence more strongly if that happened than when he told his milk-and-water tales a hundred times a year. He might also have to believe in art and magic, those mysteries he'd never cared to consider since first stumbling into a career of story-telling.

Whilever the audiences listened he never ran dry of the stories they seemed to love, because as one narrative flowed out, as his rhetoric flowered through packed and silent halls, another would be coming surreptitiously in, hesitant perhaps, shamefaced maybe, and as full of faults certainly as the one it was replacing, but an idea, a person, a plot, a flood of jokey quips puns and aphorisms would start to repopulate his emptying ark.

He knew that divinity wouldn't want to get a word in slitways among so much rammel and trash that he pumped out. There was no godliness in his squalid house. The Bible couldn't prosper in his arena of con-man narrative and verbal arabesque. But he was only doing what his very own belly-god demanded, yammering yarns to anybody who would listen and slip him the odd few tenners at the end of it.

Now that breakfast was over he felt less afraid of the West London world outside his window, and went back into the bathroom, to do his exercises so as to limber up his body for whatever perils the day might bring. On his way he knocked over a half empty milk bottle and spent five minutes with a floorcloth wiping it up. His wife hadn't taught him much, but their separation had made him houseproud. The least he could do was drive up one more time and see her, and thank her for it, before he went away for three weeks on the good ship *Psalmanazar*.

12

The main doorknob of the Miners' Club stuck to his fingers. He couldn't get them away. He countermarched through himself. The skin came off. He walked in. He felt as if he were in the Wild West riding towards the Fall but without his ivory-handled guns. They weren't students, after all. They were coalminers, the sort of people he'd grown up with. They would expect him to let the skip down into the deepest seams of his feelings, and even in sleep he didn't know that he had ever done that.

Tim Badder's father had been a miner. When he was five, and the world beyond the eyes so mysterious that his senses could not get out of his skin, he played in the street one summer's evening. The light went on as if it would last forever. He was waiting for his mother to shout him, but she didn't. When Tim Badder's mother called out suppertime, Ernest followed him in. It was peaceful. There was ease and repose. Mr Badder sat by the fire smoking his pipe and reading the paper. Ernest, who in those days always felt a stranger when in anybody else's house, stood by a corner of the table. There was a mug of hot tea and a plate of toast. He didn't move. They'd tell him to go if he did. Mr Badder put down his paper, took a spill from a plastic vase on the shelf, and put it between the bars of the fire. He then smiled in the general direction of the table when he lifted the flaring spill to relight his tobacco.

Tim was eating supper. "Don't let your tea and toast get cold," his mother said, and had to repeat it before the outside world came sufficiently into Ernest to make him realise that food had been set there for him. He hadn't seen it appear, but it tasted better than anything he had eaten before or since. "Your mam's gone to hospital to have a baby. I'll just nip round to see your dad, and tell him you're here, in case he should ferret about you. You can stay with our Tim tonight." She turned to her husband. "I'm surprised they never told him."

He grunted agreement, and in case anyone should think him in a bad mood because he hadn't wanted to be disturbed from his newspaper, added, "Some people are like that."

His father had been out, was neither at home nor at the hospital. Looking back into the mist, it was easy to imagine where he'd gone to hide.

Ernest remembered wishing his father had been a coalminer. His mother came back from the hospital without a baby. He used to think there were some stories even a storyteller couldn't tell, but he didn't believe it anymore.

Tom Baker's brother, Bernard, was also a coalminer, who had put it around that one day he would cut Ernest Cotgrave into little pieces, because when his wife left him Ernest had lived with her, till Ernest came back late from a gig one night to find that she had gone away with somebody else. She was the sort of woman who, because she wouldn't put up with much, every man wanted. In fact it was she who wanted every man (if he was any good) but they, poor fools, didn't know it. "Even though Cotgrave is a worm," her husband was heard to say, "the bits will be so tiny they'll never live together anymore."

Coalminers were angels like the rest of us when in their weekend best, though it didn't do to say so if you were in the middle of half a dozen stories rolled into one vast onion. After working in the underworld they came up black as midnight, except for the whites of their daylight eyes. Often they were laughing because they brought their own good luck at having got clear of the face without blight or damage.

There was no reason to be scared, unless the storyteller in him envied their awesome experience, though he could imagine them swapping theirs for his (with laughter) any day, because while he was usually in sight of the sky, they were hacking at coal a thousand black feet under.

The secretary had only one arm but Ernest, as the storyteller, was easier to spot than if he had one leg, because the secretary came up straightway with his good hand outstretched. Ernest had hoped to seem less of a stranger in this miners' place of leisure. He knew he didn't look etherial or clerical or sedentary – as a storyteller might be expected to appear – but he was different nevertheless.

"I'm Will Gomery," the secretary said. "Striptease is all but finished."

Only half the audience were noting her. Gomery led him to the bar.

"What do you recommend?" Ernest asked.

"Yer can 'ave a short, if you like, but I'm having a black velvet."

At least he wasn't offering a no-option lemonade. She was down to her last pair of panties, and he turned at Gomery's nudge. "Black *what*?"

His good arm had strength. He was a burly man. "Velvet. Pint o' stout, with a bottle of port-style wine splashed in."

"Is it good?"

"Good?" Gomery laughed. "You'll come down from three-o-one, and go straight through the floor."

Ernest's arm ached for the one the secretary had lost. A sharp pain at the elbow went to his wrist, as if a blunt knife were ripping at flesh from the inside. The secretary held his double black velvet: "What's up?"

"I feel a bit . . . you know . . .?"

"She's not worried. Look at her!"

Ernest grabbed his right arm to stop the burning, rubbed it from wrist to elbow as if to trace, then localise then eliminate the pain. "Must have cramp," he mumbled. The sight of the black velvet made him sweat, and he wondered why he had developed gangrene in the arm. It could be no less. Yet he knew it wasn't. He once fell in agony when he saw a man with a wooden leg. Passing a blind man, tapping his way along a Parade of shop fronts, he clutched his eyes and ran screaming into the road. Two cars almost collided. He hit a wall.

"Drink up." The secretary was affable. "It don't come out of your fee."

The tinted liquid slid in. He lost his neutral English, and dived

163

like a salmon back into the lingo-river of broad Notts, trying to stay jovial under the pain: "This is a good dose o' booze."

There were cheers, and whistling, as the dancer finished. Her pubic bush was ginger, but her hair was blonde. She waved contemptuously. If striptease didn't succeed, how could he? Smoke lifted above the parapet. Storytelling wrenched him into a dozen pieces. The same amount of emotional gut-ache in any other occupation would surely give more reward than was to be got by this procedure of fear and misery. It was almost as bad, he imagined, as living would be should he ever face up to its consequences like someone who actually existed. The black velvet threatened to sluice over his boots. He held it in.

"Nervous, lad?"

Up to now he'd concealed the turmoil from his sponsors. He forced a smile that stretched his lips, and showed teeth. Coal-miners, he told himself, are a good-natured lot, but can they be relied on for a non-violent hearing? "It's part of my trade to be nervous."

Such unaffected truth bolstered his pride and was more of a help than he'd have expected before he'd spoken. It healed his courage sufficiently for him to add, "We'd better make a start, then."

Pint jars are soonest emptied. "We all have to take the plunge," Gomery smiled, "and I can see you're game."

As Ernest mounted the stage he noticed that one of the skull-and-crossbone buttons of his leather overcoat was missing. He speculated on whether it signified Marion, or Eileen, or Tom Baker, or Bernard, or even Leonard Orgill – or even perhaps himself who was lost. Maybe he'd find it next time he vacuumed the car. Anything to hang a tale on. Each lift of a few inches above the floor encouraged him to believe it would be easier to think of a lie that would launch him into a story.

The microphone, provided to drown the laughter and back-slapping, stamp of feet and rattle of glasses, stood hypnotically like a cobra uncertain whether or not to spread its hood and kill. He'd be better off without the fear of being struck dumb for the rest of his days.

Gomery pulled it away. "Ladies and gentlemen, we've got

164

somebody with us who's no stranger in this county — nor in any other, if the truth be known. He's a lad we've all heard about, even if we ain't had the luck — not till now, anyway — to see him and hear him. His speciality is — believe it or not (as if you didn't know!) — telling stories. But these are different stories, lads. They'll wring your hearts and curdle your stomachs. I know it. I heard him in Yates's a few months back. Maybe you've read about him, in any case. He's had many a write-up in the local as well as one or two in the national press, and it's my opinion that we're privileged to have him with us tonight. You know who I mean. You can see him as large as life, and in a minute you're going to hear him tell one or two of them marvellous tales for which he's famous. Ladies and gentlemen, lads and lasses, you didn't come here to listen to old Lee Gomery, but to hear instead that Master of Storytellers — ERNIE COTGRAVE!"

When the noise of planks splitting beneath and above him had ceased (he held up his left hand to stop their generous applause), he pushed the microphone aside as if to have one obstacle less between him and them. He looked from side to side of the hall and back again. His limbs moved but not his voice. His feet scraped. The leather soles had been once part of a cow's hide, and maybe it hadn't forgiven him for having been shambled and eaten, but sent that pain shooting up each thigh to his arse by way of a reminder. He was more awed by the fate of the cow than by his own silence, and wondered whether he shouldn't flee like a jack-rabbit, out of this coaldust desert to the salad-valley of the Trent, instead of staying here to do a striptease of the soul.

He dropped his overcoat on the floor. A few people laughed. He smiled. He was so pale they saw no freckles. He couldn't feel them, either. Rugged clapping spread again across the hall.

"There's an old saying," he began casually, to prove he was in it up to his neck, "which tells us it's better the devil we know than the one we don't. But if both devils are inside one body, how do you handle *that*? Eh?"

Being afraid, he'd tell a story that would frighten them half to death, though to be effective it would have to scare him even more:

"Enoch Chadburn, who'd split from his wife, had been living

six months in London, and one night, on an impulse, he decided he must either kill himself, or go back home to try and get his marriage working again. He couldn't even wait till next morning, but left his flat in Clarundel Road and set off north into the foul darkness.

"Our tale opens with him driving along the motorway in his new car, through high wind, blinding rain, and forked lightning. He had to do more than a hundred miles to get home. Water battered the windscreen, and at ninety miles an hour it was like being in a flying boat. Hands gripping the wheel, he looked often through the rear mirror to make sure the coppers weren't on his tail. Sheet and zig-zag lightning lit the fields on either side. When it wasn't flashing, which was rare, the headlights showed the wide tarmac-cavern he drove through. In his mirror he saw the final red spark of another car's rear lights vanish on a distant curve behind. He was going so fast the motorway had bends in it. The truth was, he couldn't stop himself, couldn't hold back, and kept his speed up as if he thought his wife wouldn't be there if he pulled in for a rest and left it till morning – or went at a civilised sixty. It was after midnight, and the road was empty. There wasn't another car in sight on such a night, which was just how Enoch liked it – though don't we all!"

They wondered what was coming. So did he. But they were quiet, as he stood in his spotlight. "Hail played a loud tune on the laminated windscreen, singing a song called 'The Filthiest Night of the Year'. Even Dirty Dick wouldn't be seen dead in it, and here was our Enoch lighting a fag as he went at ninety-five, trying to keep the car steady so that it wouldn't sprint up the bank, hit a post or tree, throw him through the windscreen like a cannon-ball, and roll him to Kingdom Come.

"I said he was alone in that car, on that motorway, at that time of night, in the rain hail and lightning, but he wasn't. Somebody was sitting beside him."

His voice, though declining in timbre, was loud enough to reach every corner, even to wrap itself around bottles and beer pumps. They strained to listen, nevertheless. It was not funny, or bawdy, and not all that interesting (he thought) but multiple hooks of emotion in his voice snared them and wouldn't let go.

"He had got into the car alone. That was for sure. He hadn't stopped since. That was certain. The doors were closed. They couldn't open in a gale.

"Someone was sitting as solid as life on the seat to his left. She was garbed (as far as he could make out: he didn't have to look square-on to know) in a dark and flimsy dress. An ostrich feather grew out of her hairstyle. She was plump in the face. She was chalk-pale in the gloomy glow from the dashboard and the flash-back of the headlights. He was intrigued, after his surprise had worn off. He told himself he ought to have died of shock, but decided it would have been an unnecessary thing to do. If he collapsed from fright at the sight of his unwanted passenger he wouldn't live to tell the story to his wife. It would terrify her. He wouldn't even live to tell the tale to himself, and that was worse. Living to tell the tale was the only thing that mattered to a bloke like him – except maybe getting back in one piece to talk to his wife and ask if he could live with her again.

"He turned his head to get a proper look and felt a bump under the car as if he'd struck a shallow dip in the road. He was scared of going into a spin and hitting a bridge-support whose concrete would strike his fuel tank. He'd topped up before coming on the motorway because petrol was cheaper off it. So he was more scared of getting barbecued than of whoever had colonised his spare seat.

"He turned his head frontwards to regain control of the car. He drove with more care. He tried to get another look. Not that he docked his speed, though he did keep his hands firmer on the steering column. His eyes attuned themselves, through the metronomic swinging of the windscreen wipers, to the ever-rolling band of the road which was still being sandpapered by rain and hail.

"When he passed a lit-up service area he hoped that at the sight of its lights she would vanish as quietly as she had come. He remembered an uncle who had worked all his life at Wilford Pit once telling him how a miner at the face had seen a woman in black crouching close by, watching his every move while he worked. There was no doubt she was there, none at all. A few days later – he had told everybody about her, and they'd laughed at him — a prop split and he was a goner. This tale came into Enoch's mind as he gazed at the road. He overtook a couple of cars, sorry he didn't have a walkie-talkie to radio them about the predicament he was in.

"He was on his own. His speed was a hundred but he couldn't slow down. It seemed a safe speed. He increased it, without intending to. On overtaking he was flying blind for a few seconds due to the backsplash of the vehicle to his left. It was like being in an aeroplane. He had a cool eye. He stayed straight and level.

"He was puzzled by his unwanted visitor. He recalled those tales of 'The Madonna of the Motorway' when the MI was opened back in 1958. Haggard and dressed all in black, she was the rider in a powerful sports car down your lane from the opposite direction, and would send you slithering onto the hard shoulder, or haring into an oncoming juggernaut. Many accidents were put down to such apparitions, as he remembered. When everyone got cars and could travel at high speeds for the first time, they had to watch for the 'Witch of the Straight-and-Narrow' or the 'Warlock of the Arterial Lane' or the 'Ghost of the Trunk Route Murder' or the 'Ministry of Transport's "A" Road Footpad' — all of whom could be after your soul. Maybe the 'Black Widow of the Bypass' would sit beside you when you were driving through Epping Forest, where her lover had been killed by a highwayman. She'd lure you into a tree or lamp-standard. Not a few drivers ended up in the looney-bin, or barely survived death in the hospital.

"Such reflections ran on as he ploughed a way up that dark tarmac. He wondered if she would get out and vanish if he stopped for a rest. If his number was written small and square in Indian ink in the inside of her left index finger there was nothing he could do about it. But was his number on it? Maybe it was somebody else's, and she had got into the wrong vehicle by mistake. His wife would like that touch to his tale. His hand shook as he swung to the outer lane, aquaplaning the slush. Following his heart, he slithered too far back, grinding a few hundred yards along the hard shoulder before he righted the ship and was safe.

"He sweated at such a close brush with gravel and grit, or burning to death in the rain alone at midnight. There was a cold place on his neck, as if a suspended hand held a test tube of iced water and filtered the drops onto it. That cold spot was like an island fortress which nothing could get rid of. Out of the corner of his eye he saw that she wasn't moving. Her face, like his, was straight-lipped.

"The cold area remained at the back of his neck. She might be using her other arm to rest a thumb there and rub it lightly up and down. He said to himself it was impossible. Keeping a tight hand on the wheel, he looked again. It was a fight to hold the ship steady. Some force was dragging it away from true. Her face became thinner. She was smiling. For a moment he thought it might be his wife. That was a part of the tale she wouldn't like.

"The rain pounded more heavily. He couldn't see beyond a couple of hundred yards and so, prudently, even in the middle of his mortal peril, dropped the speed by ten, and switched the wipers to top-rate. A quick touch at his neck told him there was no leak in the roof. The icy place was dry.

"He looked through the mirror but saw nothing. Whoever it was must be lurking below the level of the seat. The shaking that began in his arms could not be stopped. Her lips were stretched in a smile as if, another fraction of an inch, he would begin to see her teeth. His hair itched and shivered as he remembered reading somewhere that you couldn't see a ghost in a mirror.

"She controlled the rain which poured so thickly down that the wipers barely pushed it aside. Even so, the lightning lit its way through and dazzled him. The icy spot at his neck turned to pain, as if a needle were pressed there. It needed all his effort to hold the wheel and stay on the road.

"Sweat runnelled from his forehead. The car swayed from lane to lane. In such weather, there was no other traffic. She was doing everything to kill him, while he struggled to stay alive. The sharp point was entering his neck. The flesh became warm. Only a trickle of blood could provide such heat.

"The car was steadier. Enoch turned. He hadn't spoken because he had been afraid. It would have seemed like talking to somebody in a dream after you've wakened up. It would make her more real, and she would then find a way to end it all.

"An inner voice cautioned him to say nothing. In a calm but

elemental moment he turned and looked. The first noise since she had got into the car ripped itself out of his stomach wall.

"The skin of the corpse-like face was tissue paper. The skull glowed through, yet it was alive. It was a man's head. He wore a morning (mourning) suit, with a white high-collared shirt, and a tall hat. The smile was a grin of maggots.

"His scream established primeval communication. Mutual acknowledgement allowed him to control the car. The wheel needed a light touch. He was wary, ready to re-impose the hard grip. At the back of his neck, warm blood had taken the place of anaesthetising cold pain.

"He looked again. The grin had widened to either side of rotting teeth, except for a white one that drew out blood. Eyes were luminous, everything real. He questioned nothing. The glare of the headlights showed another parking place. He flicked on the blinkers. But he didn't. A dozen thoughts came. He had to be cunning. His wits were unsullied. It was better not to be alone in some dark lay-by. He was already feeble from loss of blood.

"He wanted to keep on living, to tell this and other stories. He swore he had never harmed anybody, not even himself – nor his wife and children – not intentionally or maliciously. And if he had, he'd suffered by it at least as much as they had. He looked at the clock, to find out how long it had been in the car. He was sharp-eyed but both the minute and the hour hands were of equal length.

"All he wanted to do was live. The world of the spirit must not die. The evil was part of him. It was built into his bones, and the machinery of the car. It was a cross-section of rain and lightning. The blood-drinking half-corpse had its own unmistakable features. A cliff of maggots ate his head. They rustled among the parchment of the face, which tried to grin under its pain and shame. Only the single blood-tipped life-line of the tooth was free. The car swerved but he didn't care anymore whether or not it burst into pieces and took his corpse into purifying death. Tears merged with the cold sweat. His rage was evil. It intensified his fear.

"He pressed the radio-button and heard bouncing caterwauling bongo-music which was frequently interrupted by the highjinxing, jokey voice of the disc-jockey. Enoch cursed. He roared his counterweight of curses out. Enoch sang all the dirt and filth that came into his head. Such bile erupting would do no good, but he cursed and roared his vile words till he could roar no more. Then from the silence came his whisper: 'The ear trieth words, as the mouth tasteth meat,' a soul-preserving statement from ever-enduring Job. He repeated it till he reached the next rest area and, following signs and arrows, went in.

"He was careful not to switch off the engine, in case he lost the shriving tatter-noise of the wireless. The air from his lungs grew into a roar: 'The ear trieth words, as the heart tasteth meat.' He raved till whatever had kept him company was gone. He roared it beyond recall. He had tried to kill himself. His spirit had defied it, outdistanced it, drummed it away. He had grown older. It was no use going back to his wife. At the next roundabout he would turn south. He had been in a dead end, but had found a way through. He had tried to live a story instead of telling one, but saw that such a tale was not the one he was destined to live by. He fed off all people, but there was a limit to the extent to which he could feed off himself.

"He had been tempted, but had not fallen – not through any effort of his own, but because his unconscious spirit had not permitted it. He hoped that he would be able to rely on the same inner power for ever, if the threat should come again, but he knew there was no guarantee. He rested his head, and slept till dawn."

13

Not good enough. Try again. He was still the voracious blood-sucking storyteller fuelled by an insatiable backbone hunger since birth. Even when not actually drawing the marrow from people by getting at their stories, he had only to walk the street and spot faces. One flash, and they were in. He got tales out of them when they least suspected him of it, even while he himself was yarning.

His nose itched, so he scratched it in order to change expression. He wanted to stop for ever, buy a cottage in Wiltshire and never perform again. Stories pulled him down through layers of pain he never actually felt. He only half suffered because he had taken the easy way out by telling stories to save his skin. He made his lies respectable by calling them stories, and he belittled his stories by saying they were lies. He performed so as not to die, though it might have been better if he suffered the misery of National Assistance, or went through the more acute and aching come-down of sweating on motorway construction, or skulked in a factory – or tunnelled in a coalmine.

Since he was up on the stage, and visible to everybody, he must speak, move his leaden arms, shift his anchored feet, as if some unseen force worked, talked and tormented him into producing a story. With life and breath drained, he waited to be held from his spiritual death-plunge by the parachute of their applause, wondering whether he'd ever again find the resilience necessary to walk on the stage and flop out his technicolour guts for the humour and delectation of an audience.

Among the calls for more drinks came the sound of a solitary echoing hand clap. Perhaps Bernard was in the audience, hoping to lure him into beginning a story about the one matter Ernest wanted to avoid. If he lifted his head he'd find he'd gone blind. Each second was an hour. When he did look, ceiling lights were dazzling.

"To think we work underground, day in and day out," a voice called, "to listen to summat like *that*."

"Shurrup, Tom, yer ain't wokked for years!"

The secretary gave Ernest a double rum. "That was a good effort, lads. He had *me* terrified for the odd moment. I'm sure he's got summat even better up his sleeve." He put a huge hand over the microphone. "Now, drink this bloody jollop, and let's have a laugh, for God's sake."

Ernest raised his tot, turned the glass from side to side as if it contained pure piss, then held it towards them. His head went back, and the fire rushed through his gullet. Such miming brought murmurs of sympathy. It wouldn't need much ingenuity to reach their good will.

He must tell such a story as would make them feel happy once the session was over. He'd bring the show to an end with Bernard. You win, he said. He didn't want to tell the tale, but Bernard had him in a corner, wherein he must spin the yarn or get violence done against him. It might not happen, but if Bernard (who was lurking in that dimned-out lake of tables) led the pack, it was bound to. Even Lee Gomery's quiet advice – he must surely be one of Bernard's old friends – on handing him the rum, covered a threat which he must take seriously if he was to live the night through.

"My old pal, Bernard, is a coalminer. Well, up to last week he was. He's still my pal, though."

That 'till last week' already made it a story, because they wondered what had happened to make him lose his job. Had he got the push? Been killed in an accident? Won the pools and packed it in for a Jaguar car and a bungalow on the beach at Ingoldmells? Got married and given up the mining life for his wife's sake? Hopped it to Germany where the pay was better? Started his own business as a driving instructor? Been taken on as a full-time union man? (Lucky bastard!) Gone redundant because the pit had closed? Retired early and found work looking after people's gardens on three afternoons a week to keep his strength and beer-money up?

He suggested each of these queries, which they may or may not have put to him. "Bernard was married. He had two kids, a Coal Board house, a nice wife, an old banger Zodiac he'd given fifty quid for, and a greyhound he was always careful not to over-feed because he knew that if you couldn't see its ribs it meant it might be turning into a Great Dane. In the front room he had a mock-walnut, glass-fronted cabinet in which was kept his collection of daggers and bayonets."

Don't tell them about his passion for blades. But it was too late. He'd have to watch out. Be more careful.

"He worked his little front garden with flowers, and planted his vegetables at the back. He had a budgerigar, and a couple of thriving geranium pots in the kitchen window. It was one of those families you might think wanted for nothing, but we all know there ain't no such thing, don't we?"

They certainly did.

He had waited a long time to give Bernard's story its first run in public. If he was in the audience it would not only serve the bastard right, but might also make him stand up and bring his vengeful machinations into the open where everyone could witness them. Since his affair with Bernard's buck-toothed, passion-smashing wife Ernest had expected to be stopped any night and chopped into meat-pie meat. But let him try, and see if he worried. If it was a question of 'die now', he could always sleep later.

"Tom Baker's brother, Bernard, was a coalminer, and was – like all coalminers – a hard worker. He often sweated and soaked in a thirty-inch seam, though he never complained. He wasn't a particularly big or brawny bloke, but he was as hard as they come and at forty-odd was in his prime. Of course, he had his faults, not least among them being . . ."

From the beginning of storytelling it had been obvious that it wasn't the tale you told so much as the way you spun it. Gestures and tricks of mimicry could spellbind even the most truculent. Reciting part of a dictionary or telephone directory might keep them equally still, if it were acted well – such as concluding by tearing out a few pages and eating them. A wink was as good as a word, a nod as blue as a bit of swearing, a bleak smile as empty and anguished as the final phrase at a funeral before the violent booze-up began. Perhaps sounds could be booted out completely, though he thought not, because his audience, being human, needed words to batter and then soothe their souls. An actor-storymonger unrolled his tall tale in such a way that it never palled. Ernest was now and again tugged at the elbow and asked how much he paid his scriptwriter to furnish plots and people, and was only half-believed on replying that he himself was plots, people and performance melted into one. He might have told them that certain bullies foisted themselves on him and demanded to have their tale unspun, or their fortunes told, otherwise they would leave him a gibbering wreck at the mercy of those before whom he was endeavouring to perform. Audiences loved a storyteller, thank God, but if he failed or faltered sufficiently for it to be noticed, then that mob, as soon as the interior bullies who were called characters sneeringly abandoned him — as they invariably did at the upshot of trouble — would frighten him in no uncertain way almost to death with their show of an ugly mood.

"It used to be said," he went on, "that everybody loves a sailor, but as far as Bernard was concerned, it was a collier that the world was sweet on. His biggest fault — every bit as geological as it sounded when the final reckoning came — was in thinking too much of himself. What else can you say of somebody whose hobby was collecting bayonets, claymores, cleavers, daggers, dirks, knives, krisses, kukris, matchettes, pangas, rapiers, razorblades, sabres and scimitars, eh? Slogging his guts out in black grit underground he hoped for the day when he'd be rich enough never to go down to the dust anymore, so that he could smoke his pipe and spread his sharp hardware on the parlour carpet and play at sorting it out for ever.

"Bernard was the sort of person whose machinery of discontent stoked him up and kept a glitter in his eyes. His expression made people think he was heading for a hernia. I'm sure you've met the sort. He was a good father to his kids, and generous, yet they never stopped being afraid of him. At the same time there was no better mate to have beside you at the coal face. The one person who really couldn't stand him was his wife, and one day he came home off shift and found she'd gone and taken the children with her.

"The house was empty, except for the dog and the budgie. Eileen left a note saying she'd always hated his cheerful ways because they'd been too dominating ever to let her come out of her shell and know what she was like herself. She was fed up hearing him tell unfunny jokes, and spoil the kids by giving them all the treats and outings, so that they thought she was good for nothing better than saying 'no' when they nagged her to buy things which cost too much. She was fed up with being the doormat of the house. In any case, she couldn't stand that stinking pipe that Bernard even puffed in bed on Sunday mornings. The house reeked. It was soaked in tobacco. The walls sweated nicotine.

"The goodbye letter was a patchwork-quilt of misery and recrimination, a paragraph in ink, a few words in pencil. It had a line here and there in biro, as well as the occasional touch in different coloured felt-tips. She'd been putting it together for weeks.

"Among other items, she complained about his conduct during her harmless — and futile — affair five years ago, when she went away for a fortnight with a certain you-know-who story-teller. She also lit off with someone else a few months afterwards. When she went back to Bernard, it was the storyteller he vowed to track down and kill. *Slaughter him* was the phrase he had used. Bernard would forget his quest for months at a time then, at Sunday breakfast, or in the middle of the night, his already pale face would go even whiter, and he'd rave about how he was going to set off armed to the teeth with his best dirk and hunt around London (or wherever) for the bastard who had lured her away.

"She could understand his need for revenge only too well, but she could never forgive him for thinking it had all been the man's fault and that she couldn't have gone into it by her own choice. It was a great bruise on her spirit, and she wanted to heal it. If Bernard wasn't knowing enough, and sufficiently generous to allow her this, then she didn't exist, and so she had to get out.

176

"When he came home to an empty house it was such a shock that it had no effect on him. He could either chase after her (having a fair idea where she was, though he was wrong, because she certainly hadn't come back to me) or try to forget her. He had a firm notion that she'd never come back, because she'd left a letter saying not only that she had gone, but also why she had gone, and she had never done that before. There seemed nothing else for him to do next day except go to work as usual.

'Well, that's one way for a married couple to split. Some couples hate each other like poison all their lives, but never come to parting. I knew one such bloke, poor bastard, who was married to one such woman, poor bitch, and one day, after a bitter but almost silent quarrel (with dagger-looks, underbreath swearing, and barely audible grunts on both sides) he gets up courage, or feels desperate enough, to go through that traditional predeparture ritual of tipping up the laden dinner table. It's always the dinner table that gets it, because meals are usually the only time such people come face to face. The husband can also get directly at something that means a lot to the wife: the food she has prepared for him, that usually being the last real contact between them. To tip up the table, therefore, besides being a test of strength, is so final a barrier between them, so violent and brutal an act, that the husband who does it, or indulges in it, knows he can never cross it again for any sort of reconciliation. As the table is tipped up on the floor, neither can the outraged wife get at him with her fists (though she can hurl a steaming tea or stewpot like a lethal grenade going over a bastion at Badajoz) and it forms a barrier too (if the husband has thought tactically beforehand — though if he had acted tactfully it would never have come to such gravity) to cover his retreat to the back door.

"This chap, I've diverged from my story to tell you about, also tipped up the table because he'd rather let that go smash than turn his violence onto his wife. If he savaged her instead of the table there was always a chance he wouldn't kill her, but would get sent to clink, so that she'd be free and the winner — after she came home from the hospital. So it was the table men like him took it out of when they couldn't stand things anymore. Well, the fact was, this bloke in question didn't hop it, because a laden dinner table is a pretty hefty thing, and not everyone finds it easy to turn over when it comes to the point. The upshot of this aside is that as he was heaving to get the table over (he was already struggling a bit), he had a heart attack. It would have been better for him if he'd died, but he lingered for another year before death mercifully took him – as they say. His wife showed him proudly around the housing estate in a wheelchair, as if he'd been born again. Her love knew no bounds: she pushed him into town, took him by train to Leicester, and wheeled him on excursions to Newstead Abbey . . . But I also knew another chap who did actually die straight off, no bloody messing, of what they call 'massive cardiac arrest' – right in the middle of trying to up the table. It didn't even go over, but fell back on its four legs, and trembled a bit, when he dropped.

"Bernard, who was spared such a disgrace because his wife was so civilised that she left him first, never mentioned to his mates and the neighbours what had happened, though within a couple of days everybody knew. They didn't notice it from the way he behaved because he didn't change in any way. This fact worried people, who said that the effect would have to come out sooner or later. They didn't let their kids go to his house anymore to see the elaborate birdcage he had been working on bit by bit for years. In a month or two his hair went grey, but that was the only evidence of his disaster.

"He walked home every night and sat eating his supper while listening to Radio Nottingham (or Radio Trent, I forget which) as if one of them might put out a message saying he'd won the pools, or that he'd come up on Premium Bonds, (which he hadn't got), or that an uncle he'd never known about had left him half the sheep in Australia. Yes, he was a bit of a dreamer, as well as being a shade hard at the head. Or he'd sit in silence as if his wife might come in with the children and ask tartly why he hadn't put the kettle on while she was out at the shop getting twenty cigs and a packet of frozen peas?

"Once a week he'd shake his head and go out to get a supper of Mongolian hotpot from the Friar Tuck Takeaway, and come back to eat at the parlour table. Now and again he'd throw bits to the dog. Just before bedtime he'd realise that there wasn't much likelihood of his wife showing her face again. When she was with him he hadn't been acute enough to cotton on to the fact that she was ready to leave him, though now that she was no longer here he was at least sensitive enough to know that she'd never come back. She had done him that much good. Or he'd done it himself, depending on how you look at it.

"Hearing no news of her meant he didn't have to pay for the children's upkeep. He did wonder how she was managing, and certainly would not have been unhappy to fork out part of his wages. Not that he got much, of course. Miners have rotten pay."

Cheers!

"But he heard nothing, so assumed she was coping in her usual incompetent though finally effective way. Maybe she'd taken up with a bloke who had a good job, and who was keeping her even better than he had. It seemed a likely answer, though he didn't know who it might be because, looking back, he couldn't recall a suitable candidate, except maybe that shit-house of a storyteller she'd gone with before; but that hadn't lasted long. And maybe it was not having to chuck in shekels for her upkeep anymore that didn't exactly encourage Bernard to send out tracker-dogs. After six months he had a fair bit of money stashed in a biscuit barrel under his bed.

"Whenever something fundamental happened to Bernard Baker he was never able to say whether it was a disaster, or the reverse. If the world fell in on him, he'd merely rub his head and wonder what had happened, providing he was still breathing. Thank God for such people. Without them the world would stop. At this time, if you'd asked Bernard what he wanted, he'd have answered: 'Nothing.' He didn't even want to add to his cut-and-thrust collection anymore. The great unconscious was working its wonders to perform.

"He took his greyhound to Edwinstowe one afternoon. Parking his old banger on the edge of the Forest, he opened the door, and the daft bloody animal — as he described it afterwards with never a tear in his eye — ran into the road. A great truck came hurling by. The dog never knew what hit it.

"The accident had an effect on him, all the same. He didn't

have to feed the dog anymore. He then put an advert in the local paper: MOTOR CAR IN GOOD CONDITION. SELLING DUE TO OWNER'S ILLNESS. He spun a good yarn, and got £250 for it. From then on he didn't have to bother with road tax, insurance, MOT tests, and the odd spare part or repair, so that his money-roll fattened by the week. Our Bernard was a darker horse than midnight itself. He turned up regularly for work, his hair a bit greyer, and lines deepening on either side of his mouth. But he was the same old cheerful Bernard. He kept clean, and drank an occasional pint at the Institute. He swept the kitchen floor at home, made his (single) bed every day, and changed the sheets once a week. He thought less and less about his wife, and even got accustomed to being without his kids as the months went by. He'd heard nothing from them — 'not even a postcard', he said, which eventually stopped the matter biting him so deep. One day, he gave his notice in at the pit.

" 'What the hell for, Bernard?' they wanted to know.

"He didn't even stare at them. 'I've had enough,' was all he'd say.

" 'What, art fed up on it?'

"He swivelled his lit pipe along the parapet of his false teeth. 'Aye'.

"Peter, his mate, always laughed broadly when something puzzled him and he didn't know why. You've heard the sort. (Ernest imitated him, anyway.) 'We all are, aren't we, lads? But we must endure, come what may.'

" 'Are you getting a new job, then?' his other pal tried to find out.

" 'I don't know yet.'

" 'Y'aren't going on't dole, are yer?'

"Bernard was a secretive bloke, as you're going to hear. 'Not bloody likely.' Seeing as how he had been born with a need to keep his trap shut, they left him alone. His point of view was that if he told them what he had in mind he might not do it, while they considered that if a man had decided on some private matter of his own, there was nothing to be got by prying.

"Bernard had learned the hard way, latterly from his wife, when she'd decided to get shut of him. He's the sort of person it's

180

a treat to tell a story about, because when things go wrong he just clams up, and makes his own underground way towards an alteration in his circumstances. He wasn't a coalminer for nothing.

"He'd been preparing the move for months. His doctor signed the form so that he could get a passport. Then he sent for brochures from Cooks', and one Saturday morning he went to their office to fill in applications and pay his deposit. He read books about Greece from the library, and bought a tenpenny map from the bin of a secondhand bookshop, in order to know where exactly he'd be going. He called at the Co-op to pick up a suitcase, as well as purchase a mackintosh, a pair of boots, a plastic Panama-style hat to keep off the sun, and two pairs of swimming trunks. There'd be a pool on the ship, and since it was in the price of the ticket he thought he might as well take part in what horseplay and watersport would be on offer.

"In the travel office he was stopped dead by a poster advertising Mediterranean tours showing an elegant tanned woman in a pale bikini stretched against a rock with a ruined temple in the background composed of blocks and columns like those in the brick game he'd played as a kid at school. Her body was firm and slender at the navel, with beads of sweat or water on the skin. The lovely breasts were barely covered, and her half-closed eyes suggested she had just been well and truly done by a man who, though absent from the picture, might not be far away, and that a future lover could even be in Ashfield still, and about to walk out of his life forever – towards her.

"He could hardly believe that his plan would unroll into real life. Like all of us, he'd lived too long from day to day to have much faith in the inevitable, but now he wanted to change all that and sample a bit of hope, to dope himself with expectation. Once Bernard got an idea into his hard head there was no stopping him, nor knowing where it would end. He dreamed waking and sleeping about his forthcoming Mediterranean zig-zags, not concerned about what would happen if and when he came back to Ashfield.

"It was a project worth spending money on. What remained from paying the agent was changed into travellers' cheques. The week before leaving was the slowest and most worrying he had known. He hardly slept in case somebody smashed a panel of the flimsy backdoor, or quietly sliced a hole in the kitchen window with a diamond-cutter, or shinned up a drainpipe and got in that way to pinch his passport, tickets and money. The buff envelope under his pillow crinkled enough to wake the living when he turned over. He finally fell into a doze about dawn. A razor-sharp panga hung by a string from the bed rail.

"If his wife and children were to turn up, this was the time they'd choose, and if so, he didn't see how he could sneak away on the cruise he had worked so long for. He had waited for it ever since he had been born, and this idea pushed away some of the guilt at leaving his mates sweating down pit while he would be looking through Japanese field-glasses at some exotic port the ship steamed to.

"He was afraid to go shopping in case he got run over by a forty-ton rogue juggernaut on that narrow twisting lane between Bagthorpe and Brinsley that he had no reason to walk on because there were no shops there anyway – though you never knew. So he hardly went out. Even so, he had visions of screaming on the floor in pain and spinning like a shot poppy in full spate because his appendix had burst. Or he'd wake up, after daring to fall asleep, stone-blind, and regret at last that his dog was dead. He might go to sleep one night and never wake up again. All the daylight there'd been in the world since it began would fold itself into a bubble, get into a vein, and black him out forever.

"He felt no anxiety during his last week at work. He wasn't worried that a prop would give while deep underground, or scared that a truck might squash his guts, or sunk in trepidation that a blinding white flash from firedamp would be the last brief thing he'd ever see, or that the skip cables would snap and drop him to the bottom like a blob of corned beef. Such accidents were Acts of God, whereas anything above the earth which stopped him flat in the track of his Great Plan could only be triggered by the sniggering malice of the devil.

"The great day came, as it generally does when worse things are in store. He got out of his armchair to the singing of a copper alarm clock as big as a saucepan, and made breakfast with the last of the tea, sugar, milk, bread, butter and bacon. He put on his jacket and mackintosh, and looked around at the desolation he was saying goodbye to. He nodded at the geraniums, poked the warm ash out of the fire-place, turned the photo of his wife and kids face-flat on the table, set the big clock to the wall, and emptied the last of the tea leaves down the sink. Good riddance. Outside, he locked the door and put the key under a flagstone. Let squatters find it if they could – though what they'd want in Ashfield he couldn't imagine.

"His collection of steel blades had been sold for solid cash to be used should he abandon the ship somewhere and need to support himself. A buyer came from London in a red Italian sports car, on reading Bernard's advertisement in *Exchange and Mart*: FIRST OFFER OVER FIVE HUNDRED CASH CONSIDERED. Bernard indicated that he had already been given the hint that six hundred was a fairer price, and so the man parted with five hundred and fifty. Bernard's money-belt was padded with twenty pound notes. He had kept back a bayonet and two knives to pack into his suitcase and take with him.

"The early bus to Alfreton Parkway was almost empty. When he gazed out of the train window the land was familiar. Exaltation came when he went into a daydream and saw nothing for a while of either land or sky. His hand shook, and he told himself it was only a holiday, all said and done. The fact that it certainly wasn't made him happier, but only in a bemused sort of way.

"His suitcase stayed on the seat because he didn't want it out of sight, and he hoped the train wouldn't become so full that someone would ask him to shift it, for if they did he'd tell them what to do with their big ideas. On top of it lay the same old haversack he'd always shouldered to work. He had boiled it in detergent, and hung it on the clothes-line to dry in the wind. The ingrained dust had gone, and it was light grey instead of khaki.

"He had made cheese and potted meat sandwiches of the kind he normally took to the pit-face, and the first taste brought back the smell of dust and machinery. But he had changed his life. He was on a moving train, smiling at his own pale features in a tunnel, the face that would never go away whilever he looked at it.

"He was a man who could only get on a moving vehicle and see different pictures of towns and landscapes. It would take more than these pictures to alter his ideas. Maybe he was lucky. Those who are changed by travel keep on changing, so that whatever journeys they make, the moment of truth never comes, and they actually forget who they are, and what they were like before they had done any travelling at all.

"With Bernard, hammering at dark sides of coal, and shovelling into conveyors what the cutters couldn't get at, he'd seen towns and landscapes as if on a screen, but had then hacked them to pieces because he couldn't tolerate being unable to see and smell them in reality. Face to face with the actual exotic scenes they would not, however, have the immediate and vivid colour that enriched his conjured brainscapes a couple of thousand feet down the pit.

"He knew even more that he wasn't travelling when he got out of the taxi at Southampton, and saw the enormous white flank of the ship. The vessel had come to him, though he had willed it to. This only proved that there was some responsibility attached to his long-planned arrangements, but not that he was travelling. He went into the customs' shed. The bayonet and two knives were packed under the shirts in his suitcase. He had to go through the hall as if he were two people, and hope that the man setting out on the hard-earned trip of a lifetime would get the upper hand of the heavily-armed would-be slaughter-house butcher.

"The potential cruise-goer didn't smile, but pushed the Ripper-man under with his left foot, and put on an over-realistic limp under the long white dazzle-lights hanging from the ceiling. It seemed that whoever looked could not fail to see the other person he was hiding from them (and from himself) as he went in freedom to the quayside. He certainly couldn't claim to be a *bona-fide* traveller — as the phrase went — while he had to hold down, in any situation whatever, the sadistic killer who had been

his constant companion from birth, and whom he was now
taking with him onto the good ship *Psalmanazar*."

14

There were many stories attached to his dressing-gown, and even a few to the chairback he laid it on. Tales also inhabited the bathroom, and many took place in the windows of other houses. Most tales played themselves from his own pirate radio station, and tomorrow he would take them on a long sea trip from spume to chop and, hopefully, back again. It would be no mere Channel hop or Holland crossing, but a three-week post of resident storyteller on a Mediterranean cruise-ship, shaping into the cul-de-sac of all his yearnings.

He jumped, opened his legs and stretched both arms, then brought arms down, and feet together, back to the floor – two dozen times as a start to the morning. After such leaps his breath was still shallow. If anyone in the flat below wondered at such regular thumps (as they might during his absence when they stopped) let them make up a story as an exercise in self-improvement. Touching his toes twelve times put an ache at the base of his back and behind his straight legs.

At sea, he would leave Baker for good, but his knife-swinging brother might get there first, unless he could be stopped, tricked, or kicked aside from his dead-reckoning course of Jack the Ripper impact. Ernest had defeated Tom Baker at school and had worked beside him in the plywood factory, but from then on his visage, having turned into that of a storyteller, had receded – not yet far enough, however – certainly never far enough, for Baker was part of him, and Baker would not go away, though the terror-dream of defeat at the knives of his brother Bernard haunted him far more. The only time he was free of Bernard and similar faces was during the patient threading of a story. The threat went. The sweat of fear receded when dauntlessly expatiating to an audience in thrall.

Driving through Camden Town one day he cut a car too closely to reach an inner lane and turn left. The other driver was so annoyed that he edged Ernest towards the kerb and made him stall. He got out, came to Ernest's car and tried to thrust a dagger through the open window. Ernest lifted a heavy wrench from the opposite seat so the man scowled, then effed-and-blinded it, before running away. Ernest was convinced that the man had been Bernard, though how he had tracked him to Camden Town he could not imagine. He would make a short enough job of him in open combat. At the worst it would be a pyrrhic victory, with the loss of some blood and a few bone-chippings.

Walking to the laundrette, in the morning traffic-flow at Notting Hill Gate taking executives and managers to the West End at half past ten, he felt Bernard's knives against his neck. He smelled catastrophe. His left little fingertip dripped it. He kept his eyes angled at all high windows and chimney pots in case a man wearing a roll-on over his head, behind cover and aiming a rifle with telescopic sights, thought to snipe him dead. Or perhaps a Levantine terrorist bomb-butcher garbed in a camouflaged body-stocking would lob a grenade from a balustrade because for some reason his mob – as with all such – abominated storytellers. So people ran, as chipped paving stones flew at flesh, and changed plate-glass windows into razor-blade gravel, and Ernest Cotgrave clutched a Belisha beacon pole before sliding down covered in his own true crimson blood.

He ran into the laundrette. Three women and two men were pushing coins in slots for soap powder, or watching spindriers, or folding baby-rompers from red plastic buckets.

"I've got a story to tell" – they hoped someone would come in and wheel him away to a Funny Farm – "about a burglar who was pursued by the police, and stashed his swag in a spindrier."

A Pakistani child laughed. A Chinese girl smiled. An Arab sheik peered mournfully through the window. It could not, under the circumstances, be rated a good performance. Yet they listened, and between improbable holes and corners in his story he pushed his clothes into a machine. He had a mac to cover his vest, pants and moneybelt, and nobody minded the gaunt ginger-haired man watching his outer skins turning in hot water. Two of the women had seen him before and assumed he was not certifiable. Another wondered if he'd been on television. The rainbow swirl of his clothes in the washer was the slopped-out stomach going round and round after Bernard had done with him. It wasn't the first time he had secured himself from both physical and spiritual annihilation by the telling of a simple-minded story.

The Kalashnikov Kids who worshipped Raskolnikov, idiots with soulless eyes and nicotined teeth drew up – meanwhile – in a car with technicolour Love-sticker stencils and day-glo Flower Power posters over bonnet and wings, spilled well-drilled from both doors then sent the hit section in to do their assassin stuff – only to find the police had got there first and were already searching him for cannabis which he hadn't got and had never had.

In the full spate of a yarn he was free of Bernard but (and this was the safety-catch) he was no longer himself, was in fact as far from being himself as he was ever likely to get, which was one way of establishing limitations that enclosed a galaxy of uncertainty. He wasn't himself while afraid of Bernard, nor at the telling of a story, having decided a long time ago that not being himself was, in truth, the only way for a storyteller to be himself.

The first real test came with hands and feet on the floor, palms down and the body as straight as a board, its whole heavy length descending towards faded oilcloth flowers till the tip of his nose touched the lino, and then pressed up to the fullest extent of his arms. Failure would be perilous to his self-esteem, for each vital jacking up and down proved that he had life as well as strength left.

A dozen was his limit, and if that were a story to end stories his heart might tear loose from its adhesions during the final pump action, a life-like slice of reality that would be sure to get him howled off stage by those volatile gawpers in his audience whose powers of concentration (and therefore intelligence) were limited.

He didn't die. It wasn't time. With arms at the horizontal, he swung his trunk left and right in order to feel an urgent breath-lessness in each lung, an ache to every limb. His ten-minute torment on all days but Saturday was to rigorously limber the body for any emergency of self-defence.

Next came an up and down trot on the spot two hundred and fifty times. Clenching his right hand, he released one finger at the end of every fifth. Having swallowed so much tea at break-fast a canal lockgate was about to crack in his stomach and let the tadpole waters through. The imperative necessity to belch made him think that the sharp pain would slice his heart like salami if he didn't pause to give the air a chance to find its course. Yet to stop for the vacuums already bursting in the cavern of his mouth would ruin the continuity of his run, so he kept on, hoping it would filter away through any available orifice or pore.

During the final fifty he thrust his fists with all possible force to north-east-west-and-south, such unexpected changes of direction keeping off whatever quartet of imaginary adversaries might try to encircle him, a tactic taught by the teacher who had given him the nose-bleeding clouts after he had pounded Baker in the playground. Every sad happening had at least one advant-age. The tales he told for a living might also, sooner or later, shake off their hidden benefits.

He turned on the bathtaps to let water run in during the con-cluding part of his exertions. When the idle took pride in saving time there was hope for them yet. He stood straight, hands by his side and back vertical, then hinged at the knees till his fingertips touched the floor. Then he stood up and went down once more, counting each descent and ascent as one movement, the strain painful in knee-joints, thighs and the balls of the feet.

He reckoned each amount in percentages, fractions or deci-mals of the whole, cross-breeding the numbers so as to ignore the existence of his aching legs, and to keep his brain numerologic-ally nimble. Five haunch-bends were ten percent of his stint of fifty, a tenth part of it, the interest on investments or a bank loan. A dozen was twenty-four percent, and by the time he could call it a quarter he was up to sixteen, then eighteen, after which age he could vote (these days), which made it a dozen-and-a-half, and suddenly it was twenty. So far, so easy, but by twenty-five (or fifty percent which, if ever he had been so good at school, would have been a pass mark in any exam) it became more difficult, and he wondered whether he'd do the other half.

Thirty. More than the demi done, but still there were twenty to go. Could anybody in the world do so many? Whatever he managed would make him strong in the legs, so that from a harmlessly crouching position, pretending to tie his bootlace, he'd spring with solid hands and deliver a barrage of shock-blows, thereby surprising any would-be attacker. Since they were after him, it might one day be necessary. He'd have to struggle for victory but, after his Israeli-style attack, it would be possible as long as he endured longer than those who had come to slaughter him. Maybe he'd take up bayonet exercises for the fun of being able to use a few in his collection. Or perhaps he'd march back to Nottingham and join the South Notts Hussars for a spot of gun-humping or parachute-jumping, or just plain leaping off lorry-backs at thirty miles an hour, not to mention some rifle and pistol practice.

If he stopped now, there'd be no shame to it. He's already passed, they'd say, lifting him up like a stinking old floorcloth after a heart-crack hadn't even left him with enough gumption to crawl to the telephone. Such physical conundrums made it easier to stand a couple of hours telling stories, to disperse the oxygen around his brain, to unclog his cogitations, and defoul the hoped-for inventiveness of his tale-wagging. It might also get him free of verbal cul-de-sacs, and the thick soupishness of too-involved plots.

A sharp blade came out with alacrity. His head in the mirror bobbed up and down. A born flick-knife. He turned away. Some things were better left unseen. Forty-five guardsmen. Call it Victory Year. Falling over, he fought into balance. Weak baby. Four dozen. Revolutions are finished because they're ten-a-penny. Forty-Niners for the goldrush. Empire Windrush. With fifty he was a hundred percent fit, providing he survived ten minutes of recuperation.

On the scales he weighed the same eleven stone, neither too fat nor too thin, not bald, though far from bushy. He looked at his chest for cancer-moles, scanned his belly for growths. Anything suspicious, and he would put off getting it seen to for a couple of years: if he hadn't died of it by then it would be safe to go to the doctor and get it cured.

He needed to be fully awake so as to pack all impedimenta from field-glasses to toothpowder, and then lift his bags into a taxi for Waterloo station, en route to that big white liner – a final device to get free of Albion Island and avoid Bernard, who was determined to play Wild Young Dirky and stick his kidneys in the same way he used to spear black puddings on Saturday night in Tommy Scollop's tripe-shop.

A handbrush tapped at the skirting board of the next flat. Could Bernard be so close already? Pictures of times past were fruitful to recall. Without scraping at the ashtips of the past you couldn't get anything worthwhile for your stories. There was nothing new in the world except that which came out of what had already gone. He let in more cold water, hand-paddling the invisible streams together.

He'd rent the next door room as an office, thereby getting rid of whoever had slammed up the squeaky window to let in air, or to signal more effectively to someone on the street that Cotgrave was trapped in his cheese-box at last. If they poured oil on the sash cords it might make less noise.

Such a ragbag as Bernard would have neither the money nor the dedication to lay seige in such a systematic way. More likely the room had been taken by those who, during his last session, at the Jelly Baby Bingo Club, had threatened to cut his liver out and jump on it. The reason they didn't do so then was because he hadn't yet been sufficiently pursued and terrified. They would strike when they were ready: a known storyteller could never hide from a bunch of his own all-knowing neanderthal characters.

The idea of his enemies pounding the surrounding walls would normally send him looking into shops on Regent Street and Piccadilly. He'd eat at Bianchi's or Bertorelli's, then wander into a porno-movie, and by evening (having lost his spoor-trackers in the alleys of Soho) come back to find the adjoining room quieter because they had relinquished the scheme of killing him and, for the time being, gone elsewhere.

If he withdrew from the trade out of fear, what would happen to those he had created especially for his tales? Being responsible for their lives, he would sooner or later have to pay for the humiliations and misfortunes he had forced on them. When the moment was opportune, and sufficiently inconvenient, they would surround him and get vengeance.

But peace was necessary, so that he could work out a long interconnected spatter of tales for the ship's passengers. He would rattle his yarns as if he were an inspired shaman in from the snowy forest, button-holing his three-week audience out of a manic love of life if only to prove to himself that, as it says in Job, 'The ear trieth words, as the mouth tasteth meat.'

He bent forward and put his head under for two full minutes, training his breath should he be one day chased into river or marsh, or be forced into the sea from next week's cruise-liner tracking its way through the Mediterranean, pursued by passengers who could no longer endure the merciless lacerations of his never-ending tale.

He shampooed his hair, and suffered one more dip to clear the soap. He washed, then slopped in and tried to relax. He couldn't. His heart pounded at the thought of an approaching stint on the *Psalmanazar*, the longest assignment of his life. It was hard to throw off the shame of having told so many tales in pubs and clubs, which had started by the shame of being born. They might cheer till midnight but, having exploited both the people he used for his stories and, through them, his audience, he had tried never to perform in the same place twice if he could possibly dodge it. Every entertainment was a defeat, each gathering a humiliation that stopped one more vesicle of the heart. Any success robbed him of flesh and blood. At the same time, each hangdog harrangue was an attack on his audience, from whom he expected a lynching before he could get out of the hall. The relations of those in his stories who had had seizures and died, had broken their legs, got divorced or betrayed, been run over and killed (or, which was worse, maimed), been sent into hospital, sacked, mugged, ruined, raped or murdered were closing in on him. They, and their helpers, (as well as Bernard) lurked in the flat next door, only waiting till he fell asleep before breaking through to inflict on him what he had so glibly wreaked on them. They had foolproof devices of making it seem an accident. He still couldn't believe that the ship would sail with him on board, and that if it did he would walk off at the end and be the same person.

He squirted water over his hair, praying it wouldn't seep into his brain and poison him, or send him bald if it suddenly came out scalding. The longer he lived the more he knew that if he hadn't become a storyteller he would have been dead already. If he hadn't followed the deepest impulse of his stomach he would have betrayed himself, and if he did so now God might run him over with a forty-ton, swiftly-accelerating truck, turning the red traffic light to green when he was only halfway across. Or he may give him a gnawing disease he wouldn't know he had till the week before he died. Worse still, He could let him linger a normal thirty years of low-grade misery, only allowing him at odd moments to sense that something was wrong but never what it was, giving him all sorts of minor ailments both mental and fleshy and then, when He is ready and you are clearly not, killing him in some memorable way. Storytellers are the only people who are never allowed to guess their fate, because they cannot possibly know which of their characters they'll be when the time comes for them to die.

With a towel around his middle, he stood by the mirror to shave. Then he would put on clean clothes, and let himself into the rain to buy a newspaper and cigarettes, before coming back to do his final packing. He knew that he alone was responsible for all eventualities which may or may not bring their own quietude; and yet it was also true that even if you are in perfect accord with all God's works and ways, He still decides exactly when you are going to die, and what you are going to die of, or the manner in which you will be fragmented so that you no longer know who you are or ever were.

You can be puffing out the breath of immortality on a clear-skied summer's morning, but in a week you could be stepped on by something or other (usually the other) and lavished with a blackness you will never sit up and rub your head at. It was certain that a man who told stories for a living, who juggled with his own fate, but mostly with that of others, who moved his people about always within sight of their own deaths, and held their destinies in his puppet-wielding hands, could not but believe in the presence and power of a God who wielded *him*.

Part Two

15

Bottle-green seawaves surged against the cruise-ship *George Psalmanazar* as it crossed the Bay of Biscay. Ernest Cotgrave stood as close to the stern as he could without trespassing on the crew's bounds. It was only possible to get the backward view, unless he was on the bridge, which was an area even more forbidden than the crew's quarters. Walking around the ship, however, showed how the rise of water fell before beginning its run under keel and flanks. Waves were parted, but the ship nevertheless lifted. They resisted, but were forced back sufficiently to let the enormous vessel over and through. It ploughed to the roaring of the wind and the tinny red-thread sound of music from the saloon.

Waves were on the boil, unable to lie flat, an endless shifting of crests and valleys small enough not to break the generally flat line towards the grey horizon. It was soothing as long as you weren't seasick. He wasn't. It was deadening, if you wanted to go to sleep. He didn't.

His existence was no longer as simple as it had been when he talked in pubs and clubs. His thoughts could nevermore be so direct as they were when he was addressing children or students. He would never again quarrel with Marion, because both now realised that they had parted for ever. He recalled setting off north one night from London, and turning back because she and his own death had sat beside him in the car. He was cut finally free as the liner slipped its cables and went down smooth Southampton Water. His thoughts had become plain again, so that he could let them roam into whatever complications they might encounter.

He retained the primitive Box Brownie photo in the mind, the live tale walked through before leaving, which had been a last reality for his aunt, and a final one also for her husband Percy. Like all others, it was a story he had stolen. He went to the funeral, so had a right to the common tale, though he hadn't told it yet. Is any story safe from a storyteller? No one could stop him looking at those faded snapshots of death and the burials he would carry forever. Winnie had spent her life making peace with God, which had meant attaining peace with herself, which also signified keeping peace with her neighbours which, being achieved, gave her a peaceful life, and therefore made it easier to secure peace with God.

Percy, though a Flanders lad like so many others, had never considered that she might one day *go*. She died on her feet, and then fell – on coming in from the scullery with a shirt she had just washed. Percy told her to get up, but she wouldn't. "Come on, my bonny lass, you show the boggers what you can do."

He tried to eat his fingers, and felt impoverished at the taste. The next-door legs of them blackies would come in soon to say, "You all right, Percy?"

No, yes, no, yes. "*She* ain't, though. My owd lass has fell, duck. Lift her up for me, there's a good 'un."

"Bloody hell! Jenny!" – Albert's head over the fence – "get the doctor. She's gone. Old Winnie's gone, all right enough."

"Not half. A long way. It's a long way to Tipperary, it's a long way to go."

Percy knew, and Percy didn't. Pushing him through the cemetery, the wheelchair squeaked, kept wanting to go in all directions, and it was the best I could do to keep it on course.

"Get some bleddy oil," Percy said in a mardy, rasping sort of voice, as if he was on a picnic and not at a funeral, "out of them social services. Three-in-one, it's called."

"Goodbye, my love," he said at the grave. He bloody-well knew all right, not too unhappy because he wasn't far behind.

Down the steps, down the steps, down a bit more. I'll look like Albert next door. Tried to stand up, and pulled a lump of coal free. He mined it. Behind the coal was a tin-trunk-box. Snot, soot and sweat on the nose. His fist painted the itch off. That's right, my bonny lass, I can wipe it myself. Violins when I sneeze. Jenny from next door had come in with his goodnight cocoa, and tucked him in bed. "Social services tomorrow, Percy. Meals on wheels," she said. "Teas on skis in winter!"

Smiled like a baby. "My love to lovely Lucy."

Light on, but dark, a one-watt bulb. He swallowed grit. He shovelled, lying on his side, pulling lumps and slack out with his fingers, kicking it back with his feet like a dog. He cried in the dust. "Never mind, my bonny lass. We'll show 'em!"

Knocker-post, his shunter's fingers found the lock and pulled it off. Gripped the catch up. Full of old rammel. Pushed open the lid. Up the Lancashire Fusiliers. Found his cap with the badge still on, but gone black and green, then his waterbottle and uniform tunic. The rustling paper was his paybook. Three medals fell out. Huge coins: Mons, General Service, and Victory. His Military Medal was lost. Let 'em go. Thought I'd chucked all of 'em away. Throw nothing out, Winnie said. O my love, we'll show 'em yet. It came free, scabbard first. Up and at 'em. Ninth of October, and we was nearly there in 1917.

"You've let me down, you lads have," the colonel said, and cried in his brandy. I could have blinded him. You let *me* down, my bonny lass, to go over the top before. He pulled blade from scabbard, using both hands. Now to get back up that stony hill, and out through the coal. The door was at the top of the sky: no lift to rope me up. His legs were like two sacks of flour, each as big as the mill, and weighing like the stone. He pulled them with no strength, clawing the steps one ledge at a time, up knuckle by knuckle, grip of iron on his Passchendaele chiv. Up the wall, like a moth with one wing. Anything's better than mud. Take my dagger to the Old Folks' Home? I'm (not bloody likely) twenty-one today! The key o' the door is in my claw, my lovely dapple-handled dagger safe in my fist and sound, eh, my lass?

He farted, and lay on a step, and laughed. The last post. Last trump, more like. And got to the top, and saw daylight coming through the front room window. Albert would bring in tea before he went to work. You could fill it with sugar and back again, but it wouldn't taste sweet anymore – eh, Winifred? I'm nearly always wrong, but this time I'm coming all right because –

I'm coming then, lads.

Albert found him at the bottom of the cellar stairs, blood mixing with coaldust, and Percy died that afternoon, five days after Winnie.

The ship cut the crust of the swell into a spume. He imagined multifarious fish under the surface that fed off each other and the dust of plankton. Cold and warm currents crossed and threaded. Further down it was darker, and more still. The dead from the war had long since been got at, thousands of carcases consumed. Hundreds of ships had been sunk, holds and galleys crammed with food that the fishes reached. The bigger fish gorged off the delectable bellies of smaller liquidynamic trackers through the water.

Two thirds of the passengers stayed with their palms flattened against bunk surfaces. They clung, and hoped for a sunbeam. It was rougher in the fish-jungle. The stalking and snapping, the perpetual terror of feeding and being food went on as if there were neither day nor night, neither good nor evil under the skin of the sea waves. The ocean's subconscious spread down and across in all directions. It dictated whether the state of the top should be an expansive rash of powerful water, or smooth as milk-skin on a pan that had already boiled.

The depth varied, but it lapped much of the world, rising and falling so slightly under the moon's influence that the profundity was hardly touched. Beyond a few fathoms the moon had no pull on the subconscious of the oceans. Echometers, lead-lines and radar depth-probes hadn't yet plotted the seabed contours in many spots, so no complete chart of the ocean existed — nor any map of the upper spirit either.

The visual disturbance of the sea did not frighten, though the uncertainty of his soul put him in awe at its power. When he got to dead Percy's place next day, Albert gave him the dagger. Percy bequeathed it, scabbard and all. The ship seemed balanced on the knife-edge, yet the sea was unable to suck it down and pummel it to doom. Ernest could admire such violence that could not eliminate either the ship or his high perch. Albert said that Percy had wanted him to have it. He had it. He had it on board.

Waves ate the waves, fought each other in continual tournament. They choked on each other. They swallowed each other and threw each other up. Then, each gobbled its own cannibalised and vomited remains. Spray spat in his eye. Beaufort drew up his scale from one to twelve, from calm to dreadful chaos of the deeps and darks, from flat water to fifty-foot ridges, so neatly compartmented on the page, but shocking when a needle descended the millibar clockface and savage chops began. Where did it come from? The fearful tumble was meteorologically explained, lunatically sound, scientifically apt but, all said and done, when the deck shuddered, and the funnels trembled, and the wires howled on even the largest leviathan vessel, the heart shrank, and in self-control he could only marvel at the heaving waves and Ezekiel wind that sought to pin everything at its mercy. A ship which seemed to be in perfect order steamed through chaos.

Waves came from one direction. Another line, miles long, emerged from another. Battle formations were set in motion by the profound unconscious in separate parts of the world. They were created by stolid blocks of rocky land through which water was hag-driven, seams of various geological age, solid enough to form primitive channelling systems, beaten on by raucous but consistent gales, caught up farther out by currents and, hundreds of miles away, set to meet and smash a similarly prepared force of water.

The clouds sucked up and threw down. Heaven and Hell had equal voices. Spray soaked his mackintosh but he didn't feel cold. Elbows were dipped in water but his feet were warm. Eyes stung. Even the greatest tonner of a ship could be lifted by this megalomania of water. He licked salt from his mouth. It had taken a long time to find out that only inner conflict kept him alive, and that what kept you alive would finally kill you.

He gripped the rail, feet lifting and falling. He felt like dropping stonewise under to see how fish lived in it. After the terror of sinking, and the possibility of not getting out, he'd wonder whether it was really necessary to dive deep and commit suicide in order to know what shifted the unconscious forces below the surface of the turbulent nine-tenths water of the body.

Prolonged berserker staring into the waves created a change in him. Percy had killed himself, but it had been to some purpose. No old folks' home for him. He'd had an accident, said Albert, but Ernest knew how it had been. The storyteller shall inherit the earth, and die from it. Continual movement honed his spirit, finalised a new direction he had shifted against without properly marking it.

He was committed to spinning more yarns out of his own backbone during the voyage, but felt a weariness, an end-of-the-tether fatigue, yet couldn't drop into the water and end it. To come on a sea-trip with such feelings was close to letting a madman sleep with a gun at his bedside. Any bad dream would trigger it off. If he listened, it would roar into his ear like a gale beyond any Beaufort scale.

To tell stories was out of the question, yet the stop had not yet come. To continue living, he had to turn into a story himself instead of making up endless yarns in which he could never have any part. Telling his story in the school playground to save himself from bully Tom Baker had been the first vital mistake. The impulse to escape the pain of existence had been accepted without thought. Self-congratulation at finding an effective way to defeat fate had pushed aside all the agony and happiness that life would have unloaded onto him. He had told his first stories out of fear. It did not seem possible to avoid it anymore. You could not tell lies to the sea.

Having taken the wrong course early on, he wanted to get back to the life he would have stayed with if he had never told a story. The first step was to create another person who would live for him, conjure someone out of his ever-fertile invention and see whether or not he couldn't make him so real that he'd be able to step into his body and live out forever what fate he had at one time performed for him.

His brain was a Force Twelve hurricane, the air filled with foam and spray. The sea was white, visibility closing in. If he breathed life into someone whose body he could invade, reversing the normal way of a storyteller, he might live the rest of his life close to what it should have been in the first place. Such a person was already on the ship, and it needed little effort to draw them towards each other.

He was afraid it was another device for a new twist to his next story. The wind was without compass, the sea beyond control, and neither had a place in any tale he could weave. Events were putty to them and he, being part of their story, could not know what pain they were divising in spite of his tricks.

If he told the passengers a story which involved a gale, they would not be amused, and might throw him overboard soon after he began, causing him to experience too closely what he only cared to imagine.

Hired to spin a yarn every evening, when they needed some contemporary tale as a counterweight to having tramped all day through the stark bomb-sites of the Graeco-Roman world to the accompaniment of Sir Jason Wright's lecturing commentaries, they wouldn't want to hear about the forces of nature and the possibly primitive integuments of the subconscious. They'd crave, he hoped, a narrative that would hook them, a few homilies here and there, an occasional laugh baiting the storyline, and such a thick-twist ending as would make them feel they were still topdogs of the world. A story of shipboard disaster must be put aside for easychair comfort on land. The audience on the ship would be no more harmless or dangerous than those in the pubs, clubs and common rooms he had so far performed in. But his occupation had its hazards, wherever he was.

He had taken the job for a holiday, but the Entertainments' Director demanded, soon after he came on board: "Tell whatever stories you like, but tell us something new."

"Excellent whisky," Ernest said. "I'll try. But there's nothing new under the sun. You know that, don't you?"

The Entertainments' Director squinted at him as he poured himself another half-tumbler. "True enough. Yet there may well be a bit of a twist to it on the old *Psalmanazar*."

Ernest hoped he wouldn't be lured into weaving a tale that would disturb or provoke. While he knew his limits, he had not yet experienced the fullest extent of his malicious temptations. On this trip, he decided, he must control himself, and not give in to the febrile mockeries that had marred some of his dry-land performances.

He recalled his recital at the Miners' Institute, which he survived with neither chopped-off finger nor broken limb. His audience had been disappointed at the somewhat glib finish of his tale. Bernard, he told them (in an attempt to head him away from the journey he would shortly be taking himself) slipped off the gangway when going up the side of the cruise-ship, and spent three months in a Southampton hospital with a broken arm, a smashed leg, and an impaired memory, before being shunted back to Nottinghamshire a sadder and a wilder man, to be given a menial post at the nearest mental hospital, where he will now work for the rest of his born-days. They had expected a salacious and knockabout account of his misdemeanors in foreign whore-shops and semi-tropical knocking-houses, and at not getting such (or anywhere near) they stormed the stage and humped Ernest bodily out of the door as if he'd been a bankette of coal that had done two of their mates an injury for life. They then went back to drinking, and to discussing the faults and merits of his tale now that he was no longer there to interrupt by trying to explain what had *actually* happened. They didn't want to know. They preferred to make up their own minds, and had sent Bernard onto the ship anyway, in spite of Ernest's attempt to switch him from such a course.

He turned his back to the waves. Eyes ached at such motions. A man up for some air and a view of the vast outside stepped from the saloon and swayed along the deck as if he also thought it might be pleasant to chat before going in for lunch. Ernest felt an immediate affinity with the post-rickets walk, and with the self-assured tilt of his hat which stayed on in the gale as if pinned to his skull.

There had been little talk since setting sail. Various bunking and feeding problems had priority. The shock of leaving home took effect. Speech was hoarded. Even lifeboat drill hadn't made for easy conversation. And then there was seasickness to hold back, or hide. In view of all difficulties, the spiritual strength to get acquainted was lacking. Mutual retching was not a pretty method, for there was a point at which the spirit no longer had control, and it was as well to avoid any embarrassment before meeting again in calmer waters.

The man who came on deck had no thought for such matters. He wore a tightly belted mac, a jaunty hat, and a scarf pulled across his throat. He approached and stood a few feet from the rail, not so willing to examine the sea as Ernest had been. His accent was unmistakable. "It's a bit of a bloody ocean, this is."

Ernest looked into his pale and craggy face. The only time he didn't mind someone being right in his opinions was when they were merely stating the obvious. "It certainly is."

Even a green bottle would turn bilious. Bernard puffed at an old pipe that stank as if he were smoking a tin of broken biscuits. He didn't take it out while talking, either. "I don't fancy getting too close to water such as that."

Ernest had seen him before, and wondered why he had come so far from home to meet him again. He'd known him perhaps in times as far off as his schooldays, when he'd certainly had a pale face, but not the blue veins down his nearest cheek. The sting of wind and rain had puffed his skin, and gave the button-blue eyes a look of critical exhaustion. His half-mad smile, being so close, seemed more important than it should have, under the circumstances of a sea-cruise. The man's eyes smiled through his own stare. It was an inward and outward expression, the smile being for himself, and the stare for whoever got in his way. And God help them, Ernest thought, who weighed him up in an instant, as one Nottinghamshire man can weigh up another no matter how far in time and distance they get from the place. But he was wrong. He had to work harder on this one because the man was as close as his own blood, and even as close as the stare in his own face.

The smile told him nothing. The stare didn't show much, either, not even where the lifeboats might be if it came to a sinking. "I'm on holiday," Ernest had to tell him. "A sort of working vacation."

"Working-class holiday, like?"

He could even make puns, in his intuitive crackbrained way. "Not on your life. And don't start that bloody stuff."

"I'll start what I like, mate."

There was no doubt that he would. The fact that Ernest knew more about the man than the man knew about himself would make things difficult, though, because he seemed to be in the man's body while talking to him, he thought it likely that he'd be able to control the situation. He knew precisely what the man with the coal-blue veins and staring eyes must be seeing, without the necessity of looking at himself in a mirror and from a mirror. Ernest saw through the man's eyes as they looked at him, without having to look at himself in the mirror to get the same effect. It was something he'd tried many times to do, but hadn't succeeded in till now.

He described himself from the man's eyes, and hoped to recollect the details for a future story. He then concentrated on looking at the man (without appearing to do so, otherwise it might have provoked a shark-fight to the death) in order to draw on the picture later. It was a perilous and forbidden process he indulged in, for the man reminded him of what he, Ernest, might have been like if he had not become a storyteller. Ernest wanted to break this vivid meshing of forces, and it would have been easier if this man relented sufficiently in his stare to ask what type of work he was doing on board. But he didn't: it was as if he knew what Ernest wanted, and was determined not to accede. He would not enquire about Ernest's job because he didn't want to be asked questions in return. His rock-hard unwillingness to smile like any victim and enter one of Ernest's stories showed that he already knew his fate. Being a pallid denizen of the earth he would not enter knowingly into his scheme. But Ernest had never asked permission of anyone before putting them into a story, and considered himself too old a hand to do so now. His stare was as good as the next man's. This time, however, he had gone into a dangerous area, though he couldn't let that stop him. The warning mechanism invariably did its job, but was frequently ignored. His courage saw to that, but its appearance occasionally took unexpected turns. It was often useful, but could not always be relied upon to do the right thing by staying under his control, he speculated, beginning a story which he would nevertheless foist on his audience of sea-passengers.

He held out his hand. "I'm Ernest Cotgrave."

"My name's Bernard."

He had to be absolutely sure. "Baker?"

206

"Yes."

"Didn't expect to find *you* here."

Bernard pretended to be even more surprised. He couldn't grin when he wanted to. He also found it difficult to speak, though a noise came out of his throat when he took the pipe from his mouth. "I don't suppose you did."

"What's your game, then?"

"No game," Bernard told him.

"As long as there isn't."

"I'm cruising for my health, that's all."

Ernest knew that Bernard was afraid, but he also realised that he was aggressive, and certainly dangerous which, Ernest reasoned, was typical of someone who had been full of fear all his life. There had been fear of the air when it hit him on coming out of his mother. There was – Ernest knew – fear of school in case they had something to teach him which was absolutely essential to his life but which he wouldn't learn because he didn't trust them and hadn't got the brain to take it in anyway. There was obviously fear of work, because whoever employed him might, he felt, be robbing him of money rightly earned; as well as fear down the pit because there were real reasons for it. There had also been fear of his wife because he couldn't or wouldn't trust her, for if you distrust one person you distrust everyone. And so she, sniffing this fear of his even before they were married, made up her mind that since a man liked to be right in everything he was going to be proved right in that as well. Bernard was also encumbered with the fear of his own strength because it kept him from ever striking anyone either in self-defence or from motives of revenge, thinking that if he did hit whoever deserved the bullet-end of it, he would kill them. There was fear even of telling the story of his life to Ernest, who might one day care to ask about it out of love and the goodness of his heart, wanting to try and understand Bernard and all the fears with which he had been born but with which he would no doubt die.

Ernest felt this tail of thought pass between them, but could only say, "It's my sincere wish that your health does improve as a result of this excursion."

"Happen it will. But I didn't know I'd be listening to stories from you — the great Ernie Cotgrave — when I made my booking."

"As long as you see it my way." Ernest remembered being held in a corner of the school playground by Bernard's brother. It wasn't like that anymore. The ship was bigger than any such place. It was, in fact, an advantage to have Bernard on the ship, knowing where he was at last. If Bernard meant to kill him (and he did: there'd never been any doubt about that) then he would kill Bernard first, get rid of him once and for all. "Just keep out of my sight." Ernest said.

Bernard laughed, showing no fear. "You're a bit of a card!"

Ernest felt that if he continued to look at his face he would be seasick. He'd rather have eaten too much smoked salmonella at lunch, which at least would be a better reason. "That bloody awful pipe of yours is turning my guts."

"Is it?" He was pathetically grateful when anyone took an interest in him. "When my wife was at home it smoked like old socks and rusty nails, but as soon as she cleared off, and even more when I came on this cruise, it tasted like ambrosia: I used to think I had stomach cancer, but all I needed was for summat to *happen* that would change my life. There's a lesson in that for you."

Wishing to be on his own and before Bernard could spout any more wisdom to the extent of changing character, and also to get away from the awful pipe smoke, he said goodbye. The slight feeling of nausea had ceased to bother him.

16

In the nearest library to Clarundel Road he had read books on
seamanship, and browsed through manuals of navigation. Their
no-bloody-nonsense prose cleared the cumulo-nimbus clouds
from his psychic disorders. Or some of them had, and for a while
such books and almanacks showed how certain facts could be
considered true beyond the realms of intellectual argument. It
was a world without dispute, clean and mathematical, and the
clarity of these premises refreshed him, so that he wondered why
he didn't go back to school or polytechnic and stay in the world
of an engineering trade for ever. But if he did, the figure-
dabbling would lose its playtime joy and turn into an effort of
dedication. He preferred to flip through the tomes like a tyro, in
order to reinforce the background of what shipboard tales might
concern the cruise itself. In such a matter you couldn't be too
thorough, or too clever, or too fluent, or too professional, or too
loving, or too responsible.

The line of water rose inexorably, as if a soul lurked somewhere in it. The water lifted bottle-green and with uncanny
evenness up the ship's flank from stem to stern. If God existed at
all, it was to work this earthly ocean into the scheme of man and
Nature. The rising line of water was more real than any story he
could tell by artful words and erstwhile phrases. As he gazed
with bottle-green eyes, and turned his freckled cheeks one way
and the other, he thought that the bottle-green line would never
stop coming up, but would go on lifting for as long as he paid eye-
service to it.

"True enough, ladies and gentlemen, it rose, oh ever so slowly,
but nonetheless, distinct and inevitable, it came across the jug-

whites of my staring eyes, not even clicking at the crimson hair-veins as it slid over them like needle-gauges on a steamboiler searching for danger points.

"Now that I have you in this agreeable first-class saloon, with the world of water lifting forcefully under our feet and table-legs, in a temporarily unsociable Mediterranean between Spain and Morocco, I'll work my way into your classical-oriented souls with a further instalment of my story that should keep your minds off the irascible briny for a couple of hours.

"What I'm telling might seem to mirror certain moments that we're living now, though I hope it doesn't. It would be too blatant. But even if it does I pray that the end will be different. It isn't rare for a storyteller to crack a tale of what (unbeknown to him) will happen to his flesh and spirit in the future, just as a mere talker will often gabble out his yet-to-come. But that is bewitchery, not art; wishful thinking, not work; and nothing, I hope, to do with such as me.

"My present tale concerns a luxury liner running through the moody Med, a cultural-historical point-to-point for a few hundred passengers revisiting the sites of the ancient world. It is not about yourselves, or this bonny ship, or me; but simply part of a novel-tale which I see as if on a screen, and which thus becomes my story. You might ask who put such pictures on for me to pick at? What imperious but invisible victimiser, what devil of a warlock or bitch of a witch, or sod of a god set that BBC One-Two-and-Three screen flickering at my eyes and not yours? With such as yourselves I can flesh a preamble that in times past I wouldn't have had a hope of getting out in pub, club or even a students' den; can ask a primitive question in a wrapped-up civilised way, though for an answer you'll have to wait till the bitter end of whatever is yet to come.

"But if I'm to give you a clue, it may be in that razor-sharp line of bottle-green water rising and falling, slopping and dropping along the side of our isolated, high-powered ship-home. Separating our skins from the sea outside, our dry-cleaned clothes and happily-spoiled stomachs, and this big-lit lounge with fixed tables at which you sit with legs open or primly together sipping brandy and cointreau and coffee, or smoking cigars after a day spent mostly on deck with field glasses spying out the rugged mountains on either side of the Pillars of Hercules; protecting us from the water, are the steel and riveted flanks of the ship, the impermeable hull, the engines and superstructure, the fine unfaultable British construction, our help in ages past and (we hope) to come, holding us from the bottle-green elemental gale, stopping the cold water from rushing up jacket-sleeves and skirts, from swamping trouser-bottoms and dresses, preventing fish-teeth nibbling us as the cold impersonal salt-liquid pours into our mouths and floods the ripe lungs till nothing's left of any entrance or exit, and God, finally, clobbers us with the old one-two of blackout and whatever is beyond.

"Don't be alarmed if I pause after that no doubt ungrammatical and certainly mish-mash paragraph. It is but a slender and elusive clue. We're close to being born, but nearer still to the other place – or some of us are. On certain occasions from the past I'd have been on my face in the mud by now, ignominiously bundled from the pub back door, a bootprint on my backside and a black-eye where it should be. But in the point-to-point of life there's but a straight line, no matter how many zig-zag tracks occur before we get to the fullstop of our itinerary. Being on a ship, we sample such neo-neon-luxury which is the civilised end product of this whitely-lit saloon. At the same time, the pertinacious hunger of the neighbouring sea is one of the main attractions of the voyage, for which we were willing to tip out hard-earned salaries or hoarded savings or inherited wealth.

"You're right – I haven't finished paying *my* fare yet, though this is one more instalment of it. Each of my story-stints is a contribution in acceptable currency, though my book of traveller's cheques can't go on for ever. Such tales barely fit in as part of the superstructure of this powerful ship. They are just a small knob of it, a minor handrail, yet maybe a transistor in the vital radio, perhaps a hidden section of the deck no one ever steps on, an extra bit of torque on one of the screws propelling us along – but sufficient nevertheless to make the cruise memorable enough. My story-chain is part of the ship, maybe a concatenated anchor, or a slice of you, or a plankton net in the aforementioned bottle-green water, or a wedge of the sky which at the moment is full of wind and cloud that boils the spume and shoots us along.

"I give my clue as a tribute to your Charing-crossword brains, and hope that before the end of the voyage it grows into more than a port of call or a peaceful bay or a concealing promontory, more like a country you'll be able to remember me by, but mostly resembling an ocean floor of corrugated hills and valleys that we'll have fathomed here and there before we're done.

"So my story continues with the most anonymous person boarding a cruise ship at — let us say — Tilbury. He is a middle-aged man in a belted mac, the extraordinary ordinary person, the fish in water that other fish eat in passing, when and if they get a chance. Anyone who notices him can't believe what they are seeing, and if they do they decide he is too insignificant to be remembered. He boarded the ship when they came on. His luggage followed in the same way, though he had less than most. That person is strongest who lives longest, and he looked it — let me tell you. His arm strained at a large cheap suitcase, a bleached-out haversack on the opposite shoulder — making less impedimenta than anyone except the more humble marineros among the crew. He infiltrated the ship rather than came on like the rest of us. A certain person who shall for the moment be nameless, tried to stop him getting on board, but he had pre-paid his passage, after all, and so shook hands with the purser before being given a ticket for a cabin and his seat at table.

"In view of the crucial revelations yet to be made in my tale, I want to make clear that it wasn't this *Psalmanazar* ship that the second character of my story-serial sailed on, though you may (if you like) imagine it sailing or, more accurately, turbining, as closely parallel for our voices to reach those on board by loud hailer, or, when our actual physical ships look like colliding, by radio telephone. And if such communication becomes impossible due to internal chaos and inexplicable technical breakdowns caused by the loss of blueprints and instructional manuals, and malicious bouts of self-induced amnesia among recalcitrant operators at critical moments; or by strikes, mutinies, and acts of God, then only morse-flashing or flag-wagging of the most soul-saving phrases and such-like pieces of information will prevent either one ship or both from sinking with all hands and passengers together. The best and most infallible form of ship-to-ship and body-to-spirit contact will be through me, via the Land's End aerials of this set of stories which are already half gone. I am the transmitter of whatever intelligence needs to be pulsed or flashed across the water by day or night, twilight or dawn.

"Our fellow-passenger with the trilby hat and belted mac, allowing us to take breath, took his ticket from the purser and followed the cabin steward along the various corridors with his weighty suitcase and bleached haversack. The way was complicated, and directions frequently changed, but due to his previous occupation he had no difficulty remembering every turn and flight of steps necessary to get back to where he had started.

"Bernard knew that even the old-fashioned rich of the world occasionally travelled with cheap suitcases. They might also wear trilby hats of the commonest kind, and be dressed in belted mackintoshes. A blue streak down one cheek could be hard to answer for, but their faces might be pale and craggy, much as if they had, in their eccentric way, bicycled to Khatmandu and back. Such a one might have been robbed in Turkey, and then sent sufficient money from home by a rich but parsimonious aunt to get himself re-kitted. He could purchase a rough and ready rig in Istanbul, clothes which had belonged to a tourist from South Wales, sold by the thief to an old clothes dealer whose stall was between the carpet and candelabra niches in the Grand Bazaar.

"All I'm trying to say is that Bernard did not feel out of place because it did not occur to him to do so. He didn't seem so to the experienced purser, either, who saw him come aboard, because the purser had much accustomed himself to all types after thirty years at sea, and wasn't put off by the suitcase or the mackintosh, or by Bernard's somewhat puffy visage with bluish marks down one cheek as if he had been through a weird shamanic ritual in a secret valley of the Pamir Knot. The purser's expression was non-caring, possibly (at the worst) contemptuous, though the faintest of smiles led it to the proper side of unpleasantness. Bernard even gave a pound note to the man who put the suitcase under his cabin bunk — as was expected from someone who wore a small blue-and-green feather in the side of his trilby-style hat.

"When paying his deposit at Cooks' his general expectations so occupied his vision that the reality of living and sleeping during his cruise hadn't been considered, as it might if he'd been brought up differently. He'd always found it difficult to picture the future, and realised, as he looked around the narrow and dismal space of a cabin, that he would have to improve in that respect if his mission was to be successful.

"He'd never known anyone who used toothpowder before: it was on the shelf above the sink. A suitcase of real leather, and decorated by round and triangular labels, had been stowed under the opposite end of the bunk. To share a cabin was a mistake. He'd bought the cheapest ticket, when a more expensive one would have given him the luxury of seclusion. To have another man sharing the same oblong floor-space, and perhaps arguing to get at that single round eye of a port-hole, didn't bear thinking about. Why had he come on a cruise with a large radio-tape-recorder combination? A pile of books and notebooks had been slewed aggressively across the top bunk to show he'd had the luck to get there first.

"Bernard felt cheated. There was no one to blame but himself. He had a lot to learn in the new world he had cheap-skated into but, being a slow learner, instead of this making him determined to improve matters, it merely brought out a further instalment of self-bitterness. Though he felt rabid at whoever had forestalled him in getting the best part of the cabin, he knew there was nothing to be done. What was left of his calmness and curiosity told him that he should go on deck and watch the departure, observe other passengers instead of himself.

"It was a fine day in May, with everything so soft and beautiful, giving a pleasant memory of what he would never see again. He stood by the rail, near one of the richest passengers on the boat – as he discovered later when he sat by her in the bar. 'You can see there's no coal under that flat land.'

"It was a strange remark, and she responded, in an American accent: 'How do you know?'

"She was a tall and well-built woman, which was why smallish

Bernard spoke with such ease: 'Because it's flat. And saturated. Gravel and sand, I expect. I can't imagine coal under it, can you?'

"'I suppose not.' Her voice was cut by the ship's hooter. When the air was clear again, she said: 'Why are you interested in coal?'

"He moved a few inches closer. 'I did geology at night-school. We went on a field trip – down a coalmine. It was the most interesting day of my life.'

"A seagull flew alongside, its button-eye turning north, then south. His life must have been a dull one, and she wanted to know more. 'I suppose you expect this to be a *really* interesting trip?'

"To think in such a way was beyond his experience. Life was an exercise in economy of spirit. You only ever pursued what was vital to your purpose. That was why he was on a great white ship pulling its own length along the estuary. People waved from the shore, though not to him, he knew, while he talked to this American woman with straight grey hair whom he thought much older than he was. He had reached the age when he could no longer say with accuracy how old anybody was. He could only try to decypher their hope or lassitude, and decide whether to share it or end it. Nothing else mattered.

"Gaps of blue sky between the clouds were openings onto countries he'd never reach. There was land up there which nobody else knew about, a continent of deserts that went on for ever. The land was striated by purple and beige escarpments, beyond which were conical mountains of white egg-timer sand. To the left, if he veered so far round, there were depressions as far as the eye could see, full of pale blue water. In reality they were ash-dry. He flew over a new vast earth that he had discovered all by himself. Real water ran between clumps of trees, but he was unable to land anywhere, not even to save his own life, which in any case seemed worthless now that he had left the country of his heart. The feeling that his life was of no value also made it seem enjoyable and worthwhile again. He had died, but was trying to come back to life.

"As the ship went along the grey river he looked at himself (and the ship) from its banks, and then he came back into himself, and took in the view from the ship, of oil refineries or storage tanks packing the sky on the other side of the river, which was the one the America woman seemed most interested in and which, because of the ship's manoeuvres, they now faced.

"The land repelled him. After so long on soil and pavement it had betrayed him. Having passed so much of his life either on or under it, he wanted to look at the sea. He couldn't wait to get away from the land, which was hard underfoot, and full of treachery. He'd been deceived and used beyond the limits of toleration, as much by himself as others. Nevertheless, he wouldn't put up with anymore of it. Apart from the boat, he'd see nothing but water. The widening river wasn't enough. Land bothered him, threatened him even more now that it was possible to get away. It could be pushed out of sight. He never wanted to see it again, certainly not to stand on or touch it. He had come to the end of land, and whatever it demanded. He could no longer put up with its anger, and assumed that once beyond its view he would never go back. The land wanted his life, but the sea welcomed him. He belonged to waves, not teeth. She wondered why he laughed.

"He might not have felt this if she hadn't been nearby. Truth could not be ignored, though he did not think it worth mentioning. It was his secret. He preferred to talk of coalmines and oil wells, rather than the area of water gratifyingly widening around the ship. She was responsible for the decision that he belonged to the ocean, and that he would never go back to trees and runner-beans. He did not laugh again, in case he should frighten – or warn – her.

"'I always expect to meet interesting people when I go on a cruise,' she announced.

"He was surprised to find himself so classified. It was a big promotion compared with a few weeks ago. 'Do you often go to sea?'

"One of the officers walked by. Bernard had seen a coloured chart of the various ranks and jobs in the Merchant Marine, so knew him to be a Radio Officer. The man looked at him, and seemed about to speak, but then changed his mind and went on. He was busy, no doubt, and had somewhere to go. Bernard felt that since people had only to look at him to guess his purpose on board, he had better start work as soon as possible, so that they wouldn't have time to compare their observations with each others, and prevent him doing it.

"'Last year it was the Pacific,' she was saying. 'Before that I went to the Carribean. Next time I'll try South America again. Or maybe India.'

"This led him to ask: 'Do you like being at sea?'

"'How do you mean?'

"'Do you like the sea?'

She laughed: 'I can't stand it at all!'

"He was confused. 'Why do you come on a ship, then?'

"She only laughed to show her good teeth, he thought, and the clean-looking insides of her mouth. His pegs were half false, having lost their grip in various brawls. Muriel, who had seen more Englishmen of a certain sort than she imagined he ever would, put it down to the national defect of bad diet.

"'It's a convenient way of getting around,' she told him. 'I don't like trains or planes, or cars or hotels. The best view of land is always from the sea, anyway.'

"He scratched his leg lazily, as if it were a nervous motion he'd had since birth and so had got used to, but in reality to check that the short razor-sharp knife was snug in its scabbard tied firmly to his left calf. It was a comfort when he felt threatened by someone who disliked the sea as much as he considered it vital to the last weeks of his life. Maybe there were others on the ship, men as well as women, and perhaps members of the crew, who were ready to swear that the sea was not fit to girdle the earth. The voyage would be too short to chat with everyone in order to find out. In any case, he couldn't kill them all. As for the woman by his side, she was no pipe maker's dream, though as his first candidate, she would have to suffice.

"'That's what my wife always felt.' He was unable to make up his mind whether the buttons on her coat were made of wood, or of painted stone.

"'Felt?'

"'She died six months ago.'

"'I'm *sorry*.'

"Maybe they were plastic. He wanted to touch them. Yet he didn't think they were, not on such a coat. 'It was all for the best.'

"A very tall, gaunt, though well-built man with grey hair and a flowing scarf limped towards a flight of steps leading to the promenade deck. 'I believe he's the professor who'll take us around the various ruins,' she told him.

"'Oh, ar? I sensed it was, though. Looks like 'im.'

"She thought it would seem a hasty question, if not actually indelicate, to ask why it had 'all been for the best'. At least a year was needed to recover from a death in the family. Being well travelled she had a certain amount of sensibility. Had she asked, as he expected her to, and as he'd hoped she would, he might have answered that his wife had died because she didn't like the sea, and that though it hadn't been entirely her fault, she had lived almost as far from the sea as it was possible to get in England. He would have admitted that, by working down a coalmine seven hours a day, he'd been even further from it, but in him it was allowable because he loved the sea anyway. Being a few thousand feet underground, and a mile or two from the skips, you felt closer to the sea than to the land. Ask any collier. The danger at being underground made you think of the perils of the deep. When the colliery brass band played 'O God Our Help in Ages Past' nearly everyone was in tears, or close to them, at the awesome words that clogged the heart.

"As for what had really happened, there was no one he could tell the truth to. Maybe the sea would wash the crime away. His wife hadn't left him, as he had told everyone. The sight of the sea drew out the truth that he had killed her without meaning to. The brass base of the lamp was heavy, and the blow had smashed the bulb as well, so two lights were extinguished.

"When the police came three weeks later, he gave out that she had left. He didn't really care. What she did was her business. It allus had been, anyway. She'd once gone off with Ernest Cotgrave, and if they wanted to check on that, it was all right by him. Serve bleeding Cotgrave right anyway if the coppers asked a few nasty questions in front of his wife. No, mate, he said to the copper, she just left. Beats me, it does, but what can I do? And then the copper went. Nothing of her remained. No trace. Not a stain. They could pull up the floorboards, and turn over every inch of the garden. It wouldn't take them long. They could climb into the roof and search the chimneys. They did, when they came again. They found nothing. If you're curious, he said to himself, I'll tell you how it was done. Everyday he took a bit of her in his snap tin and tipped it in a remote end of one of the galleries down the mine. No one saw him. He worked shifts for a fortnight without eating much, though he did manage a sandwich in his trouser pocket, which he removed as if it had come from his tin. Lights at the coalface do not dazzle. And if he got thin it was only to be expected, pining as he was (and who wouldn't be?) for a wife who had left him.

"He didn't want to torment his American acquaintance, whatever other plans he had. 'It was all for the best. Cancer is a terrible thing.'

"'My husband was from Yorkshire,' she told him. 'He owned land there.' The First Officer came by. Even the owner would be shit to a bloke like him. At least the Captain deferred, or acted as if he did. But the First Officer looked at no one, though Bernard wasn't deceived, knowing that in his superior way, the officer was nevertheless ready to spring if the woman Bernard appeared to be speaking to suddenly needed help. Or maybe he was checking on a description that had been given before the ship sailed. They'd caught Crippen like that. Too late. Bernard knew, however, that they were sizing him up, and waiting to see whether he acted in any way to give them reason for shackling him to the post in the middle of the padded cell eight decks down.

"The estuary was widening. He buttoned his mackintosh to keep the breeze from his chest. He should have brought his muffler up from the cabin. 'Was there coal under it?'

"'Yes.'

"He was wistful. 'Must be marvellous, to own coal.'

"'Nobody does anymore.' He touched his face again, then went on to scratch his leg. She detected a mannerism, rather than a need. 'He had an income from it, at one time.'

"'Compensation. I don't expect *he* liked the sea, either.'

"She wouldn't settle his curiosity, having lost just enough of her American spirit by having been married to an Englishman not to do so too readily. The man by her side frightened her, she didn't know why. If someone scares you it's always a while before you get the reason for it. Otherwise they wouldn't have that kind of effect. He was too close. There was no other island or land mass like England, in which places could be so distinct and therefore isolated – she thought. People who lived in them spoke little, and often hid their feelings only in the hope that they would be able to find out more definitely what they were, or whether they had any at all. They never did find out, of course, but it didn't seem to make them too unhappy – only dull, to an outsider. She had detected such traits in her late husband. His self-investigations were so intense that they had actually killed him. She, on the other hand, had always believed it necessary to share your observations in order to find out what you thought. However, she wouldn't go so far as to divide them with this small dark Englishman at her side.

"The white ship turned into wind and rain. Stabilisers took the worst of the gale, but she had to leave the deck, because he looked at her with an intensity that could only be diverted by a blow. Perhaps he wanted her to strike so that he could then retaliate with something worse. She wondered what it could be, and was sorry they were on the same ship together. She was frightened of that little man in the belted mackintosh, who had talked to her for only a few minutes. It was crazy to think him harmful, yet her instinct had never deceived her.

"He observed her from a distance. Thinking into the future, she knew he sometimes followed her. He waited at the door of the dining saloon, so she turned to another exit. Refusing to be intimidated at this stage of the voyage, she swung back to go out by the way she had originally entered.

"He was no longer there. Against her will, she looked for him so that he might talk to her again. She hadn't been at all afraid when he was close and trying to amuse her. He might be the most interesting man on the ship. Whatever he was, she was trapped.

"She lay on her bed, full from lunch. The boat swayed: seasickness is mostly fear, though it did no good to think so. Instability under your feet makes you wonder whether the floor is caving in. The sole of each foot has direct and sensitive contact with the stomach. It was important to lie down. Lunch had been good, and she had enjoyed it. It was part of her, and she did not want to let it go. The cabin, with its one bed, lights on, and private wash and shower place, was worth belonging to, and would be her home for three weeks. Then she would go to New England for the summer. The passing of time was a combination of mobility, and fixed residence, neither lasting so long that she ever became bored or disgusted with her life. O lucky woman! Her husband was decently dead, and there was enough money to live on, without pushing someone out of a job.

"Her things were unpacked, clothes hung, make-up pots, tubes and bottles arranged. For books she had a Bible, half-a-dozen thick small guides, and a few novels. Her writing case lay open on the table. She reached for her diary, not so violently as to disturb her stomach, and wrote into it, speculating mainly on the passenger whom she had begun to fear, but whom she was afraid of no longer now that she was trying to describe him. He hadn't told her his name, and she wanted to know.

"Her thick Mont Blanc fountain pen carried red ink, for she liked to see the pages of her travel diaries neatly entered in red. Those at home were done in blue-black. Such swaying softened the world, made the peace so real that her eyes closed, and the pen dropped, its nib staining the sheet.

"It was a harsh, grey sort of sleep, impossible to say how long, but she was in a similar world, and dreamed there was a huge and glow-eyed cat trying to get into her cabin. It banged at the walls and the door. Waves were hitting the ship. She opened her eyes. Everything was the same, except that it felt cold – though the pipes were hot. She closed her diary, and screwed the pen shut, and hoped the sea would be calm tomorrow.

"There was a definite knock at the door. Had she locked it? She thought she had, but leapt out of bed to make sure. She was putting on her dressing gown, but the door opened before she got there.

"Bernard started a letter to himself, with a black biro in his red covered exercise book with a lion on the front and arithmetic tables on the back. 'Dear old Bernard, only friend of my life, don't ever forget that that person is strongest who lives longest.'

"The ship went up, and it went down, and he hung onto his bag of knives for comfort. He stayed with his razor-honed daggers, and an old bayonet which was the pride of his collection. It had a long comfortable handle, ease of swing, even balance, and was a possible swathe of death when sufficient force and intention was put into it. As a machine, it had a life of its own. It fitted the hand. It obeyed without a murmur. It could cut flesh as the ship cut water, cut sky as quick as any lightning flash. It would cut the squeal out of a pig. A whippet that ran head-on into it would have a twin brother. It didn't bear thinking about. He could hear wind thumping, and a weird crinkling noise as if the ship were made of cardboard. He was frightened when not thinking about his knives. Water was forceful. The ship's sides were too thin. The ocean gurgled along his cabin walls and sounded as if about to penetrate and flood in.

"A man's way through life was similar. Circumstances broke through the thin skin that covered blood and body. So he had always felt. At times it bothered him more than others. He had noticed it down the pit rather than when walking the street. In his cheap cabin, lying doggo in the guts of the ship, this was no surprise. Darkness in the coalmine was like night in the ship. Fear in both was the same. Water could rush in and suffocate just as dust and rock might bury the lights out of your fingertips. But here he had knives to curve a swirling claymore tunnel through flesh and water as soon as the idea of being smothered by the world became too much to bear. He wrote another sentence: 'I'm going up to kill her now.'"

17

The mulligatawny was just hot enough to suggest its Indian origins, though it may have been dragged a little bit through the ovens to get there. "You may wonder how I know what's going to happen," Ernest said, "and if you do, perhaps I'll tell you."

He sat next to the Regius Professor of Greek at table, who replied, from his leathery wrinkled face: "I do wonder, but I know you won't tell me the truth, so don't bother."

"The fact is," Ernest admitted, ignoring the contempt that spiced his bonhomie, "I don't yet know myself."

"I know you don't." The elderly professor smiled. "I suppose the whole art of storytelling rests on not worrying too much whether you know or not."

"It does." Ernest felt no amusement. He was a perceptive old bastard. "The first duty of a storyteller is to *forget* nothing. Everything rests on that. Otherwise I don't regard my 'art' as so precious that I won't reveal a thing or two in advance of the main narrative."

He did, though. Tell everything, and you need give very little. Say nothing, and they feel free to guess. Drop one or two clues and they've got the whole picture – so they think. Therein lies the danger. But he wouldn't tell anything, if he could steel his heart not to. It should be possible because he had two hearts. To have one makes you vulnerable, but with two you played one against the other and became impenetrable.

The professor noisily drew soup out of the spoon with his lips. Spoiled as a kid, Ernest decided. Or terrified into hurrying. Habits are formed from constant fear – though he certainly looks craggy and fearless enough. I expect he had an upbringing twenty times harder than mine, even though he was that much richer. The wealthy kids have to get bullied and broken, otherwise they would never get through life. Afterwards, they're as tough as nails, and need to be, to keep their fragile pride, their vulnerable position, and their money.

Ernest sprang it on him. "I share a cabin with this Bernard chap. I've seen his knives, the German bayonet, his tenpenny red notebook, and a framed photograph of his dead whippet. With a glint in his eyes, he does eight minutes of physical exercises every morning *before* breakfast, mostly knee-bends and arm jabs."

There was still a slight push under the feet. In daylight he'd have been keeping an eye on the horizon-line going slowly down the circle of the port hole. He would have noted its absence for sometimes as long as a quarter of a minute, and then felt relief at its reappearance, and its equally slow climb. The metronomic dip and rise of the ship kept him up to his purpose.

"I suppose your tales are real enough to you," the professor said. "Damn real for us, too. You tell 'em unconscionably well."

"It's my trade." And my backbone, though he didn't add that. I've got two hearts and two brains, and twin stomachs for the fight.

"I'd have imagined that a high-class sort of entertainer like you would have a cabin to yourself."

"I should have thought so, too." He refused to admit the inconvenience, and his disappointment. He didn't lack pride, any less than the bloke beside him. Perhaps it was good to have company below — as long as it stayed down there — silent so far, inactive, bone idle and dust-raddled, except that physical jerks were meat and drink to him. He knew where to find him, when he needed to call him into the open.

The professor wondered whether Cotgrave did share a cabin or not. He was a wiley old scholar, with faculties that jumped on conundrums with alacrity.

"You like doing crossword puzzles?" Ernest asked.

The professor was startled, but that galvanic inner bump showed no flicker on the eyes. Ernest in daylight had swung his Japanese binoculars from the horizon, and then accidentally, across the forward deck. The professor had been looking at a newspaper folded so small that he could only have been either reading the death announcements of his acquaintances, or doing a crossword. He appeared to settle all the answers to the clues in his mind, then write them in altogether, so quickly that he seemed to be scribbling. But why had Ernest mentioned cross-word-doing at the precise moment that the word had entered the professor's mind?

The most cunning ploy was to be completely open, the professor decided. "I do *The Times* everyday. Can't seem to live without it. For three weeks before leaving I gave up the pleasure, saved the back page, and numbered them one a day for the cruise. Better to sacrifice 'em at home than be without them here."

He'd already finished his soup. Ernest had barely started: "A helicopter should drop a few hundred copies to us every morning. You'd think it could be arranged. Or they could send the cross-words – clues and answers – by radio. If they'd paid me to do it I could have devised one every day."

"You make a story out of everything." The professor spoke half in admiration, yet somewhat with distaste. He found nothing likable about Ernest, but he was curious, so couldn't ignore him. In any case, he liked people he didn't like rather more than those he did. 'I'm glad the tradition of storytelling is coming back. We want a few of the old English folk-skills, to break up the poisonous oil-slick of modern living. It's good chaps like you who help us out. There's too much technology, too many machines, too many motorcars."

The brochure specified that the ship had a thrust of so-many thousand horsepower to get it through what stormy water it might encounter. Ernest had been glad of it in the recent gale. Even with stabilisers fully out, the decks had been almost depopulated by the opposing power of the sea. The professor had hobbled speedily around the boards helped by his ivory-handled walking stick. Ernest was curious as to how he had become lamed, and hoped that one day he might, by a side-on question, lift out the tale of it. Each time in passing, the professor grunted.

Another person out during the storm was the pallid-looking joker in the belted mac with whom he shared a cabin, who had not even looked at him the many times they brushed by. Having already introduced themselves, it broke no friendship. The contact was deeper. Bernard was quiet and surreptitious, would vanish around the stern, and only reappear after Ernest had decided to dodge him by crossing from port to starboard via the night club saloon nearest the bows. When he thought about him, he would materialise, whereas an hour or more might go by and he did not turn up only because he hadn't come to mind. It galled Ernest that life was at times so simple, that it was often at its most complicated only because you did not believe in its essential simplicity — and who could be so simple as not to see that? Faith in life itself was all that mattered to a storyteller.

"I suppose there *are* too many machines in the world," he said, when the fish course was set down. The professor extracted the slice of lemon from the metal squeezer and pressed it between his big fingers, spraying liquid over the table cloth and Ernest's left hand.

It was a question he had often gone into, so he flipped — perhaps deliberately, but who was to know? — onto the subject of surnames. "Cotgrave? Where does *that* come from?" — as if it were a particularly bedraggled sort of rat that the cat had pulled from under a derelict lorry.

Ernest had never thought about it, seeing it as too much like wondering how he came to have a little finger, or a left ear.

"Cotta's grave, I expect," the professor decided, after a while. "We're all born into the skin of our own grave, though. Don't know who Cotta actually was, however."

"Maybe he manufactured cottapins, for fixing pedal-cranks to bicycles," Ernest flippantly suggested. "It's the name of a village in Nottinghamshire. I don't suppose *our* family ever owned the place, though."

The professor shook his head in agreement. "They must have been Cotta's serfs."

This idea, though no doubt pointing towards accuracy, annoyed him. "I expect all our family, as well as yours, were serfs in those days." Ernest felt as if he were destined to be a serf from the cradle to the burial ground, not to the world or anybody outside necessarily, but a serf eternal to himself because he felt that

226

within him were two people in complete bondage to each other, occupying him till in life he put an end to one, or his death did for both. If one died, the other would be condemned to silence, because there would be nothing left for it to consume. And because they were so dependent on each other, one was always lying in wait to kill the companion-serf who existed in the same body and spirit. It was a marriage in one mind, a brotherhood in a solitary brain, a disaster in a single body. Only storytelling, or murder, could relieve the pain.

Ernest's last words were too *distinct* to be noticed by the professor. He was more adept at picking up half-said phrases, at correctly interpreting the *sotto voce* remnants of someone's thought, while plain and open words were merely the cannon-fodder of ongoing conversation. He drove, therefore, along the rail of his hard-set opinions. "I'd have been quite happy if invention had stopped at the bicycle and the gramophone. We could have done without jet planes and motors. Likewise with teabags, and automatic shavers, and portable radio-sets. The quality of life has really gone down a one-in-eight hill."

Ernest sensed a tremor of agreement, but knew he was not yet old enough to voice it, and hoped he would never feel so, though he wondered whether such an attitude wasn't barring him from deeper wisdom – of a sort.

"Take the telephone," the professor went on. "A loathsome instrument. Nobody writes letters. They can't describe anything in proper English. Aren't able to express themselves on paper. Won't bloody *spell*. They're too lazy, and Bolshy. No discipline of mind. And none of bloody body that I know of. They prefer to babble over the telephone. Look how idle everyone is when it comes to getting from place to place. They have rubber legs, and paper lungs, and balsa wood hearts. They don't walk or cycle. They get on a bus. They climb into a *motorcar*."

It sounded a nice sort of world, though Ernest couldn't imagine England consisting, industrially, of little more than a rash of push-bike and wind-up gramophone workshops in rural back-yards, while D.H. Lawrence strode about in an Indian poncho under the greenwood tree. Human ingenuity was rather more complicated, than God, than two wheels and a sprocket, plus a

227

few blown up inner-tubes. He told the professor that he liked being carried on a ship of so much horse-power, enjoyed seeing radar scanners turning continually above the bridge, and knowing that a first-class radio officer was always available to keep them in touch with the shore. You could never tell when mayhem would break loose, or a leak be sprung, or the ship get turned turtle by a freak tidal wave as in that movie he'd once seen. No doubt lifeboats were motorised, and had pre-tuned emergency transistorised radios, as well as hard-tack, and self-heating cans of hot sweet tea stashed away should they have to wait an hour or so in the boats and feel peckish or out of sorts in the meantime. Or there'd be signal rockets tucked in dry lockers if the lifeboats, by a negative sort of miracle, started to go down as well. And if anything did happen to the ship, there'd be aeroplanes over within minutes, a Piccadilly Circus of the air and sea as launches and helicopters queued to pick them up. Efficient engines would, in no time at all, throb a dozen to each ear, while technically-minded men and competent officers would haul them to safety with easy-going laughs and mugs of steaming cocoa.

The professor's barking drone pulled him from his pleasant fantasy of disaster: "When I was a child there were six of us, and we had a pony each. The spare stable was full of bicycles. I fed a horse at three, and mended my own puncture at six. You'd think we never walked, but we did. We had time for everything. At school I had to write a letter home every three days, and if it was less than five pages my allowance was cut. My parents had to know all that went on, inside and out of us. I sometimes wonder how they had time to read the thick letters we sent. Do you know, Cotgrave, they'd write the same amount back to all of us, but they never seemed short of time, even though my father worked hard as a barrister, and was up in Town much of the week. He used every single minute of his day, that's how he did it. He earned thirty thousand a year — which was *money* in those days."

"You say you walked a lot," Ernest put in, "but were your legs like that, then?"

A storyteller could ask questions that might bring a black-eye if anyone else were to put them from mere curiosity, though he still had to guage the temperament of the person before doing so.

A question forced people into making a decision as to whether or not to tell the truth, and such undue pressure sent certain types berserk. He once heard a man in the plywood factory ask a new-comer the date, and the response wasn't fit to be printed. The person who was asked for this information didn't want to think back an hour to when he'd seen the date of his newspaper or calendar, or heard it given on the news, because his wife and children, or lodger, would inhabit that minor flashback and recreate the awful misery contained in it. Ask a man the time, or the date, and you throw his tender equilibrium back into anguish and instability. In any case, perhaps it was merely that the man found it easier to be creative in bad language than to accurately judge the placing of two hands on his watch dial, or the shape of black numerals on the calendar. Had the question been more personal, uproar might have taken place, especially if the person thus unfairly interrogated did not have the intellectual spread or emotional probity to respond in a civilised fashion. A well-developed mechanism of responsibility was necessary with regard to asking questions, though it was clear that no such rules would work with Professor Wright.

"One thing I will say, Cotgrave, they feed us well on this cockleshell. Salt air stokes the appetite, and good cooks slake it. So all's right with the oblate spheroid. It usually is at sea, even when the waves hurl us about."

A subtle lift underfoot suggested that one could not question the professor, only listen, and hope for the best. You might as well try to control the sea. He offered a cigar from his tin of Havanas. The professor pulled its band away, cut off the end raggedly with his steak knife, and lit it slowly.

"Good to smoke between courses. Stops one bolting the food. Lots of rules in *my* life, Cotgrave, and they fall into two sets, one being called 'Never', and the other 'Always'. I try to stick to 'em. Sometimes I can't, but I make the attempt. Now and again I add a new rule, or drop an old one, but by and large they've stayed the same over the years."

Ernest thought he would be polite for once. "Do you mind if I ask what they are?"

"I intended telling you, otherwise I wouldn't have brought the

229

matter up, would I?"

"No," Ernest snapped.

"I'll give you the 'Nevers' first, then go on to the 'Always'. The 'Nevers' are these: Never finish a bottle of wine. That is to say: never drain a glass, so as to leave a portion for Apollo. Never clear your plate, in case someone should think you were actually *hungry*. Never let a foreigner know you speak his language — unless you speak it better than he does, in which case, always make a mistake somewhere in using it. Never regret anything. It's bad for morale, and does no good under any circumstances. Never tell lies. Never tell the truth, either. Never say 'no' to a woman — or to a man, for that matter. Never smoke a pipe, but if you must, do it in secret. It's a criminal activity. Never leave less than a note at table for the waiter (though these days it has to be a five-pound note, or a tenner, occasionally) even if it's your last. Never look at your privates, neither your own nor anybody elses, unless you're on parade and it's *your* battalion, or battery; or unless it's in stone and they're in a museum (or somebody's private collection). Never — but NEVER — go to Vienna: they once made people scrub pavements there. Never express an opinion. Never show emotion. And never yawn — as you look like doing now."

With each 'Never' the professor emmitted a mushroom shaped cloud over the table. "That's rather a lot of 'Nevers' for these modern times. So now for the 'Always'. Always compliment your wife — or man friend. Always congratulate the cook. Always ask for something you know people haven't got, and then be gracious when they say they haven't got it. If they hum-and-ha over it, never have anything more to do with them. Always use the indirect approach — or, in other words, never do the obvious. Always have a cold shower in the morning, and do ten minutes violent exercise afterwards, even if you get to be ninety years of age — which I suppose neither of us will. If it kills you, there are worse ways to die. If you try to follow all those rules you'll be a good chap (I won't say a gentleman, necessarily) even if you are a storyteller."

For every 'Always' he blew out a perfectly shaped smoking-ring. He was long practised in everything. Ernest had only one question, though he was careful to request permission before asking it.

"Another *always* comes to me as I cut into my succulent chateaubriand," the professor said, "and that is: always do exactly what you damned-well like. So fire away with your awful question."

"Do you believe in God?"

"There's one thing more: never talk to yourself. Find somebody and make *them* listen, if you think that sort of attack is coming on. There's usually no difficulty in button-holing somebody – I find. Which reminds me, Cotgrave, I saw you standing near the rail talking to yourself a couple of days ago."

Ernest wondered whether he should kill him now, while he was eating and in the full spate of his insupportable hedonistic natter.

"Rehearsing?" the professor added.

"Right." He cut into his duck. Even the professor hadn't found the secret of what was forcing him apart. "There's nothing like a sea trip to put you in touch with yourself, and get you out of yourself at the same time."

The professor considered for a moment whether to slide in a quotation from Homer, or even Hesiod. He assumed it would be a waste of time, and went back to his knifing and forking.

"It's good to leave one's wife now and again." Ernest quickly ammended his tactics for obtaining information. "Though I expect it's even more of a holiday for her to be alone for a while."

The incredibly bushy eyebrows lifted. "Wouldn't know what to do with a wife. Married a woman from Germany in 1938 to get her into England. Otherwise – no. Anyway, I never travel in order to get away from anything or anybody. Strangely enough, things often happen when I *am* on my travels, though this trip's been dull so far. Can't understand it."

"I hope my story enlivens the scene."

"A poor substitute, if it does. Good of you to try, though. I don't like it when people threaten me." But he laughed as he said it.

Ernest had to keep telling stories, otherwise his brain would rot. Even death was preferable, though not necessarily his own.

"I expect something to occur when we come to Longitude Thirteen," the professor said, rippling his fingers loudly for another bottle of wine. "It usually does."

18

When the ship came to, and crossed, Longitude Twelve, Ernest
stood to starboard, and saw the green hump of Pantellaria a few
nautical miles to the south. It rose softly from a backdrop of
rainy haze, but the water between the island and the ship was
deep cobalt.

"The Mediterranean is a funny bloody sea," the Radio Officer
observed, leaning over the rail. "To judge by the colour, you'd
think we were near Spitzbergen. I never did like it. A treacherous
pond. You know what to expect with some seas, but not the
unholy Med."

Ernest thought it looked friendly enough, and considered that
the Radio Officer, unlike most people who had few opinions,
wasn't wise in what he said. He wasn't the one who decided how
to phrase the messages he tapped out. He merely sent what he
was told. But his hand was intermittently on the key of power.
He manipulated codes. Ernest knew he was a type to be wary of.

"The ancients called it *Cossyra*." The professor locked a set of
his bushy brows to the eye of a brass-bound pocket telescope
padded with leather along its length. A 'geological specimen' bag
of several instruments lay at his feet. "Not much else to say about
the place. Rocky and barren. Soil volcanic. The Carthaginians
had it first. *They* would. Then Arabs. *They* would, as well. Then
the Italians took it. Had to have something, I suppose."

"A beautiful sight," Ernest said.

"They've still got it," the professor spat.

The Radio Officer strode away: "Keep the place!"

"But we captured it in 1943," the professor told them.
"Buried it in high-explosive, so that the flower of our youth

233

could go ashore without a shot being fired. I expect they have a nice new town there now. We were a demolition squad for the whole of Europe. It was fun while it lasted. Wouldn't mind a bit of the old bang-bang stuff now, even if they took my other leg! Had my battery well-trained. Drilled my gunners like poets. In Italy we fired by dactyls. Eighteen rounds made a hexameter. I nearly had a fit one morning when the German battery opposite played the same tune. *He* must have been a classics-wallah as well. Anyway, I smothered 'em in a few cantos of iambic pentameter. Then he had to pull his guns out to avoid being cut off, so we never finished our dialogue."

Bernard, a few yards away, found the island through the Japanese binoculars that obscured most of his face.

"As soon as we pass Panta I start to smell Greece," the professor called, "though it's a day or two before we get there. Got to cross Longitude Thirteen first."

By mid-evening the ship would be over it, and Ernest brooded on the fact. It was already afternoon. The line would be unmarked and invisible, like many barriers. A meridian of longitude was man-devised, by which to tell the time and plot your position. Like all meridians it was a great circle that would slice the earth in two if any galactic knife was sharp enough and sufficiently vast. Fire would pour out of the middle, and the two halves would capsize into space. He found it hard to envisage a catastrophe that would be final even for the worms. He clung to the view of Pantalleria as if it were the last sight of a fruit he would never taste.

"History doesn't repeat itself," the professor laughed and shouted at the same time, "it *vomits* all over you." Ernest turned away in case the professor should for once in his life be seized with the idea that because he studied history he personified it.

Three-thousand feet of height diminished, when he wanted it to do otherwise, and lost the admiralty precision of outline which had laced it when the sea was cobalt. It turned pale. He yearned for indigo and the approach of cliffs, but the ship went relentlessly, mindlessly and – it seemed – without effort towards the Thirteenth Meridian of Longitude East. He wondered what other places hung on it like jewels.

The professor waved a pocket-sextant, and a hand-held range finder. "'*No man should travel without the instruments for taking heights and distances*' — or so that plebeian old bore Doctor Johnson said. I like to know where I am, Cotgrave, so lumber myself with these toys. You can never tell when you're going to find yourself in the middle of a desert, or lost in a milky ocean!"

Ernest was due to begin another instalment of his story as they were crossing Longitude Thirteen East. The slightly raised area had been used by last night's band. His left hand, lifted for silence, was padded with bandage. The throb had subsided, but sufficient pain remained to get him safely through this lump of his tale. They knew him well by now. Even the funny little pale-faced bloke at the back raised his hand and smiled, as if he and Ernest had recently conspired in some matter unimportant to one but vital to the other. Ernest turned equally egg-white at the thought of Bernard lifting *his* hand only to mimic him. It had to happen sooner or later but, because it had come now, Ernest for a moment forgot his name, not the name of the man at the back with bluish coalscars on his cheeks, but his own Ernest-born Cotgrave-name. Only now that it was lost did he realise what it had always meant to him. It had gone as if intending never to come back. Bernard Baker appeared in its place, and even when he forgot that name, he couldn't get back to his first, though Bernard Baker seemed enough to be going on with when it re-appeared. There was nothing left to do but do it, he told himself, and a name wasn't necessary for that.

A bag of tricks and possible effects lay by the stationary pair of shoes in which his feet were wrapped. The accessories to his act were contained in a cloth-checked reticule bought one Friday morning from a stall in the Portobello Road Market, that slag-heap, street-long emporium in which the loot and tat of the British Empire assembled before going back to where it had come from. He remembered his name, and was calm when his lips spoke it, for he always found it difficult to begin a story, and certainly an instalment of a life-and-death chronicle, if he did not know who he was. To have the familiar container at his feet gave some comfort. Without it he would feel like a conjurer who had lost his cards and rabbits. The contents of his bag were more vital.

"Every fatal disease brings with it the desire to go on living to the end." Nothing but the best was good enough for these privileged spectators seated in the Coliseum of Human Sacrifice, even though they were total strangers to the violent seesaw of millibars in his soul, not to mention the grind of tectonic plates behind his eyes. He looked at the few dozen faces, and Bernard's was not among them. Bernard's mobility frightened him. Maybe he was on the lifeboat deck, baying at the moon. Live for me, Ernest pleaded, and I'll tell stories for you. He felt hounded towards death by that self which was determined to live for him or die in the attempt. Perhaps they would both die. For a person who told stories, such an end was logical. As a fate it was almost just.

It was necessary to lard every session with a preamble. "I am an artist, and the more of this story I tell the more I am robbing and emptying the person I might have been. From the early days, unbeknown to me, that other person decided on revenge before it was – or is – too late. Even if the death-attempt does not succeed he is bound to accomplish the next best thing."

"And what the devil's that?" a short, dark Dane shouted. A drink was pushed into his hand. He was told not to interrupt, and grumbled as he sat down that everyone was trying to poison him.

Thank God I don't have to answer yet, Ernest thought, though when the time came to do so it might distress others, as well as himself. Every nuance needed forethought. He made notes, fixed a specific programme in his red-covered notebook, and hoped it wasn't a sign that his career was about to finish. Every storyteller scorched his talent to ash sooner or later, as Leonard Orgill had tragically related, not to mention old GP, who told me so in a dream one day, by the banks of the silvery Trent south-west of Newark.

"I must go back to Bernard. A storyteller can never forget his victim, till he himself becomes the victim, which he does because he cannot let his victim go. Bernard dreamed of those prime blades which, had he and they been big enough, he would have brought down on the earth at Longitude Thirteen (which we are now crossing) and sliced as neat a great circle as any semi-globe could afterwards boast of. He couldn't actually do it, but he wet dreamed of such a calamity at some time during the long night that followed.

"He also, in a normal dream, walked along a straight black tunnel hewn out of solidified soot, a tunnel more than high enough to stand in. It was so wide that at the left were small booths, which appeared to be workshops and market-stalls combined. He had got into the tunnel through a junkshop on a street of his childhood town. In one booth were two young women dressed in papery black clothes. They had thin noses, and pale yellowish faces, and worked with miniature screw-drivers at a heap of broken fob-watches. When Bernard looked he saw that none of the white-faced watches had hands. The women were still, and did not speak or look at him. So he passed on. After a restless night, the dream came back to him all day long."

A chair fell over. A tall, blond, red-faced man stood up, laughed loud and soullessly. "He's going to die!"

A beer-bottle rolled along the floor. Ernest stared and, after the silence, resumed: "It'll be either him, or us. Bernard didn't eat breakfast or lunch that day. The sea air fed him. It bred sweat and energy for him to live by. Close to the prow, he looked at water being sliced by the bows that seemed to be taking him and nobody else forward. He viewed the unfolding curve, the ever-turning captive deluge that had already fallen from the sky and been imprisoned by its allegiance to the earth. It soothed him but, the longer it fixed and mollified, the more it packed the turmoil back, ramrodded the utter confusion that he wanted to break loose in himself. The water, divided by the surging ship, fell against his brain and wore the fibres away. It seemed to enter through the terminal of each eye, so that when the speckled sea released him from its grip (as if the connections to his source of power became automatically detached when the maximum that his system could take had been reached) he walked like a being guided by some electro-magnetic beam, back to the cabin to get a knife and a bayonet.

"It was dark, and maybe the phosphorescent sparkle in the wavetips finally let him go. In silence, and unobtrusively so that he met no one, he got into his cabin and reached under the bunk.

"The knives came out as if newborn when he slowly took off

237

their swathes of chamois leather. One small light above the bunk shone, as he sat on the floor balancing a bare bayonet in one hand and a naked dagger in the other. He weighed them, and soothed himself. He was afraid of the sea bubbling and swishing close, suspecting that it was about to break through and suffocate only him. Crew and passengers were part of it. Looking down from the top deck he felt himself built into the sea's energy. He fed off its liquid and salt as if it were making him drunk, but down here he was menaced because its power was out of sight. There was no reason for such fear. The ship was a masterpiece of marine engineering. No detail of safety and convenience had been neglected in its construction. The pamphlet had told him so. Yet you could be sure of nothing. Hadn't the workmen, while making it, skimped a rivet? They might have done. Down here, in the guts, it was cardboard. Anything was possible. An unexplained knock against the side of the cabin nearest the sea made his heart race. It threatened him. He looked to where the tap had sounded, waiting for a rip to appear, and a grey fist of water to strike through. The only safety was in flight, but there was nowhere to run to. A walk around the deck brought you back to the same place. Down below it was worse. You could be trapped in some cul-de-sac against a watertight bulkhead with its capstan bars and huge bolts firmly in the locked position. They might spring open, and set that selfsame flooding fist of invincible salt water swamping at you. Or you might lie down by the safe-seeming bulkhead, arms and legs drawn up in the warmth, and thinking you were secure at last when, too late, that rage of white water came boiling from the way you had walked, and the trap was final.

"He sweated out his speculations, wanting dry land that went on for hundreds of miles and didn't frighten him like the sinister sea curdling along the cabin wall. It was impossible to reach land where all flesh is grass. If he leapt over the side, the sea's salty jaws would consume him before he swam half a mile. The only land was in flesh-and-blood people walking around the ship. Each live body was an individual piece of the earth billeted on the ship as they played cards or supped at the bar or spied into the slop-chop distance looking for something they'd never see, or listened to that treacherous storyteller yammering false yarns in which he tried to murder his very own Bernard's character after pushing him around in humiliating and shameless ways. The storyteller, acting like a social worker or a policeman, or boss at a factory, was one of 'them', belonged with 'the others' of the world who organised people by holding their fears and secrets to ridicule. His shameful explanations made others laugh at what we didn't see as funny at all, causing *them* to shed easy tears or feel superior at our misfortunes. There was no justice. Such people shouldn't be allowed to escape the consequences of their betrayals. They were allied to the sea as it crawled restless and relentless along the cabin walls, only waiting for a small crack to widen so as to get through and black me out forever.

"Snakes of sea water lapped your life around on a ship. Bernard wanted to get back underground with shovel and pick, and follow the dim beam shining from his helmet. He needed to feel the earth's homely dust peppering his lungs, stinging motes as old as the world itself that would settle and stay there long after he had gone. He would rather be choked with dust than water, for he would recognise his own smell in it.

"He chose a knife. When the cabin door fell to, he felt better. Humming a tune that had been in his head since his wife's departure, he walked towards the main companionway with the weapon under his coat. The signature tune of some banal radio programme raced into his mind as soon as he ceased to consider his knives, or speculate on the woman he had talked to as the boat set out (and whose cabin he'd gone into later, though he couldn't remember the red fog of that short visit), or discuss with himself the murderous aims of the sea behind his cabin wall. The domineering little tune would jump back into his head like a yap-terrier and get at him. He had no control, for whatever effort he made, the tune was always there as soon as his purpose relaxed its grip. It invaded him as he climbed the stairs. It also helped him, because it put a harmless expression on his face which suggested that he was an equable kind of person ready to help anyone in trouble. When, due to the turmoil of his mental perorations, the tune went out of hearing, it left his pale face like paper, and his grey eyes so unmoving that no good influence could get at them. At such times his thin lips were held together by inner and circular cogitations, which wouldn't allow anyone to prise them open and disturb the freedom he maintained in his fortress.

"The only way to obliterate the dominating music was to keep an intense and particular observation on everything round about. Such an effort made it seem that his consciousness was trying to show him an illuminated state of life he had not experienced before.

"This jingle-tune had been sent in as a spearhead to deflect him from the set purpose of wielding his knife. It was trying to take him over, but he fought it, and the effort of battling increased his sense of purpose, which was strong precisely because he saw no sense whatever in anything he intended to do. Sense was unnecessary. One must not interfere with the workings of the unconscious at exactly the point where it was coming into consciousness. He had waited for such a thing to happen from the day he was born.

"Bernard walked stiffly, as if he'd once had an accident and injured his leg. The jumpy little signature tune made him aware of the ordinary things of life. Whatever they might be, he wouldn't like them. They were not his. After a futile, circular discussion with himself, the tune came back to comfort him. It didn't. As soon as he got on deck and looked at the water, the tune vanished, and the salt waves took over in their rise and swish. When the tune let go of his mind it left him without memory.

"He leaned against the rail, heard dance songs above the plying waves and the rumble of the ship's huge diesels. People were dancing to the same tune, but they were free because the music and their bodies were in rhythm, matched to the movement of their feet, while their arms were around someone similarly taken up. He had never been able to dance. It angered him to watch, and he preferred his soothing grip of the rail, tacky from the salt air. Out of the cabin he felt no fear of the endlessly moving sea. It would have been better if the dance band hadn't been playing, but he had always known that you couldn't have everything in the world. It was enough that he had become a sadistic killer loose on a cruise-liner, sufficient proof that even he had his own soul to destroy, and therefore his own story to tell.

"Someone came out of the night club and walked stiffly in the opposite direction, as if wanting fresh air from flesh-smell and fagsmoke. Whoever it was would do the whole round of the deck and reach him. He waited. The handle of the long knife was a precious object he had loved since leaving the cradle. No one would rob him of his knife.

"He gripped the safe end, and stared at the sea. A distant light was like a blunt needle trying to break through a blanket. It might be Sicily, but who could be sure? Yesterday he'd opened his map, and an unexpected wind ripped one of the folds apart, so he wouldn't bother with it again. Flesh was more important than paper. The light went out. Perhaps it had belonged to another ship. When it came on again, he no longer cared. Such signalling was meant for those on the bridge, not him. Maybe it was a message warning the captain of what he was about to do. No one he knew would make an effort to get in touch with him alone, and if they did there would be nothing in it for his advantage.

"The stars were trying to replace the lights and might be saying what he'd like to hear, but he found them frightening: they were too far away to be anything more than pinpoints of blue against a blackness that he would soon know about. He turned, and set his eyes at the waves.

"The wooden rail was comforting. It was hard. The tackiness reminded him that it had come from a living tree. It belonged more to land than people on the ship. People were only flesh and blood. There was more soil, even in dead wood, than in people. He stroked the rail, as if to bring life back into its solid wood-flesh. The handle of his knife was wood, and he gripped it with the other hand. Between the two kinds of wood was a blade of razor-sharp steel.

"He did not know what he wanted protecting from but felt a rush of agony through his spirit and called on God to save him. Whatever happened, and whatever he did, would be nothing to

241

what he had already done, and nothing either to all other butcheries in the world. But he cried to be held back from something for which he knew no words. He shouted to be freed from what he had so far lived through, including that blameless and ordinary part of his life from which he did not need to be saved. He cried to be rescued from the total insignificance at the middle of himself, but it was too late. He was a watch without hands.

"He did not pray for protection from what he might do in the future, because even as little as ten seconds into it was locked by an iron door as strong as those bulkheads which were designed to keep back the violent force of the sea should the outer skin of the ship crack. Only the past was important, and it had gone, was continually going like fine dry sand through his fingers. Since it was too late, who else was there to cry to except God? And even He, being God, and therefore unable to respond to his despair, had abandoned him. There was no one left except himself, and his despairing voice ricochetted from the cell-like limits of his inner country.

"Bernard slid to the iron gutter between the rail and the wood, hands over his head as if about to be smashed by an elemental force he had brought into action but would never know why. His hair was wet and he wondered how the water could have leapt the great distance up to his scalp and hands. Eyes closed, he drew a finger to his lips. The liquid tasted reassuringly of salt. The sea had found him, even so many feet above the waterline. All powerful, it could get at him any time, in spray, wave or flood. The sea poured from the back of his hand. He drank as if he had crossed a desert.

"Whoever had come from the night club rounded the stern of the ship and walked towards him. He did not know what lay in wait. Bernard looked, even before hearing the tramp of heavy shoes. He felt rapidly round about to get his hand back on the haft of the knife. The act of searching and the sound of footsteps made him realise that the liquid on his wrist and arm was not sea water but his own copious blood. He would mix it with someone else's.

"The moon shone on the sea, as he gripped the rail, and looked across its beams. It was almost dead calm. The knife had fallen between the bars and gone into the water, as the ship was passing Longitude Thirteen."

19

When no one speaks, but glasses still move and collide, it is more disturbing than absolute quiet. But it did not faze Ernest that there was no applause. As a storyteller, the phenomenon of surprise had worn off years ago, and if it hadn't he would not have shown his awareness of it. They were too respectful to clap, he hoped; too involved with the sinuous plot of his story; too stunned by the approach of sombre and half-expected conclusions.

During the tale his hand had throbbed. He had been aware of a swift draw of steel across yielding skin on relating how Bernard had fallen against the rail while calling out to be saved. It had lasted a few seconds, but the fundamental pulsing of his injured hand under the bandages reasserted itself. In spite of his story – in which he had been too engrossed – he wondered what the pain was, and how it had got there.

This discomfort (he had not so far in his life admitted to pain of any sort) made him stay longer on stage than he would normally have done, and such hesitation, before walking through his audience to the bar for a soothing glass of whisky, gave someone the opportunity to ask a question. At his interview for the job he had stipulated to the Entertainments' Director that he did not want any to be asked at his performances. He made the point again when first coming on board. The Radio Officer, standing under the clock by the duty free shop, overheard him talking to the Entertainments' Director, and Ernest noted repugnance, almost hatred on his face. The bantam-like Marconi man, as neat in his way as any desk officer, put on a show of testy pride, perhaps to make up for the fact that he didn't spin a wheel or sight a sextant. He stood back, plainly hoping to control his sneer, yet relying on Ernest both witnessing the attempt, and its lack of success. For what purpose Ernest did not know, but he had read in a novel that wireless operators were noted for their lack of balance when it came to a refined appreciation of other people's feelings. Psychologically, they were — by and large — a rough lot, and appeared to be proud of it. Such was the telegraphic traffic that passed through the hands and eyes of these doctors of communication that they developed perspicuity concerning the follies of the world, though at times their temperaments leaned towards a snappish intolerance. Ernest figured that in company their behaviour tended to be unpredictable, and that their solitary calling made them misanthropic rather than reflective. In view of this he saw no need to tell the Radio Officer to piss off and mind his own business, since he would not have done so. Whatever was spinning into his dot-and-dash mind, he seemed to be waiting for Ernest to finish his conversation.

The Entertainments' Director, being a man of many travels and much experience, told Ernest that how he handled the job was up to him, as long as a certain number of passengers were drawn to the spinning of his nightly yarn. If no one turned up, he joked, they'd hang him from the yard arm while going through the Greek Islands, which sort of entertainment they might well find more to their taste.

Ernest was about to protest that "yarn" was not really what he liked to call his performances any more, but again caught a curl of malicious amusement on the Radio Officer's lips, and so merely repeated his "no question" rule. The Radio Officer possessed the features of someone who had left youth behind, and had set himself up as a menace to those who had not, or could not. Seeing him in the audience now, Ernest knew he must be careful to keep himself under control.

After his conversation with the Entertainments' Director, on the matter of not allowing questions, Ernest remembered other places where his softness of heart, which had probably been no more than a cover for vanity and self-importance, had allowed them to be asked, with uncomfortable consequences for his audience and himself. But the present question was cunningly aimed and he had no option except to answer. A storyteller is nothing if not deferential. He regards his audience as sacred, whose needs come even before vital measures of self-preservation.

"How come you injured your hand?" asked an American girl. She stood up politely, then sat down as soon as she had phrased the question and it was clear that he would respond to it. A flattering sort of curiosity was built into the pleasing pitch of her voice. But the question was deadly, and difficult to answer, and impossible to lie to.

"It's a long story." And you've heard most of it, he ought to have added. The rest of the audience were amused at her temerity, or envious of her self-confidence, and he wondered how many had, before she spoke, connected his injured hand with the hand of Bernard in his story. His internal query, however, seemed irrelevant. He could think of no answer that would get him out of the trap he was rapidly building around himself.

"I believe in FATE," he announced. "Everything is decided for us at the moment of birth. As soon as we steal the earth's air to get our lungs working, we are under an obligation which does not lapse till death. These things are arranged by someone – or something – for which I have no other word but 'fate'. It is even more mysterious than such an easygoing hypothesis suggests. All the future is foretold but – and here's the complication – freedom of choice is given to everyone. When we exercise that choice we are in turn being moved by someone who decided what exactly we are going to choose so freely. You may say that in such a case, there is no freedom, but I say there is, and that freedom doesn't mean *what* you choose. Freedom is being in a position to choose what options fate makes available to you. The act of choosing is at that indeterminate point where you may lose that freedom and be on the way to bondage."

He held up his injured hand, so that there would be no mistaking what he meant. "Yesterday, I decided to sharpen a pencil with an open razor. The blade accidentally slipped, and I gashed myself."

They laughed, in a subdued and free-natured way. He had answered the question with enough philosophical grace to suggest that he'd had a similar education to most of them, or at least

246

wished he had. They appreciated his gesture. So did he. They were his people, just as others, in whatever place he had performed, had also been his people. Everyone was equal in the eyes of a storyteller. Being born with a firm sense of egalitarianism was the first condition towards becoming an artist. Even talent did not precede it.

There was a place in his tale for everyone, which included the people he was facing as much as the untapped multitudes within and beyond himself. They were the reality and the mystery in him, just as he was the mystery and the reality in them and in himself. The necessity of equality was axiomatic; love or concern followed as a matter of course.

But it was perilous to admit it. They either felt it, or they didn't. He was not the man to force a principle down anyone's throat, which may have been to his disadvantage, but he held on to such a belief so that it might comfort him in oblivion when they no longer cared to listen to his stories. No matter what he thought, he was – after all – only a storyteller, and as such was far more pure than simple.

The ship lagged its way across the Mediterranean like a snail leaving the wake of their spirits behind. On some point of latitude and longitude that vicious knife had sunk, smears of blood rapidly washed from it by the ever-cleansing salt of the sea. He looked at his hand and wondered whether he was sea or the land, whether he was salt, or soil. When he cut himself the salt ran free. The blade had come out of the earth. The fight was coming to an end.

The American girl asked another question. If she persisted he'd have to marry her. "Your tale is not a simple one." He had no option but to agree. It wasn't finished, so how could it be? He felt a further instalment on its way, implying that the most pertinent interrogations should be left to the end – by which time all questions might have been answered.

"There's one thing I'd like to ask, though it's more of a discussion-point than a question."

He nodded. There was nothing else he could do.

"When Bernard called on God to save him, did it signify that God did so when he made the knife slide into the water?"

To answer it would finish him off as a storyteller. It would also put his questioner in danger of her life. But how was he to evade the issue, and tell her so?

She sat, and he must say something:

"Occasionally, I am invited to lecture on the storyteller's art, if there is such a thing." Modesty was a good beginning. The Radio Officer, so scornful at hearing him tell the Entertainments' Director that he would answer no questions, sat at a table talking to a tall angular blonde woman with an intensity of speech only broken when, after taking a drink from his large glass of beer, he looked directly at Ernest as if to say: "We all come to it sooner or later." There was sympathy and understanding in his gaze, suggesting that, being in the communications trade, he too had given some thought to the transference of information, the passing of impulses, the construction and decipherment of codes, the subtle harmonics of mixed frequencies, the technique of beamed aerials, and the theory of power-bouncing up to the Oliver Heaviside layer and back. Ernest knew he was one person whom he would never be able to put in a story. He was almost as afraid of him as he was of Bernard.

"It isn't easy to talk about storytelling. To do so can have unpleasant repercussions. It's always seemed to me that, for a storyteller, the necessity to explain is a mark of failure. Explanations only mystify. Sophisticated people may be able to explain their way out of mystification, and good luck to them, but a storyteller may well succeed in explaining his way into it which, believe me, ladies and gentlemen, is bad luck for him. If a person other than the storyteller tries to explain his stories in such a way that he involves himself and his listeners in mystification – that's all right, because it is his task, and may even be his pleasure, to lead them out again, with no harm done.

"But for a storyteller – and I tell you this out of honesty, though mostly for your own good – it would expose both him and his listeners to a possibility of doom. The tunnels into which he might take you, and which he knows better than any outside explorer, might leave you inextricably lost. He leads people into areas so remote that after a while he feels free to talk their bodies and souls into becoming part of a story from which they might never sufficiently emerge to become wholly what they were before. When you are caught in those tunnels of doubt and confusion, the storyteller no longer cares to use each of you as the means towards making a story, but he takes part of one, a bit of the other, a lump out of a third, a piece of somebody over there — in order to create a whole person. He then goes through the same process to make another, and as many as he likes, until there is nothing left except a few twitching bits and pieces — as well as a group of characters who bear no relationship to each other or to the original people who set out with *me* on the process of explanation as to how I make stories. I take a razor-sharp knife to your souls. I butcher and hack, but do my best to make something new out of them. It's not pleasant. It's the dirty business of a self-confessed murderer who robs people, sucks them dry and drives them mad. I remake them, but they still remain insane enough to dance to my puppet jingle-tune so that I can make a tragic or pathetic or even hilarious story out of their antics.

"There's a twist, though. There always is. I've been doing it so long that I have gone too far. Your crimes always catch up, no matter how quickly you run, and no matter where you run to. The murderer tries to avoid the locale of his wickedness, but how can he, when that scene is everywhere? It is everywhere because it is himself. What happened, was that all my victims — for they were no less — gathered to decide what to do about me. I had shaped their fates glibly and inhumanly, murdered and remade them to my own peculiar images so as to try to explain myself, which is another way of saying that I did it in order to keep myself alive and safe. I was empty, yet brought myself back to life by filling my emptiness with *them* and their fullness. They were innocent bystanders running their own lives as best they could, but I used them, corrupted them, dragged them into my life and made them commit crimes they hadn't thought of before I came along. They are not to blame. The inexorable laws of the universe state that since I corrupted and therefore betrayed them they are now compelled by something bigger than themselves to destroy *me*. I spoke to them and used them, instead of speaking to and addressing God — as the great storytellers must at one time have done.

" 'The ear trieth words as the mouth tasteth meat'. Corruption by words is the worst of betrayals, the bitterest harvest to reap. I had no life, so used theirs. I cut my way through swathes of people, ripped off their limbs and stuffed them into my life. I ate their hearts and consumed their souls. Full of greed, I made them live for me. And they loved me for making them live for me, because I also made them live for others, and in many ways for each other, though they didn't thank me for that. I told my stories as if they were true, but none of them could be.

"The better I became at it, the more I strutted around. And yet, right from the beginning, the people I invented were planning to get their own back. I brought many people to life, and when I had done with them they crowded at the back of my mind and would not leave. They lurked. They bided their time. Now and again I recalled one that I had used, and thought: 'How strange that I should think of *him*, or *her*;' and I would grin at the recollection of what merciless events I had put him – or her – through in the story I had made up. But such who occasionally came back to mind in this way were the ringleaders of the plot. They were reconnoitering my mind so as to know when the time would be ripe for their revenge. One of them is lecturing you now, not me. I can't get free. I'm forced to tell you this, and am acquiescing in the telling of it because I hope that by doing so I may discover a method of escape. If I do something favourable for them they may relent, and let me go before they destroy me. I can't retreat. The only chance is to go forward, and on towards any possible light. I'm trying to recapture myself from those I created, and who have taken me over like an army of occupation.

"It wouldn't have been any good for me to speak these thoughts to myself in the seclusion of my cabin, or on an endless walk around the deck, or to do it in any other way than how I am doing it now, because they insist that I expound before an audience, and tell it as I told stories about them during *my* absolute control when I so readily murdered their minds and characters. In any case, I couldn't do it alone, in some isolated place away from people, because when I try (as I have many times) I meet one of *them* who jostles me and laughs, or waves a knife in front of my face.

"*They* demand that I do it in public. If I'm sweating, it's because I'm frightened. Take no notice of me. On board ship they have me at their mercy. I was forced into this job at the point of a bayonet. Bernard got into me, came with me into the shipping line offices, and spoke my mouth and moved my fingers to fill in forms and agree to all they said. He lived my grimaces and smiles, and told me about knives and bayonets and how to clean and sharpen and look after them. He gave me textbooks on the history of swordsmanship, manuals of tactics concerning the 'White Arm'. He told me how one of his ancestors in an English cavalry regiment at Dettingen lost his way after a futile charge against a wood on the right flank of the armies. He fought off the enemy with his sabre and carbine but was then made prisoner by the French. Later he was rescued by a German dragoon who turned out to be a woman, and they fell in love and had six children and were all set to live happily ever after, until one day from their cottage door they saw a horseman in the distance. . . ."

He was impelled to run, but couldn't move. "That was a digression, not one of *my* stories, but further proof that *he* is in me, and guiding my words, and making me tell one of *his* tales for a change, though where he got it from I can't imagine. 'We want *you* to live, instead of us,' he said. He's not the only one. There are lots of them in me, and give their opinions continually, so that none of my own are left. They shout orders in the middle of the night. They tell me what to do — which they have always done, but in happier days I used them as ideas for stories. But now they want revenge. I call out to be saved, but you all think it part of my story, tale-teller's trickery to make the meandering yarn more interesting. And it is, fellow passengers! I'm the Master Storyteller, the born yarner, the card-spinner, the onion-skinner and maker of the wheels-within-wheels machine that is supposed to mirror life itself! So don't worry about someone like me. God did not listen to Bernard's plea when he caused the knife to fall into the sea. It was me who made God listen. Bernard was a puppet. He was nothing more than a character in my story. He was born from nothing, a tale of my heart. But will God listen if I plead with him to save *me*? He didn't hear Bernard. I only said He did. I showed that He did in my story, but our Bernard had more than one knife. He had several, an arsenal of weapons in his cabin, being nothing if not thorough in his dull, pre-meditating way.

"Like the rest of them, he decided on each move and counter-move, and forestalled every thought that needled into my brain. They had time for continual plotting and thorough planning because I had thrown them into idleness when I had no more use for them. They were a surly crowd of the psychic unemployed who worked me so much into their power that I was helpless. They want me to use my story-spinning in such a way as to make you believe I'm merely telling you another story. They want you to believe it's just one more strand of a tale, part of a pattern to make a solid and conclusive end before you go your different ways to bed or damnation. It's as if, among you in the audience, sits an Examiner of the Guild of Storytellers, who will decide whether or not I am to be given my Master's Certificate which, of course, I have coveted and worked for for so long. Nothing of the sort! Even that, and especially that, is part of the story they put between my lips. I wrench myself back on course, so that even if you see me destroyed, you'll know exactly how it happened.

"Just as I am the victim of these monsters who've taken me over, so *you* are acquired by them through me insofar as I am able to hold you with this story which is dictated by them. I have to defeat them, and the only method I have, pyrrhic though it is, is to let them defeat me. They are making me do something final, which means me putting myself into a story at their behest and behove, which they hope will give it, me, and them — and you — an ending. They have engineered the conclusion to involve all of us, because we are on this ship together, and the journey will end like this. . . ."

20

Bernard, don't open that reticule. Nor you, Ernest. But Ernest knew that he himself was doing it. He imitated Bernard, who mimicked him imitating himself mocking Ernest who mimicked him. I've never asked before, but I want God to help me now.

It was raining against the open upper deck so he put on his carefully folded raincoat and buttoned each button with loving care.

His audience were quiet. They waited for him to begin again — and once again begin. They were patient because, as far as they knew, he was dressing for the part before going on with his tale. He fastened the mackintosh up to his neck, though did not draw the belt to the last eyehole in case it choked his waist. He smiled at Ernest Baker and nodded at Bernard Cotgrave. He shook hands with himself, trying to make friends, and winced at the hard grip. His palid, blue-smeared face and placid eyes pushed out the free-and-easy posture of the chief narrator. It was a long time from the days when he had been able to say whatever came into his head, and guarantee a flowing tale.

He pushed a hand snappishly up to wipe the rigid smile away, as if a hornet had settled on the lips. Interlopers were moving through. His arm went like a pendulum. The smile had no intention of moving. Their applause at this part of his act should have enraged him, since it wasn't he who was skilful enough to amuse them, but he felt glad at least to be making them laugh. The ache of miserable helplessness passed as soon as they stopped clapping.

He took a trilby hat from his bag. It was obvious that other things were inside and, looking forward to still more novel entertainment, they wondered if he weren't a magician as well as a mimic. At the journey's end they might write congratulatory letters to the shipping company on the originality of their idea in employing a person who not only told stories, which was what they had expected, but also impersonated his characters with a reality that disturbed and thrilled them.

Under cover of his many masks, from the shipwreck of himself that was half-submerged in the mud of consciousness, he felt many intentions flooding the minds of his audience. His perceptions were finding their weaknesses, which he would be able to use, doing to them as he was being done by, for if you can't or won't, or don't, then what right have you to hope that God will save you when the sky falls in? Each star was the tip of a cosmic needle. If they stabbed him he would bleed to death.

He held up the hat. His keepers allowed him to relax the smile as he straightened its brim. Sweat-drops fell from his forehead, ran out of his cheeks and vivified the painted marks. He flicked dust from the crown of the hat, and smoothed the inside band. It was still warm, and slightly greasy from having been on someone else's head for an hour during many circuits of the deck. When his nose shrank at the smell, they laughed, as he'd known they would. A man of many talents had a soul of many colours. The personalities he concocted were sufficiently related to appear as real people. He was able to make them life-like because no other person on earth resembled himself. They threw off the stories with which he had so far shackled them.

The hat was held at the length of his arm. If he put it on he would be finished. It was the crown of their victory. He wanted to drop it, but he had his pride, and they knew it. They skewered him on his pride. Pride had been his enduring mistake. They were certain he wouldn't humiliate himself as he had shamed them, therefore he had to do what they told him. He had controlled them for so long that they knew him to the widest extent of his soul. Such mutual familiarity meant a contest unto death. They knew it, and he was sure of it.

The audience had become part of him, and he saw himself at the bar with a brandy glass by his fingers that rattled a tattoo on the bakelite surface with long blood-covered nails. He wore a white shirt, black tie and jacket; his hair was combed back, and he smiled, the master of Cotgrave's ceremonial downfall wondering how that silly upstart bastard on the platform was going to get out of this lovely unbreakable trap — and relishing the fact that he never would.

His reflection in the mirror showed a deep strawberry-mark down the side of his face. Arthur Bingham, the fancy-man traveller in ladies underwear from the Major Oak Lace Company smirked. "I prophesied you'd end up like this, after you used me in that pub tale for getting accustomed to the fact of Marion's affairs."

Ernest caught a whiff of the aftershave they both still used. An upward semaphore sweep of his left arm signalled defeat and death. He put on his hat, so as to dress the part. Hatless, you were an insult to God, blighted a world that wouldn't be sad to see you go. Your hair was a pestilence when exposed to the sky. Under a roof it was a scab. By his own free will he put on the hat.

His street-map mind resembled the confused lines of a jig-saw puzzle without the picture: the maze of an Israelite Jerusalem buttoned at the centre of the world, in the middle of which Elijah ruled for sure. How could you get from A to B when you were rooted for life at Position Z, and Longitude Thirteen ran through the middle of where you stood? To explore the meridian meant getting lost on complicated, large-scale charts and being forced to follow the line downwards till the plain ocean showed you no route of escape. The bigger the ocean, the smaller the cell in which the self was imprisoned. He raised the hat as if greeting his spectators for the first time, lifted it only to put it back again.

"He's a nut case."

The voice was loud, clear and common, startling enough to be heard above the still reasonably polite response from most of his audience. A member of the crew had got into the first class saloon under the erroneous assumption that he had a right to be there — or he had come in via an unobserved crack in the wood. Old Thursdon, wearing a dinner-jacket with his liquorice allsort medal-ribbons at the lapel, sat at a table with a beautiful dark-haired woman he had recently married.

"The bastard will be a bloody basket-case before I've done

255

with him!" shouted the Radio Officer.

Others shared his panic. Chairs fell, and two people ran out of the saloon. A burly passenger, excited at the smell of danger, or from a superfluity of food and alchohol, and released from his inner constrictions by the sudden lack of order in this part of the ship, picked up a table and hurled it so that an enormous split streaked across the mirror, taking Arthur Bingam's malign face back to where it belonged.

"How the hell did he get that *weapon* on board?"

It was easy to spread fear. The story had begun. Ernest swung the long dagger round till his arm ached. A woman called, "He's just a terribly good actor."

Thursdon and his wife walked, dignified, out onto the deck to look at the stars and at phosphorescence dripping from the bow-waves.

He changed it to the other hand, careful to keep his fingers latched as firmly at the haft as that healed cut of a smile clipped across his face. The thin blade was honed to a deadlier keenness than when Uncle Percy lunged with it in Flanders. From the hill-top he watched his audience scatter. A man who wanted to kill him was taken out screaming when they wouldn't allow him to make the attempt.

Ernest tried, as Bernard would have liked him to, to think of his audience as mere spectators, which they were, but they were also Bernard's audience, because Bernard was in control, and if the faces meant anything at all they were, from Ernest's point of view, relegated to the category of frightened onlookers, while to Bernard they were his allies intimidating Ernest into behaving exactly as he – Bernard – wanted them to behave.

The only way to go on with the story was to leap from the summit of his hillock. In spite of uncertainty, he enjoyed watching everyone scatter, though to prove that he himself was the story, he would have to descend among them. It was what he had always wanted, but it would be a matter to shed tears over, nevertheless — or would be if he were telling the story and not living it. He wanted to lie on the floor and go to sleep, but to do so would be like saying a final goodbye to himself, for he would never move again.

He ran to the middle of the saloon. The waiters, the Radio Officer, the Chief Engineer, and a couple of seamen jumped clear. A scarf spun around his eyes. Radio Officers of long experience possess such digital dexterity, not to mention powers of intuition, that they have even more luck than a cat. In avoiding Ernest he collided with the piano, and accidentally strummed a few bars of the popular jungle-jingle that had marinated Bernard's mind most of the day. When an elbow and one hand finished spattering the keys Bernard aimed for his backbone, which seemed to house the tune, but the Radio Officer, still in the throes of his run to get clear, spun on his heels and put himself behind the rounded corner of the bar.

The dagger, however, found someone else — who ran in panic across the Radio Officer's path. The tall thin seaman with shocked eyes, on reaching the door, clutched his forearm and watched blood pour through his clothes and tightened fingers, where the dagger had jabbed at his segment of the spinning scarf. His fingers found the wound and he fell unconscious.

With bitter regret, and in the midst of fixing his all-round defence, as well as a more circular vogue of attack, Ernest knew that this was a story he wouldn't be able to tell like all the others. A pack of tigers circled and would never give him the chance. Bernard laughed at what he had done. Bernard stabbed. The Chief Engineer came close, and felt the blade at his jacket as he avoided the worst of its force. While they stepped around, he spun twice as quickly in the opposite direction, keeping them beyond his perimeter.

"Give me that cleaver," a voice asked. The plea was venomous. "There's a good lad."

His smile wouldn't let him talk.

"Hand it over, you crazy bugger."

It isn't a cleaver. It's killed people. He shaved at the voice, and leapt back. A blow got his chin, and another his forehead, but neither were enough to knock him out, though a blackness overshadowed one eye. A shout drilled through his pain: "Kill him!"

"He's a mad dog!"

They were wrong, he knew. Let me go, Bernard. Release me,

Baker. Unlock me, Psalmanazar. Set me free, Orgill. They solidified to their deepest will. He thrust. His stomach was ash and clinker. He spun. Bernard clutched him, but wasn't absolutely to blame. Honesty surfaced. Reality bit. It was Uncle Percy's dagger, after all. He had gone to the house after the funeral, and it lay on the dressing table. He intended throwing it in the dustbin. Black Albert said, "He wanted you to have it, but wouldn't it be best to get rid of it, man?" And Ernest promised he'd do just that.

"Kill him, before he kills one of us."

A messenger came in: "They've found a woman's body cut to bits in her cabin."

The floor rocked. Would the ship dock to let him off? He didn't want to leave. They stopped moving, and watched from a safe radius. He felt a sickness at being still. Unless he moved, he was weary. They locked him in the fatal story of his own concoction, but couldn't prevent fatigue closing his veins. He was alert, nevertheless.

Tables were lopsided and tripped, drinks spilled, glasses cracked and still lying on the table. Glasses were intact on the floor. No pub or club ever looked so plundered. He laughed. A soda syphon spat itself empty on the bar counter. He waited for more cataclysmic news. Had the Radio Officer tapped out the message saying that the professor had vanished? Maybe they didn't even know he'd gone. That was when his story had begun — as a last effort to push Bernard into doing something which he, Ernest Cotgrave, would be able to hang a tale on. Bernard had done exactly as he had been ordered, driven the professor into a corner, and then accomplished all that could have been expected. But the murderous foray was inconclusive. The lunge had come too late to break into any kind of victory. Before Ernest could turn away they had pushed him into a yarn of their own invention. He stepped into it as if to show that he could do better than they had ever done, and by the time he realised his mistake it was too late to disentangle himself.

"You wouldn't *really* hurt anyone, would you, old son?"

His head was bandsawed and sanded, and caught in the hot plywood presses. He wouldn't, but only if he didn't have to. He wanted to speak. He needed to explain as if — even though it was no longer possible — it would make everything all right again, and normal life would be clocked on once more. This was the last thing they'd let him do, and he knew it. If they allowed him to speak he would only go through the same old circumstances and events, and end exactly where he was now. Even to begin clean from birth would make no difference.

Inside was panic, but his smile stayed firm. No words would come. He was safe inside himself, and would have to die in his own prison.

"We'll look after you," the Chief Engineer promised. "Won't we, Nat?"

The Radio Officer's first name was Nat, Nathan, Nathaniel, and he said nothing, kept his grey pinpoint stare, and a faint tremor at the lips as if too busy collating messages for tapping like gnats and bees back to the owners. There would be much to-ing and fro-ing before the night was finished. His lips licked danger, as if aware that he was living a story at last instead of sending it. I've got *you* weighed up — you psycho-bandit running a protection racket on your own innards. Oh no you haven't, Ernest thought, intercepting his stare.

The company should have known that the storyteller's act would terminate in blood and madness. He was preying on the tripes of everyone in the ship. The intricacies of interlacing minds in this saloon would, if fine-drawn, the Radio Officer thought, keeping well into safety, make the circuit diagram of the transmitters on the *Queen Mary* look like a map of the Wigan Underground.

Bernard leapt, as if there were steam in his feet. Ernest couldn't hold the leash. He didn't altogether want to. He watched Bernard lunge with ferret-like ferocity, and Ernest smiled, enjoying the smell of fear and chaos that seemed a little too easy to cause. Stop it, Bernard. Bernard was too glazed to hear. He scattered tables between himself and the door.

The clean breath of the sea came in, and saved Ernest from sickness. The crab-like grip of the smile didn't seem so tight at his cheeks. People in the saloon had scattered like sparks from a blacksmith's hammer. He was free. There were boards under his feet. He liked the noise. His free hand slid along the wooden rail while running for the companionway to reach a higher deck.

Shouting stayed behind. Bernard liked it. Silence comforted him. Needle-pointed stars swung when Ernest lifted his head. He collided with an air vent, knowing that paint marked the crushed skin of his forehead white. It was warm. He wanted to sit down, but his legs pulled him along. A shadow swung close: it was himself. Scattered crests were luminous from the lights of the ship. Shadows had velocity when they came for him. Over the noise of the breeze he heard occasional shouting and the running clog-steps of seamen. Now *they* were telling the story, not me, nor Bernard. Tannoy voices were getting people back to their cabins. They hadn't expected it, but you never got what you haggled for. God had had the first big word, but the world always wanted the last.

He couldn't cry out for God's help, nor call back and inform those who were searching for him where he was. The hiding place was his alone. He called on God so intensely that he thought his ribs would break. The ship's dimensions were enormous now that he had the decks to himself. There were enough lights by which to see everyone. There were also corners, and he didn't know who stood in them. There were hiding places he hadn't yet found, but perhaps the hunters were already there.

"Come on, we know where you are."

The wind wrapped words around the masts and aerials. He jumped. Was that voice close, Bernard? I don't fucking know, Ernest Cotgrave. One run of the deck remained. The Radio Officer had split the audience into search parties. A series of pincer-packs were running over the ship. He was a lynx-eyed lynchman, a family man who couldn't stand his family. You could see by his face that complications and violence were mother's milk to him. He was in touch with the aether and the universe. O lucky man! – please keep away from me.

He felt them sensing where he was. His vision always became sharper when he heard the howl of a wolf. They'd swarm on both sides. Coming to the upper deck had been a mistake. They blocked all companionways. Collaboration was a blunder. Stupid fucking Bernard. Drop dead, Cotgrave. He should have gone lower, and into the cabin corridors. He decided to try.

Ernest, or Bernard, or maybe even some of the others he'd forgotten about, were feeding the wrong information, pushing him into a situation he wouldn't get out of. Hadn't he always done the same to them? He would do it again if another life came round.

A shadow jumped. Could the fox turn on the hounds? In dodging their envelopment he struck the rail. It was dark air, a blur when cloud moved and the moon glowed. Its topography was as sharp as a map. He wanted to sleep. The pain at his ribs where the rail had struck made him crave to lie full length. He rubbed with both hands, and noticed that he no longer had the knife. It had come a long way from the mud.

Bernard and his mob would push the bitter remnants of his final story down his throat. It was no use looking for a knife that had slid through the rail and into the sea. Percy's dagger had gone to a grave so deep no one would ever find it again – not even St Peter if he went out looking.

He had to play his tale, which now became theirs. Let them drive him through the black hole of their revenge. He must get to his cabin, and pull another weapon from its shammy wrappings. You know where you are, said Bernard. All you've got to do is get 'em. But he'd only come on board with Uncle Percy's dagger-knife.

Their story was different, and led him towards a trap at every step. They had other ideas. His fate was bundled with theirs. He was a storyteller, but their stories would consume him. He had never let them know his next move when their balance had been in the offing from knockabout pillar to the last heartbreaking post in his tales, so why should they consider his feelings? His brain was a bunch of living nettles on which tiny insects of his thoughts lapsed into pain and disaster. Boots stamped on everything. He tried to throw Bernard out of himself. He spun, and sprawled painfully on the deck.

They heard. He got to his feet without wanting to, and ran. It was a few more yards to the cabins, if he could reach the aft companionway. It stared, an enormous cavern-mouth in the moonlight.

"We've got him. *Don't* let him get away."

They hadn't. They wouldn't. They wore red coats and carmine jackets. They had crimson cheeks and scarlet hands, and stabbed back at the woodwork with glittering spurs: "Tally-ho!"

"I'll believe it when we have."

"Put both boots in, Sparks."

Sparks laughed: "I wish I was a fucking octopus!"

They all laughed. They roared. They were a good audience, but it wasn't his story anymore.

He knocked a grunt down. An open mouth missed his elbow. Ernest ran. Bernard was a strong man who had laboured all his life. It would need more than two or three sailors, and a few enthusiasts of ancient Greek civilisation in full spate, to stop him on a track made good.

Ernest had time to do three knee bends before they came from fore and aft. A mob at each end left no entrance by which to avoid them.

"He's lost his knife."

"Get him. And no mistakes."

They shone a crushing lighthouse-light from a tall tower against the foundering shipwreck of his brain. A giant hosepipe was slotted into a nozzle, steel to steel, ready to send waves roaring across the deck.

"We can't be sure."

"Flush the swine."

In running down the steps, and knocking the man aside, he lost his hat. Ernest threw off his mackintosh, and hurled it against their legs. He climbed onto the rail. He was free, and fell, and took with him all the people he had ever drawn out of himself. The noise in his ears as he hit the water was that of a giant snowball dropping into fire.

Part Three

2I

The paper was blank to start with, and of quarto size. It was thick enough not to show his writing through the other side, except dimly when held to the electric light. Harriet had decided that nothing but the best was good enough. A bottle of ink, and a wooden-handled pen with a sharp brass nib, were set in front of him, but all he had written so far was: *Elijah rules*, before attempting to bring his chronicle to a proper and satisfactory state of conclusion.

He didn't need guiding-lines because with such a pen he was unable to write quickly – it being necessary to dip the nib every few words. When he began, the lines came out straight and close and black, as if he had had much practice.

He thought the penholder was wood. It may have been plastic. He believed the nib was brass, but it could have been steel. Time, as always, would tell most things. Without the cry of a wolf he couldn't see as clearly as before. The holder was painted black, and the nib was coated with its shine of ink, so he couldn't really discern what they were, and he didn't much care, though he considered it would be useful to come to a decision before getting on with the rest of it. To be plagued by needling uncertainties, while drawing complex events from a disordered memory, was hard to bear. The only thing in life that didn't change was the smell of ink.

Lines on the paper were useful to prevent his thoughts from travelling to other worlds. He wondered if he weren't the only storytelling yentering yetti outside the snows of Tibet. Butter wouldn't melt in his abominable buttonholes. When the nib snapped he thought that the swirling blade was indeed mightier than the penholder, but whatever else he believed, he was sure that, in his final days, the end also would be colonised by the word, and that he who lives by the word dies by the word.

He reflected that the purpose of such observations was to find one's true self (if there was such a thing, though he was close enough to a conclusion to decide that perhaps there was, after all) and then stay loyal to it. But during the long circum-navigating voyage you must be loyal to those concepts that set you going in the first place, because they alone will enable you to recognise your true self when you find it.

"Each word is a bag of flesh and blood," he said, winding his last interconnected serial of stories and life-tales to an end, two days before the ship was due at Southampton. "Bernard-Ernest found it so," he went on, "as Ernest-Bernard leapt over the rail with the clear intention of dying. But when the salt-water world closed around him/them he wanted air again. Coming up from the icy fire of sheath-like darkness, and avoiding the fishes by shutting his heart-valves tight from their cold-eyed con-sciousness, his arms began to shift and his sight to see.

"Every action proved that, right or wrong, it was the obvious thing to do. The rest of the world took notice when he had got out his knife. The effect was precipitate and tremendous. They sur-rounded him. He was the threat of the moment, their deadly enemy. They were *his* foe, yet when they reacted as such he almost looked on them as his friends, though such tentative amity was not returned. As their vigilance appeared to slacken, he stabbed and leapt. When they closed in with loathing, they became his friends again. But when that detestation turned into a sport, there was nothing to do but leap into the sea.

"Likewise in this final action – when he hoped it would be the end but found instead that dying was a privilege he had not yet earned by suffering, or age, or the nobility of self-sacrifice, or by a sudden and arbitrary blow which it was not his to make and which he would not know about in any case – he came to the sur-face and was assailed by one lifebelt, and then another. They still hated him for having shaken their comfortable world, though they did not want him to drown. He found lifebelts around him in sufficient numbers, as if the latest craze in deck-games was something called *Man Overboard*, by which they were lobbed at the target of his bobbing head. When the overhanging shadow of the ship's stern drew away, he pulled one and then another close so that, as long as he could grip, he would not sink into that abyssal void of water under his waving feet."

The saloon filled during his final chapter. They sat quietly. There was neither a free chair nor empty space. At the beginning of the cruise a couple of dozen passengers had come to hear what he had to say, though most preferred whist or chess or bridge. But after a few sessions, the lecture on classical sites in antiquity had to be given a different hour in the timetable, because too many deserted it to hear the serial-saga of Ernest Cotgrave's life.

In the first week it was hard for him to go through his evening's excerpt before so few people. Many missed the details of his childhood at the hands of Baker, some only came in at the beginning of Ernest Cotgrave's life as a storyteller. He told them quite early on that he and Cotgrave were different people. You couldn't be too careful with such an audience. At the same time he admitted that there were similarities in the details of their existences, (it would have been foolish not to emphasise this) though he hoped the parallels weren't so close as far as their fates were concerned. Before the half-way mark, nearly everyone came to listen, which condemned him to a lonely state on ship-board, for as he walked the decks or stood at the bar no one cared to talk to him in case they disturbed him from composing his story. He understood, but at the same time did not like being ignored. He was a quiet walker, and once overheard a group talking about what they might expect in future instalments.

This was the first time he had devised a more-or-less unified tale, but he did it only so as to make his three-week task of entertaining a shipful of passengers easier than inventing a score of separate pieces. Going by the number of listeners on this final night, as the ship crossed a Biscay which lacked the chop and gloom of the outward leg, he didn't doubt that it had been a sensible tactic. The shipping company might well ask him to do the same stint another year, perhaps on a different ship (they had enough to make it an annual holiday) though he could not believe, judging by the way he saw the end of his story, that he would be in a position to accept such an offer.

The long days on board had shown him how to rejoin his body and his spirit. The elemental force of God was seen in isolation, as the uprising and crumbling green bread of the water blackened on hitting the ship. Despite stabilisers, powerful engines, and officers in whom one could implacably trust, it threatened every nut, bolt and bulkhead with disintegration. He had also learned to talk, to live, to tell a tale, to unload his heart through the backdoor of well-disguised confession every night. Apart from getting paid at the end of the journey, there had been hints of a collection as well. Jesters were highly considered on this kind of jaunt, though in some ways he was looking forward to getting back to London.

"What will you do after this job?" the young American woman had asked as they were passing between the Pillars of Hercules under warm sunshine.

"When I was a kid in school," he said, "and heard the teacher talk about the *Pillars* of Hercules, I thought that Gibraltar and Ceuta were two great rocky *pillows* on which the giant laid both his heads every night!"

"It's no surprise," she said, "that you became a storyteller."

"Too much experience was open to misunderstanding," he went on, "so it was impossible not to. When I get home I'll visit Lonely Len in his cottage on the Yorkshire Moors. He's a squalid old man, in reality, stinking of piss and tobacco, except when he has a bath and dresses impeccably to feed the mallard ducks in Nottingham. Normally, he's as scruffy as hell, though he does wear a collar and tie while bending over a huge iron pot in the hearth to stir his foul stew of liver, lights and swedes. 'I'm glad you've come,' he'll say. 'I've got a story for thee.' They all say that, but Len goes on: 'A man were out in a winter's blizzard to check the level of the reservoir up on the moors. Two hours went by and he didn't come back. So his son of eighteen sets out from his cottage to look for him, telling his mother not to worry, because he'll find his feyther. He knew every stone backwards, whether snowflakes covered 'em or not. But the lad didn't come back, either. A month later, snow melts, and they found bodies clinging together near north side o' reservoir. One death was

268

duty. T'other was love. You can't do better than that, can you?'
'No, Len,' I'll say, 'love or duty — it won't do. It's not enough. It
just won't do. That's a newspaper story. That sort's ten a penny.
I want *real* stories, Len, soul-yarns, heart-tales, and that
summat-else as everybody's hard-put to give a name to. I can't
live with yap-crap anymore, and I'll feel better when nobody else
can, either.' 'Nay,' he says, ready to turn nasty, as only a solitary
bloke can, 'I give thee stories. I'm as good as the Bible. Brought
up on it. It's up to thee to tell 'em like that — properly. Anyway,
that man killed near the reservoir was my father, and his son was
my brother.' He seems heartbroken at such a memory, that he
dredged up for my benefit. I realise he's getting close, even
though he'll never get there, so I sit and listen to a few more tales,
then give him the bottle of whisky I brought with me, and leave
him to his stew and tea, and an evening of tears-and-swillpig all
on his own. As I walk away down the path I hear the foul old liar
kicking the guts out of his dog, and ranting death and damnation
against all storytellers who only want to pick his brains and blud-
geon his heart with a sledgehammer.''

It was no laughing matter, even though the feather-down,
grey-blue Pillars were still visible. ''I like your stories, though,''
she told him. ''This trip has been good for me.''

''Thank you'' — hoping she liked him as well.

''I've seen so much.''

Her name was Harriet.

''And heard so much. I don't know how I'll live without seeing
those wonderful sights, and hearing your stories.''

''One day,'' he decided, ''if I can get the money together, I'll
buy my own premises, and go into private practice, in Harley
Street. I'll have a notice in the window, and a brass nameplate
saying: STORYTELLER. ALL STORIES GUARANTEED
TRUE. I might have an address-card printed: 'Storyteller, traveller, and doctor of the soul' — doctor of every soul, that is, except
my own. Highborn women and Japanese tourists will flock to
hear my tales though.''

''It's a great idea.'' She wasn't certain of his seriousness, but
decided to laugh.

''The first real stories I heard was when my father told lies to my mother. He performed long, colourful, circumstantial accounts to explain his doings with other women. I'd seen him once, twice, no – three times altogether. I noticed the effect of his tales on my mother. Sometimes they didn't work, and she was in a terrible state. I knew from then on that I could do much better than my father's lies if I tried. I was glad I found out about him going with another woman because up to then I'd thought he might be queer. I don't know why I was glad, considering how much suffering it caused my mother. As a kid I was miserable for years, or just plain bored. I'd say, when I was alone: 'Talk to me. Let's have a story' – and I began telling myself all sorts of adventures, drifting my way into a happy sleep."

There was a faint corrugation in the pale blue sea where the Atlantic was, as usual, trying to get into the couloir of the Mediterranean. The ship had left it now, so it didn't matter. It often played up rough around here, even on the most promising days, the Radio Officer had told him. He'd made friends with the Radio Officer, a quiet, soft-spoken, middle-aged man from Wigan who had been in the RAF, the only officer on board whom he could talk to with ease.

"At the moment," Harriet said, "You make me want to weep, I don't know why." Her hair was jet black, and led like a rope over her shoulder. It was the part of her that came closest to him. Glasses protected her brown eyes, but he could see that they were near to letting tears fall.

"I don't mean to." He spoke into her ear, then kissed it lightly. "The infancy of a storyteller is peculiar. I never knew which leg of my trousers to get into first. I used to put my left leg in the right trouser – and fall flat on my face. I couldn't tell the time till I was twelve, because both hands of the clock always seemed the same length. I didn't know my left hand from my right till I was fourteen, because to me they seemed identical, like my legs, eyes and ears. I'll never forget the moment I learned to tie my shoelaces into a bow instead of a knot. It affected me as a revelation much like it must have felt to the man who first stepped ashore in America – or onto the moon. I was already eight years old, and from then on I hardly ever looked back in my dealings with the world."

"Tell me more." Her eyes weren't entirely relaxed when she laughed.

"I dredge my soul, even without trying, hoping to bring up ambrosia instead of life's bile. I'm falling into split-infinity. All my life I've been expecting the sun to rise in the west instead of the east. Now I feel it happening at last. I can't make it out. It comes up from America and drops away on the wrong horizon — or the right one for me. It must mean that I've fallen in love, in an old-fashioned sort of way. I think it's the only way left to me of feeling anything."

He had long ago noted the high forehead, with the faint vein showing vertically down the middle when she laughed. He saw the gentle arching of her nose, and the small mouth with slightly downturned fleshy lips. After his yarning stint last night he had met her on deck, and they stood at the door of the night club, with its flashing lights tearing at the eyes, and bongo rhythms kicking the brain. To be locked in such murder-music was a storyteller's nightmare. With the slight swell of the sea it made him feel sick. She held onto him, a hand at his elbow. They didn't speak, then said good night and went to their cabins. Three weeks had lasted months. At the ruins of Delphi she had taken his hand while ascending the steep slippery steps to the Theatre. He had walked with her in Jerusalem, the capital city of Israel. She held his hand now. He sensed that she needed something from him, and he didn't know what it could be.

"When I first came aboard," he said, "and saw you, I never thought you'd talk to me in a million years. You've no idea how insignificant storytellers can feel. It's part of their pride, the arrogance of emptiness that forces them to perform."

"Stop telling stories." Her tone came as close to a plea as she could find in herself at this phase of their acquaintance, and he knew suppressed anguish when he heard it. "*Talk* to me, instead."

But he was remorseless, though knew she was strong enough in her soul to take it. She always would be, so he could press as hard as he liked. "I only feel human when I'm telling stories on that stage in the saloon. Otherwise I'd be no more than a somewhat pathetic and apathetic peripatetic!"

"Stop it." But she was calmer now.

His chance had gone. She was strong. When the full force of his relentlessness was about to let itself go he always pulled it back. "What will you do when you get to England?" he asked.

"Take a plane to New York," she said. "Maybe go to my husband."

He gripped her arm, so that she faced him: "Don't."

Her eyes were more beautiful when she was startled, or didn't understand, or when she wanted him to imagine that he puzzled her in some way. They shone.

"Don't go back," he said.

She laughed.

"Stay with me."

"I can't do that."

"Never go back to him."

"I'm not a person in one of your stories."

"I know that," he said, "more than I've ever known anything in my life before."

"You'd better."

"I'll break out of my storytelling for ever."

She showed him the depth of her weariness. "You don't have to. Just don't involve me in them. It's no use sacrificing anything for me. I don't want any man. At least, that's how I feel now."

"You don't have to want me. Only don't let us lose sight of each other."

She hesitated, but said nothing.

"Like England and America," he smiled, "we have a 'special relationship'."

The luxury cruise was coming to an end, so he would finish his tale. Back in England he would lock again into the same round of club, pub and meeting hall. Or would he? Perhaps he'd live off this tale for ever, though he could not see how he'd have another chance of such a long-time captive audience.

By imprisoning them he had gaoled himself, and could see no livable existence beyond the docking at Southampton. He had relished his three meals a day, valued his place to sleep, and enjoyed the circumscribed parlourdrome of ever-changing views in which to walk. There had been no worries, as long as he went on quarrying into the continent of his tale each evening. Three weeks had altered him in a way that the imagination could not have warned him of. One may speculate about the future, but not imagine it. The tale had involved him too deeply to let him walk back onto the quayside, with a careless wave and see-you-all-next-year-if-we-are-lucky. If he survived the decompression chamber he would find himself back in the deepest bilges of reality. However much he changed, and whatever happened, Elijah Ruled, and he had to make sure that the victims in his story also knew it.

22

Tonight was the winding up of the Ernest Cotgrave saga. He would bring the story in from the spin of the waves and the blight of the wind. The last day on board would be needed for packing, for handing out tips, and filling in forms ready to land on Friday. So ended his tale:

"When Bernard was in the water, many thoughts went through his mind but, it must be admitted, they came mostly from Ernest. Bernard felt a crippling horror of the dark sea and receding ship. He cried out, and struggled to be saved. He called for light, warmth and food. He wanted a roof. He needed to see faces. He craved to hear speech. He wished for the friendly bark of a dog before he died. There was no heaven on earth like Ashfield.

"Ernest tried to pull him under, wondering why he should want to live. If you don't pack it in, Baker said, I'll kick the snot out of your nose. Ernest heard some of the audience baying for blood in their posh voices. They leaned along the rail, he supposed, like spectators at a dolphinarium. Members of the crew were closing in, to lynch him in real Baker style. Beyond their Scylla and Charybdis was heavy-booted justice to kick him around for the rest of his life. He saw the situation in its devastating simplicity, and closed his ears to it. He let go of both lifebelts, and watched the all-visible, intense colour lift onto a shallow crest and wash away. There was space under the water, a palace of dazzling lights, as in the time of long ago beneath the surface of Martins Pond. Sinewy monsters were settling in for the rip. His legs were like coatsleeves with no arms inside, and snakes were swimming up. He pushed his arms above his head, intending to smash the ice.

"Bernard had fainted at the previous telling of it in the pub, and preferred to wait for mid-shift, in a narrow seam deep underground, before getting stuck into his snap. He shook water from his eyes, looked at the stars, and extended his freezing arms towards the lifebelts. There was an eye in his snap-tin, and a finger. He latched onto one. It was a lifebelt with a water-activated battery. A light shone from it. The ship lay cliff-on. Ernest grappled to pull him under. In fighting clear, Bernard's leg lost all feeling. His body ended at the thighs, leaving the ache of cramp below. He screamed that they were biting his legs off. The water stopped his bawling, and it took all his life-force to stay under the stars. Shut up, you coward, Ernest shouted. If we die now, we won't face it later. Bernard was tired to death. Ernest had a vision of the whale, whose enormous open-mouthed wall was as big as the factory-side, lines of windows he had once looked at suddenly becoming the Leviathan to shelter and eventually save him. He saw towering lights, the warm presence, the ship's foul breath. It was the only thing at hand. He wanted to go down. Neither God, nor the ship, nor men in the boat allowed him to. You couldn't fight a factory wall. It stank of oil, of foul air from the vents, of paint and stale food.

"His eyes closed. A chain rattled. Satan would welcome him, as his mother had sworn he one day would if he didn't obey the Laws of Life. He tried to prise his eyes open.

"The lifeboat came close, ribs and planks sheering out of the water, a presence even more threatening than the liner's escarpment. He felt that, should he swim away, he might even have the stamina to stay on the surface till he reached land. But thinking of escape only weakened him. Bernard's heart was worn out by its long ordeal of life. Ernest was dragged aboard, to the city-lights of the ship. Full of rage, he began fighting, to throw himself back into the water where Bernard had gone down.

"'I'll keep the bastard quiet.' He was too precious to lose, the boatswain told himself. He's got a reckoning to pay. He aimed a blow, and the light that swept over Ernest became so bright that it extinguished his brain.

"It was a week before an orderly in the sick bay asked:

" 'What made you do it, mate?'

"He was the same man who, when Ernest had previously gashed his hand with the bayonet, had called him 'sir' while putting the dressing on. Ernest thought he was asking why he'd saved himself, instead of drowning like any self-respecting man after what he had done. 'I wasn't. I was rescued.'

"He didn't know why he had stayed alive, except that the salt water separated him from Bernard (and all the rest) and pushed him clear. He could not talk, so there was nothing to be said in response to the orderly's question.

"The Radio Officer worked hours beyond the call of his duty. For a while it was his story, and nobody elses. = SADISTIC KILLER LOOSE ON CRUISE LINER = MASTER + The news bounced around the world. As a press item it came before a hi-jacking in the United States. There was no need to spin it to the bitter end. Ernest told the story to himself continually, could not sleep because the talk went on and on, repeating itself with all embroidered details till he died again from exhaustion. He was the chief character, which is what he'd always wanted to be. It was assumed that he had also killed the professor, and heaved the body overboard. Two more people had gone from the ship. In his tale, Ernest caused one newspaper to speculate on what would have happened if Bernard had been on a *world* cruise. But Bernard was dead, he told them. He had drowned. They wouldn't believe him. All power to Psalmanazar. From being a storyteller he had become a sinner. He had sacrificed everything. The others had robbed him by letting him stay alive after their story had ended but, as he consoled himself during his years in Broadmoor, even a storyteller couldn't have everything.

"He regretted that they didn't hang murderers anymore. He would have had the best story of all, especially if he had been executed in public before a raving mob that streamed out of pubs and clubs and football grounds to see it happen. Yet if he had been killed for his crimes he would not have been able to tell the story afterwards, either to himself or others. On long summer afternoons he boasted how he had been hanged. It made a better climax than any he had devised in the past. Whether it happened or not was immaterial. It was the one reminder of the life when he had been a teller of confected yarns. As a solid item of self-indulgence, he gave into it because he could not bear to be deprived of what had taken him so long to earn. The eternal soul was grateful for whatever mercies God and the world inflicted on it.

"Storytellers, like electronics engineers, have to make sure no loose ends hang from the black box of their tricks. Not only that, but the black box has to work in the expected way when switches are thrown, knobs clicked, panels slid, and aerials slotted in. There is more chance of smooth working when the circuit diagram is faithfully adhered to, and all connections made at their allotted points.

"The place wherein the end of this story took place was a loony bin. The professor walked in one day, carrying a basket of out-of-season fruit. Jason Wright had a generous spirit, in spite of his idiosyncratic aspect and more than occasional cantankerousness.

"'Hello, Cotgrave!'

"'Hello, sir!'

"'I've come to take you out of here.'

"Ernest laughed at such flippant wickedness, knowing that no one could get him his freedom this side of a miracle cure for brain damage.

"'Well, one day, I may. Or somebody might. But I'll keep you in mind.'

"'Thank you.'

"'Don't take it so badly. You had a good run. Better this, than drying up as a storyteller. ''One crowded hour of glorious life, is worth an age without a name''? What?'

"Ernest smiled. He was perfectly sane, but pure, and empty. 'I did try to kill you.'

"'I know, my boy. People have. Daresay they'll try again. I can't altogether blame them. But nobody ever got up early enough to succeed. Or stayed up *very* late at night. But your meat-skewer came damned close. Good thing I jumped into that door leading to the crews' quarters. Stayed till the ship got to Jebel Tarik, then hopped it. One of the waiters who looked after me was a fetching young chap. Apollo's cousin, I swore, as soon as he pushed in the light button. Had the time of our lives. He still comes to see me, when he's ashore.' His sigh of regret was like the sound of an iron door closing on a furnace. 'I suppose I'll settle down one day, perhaps find a datcha at Delphi, or a cottage at Corinth – even a *pied-à-terre* in the Piraeus. But I'm glad your tale-yammering days are over, Ernest. Telling stories must be a terrible thing, whether you scribble 'em, or talk 'em, because sooner or later you come out with whatever's going to happen to you, and who wants to do a rum thing like that? You think you're expounding your past (not to mention other peoples') or making up stories out of thin air, but you're spinning your own future. The more exciting the matter, the less likely is it that the future is going to be a peaceful and happy one. I must, therefore, add one more "Never" to my list, which is: Never tell stories!'

"'Haven't you got just one "Always" for me?' Cotgrave whined.

"The professor thought for a moment. He didn't need to, but wanted to get everything possible out of Cotgrave's unhappy situation. If Cotgrave knew he was doing this, and he plainly would, being a broken-down and captive storyteller, then he would feel better – surely (somewhere) – at this touch of genuine life. It was bound to do him more good – providing it did him any good – than listening to a rodomontade of useless sympathy. 'Yes – I have. My last Always is: Always keep on trying to escape from this place!'

The professor left his basket of fruit. Ernest was glad he had been saved from killing him. Bernard was no longer in his heart or hands. Bernard was cock o' the walk, working underground, king of triumphs, back with Eileen and their kids, his old car, the dog and a front-and-back garden in an Ashfield he'd never left and probably never would.

"Which brings my chronicle and my performance to an end except for this. . . ."

23

He lifted the knife, and drew it across his throat. Harriet was unable to see whether or not he had gashed himself. It might have been a premonition of the approaching reality. When it came, her sensations were irrelevant. It could not be denied, however, that she was the first to shout a warning.

They imagined his stance to be a tableau specially devised for bringing his series of entertainments to such a conclusion that they would not forget his performances in a hurry. It resembled his own story all over again. Anyone could see that.

The appearance of the knife came too quickly for them to feel alarmed. People hardly ever believed what was in front of their eyes. No sane practitioner of life would expect them to. A girl was raped at a bus stop, and none of the people in the queue either did or said anything. They turned away, too embarrassed to believe that what they were seeing was actually happening. If someone was being attacked, it was none of their business. They were in the land of the free. "And if a soul sin, and hear the voice of swearing, and is a witness, whether he hath seen or known of it; if he do not utter it, then he shall bear his iniquity." They did not allow Leviticus to rule, as they should have done. Every Englishman's home is his indifference. These people on shipboard were the same. At some time in the past, their nerve ends had been disconnected, and they had connived in it.

He lifted the knife, ready to spin among them in an attempt to tear the hemisphere of coloured gossamer to shreds. I would sink the ship, except that I'm on it. We can't go down together. He couldn't tell them so. Even wireless communication had been broken. The radio operator had seen to that. It was too late to hope that the boilers would burst, the masts collapse, the bed of the sea shoot up a rock to rip the bottom of the ship and inundate it before one solitary boat could get close for the rescue-snatch. He could tell them nothing. All listening faculties had gone. Elijah ruled – if anyone did.

The splintering of applause sounded as if the ship were falling apart. The noise subsided to a buffalo-stumping of appreciative feet. His stance, with a bare knife completing the upward hook of his arm, seemed an apposite end to his series of tales. Homely and understandable, it fitted their sense of humour, and still accorded with honour and good taste. It was no vulgar joke, but a dramatic finish that matched what had gone before. It paid homage, and with an artistry they found pleasing, to his own prolonged effort of keeping them entertained during the trip. In a pub he would have been labelled a bit of a card. His storyteller-heart intended precisely that, but their amused response, and more recognition than he felt he deserved, set him on a final vector.

Perhaps it was caused by Harriet's scream. He was in love with her, so she understood him more than anyone else. She certainly sympathised with him, at this moment, more than he did with himself. This assumption, right or wrong, set him onto a certain track which he hoped to make good.

The occasion called for speed, but his inability to muster it amounted to sufficient hesitation within the passing of the moment which proved fatal. Paralysis of will had not been part of his plan. Unlike the hero of his story, he was split between energy and space. As a storyteller, with no experience of defeat, he gave in too quickly at the first breath of it.

He brought the knife swiftly down towards his stomach. The current of applause oscillated. It encountered resistance, then stopped as if turned off by a light-switch because they saw at last what was likely to happen.

The Radio Officer, a small, quiet, dark-haired man in his forties, whom one would not have imagined to be the sort of person to tackle a potentially sadistic killer about to break loose on a cruise liner, acted with speed and in silence. He moved to a position behind him, as a man would who had lived among the headline message-reality of the spheres. Knowing what must be done, he did not hesitate. At radio school, many years ago, the only other person who had been able to take morse faster than his thirty-six words per minute had gone mad before the end of the course. He grabbed his arms so forcefully that he was unable to bring his story to a conclusion in the only way that mattered.

The audience watched the struggle. Even now, they had their doubts as to the authenticity of the drama, which might only have been a pre-arranged plot on the part of the storyteller (and his friend the Radio Officer) to drag out the final thrill of his story's conclusion. Some assumed so, to judge by lingering smiles, and the occasional facial twitch of curiosity. A few thought it might be carrying things a little too far, and that such collusion could be a threat to civilised values – which should not be held too lightly on a ship at sea.

The Chief Steward, pink-faced, spruce and grey-haired, cap over wrist, walked in from the deck. He kicked the dagger from the storyteller's hand, but not till the point had scored blood from the right forearm of the left-handed Radio Officer.

In less than a minute of latitude, a squalid and humiliating end had been averted. Drinks were served to cover the embarrassment of a minor incident near the voyage's finish, it being not unknown for them to occur at such a time.

24

Detectives and police were there when the ship docked. Messages, transmitted via the glad-hand of Land's End radio in the form of electrical words, had warned the forces of law-and-order to wait for him. A vicious attack with a knife was a serious charge, yet England was reasonable with madmen, even lenient. Friendly doctors had got him to this private Lunatic Compound instead of gaol. The Radio Officer's gash was not deep enough to stop him sending morse and quickly healed. He testified in court to nothing more than an aberration on the part of his one-time friend, supposing that the three-week strain had been too much for him. He was commended by the magistrate for his courage – and his sense of forbearance towards the accused.

A late summer wind slipped in from the east. They had cut off the central heating. Mental cases had their internal supply, generated by suffering. They kept warm by working, or eating, or by propelling themselves around the grounds till they began to lick the soil. One man walked on hands-and-knees for three days. After electric shock treatment he shambled, though more or less upright. The institution was designed for getting psychically disturbed people back into the ways of the world. Some were stuck eternally in its door.

He preferred to be a spectator, and observe how they handled spades among the vegetables. They obeyed the unwritten rules of using them harmlessly, biding their time for when they got out. He wielded his pen every spare minute, hoping it would turn into something mightier than the rake, spade, fork, hoe or bayonet, kris, kukri, panga, matchette, Wapping chiv or Hastings chopper.

He buttoned his jacket. His sweater had been stolen, but he would get it back as soon as he discovered who the would-be Leveller had been, for it would be more accurate to say it had been borrowed, though whatever he called the action he was still without its warmth, and the day was raw. He would be free of the place in a couple of weeks. There was no more danger in him than in anyone standing under a railway bridge at midnight, or behind bushes, or in a room before the light was pulled on. He had been through his de-intoxication chamber, and had brought himself back to consciousness with his pen-and-ink narrative of the *Psalmanazar* cruise. Harriet told him, as part of *her* story, that maybe she would not abandon him, after all. When, passing between the Pillars of Hercules, he had pleaded with her not to go back to her husband, but to come away with him, she had intended to say no – not by words, but by action. She would go to the States, so as to forget him and his stories.

With his storyteller's thirteenth sense he knew that she had refused him when she had not unequivocally accepted his idea at the time. She was the sort in whom hesitation indicated a negative response. To consider an issue before giving an answer meant a definite no. If the 'no' came quickly, however, it meant that there was some hope of a change of mind. If she had given this positive 'no' speedily enough he would have seen sufficient hope not to have made his despairing play with the knife at the end of his cruise-ship story. The vaguest hint of an ultimate 'yes' from Harriet would have held him back. He was sure of it. Yet you could never be certain – unless you were a storyteller, in which case it might not matter whether you were or not.

Harriet confessed that for most of her Mediterranean cruise she had been in a numbed state – except during the hours of his story. She had come back to a pained wakefulness at such times. His intricately ravelled tale had put life into her. The fact that it had drained it out of him was not apparent. He seemed – at the time – to thrive on the telling. He appeared to be inspired by it. All she knew was that it had put the love of life back into her. What it had done to him hadn't seemed important. His subconscious had been working to an end of its own, which couldn't be bad in the final manifestation. She talked at length, and he had wallowed in the luxury of listening – which was all he could do.

After six years being married, Harriet and her husband had decided on a 'temporary separation', she said, continuing her story. In order to reorient her life she had set off to see the Mediterranean. It had not been her intention to meet anyone who might influence her, or even interest her. She craved to be alone. She needed freedom. She did not want to go back to her husband, except to sever a few business connections.

She had no desire to see him after the boat docked, but the performance of his final excerpt changed her mind. He had played with illusion and reality once too often. Such an exhibition made a sufficiently deep impression for her to become fixed in a trap from which she could not escape. It didn't alter her. But she stayed, caught by his final act of folly, fealty and courage. What he had done out of despair because she would never see him again had caused her to stay with him after all.

He was afraid to enquire how long she would wait. To do so might bring an answer that would make his life insupportable. She saw that he relied on her. He realised that she was beginning to depend on him. What started in mutual attraction might end in the freedom of compatibility.

"I'm glad you stayed," he wrote, one afternoon in the visitors' room.

She laughed, saying that all she'd done was provide the ink and paper, and he'd damned-well better use it. She took nothing in earnest, it seemed, and there was enough therapy in such an abrasive spirit to last a long time. Flexibility returned to him under the barrage of her wit and scorn. She showed him how to negotiate the treacherous by-ways of illusion and reality with the sacred proportion of intelligence and humour.

Harriet had more than enough for both, and because he took to it so readily she stayed longer than she'd intended. "I've got money, so I can afford to," she said the following week.

He was planning his next story, in which neither he nor anyone he knew would take part. "We'll find a remote cottage, and in the evening have a poacher's supper," he wrote quickly in block capitals on the small lineless sheet of paper.

"What's that?"

He was still in danger from his stories, and she watched him bend his back to the pad. He carried stubs of pencil in every waistcoat pocket. "Rabbit stew and rhubarb pie! It'll be autumn, and cold, so I'll light a fire. Getting a fire to go is an act of love."

"I know," she said. "But you need more than fire."

"The highest expression of love." It was as good a way to tell her as any. He thought before writing: "Mutually beneficial – if you'll allow me to say so – you get wood and paper into position like a bird building a nest. Then you light it, and manoeuvre the sticks so that they catch. Placing the logs needs great care, but flames soon warm the room."

She held his hand: "For God's sake!"

"I don't care where that room is. To know what you want in life is the only victory." He went to throw his bits of paper out of the window, but she took them from him:

"They're mine, now."

He watched a man who was watering the vegetables lose control of his hose-pipe. It spun from both hands like an anaconda because someone at the tap around the corner of the conservatory had turned it on to its fullest extent. The nozzle lay among rows of peas, while it spouted and made mud. He held both hands together, and smiled, but looked as if he were in pain, and as if it were the first problem he'd had to tackle. Five minutes later he set off with a murderous look, to find the man who had turned up the water pressure.

He remembered that as a child he had known spiritual servitude. And even before that, his soul had been in bondage. It could never be any different for a storyteller. Everyday he thought he saw Harriet walking along the drive.

"You're leaving," she said, coming out of the main office with papers in her hand. "I've got plane tickets for tomorrow."

He shaped the word 'where?' with his lips. The storyteller in him had won. He had come through the jungle into a garden, and had one more story to tell.

GENERAL FICTION

CYRIL ABRAHAM

Δ	042616184X	The Onedin Line: The High Seas	80p
Δ	0426172671	The Onedin Line: The Trade Winds	80p
Δ	0352304006	The Onedin Line: The White Ships	95p

BRUCE STEWART

| Δ | 0352305738 | The Onedin Line: The Turning Tide | £1.25 |

TESSA BARCLAY

| | 0352304251 | A Sower Went Forth | £1.50 |

JUDY BLUME

| | 0352302712 | Forever | 75p* |

ANDRÉ BRINK

	035230703X	A Dry White Season	£1.95
	0352305916	Rumours of Rain	£1.95
	0352306904	An Instant in the Wind	£1.95

ADRIAN BROOKS

| | 0352307773 | The Glass Arcade | £1.50 |

JACKIE COLLINS

Δ	0352395621	The Stud	85p
	0352300701	Lovehead	95p
	0352398663	The World is Full of Divorced Women	£1.25
Δ	0352398752	The World is Full of Married Men	75p

CATHERINE COOKSON

	0426163796	The Garment	95p
	0426163524	Hannah Massey	95p
	0426163605	Slinky Jane	95p

HENRY DENKER

	0352396067	The Physicians	95p*
	0352300523	A Place for the Mighty	75p*
	0352303522	The Experiment	£1.50*

GENERAL FICTION

		KELLY STEARN	
	0352306378	**Consequences**	**£1.25**
Δ	0352302968	KATHLEEN TYNAN **Agatha**	**75p***
	035230183X	DOROTHY UHNAK **Policewoman**	**75p***
Δ	035230684X	GERALD WALKER **Cruising**	**95p***
	0352301570	MARGARET WALKER **Jubilee**	**95p***
Δ	035230667X	DIANE MASTERS WATSON **The Rose (Colour illus.)**	**£2.95***
Δ	0352304421	DAVID WEIR **The Water Margin**	**£1.50**
	0352303271	ALAN PARKER **Puddles in the Lane**	**70p**
	0427004470	GRAHAM PARKER **The Great Trouser Mystery (Large Format illus)**	**£3.95**
	0352304533	MOLLY PARKIN **Fast and Loose**	**95p**
	0352300809	**Love All**	**95p**
	0352397179	**Up Tight**	**95p**
	0352302631	**Switchback**	**95p**
	0352302151	**Good Molly Ms Molly (illus) NF**	**£1.25**
	035230331X	**Purple Passages (illus poetry)**	**£1.25**
Δ	0352303581	JACK RONDER **The Lost Tribe**	**£1.50**
	0352398779	FIONA RICHMOND **Fiona**	**75p**
	0352303808	**The Story Of I**	**75p**
	0352305215	**On The Road**	**75p**
	0352305568	**The Good, The Bad and The Beautiful**	**95p**
	0352307471	**Galactic Girl**	**95p**

...m Books are obtainable from many booksellers ...sagents. If you have any difficulty please send ...e price plus postage on the scale below to:

Wyndham Cash Sales,
PO Box 11,
Falmouth,
Cornwall

OR

Star Book Service,
G.P.O. Box 29,
Douglas,
Isle of Man,
British Isles.

While every effort is made to keep prices low, it is sometimes necessary to increase prices at short notice. Wyndham Books reserve the right to show new retail prices on covers which may differ from those advertised in the text or elsewhere.

Postage and Packing Rate
U.K.

One book 22p plus 10p per copy for each additional book ordered to a maximum charge of 82p.

B.F.P.O. & Eire

One book 22p plus 10p per copy for the next 6 books, and thereafter 4p per book.

Overseas

One book 30p plus 10p per copy for each additional book.

These charges are subject to Post Office fluctuations.